To Mary and BJ, Best wishes with Love + Katia Petrova xxx July

Tatiana's Day

TATIANA'S DAY

Katia Perova

iUniverse®

TATIANA'S DAY

iUniverse books may be ordered through booksellers or by contacting:

iUniverse
1663 Liberty Drive
Bloomington, IN 47403
www.iuniverse.com
1-800-Authors (1-800-288-4677)

ISBN: 978-1-4917-9153-0 (sc)
ISBN: 978-1-4917-9154-7 (e)

Library of Congress Control Number: 2016904823

Print information available on the last page.

iUniverse rev. date: 03/25/2016

For George.
And for Russia, with love, and pain.
July 2022

Be thou my angel sent to guard,
Or source of sly, deceiving fraud,
I beg release from my confusion:
All this, perhaps, is empty, false,
My callow soul trapped in illusion!
By fortune meant for something else.

Aleksandr Pushkin, from “Tatyana’s
Letter to Onegin”, *Evgeny Onegin*

PART 1

Chapter 1

1990

"What are you doing tonight? We're celebrating with beer and nearly fresh chocolate cake. There are about ten of us going to my place—and my parents have been warned and are willing to cooperate. Want to come? I'd like you to come."

Grey eyes sparkled at her. A big smile worked some magic. Tatiana didn't realise at first that Oleg was talking to her.

"Me? You're asking me?"

There were a lot of people hanging out, all of them smoking and chatting. Exams were over, so spirits were high. "You, of course. I'm asking you. What's your name, by the way?"

"Tatiana."

"And that in itself calls for celebration! 'So she was called Tatiana!'" he quoted teasingly. "Hey, guys, on the lucky day of St Tatiana, we are going to have Tatiana with us!"

Tatiana just wanted to disappear—urgently. She wished she could fly away with the myriad snowflakes that were generously falling from the January sky. Ever since she'd found out she was named after the heroine Tatiana Larina, from the doomed love story in verse *Evgeny Onegin*, Tatiana had dreaded the association. O how she wished they hadn't chosen that name, her Pushkin-loving parents. But the name Tania was even worse—far too common and simple. She preferred the name Tatiana.

But of course there was St Tatiana, the patron saint of students. *Damn. Damn 25 January—my name day and her name day. I'm going to get teased for the next four years!* Tatiana thought.

All eyes were on her now, and she did not like it. Being the blue-eyed girl whose youthful looks hid her real age, she was only ever good at talking in the classroom. And that was because she always studied, did her homework, and knew exactly how to answer the teachers' questions.

Oleg's friends were all smiling at her confidently. They were the ones who laughed the loudest, told the rudest jokes, and drank beer—both boys and girls—as if their only purpose was to have a good time. Studying was not top of the agenda for them, yet they were bright and charismatic. Tatiana knew that they could all pass their exams by cramming the night before. What she didn't know was why she was standing next to them in the "Smoking Square", which was opposite the university.

Since almost everyone smoked, the place was tightly packed with students from every year. Smoking was something that one had to do to be accepted. A cigarette was the ticket one needed to belong here. It was even better for someone who didn't have a light, because asking for one could start a conversation.

Tatiana found herself standing next to Oleg's group because she knew one of the girls—one of the witty, loud ones—from her class at school. No one had ever questioned her right to stand there, but no one had really spoken to her before either, not since September, when the year had begun. And now the first person to address her, invite her even, was the Man himself, the group leader, Oleg Isaev.

He was at least two years older than everyone, people said, although no one knew for sure. He was in the army before, almost definitely deployed to Afghanistan, and he was the best at everything—jokes, witty banter, pulling pranks, playing guitar. But he was tight-lipped about his past and never gave anything away. He also had a strange sort of poise or charisma that meant nobody ever questioned his authority.

So when Oleg asked her to join the party, Tatiana just took it as a command, not an invitation. In fact, she felt honoured, if not a little confused. She knew all about him, but he didn't even know her name.

"Me? You're asking me?" These were her first words to him.

Snow kept tumbling down—huge snowflakes, each one beautiful and unique. Tatiana loved winter days like this. The temperature was just right, only a few degrees below zero. It was not too cold and not too windy; all was quiet and magically still. Ever since she was little, a fresh fall of snow excited her. Even now, she loved to pick up a small heap from the ground, all the individual snowflakes still visible, and press the snow between her mitts. But the snowflakes wouldn't stick together—it was too cold for that.

It was a fluffy, soft snow, just right for sticking your tongue into or for cramming into your mouth and letting it melt on your tongue. And that was the best taste ever. In her mouth, snow turned into the sweetest of all waters. If only it could be bottled and sold as snow water. Tatiana could even picture the label on the blue bottle, all silver with a scattering of snowflakes.

Today, the snow was magnificent—Mother Nature on her wedding day, the time when the huge grey metropolis of Moscow turned into a spectacular bridal party, white, festive, glamorous, and quiet.

The snow had muffled the city's traffic and sirens along with all the noisy city buzz. And the ever-rushing Muscovites had become fairy-tale wedding guests as the falling snow adorned the tops of their hats and the shoulders of their coats, sparkling like Swarovski crystals under the street lights. The spectacle dazzled Tatiana. It would be a shame to go home on a night like this.

"OK, I'll come. But I need to call my parents first."

"Good girl." Oleg took a coin out of his pocket. "Go on then, make a public phone feel useful."

Oleg lived with his parents in a small two-bedroom flat in the south of Moscow. It was empty when the noisy group of excited students reached it. They walked up to the fifth floor (the lift was out of order) with armfuls of beer bottles.

Inside the typical Moscow apartment, with its small rooms and narrow corridors, the first thing Tatiana noticed was the books. They were everywhere. There were thousands of them. An old piano took a proud place in the centre of the living room.

"You can smoke everywhere," Oleg said, giving permission. "We just need to open the windows before my folks get back."

Inhaling the heavy fumes, all of the students quickly got drunk on their favourite: vodka with a beer chaser.

Because she drank with the others, Tatiana didn't have a clear memory of the night. She remembered they had all been singing, at the top of their voices, popular wartime songs about faithful girls in blue shawls waiting for their soldiers to return, and some childish Soviet rhymes from the 1970s about drunken hedgehogs and Thursday departures from Liverpool harbour.

She also remembered Oleg playing the piano, first to accompany the singing, and later, after he had gotten more serious, slipping into some kind of jazz. He played with skill and passion, moving up and down on the stool in time to the rhythm. Then she remembered sitting on his lap at the top of the table when the sky outside the window was turning pale pink. The smoke from the nearby power station was rising up high—the unmistakable sign of freezing temperatures outside.

The conversation was dying out and all the faces were turning pale when Oleg gently pushed her off, saying, "Let's make coffee for everyone, Sunny." There, in the tiny kitchen, they kissed.

Tatiana wasn't even sure if it had really happened or if it had been a part of her dream. She was tired, a little drunk, and hazy after the most exciting night of her life. But she did remember the two of them counting the number of mugs and spoons of instant coffee, as familiar as an old couple.

Oleg called her two days later. "Hi, it's me. What are you doing tonight?"

He doesn't even use my name! she thought.

Before she could answer, he simply said, "I'm coming to pick you up at seven. Bring your swimsuit with you. What's your address?"

Tatiana had never been spoken to like this—not by a boy, certainly. He just gave her orders, but in such a way that she couldn't protest. She heard him smile on the other end of the phone. It was a game, with rules she had to follow. And somehow it felt right. She wanted him to take charge. She had spent years studying and mapping out her future. Only recently did she begin to realise that she had never enjoyed herself, had never let herself go.

All the young people around her were having fun and didn't seem to have a care in the world. But Tatiana had turned herself into a nineteen-year-old bore, the oldest teenager in the world.

Enough of that! All these responsibilities—they're not real. Stop acting like you think you should act. Surprise yourself! Go with him. And as if a tightly strung guitar string broke inside her with a loud ping, Tatiana suddenly felt herself relax.

"Do you have a pen? I'll give you my address." She tried to hide excitement in her voice.

She got dressed while wondering about the swimsuit. Who needed one in the middle of winter?

It was always a laborious affair to get ready when it was –17°C outside. That was the only thing she didn't like about winter—putting on layers and layers of cotton and wool. After managing to button up her coat on top of those layers, she felt, as usual, like an asexual object—a vegetable, something like a cabbage. And the trouble was that everywhere indoors the heating was at a maximum. She always had to rush straight to the cloakroom to take off the layers, doing the whole thing in reverse.

At 7 p.m. the doorbell rang. Tatiana was ready. "Mum, Dad, I'm going out now. I might stay over at Lena's." She didn't even give her parents the chance to reply before shutting the door behind her and taking the lift down. Saying that she would be staying at Lena's was convincing. Her parents knew that her college friend lived on the other side of Moscow.

I should still call Lena in case they check, she thought, making a mental note.

Outside the front door, a large Volga taxi was waiting. Immediately Tatiana felt like a princess going to her first ball.

"Hi, Sunny. Let's go." By the change of his tone, Tatiana realised that the first sentence was addressed to her and that the second was addressed to the taxi driver.

Does he remember my name?

Tatiana sunk into the faux leather of the back seat. Oleg said, "Tatiana's Day was fun, wasn't it? You don't mind me calling you Sunny, do you? I like your smile. It's so warm; it reminds me of sunshine."

She smiled at him with relief. *He does know my name.*

He put his arm over her shoulder and drew her closer to him. She felt the full blast of the heater blowing hot air around the small car. She noticed the driver's fur hat and his jacket on the front seat and felt conspicuously overdressed.

Damn these layers. What was I thinking, that he was taking me to the North Pole? She felt silly. *Of course he would hire a taxi. It is −17°C out there!*

"Where are we going?" she asked softly.

"It's a surprise. I hope you like rock music."

Surprise. Ever a magic word for little girls. Tatiana always felt she had a little girl inside her. Now the little girl inside her rose to her small feet, clapping her tiny hands and jumping up and down like only children do.

"I don't know much about rock music." Tatiana tried to maintain a mature, calm exterior. She carried on sweating through her damn layers.

"Well, OK, it's a good time for you to learn then." And with this single comment, Oleg reminded her who was the boss and the grown-up in this situation. "Step on it, chief! We're going to be late," he barked at the driver.

Still wondering why she needed a swimsuit to go to a rock concert, Tatiana began wondering about the man beside her. She had only ever seen Oleg at the Smoking Square. She could always tell he was there even if she couldn't see him. When he was around, the laughter was louder and there was always a commotion in the group.

Everyone became more animated when Oleg was in their midst. He was the centre of everyone's attention. They all laughed enthusiastically at his jokes. They all listened carefully when he spoke.

Oleg Isaev was not a handsome man. Strong but shorter than average, he had grey eyes and curly brown hair. He always wore the same pair of jeans, maroon polo-neck jumper, and brown parka. But somehow his ordinary appearance was nothing like ordinary. He had power in his eyes.

Tatiana could feel when he was looking at her. The gaze of his clever, steel-coloured eyes was almost unbearable, as if he were looking right through her and was able access all that he needed to know about her.

Not in a million years could Tatiana have imagined herself sitting next to this man in a taxi, let alone kissing him in his small kitchen. She was still unsure that the kiss had even happened.

So far on this date, he hadn't tried to kiss her. Only his arm was resting over her shoulder, almost a reminder that something was going on between them.

But what does he see in me? She wanted to know because she didn't know it herself.

"We're here, Sunny." Oleg's voice interrupted her thoughts. "We'll have to walk now."

Oleg paid the driver. Tatiana noticed that the meter was already switched off. The two must have agreed on the fare beforehand. It had been quite a journey, from the south end of the city where he lived, over to her place in the east, and then back to the south side.

She recognised the place where they had stopped—the huge Olympic Park on the banks of the Moskva River.

As they walked towards the covered arena, Tatiana quickly stopped, regretting her layers. The snow was squeaky and dry under their boots. Tatiana looked at her feet. Ever since she was small, she loved to play this game. She carefully tried to step on an untouched patch of snow because it made the loudest noise. From all the winters she had lived through, Tatiana knew what this crunching melody meant: a dry, biting frost, a proper Russian freeze.

The concert was loud, as she had expected it to be. Tatiana recognised only one ballad—intensely powerful, full of pain and emotion. She looked at Oleg. His eyes were shut and he was lost in the song, his hand moving perfectly to replicate the chords of the lead guitar.

Of course he plays the guitar! Tatiana liked seeing him like this—emotional, lost in the music. For the first time, she felt close to him. She wanted to know him better. And because his eyes were closed, she was able to take a good look at his face, noticing a scar above his left eyebrow.

When the concert was over and the crowd began slipping through the doors, Oleg took Tatiana's hand. "I loved it! How was it for you, rock virgin?" He didn't wait for her to reply. "Are you ready for a swim?"

Maybe it's a trick question.

"Swim? But where?"

"Trust me?"

His eyes looked sincere. He had a boyish grin of excitement on his face. Tatiana smiled and nodded. This time, SURPRISE! flashed in neon letters in front of the little girl.

"Wrap up! It's a bit of a walk."

They made their way out and quickly parted with the crowd that flowed steadily in the direction of the metro station. They were the only people heading the opposite way, deeper into the Olympic Park and towards the Grand Arena. While they had been indoors, more snow had fallen over Moscow. Tatiana couldn't hide her joy. The little girl swirled to the "Dance of the Sugar Plum Fairy" as Tchaikovsky's festive music tinkled in her head.

Tatiana freed her hand from Oleg's grasp and began to waltz down the untouched white runway, which was lit on both sides by bright street lamps. She laughed and laughed, feeling liberated.

"Come, catch me!" she teased.

"Oh, be careful what you wish for, Sunny!" Oleg replied.

They raced down the alley, Tatiana first, still giggling and holding down the shoulder bag that flapped and bounced on her hip. Behind her, Oleg increased his pace. In that instant, Tatiana knew that she wanted to be caught.

Still laughing, she slowed down just a little. Sure enough, she felt his arms on her shoulders. She was still giggling when he stopped her, turned her body to face his, and began kissing her whole face, including her cheeks and nose. He kissed erratically at first, but then his lips found her mouth. When their tongues met, the world slowed down.

They stood there, two small figures joined together under the cold, magical light—the two tracks of prints behind them eventually becoming one.

This was their first real kiss. Thereafter, Tatiana thought of it as a scene from a painting, or the end of a black-and-white film when "The End" appears across the screen. Only it wasn't the end; it was the beginning.

"We can't stand here for long. We'll freeze!" Oleg broke off their embrace. "Let's go!" Tatiana just managed to catch her breath. She inhaled deeply and immediately felt freezing air cutting sharply through her nostrils. Kissing outdoors in the middle of a Russian winter was not the best idea. Her lips, still wet from the kiss, began to tingle with pain.

They started walking briskly, holding hands. At the end of the alley stood a large dimly lit building. It looked deserted.

"What's this?" Tatiana had lost her bearings; she had been in the park only once before, on a bright summer day. It had all looked very different then.

"It's the old Olympic swimming pool. They used it for the water polo matches in the 1980 Olympics. Come! Let's go inside!" Oleg hurried her.

"But how will we ... get in?"

"You don't need to worry about a thing if you're with me," Oleg said, visibly proud of himself. "I've got it all under control. Relax and trust me, baby."

Baby? Ouch. That's even worse than Sunny.

One of the side doors was unlocked when Oleg pushed it. "A good friend's the gym manager here," he told her. "He owes me a favour, that's all. Don't worry, there is nobody inside. They don't have security—no need for it. There are guards on all the gates to the park, so they just lock it up in the evening and go."

Oleg flipped a switch on the wall. Dozens of buzzing lights came to life. Tatiana saw a long, narrow corridor that wrapped around the building's interior. Oleg started walking with the confidence of someone who was familiar with the place. He didn't stop to read the signs on the doors until just before he pushed one of the doors open.

"That's you." He flipped another switch. Tatiana walked into a large changing room with white-tiled walls and rows of numbered lockers.

"There should be a towel for you on a bench somewhere. The hot water's on too. See you outside in ten?" Oleg continued moving further down the corridor.

Tatiana only just stopped herself from asking, "Outside where?"

He meant the pool, of course.

After showering and putting on her swimsuit, Tatiana began to wander inside the huge changing room in search of an exit to the pool. There was no such door. Then she noticed white-tiled steps covered by water. At first, she thought they led to a small footbath. Only when she took another look did she realise that the far wall of the bath did not reach the floor. There was a gap. When she bent down to see better, she noticed light coming from somewhere behind. It wasn't a solid wall but an opening—the entrance to the pool outside. The only way to get there was to swim underneath.

She was suddenly struck with her childhood fear of underwater tunnels and caves. Tatiana held her breath.

Stay calm! It's only a short dive under; it won't take me more than a second to get to the other side. But what if there is just a blank wall at the end? Will I have enough air to swim back?

Tatiana was shivering. She hated what-ifs.

Be brave! You don't want to make a fool of yourself on your first date! Don't be a wimp—it's already a mystery what he sees in you!

Be brave. She had said this to herself many times before, such as when the dentist had to pull her tooth without anaesthetic; when those schoolboys had wanted to snatch her satchel; when the professors at her university interview had thrown tricky questions at her. Her mouth had gone dry, just for a second, when she was asked those tricky questions, but she'd pulled herself together and smiled her way in. Exams were always the easy part.

"Be brave!" Tatiana said it now. "You can do it! He is waiting." She stepped into the warm water, closed her eyes, and dove in. She must have given herself a powerful push, because she popped up on the other side like a fishing float.

She opened her eyes and paused in wonder. At first, she could only see thick vapour rising from the water's surface. Her head felt immediately cold. The contrast in temperatures was sharp. She noticed that the area was bright. *The pool must be lit by powerful lamps somewhere high above,* she thought.

"Is that you, Sunny?" Oleg's voice sounded like a strange echo. "Swim towards the middle." She took a few strokes in the direction of his voice. Then she saw his smiling face, his wet hair flat and stuck to his head.

Oh no, I must look like that—and on our first date!

She swallowed her vanity and smiled back at him. "How big is it?" she asked. She couldn't make out the pool edges through the steam.

"Well, it is the Olympic pool, so it must be fifty metres long," Oleg replied in a schoolteacher's tone.

Does he have to be patronising? He makes me feel clueless.

"And what's over that side?" Tatiana asked, pointing to a spot over his head.

"There's a smaller lap pool. There's only a narrow walkway between the two. But I don't think it will be a good idea to get out of the water now—a bit chilly, isn't it?" They both giggled at the understatement.

Tatiana dove under to keep her head warm. When she surfaced, she looked around again. She had never swum in a professional pool before. This one was definitely special. She could see rows and rows of spectator benches climbing high on every side. She couldn't see the very top, as a mix of light and steam obstructed her vision. The place seemed fuzzy and surreal. Tatiana swam closer to Oleg.

"Look up," he whispered. At that moment, impossibly giant snowflakes began to fall. She felt the air getting thicker and slightly warmer, as it always did when it began to snow. There was no wind. Tatiana and Oleg, both looking up, could trace the trajectory of each snowflake as it danced its way down, dissolving instantly on the warm surface.

"So pretty!" Tatiana said as she gasped.

"Pretty like you, Sunny."

Oleg pulled her towards him with one arm. They kissed again, their mouths exploring, their tongues swirling slowly. Tatiana screwed her eyes shut, lost in the sensation. Their weightless bodies pressed together, their legs dancing through the water. She felt the snowflakes gently landing on her head, patting it softly: *tap, tap, tap.*

It was impossible to maintain that balancing act for long.

Once again, Oleg was first to pull away from the kiss. With a pang of disappointment, Tatiana opened her eyes. "We should go inside now," Oleg whispered. After clearing his throat, he said in a louder voice, "Before we get meningitis and die!"

Tatiana laughed and nodded. "You're right!" She tried to sound cheery. "We don't want that to happen!" She turned and began swimming away from him. The prospect of diving under the wall didn't scare her any longer. The fear was gone, having been replaced by the promise of something wonderful.

"Make sure you dry yourself really well, Sunny," Oleg called after her. "I'll go and book us a taxi from the office."

Dry myself well! Will he ever stop? He sounds more patronising than my dad! But then again, she thought, *he is right. It is the middle of a Russian winter.*

Chapter 2

From that extraordinary night in Olympic Park, Oleg Isaev dazzled his way into Tatiana's life. They spoke on the phone almost every day. He took her on many dates.

Each of their dates began with Oleg's grand entrance. He strode into her family's fourteenth-floor apartment, fresh and glowing from the cold, his eyes gleaming with excitement.

He never came empty-handed, always bringing something special for Tatiana, like a box of her favourite chocolates, a new record, or a jar of rare Chinese tea.

Tatiana loved these theatrical arrivals. She felt like a child expecting Grandfather Frost on New Year's Eve, who was also known for his dramatic entries.

"Hurry up, Sunny one," Oleg would command from the hall while Tatiana was still fussing over yet another gift. "Your carriage is outside. The chief is waiting."

Tatiana quickly got used to the luxury of being picked up by a taxi. It had never occurred to her to ask Oleg how he could afford it.

"Where does he get the money from, his student grant?" Tatiana's mother had asked once. "Really, where is the money coming from?" But Tatiana had had no answer. She wondered that herself.

Oleg took her on adventures. It was never just going to the

cinema. Instead, they'd go to an Art Society screening of a controversial Japanese film—invitation only. Or they'd go to a black market somewhere outside the city, where one could buy or exchange banned Western records.

And then he would take her to a restaurant or a smart cafe. He always knew someone there, and they were shown to the best table. Oleg, without looking at the menu, would always ask for "the special".

"Menus are for the average crowd, Sunny," he'd remark. "Look at them! So pleased with themselves, drunk on Russian vodka." He meant the foreigners, the average crowd in those places—clients of Intourist.

Adventurous, and brave enough to sample Russia in winter, the average crowd danced to live music. They looked merry and exhilarated as if they had gotten away with cheating Death himself. To Tatiana, they were not average at all. She didn't see many foreign people on the streets of Moscow. The people she saw when she was out with Oleg spoke different languages, looked exotic, and appeared somehow to be more casual and at ease with themselves. Tatiana envied them.

The average crowd, for her, meant friends and family. And her friends and family never went to such places. They simply couldn't afford to.

Before she met Oleg, she had never even visited a restaurant before, except maybe for a wedding.

Where does he get the money from? The question popped into her mind again and again. Because she never saw a menu when she was out with Oleg, she had no idea how much everything cost.

Without asking for a bill, Oleg always put some folded notes into the waiter's hand. They were served by the same waiters in each place. "My people", Oleg liked to call them. "My guy's not in today. Let's go somewhere else," he told Tatiana once, after which they left for another restaurant.

One night, after finishing a bottle of Georgian red, Tatiana plucked up the courage to ask him, "Are you secretly rich?"

She already knew this couldn't be true. Oleg looked nothing like the privileged son of a powerful political family. She knew the type; there were two at the university. Those boys never smoked in the square with everyone else, in case they got asked for a cigarette (they smoked real American Marlboros, not the cheap, stinky Russian puffs). They wore beautiful clothes that had been bought abroad by their well-travelled parents. They even spoke as if Russian weren't their native tongue, using a secret lingo spattered with foreign words that was impossible to follow. To the average person, they looked, smelled, and sounded like aliens. No one really liked them, but everyone was jealous of them—envious of all the cool, shiny things they had access to.

Oleg was not one of those young men. Tatiana had seen his apartment—the typical home of an intellectual, cramped and full of books. He always wore the same old clothes. He clearly was not well off.

"How come you can afford all of this?" She waved her hand around the restaurant.

"Well, if you really want to know, I play for it," Oleg said simply, looking straight into her eyes. His tone was sincere. "Russian Préférence mainly."

Tatiana took this in. She knew the game, although she'd never seen it being played.

"But you can't always win?" she asked, still absorbing the information.

"But it's unlikely for me to lose. Do you want to hear the story?"

"Yes, go on." Tatiana perked up in anticipation.

"I have a partner—a bit of a genius. Alex and I were at school together. Cards has always been his thing. Don't get me wrong. I mean, I'm not bad myself, but he's in a league of his own.

"The really great thing about Alex is that he's mad. Officially crazy. He's properly registered and has official papers saying 'diminished responsibilities' or suchlike. He checks himself into hospital from time to time, when he gets too anxious. He says the food is good there, but I don't believe him."

Tatiana took a sip of wine. "Sounds like an interesting character, your friend."

"Oh, that he is!" Oleg continued. "Alex likes to disappear from time to time, when things get out of hand. You know, all these changes in the country, arguments with his mum .... But this is between us, OK? No one knows that about him."

Tatiana nodded. "I would really love to meet him. I'm intrigued!"

"And you will Sunny. One day," Oleg agreed.

"But don't you need a third person to play Préférence?" Tatiana asked. "How does it work?"

"You're absolutely right, clever girl. You're paying attention!" Oleg looked amused. He reached out and gently squeezed her hand atop the tablecloth. Tatiana blushed at the compliment. Oleg leaned forwards and continued in a confiding tone, his eyes burning into hers, "That's where I step in! I use my charms and connections." He nodded in the direction of the passing waiter, one of "his" people. "They help me to select the right candidates, the guys with cash and an ardour for cards, but little experience! And you know what's funny?" Oleg straightened up and tapped on the table. He looked self-assured, with his usual I'm-in-charge demeanour. "Most of these guys know that they have very little chance against us, but they still do it anyway. Dostoevsky said it in *The Gambler*: 'It was not the money ... I wanted to make this mob wonder at me.' It's human nature. The excitement is in the process. These guys don't care about the money. They just want to learn from us."

Tatiana listened intently, gazing in awe at this revelation. Oleg had never talked so openly before.

"It's like my neighbour Konstantine," Oleg continued with excitement. "He's a student at Diplomatic College. His parents are never home; they live abroad most of the time. Konstantine is privileged, loaded, and bored. He spends his free time playing tennis and golf. Golf! In Moscow!" he exclaimed.

"Sorry, you lost me there," Tatiana said. "What is golf, some kind of card game?"

"My point exactly, Sunny. It's a kind of sport, by the way, played mainly by rich foreigners. But it's winter now. The golf course is under snow, so my poor neighbour has nothing to do. Alex and I keep him company. Konstantine loves Préférence. He's bad at it, but he doesn't care." Oleg raised his glass. "To Konstantine!"

"But what happens if he gets really good and starts winning?" Tatiana still couldn't comprehend.

"Not before his money runs out." Oleg smiled a devilish smile. "Besides, there are plenty of others."

"I am not sure it's, well, you know, a sustainable life plan." Tatiana shook her head. "You can get yourselves in trouble."

"Oh, don't worry, it is just one of my schemes to earn some pocket money. I've got ideas. I will tell you one day." Oleg began looking around. Tatiana understood that the confession time was up.

She felt a pulsating attraction to this man. He was different, appearing to be someone who was in control of his life, unlike the other boys at university, who were aimless and dependent on their parents. It was only on the surface that Oleg played a fun-loving joker with a sharp tongue and a guitar.

She felt blood rushing to her head. "It's hot in here," she murmured, unbuttoning the top button of her blouse. *I want to be his. I want him to take control of my life, too.*

With reddening cheeks, and being almost breathless, she stood up in front of him. "Dance with me, please."

"Whoa, Sunny! What did they put in that wine?" Oleg tried to joke. The sudden rush of her desire had clearly caught him off guard. "Er, OK, I can't say no to a lady," he mumbled and then led her to the dance floor.

The music was loud. The lead singer, flaunting her Hollywood cleavage in a tight dress, was singing a cheesy radio hit about raspberry-coloured sunsets and raspberry lips. "This is not my kind of music," Oleg almost shouted, holding Tatiana close to his chest as they started to move slowly, her hands on his shoulders and his on her back.

Tatiana noticed with disappointment that Oleg had put his hands quite high up her back, as if he were dancing with his sister. She didn't have a great deal of experience with boys, but even she knew that most of them would seize an opportunity like this and try to feel her up under the guise of dancing.

Tatiana raised her arms and locked them over Oleg's neck, pulling herself closer to him in an embrace. "We can go home now," she said loudly. "We can dance to your kind of music there."

Oleg just smiled and closed his eyes as they continued to move. The moment was gone.

If it hadn't been for the wine, Tatiana would have felt embarrassed. *Maybe he doesn't fancy me?*

But Oleg must have read her mind. "It will all happen, Sunny, but not tonight. I need to focus on my meeting tomorrow."

He gently kissed her earlobe. It tickled, so Tatiana began to giggle. His ambiguous promise made up for her disappointment. She was completely intrigued and smitten. She had so many questions that would have to keep.

But things changed after that night. They continued to speak on the phone, but they didn't see each other. He kept saying that he was very busy with a new venture. She bumped into him a few times at the university, but he would never stop for long.

He began to skip lectures too, only turning up to collect assignments and any seminar notes prepared by his fans, as Tatiana called them. These were young women who wore bright lipstick and black eyeliner, and swore a lot. They seemed to worship Oleg.

"I had a fight with my ex yesterday," said one, a tall blonde whom everyone called the Rocket. Everyone knew the Rocket because she moved with astronomical speed, pushing everyone out of her way and shooting out words as if they were bullets.

"He came to my place to beg me to take him back. We had a drink or two, and then we got into a fight. And this is nothing," she said, pointing to the fresh bruise on her cheek. "You should see his arms today—all black and blue. I punched him hard."

Everyone was listening. The Rocket was taller than most of the young men in her class. With her cropped blonde hair, bright lipstick, and broad shoulders that looked as if they belonged to a discus-thrower, she was an intimidating presence.

"So then we had mind-blowing sex, and afterwards I threw him out. And that's the way to treat your ex." The Rocket bowed as if on stage.

The young women cheered and clapped, but the young men went quiet for a minute, contemplating the fate of their comrade.

No one had seen any of the Rocket's boyfriends. Moreover, Tatiana wasn't always sure she believed the anecdotes. But deep down, she was a bit jealous of the Rocket and her ilk. They were all very confident and charismatic. Tatiana was nothing like them. She didn't wear much make-up, partly because she didn't know how to apply it. Why would Oleg choose her over someone like the Rocket?

Tatiana wasn't surprised when Oleg began to feature less and less in her life. She accepted his apparent withdrawal and wasn't even that upset, because it all made sense.

She told herself she was too plain for him.

Then one evening, while she was curled up under her favourite itchy throw with a tome on her lap, the phone rang.

"Hey, Sunny. Did you miss me?" Oleg asked in his usual half-joking, half-patronising way.

"Depends on what you have in mind." Tatiana tried to keep surprise out of her voice.

"Well, 8 March is around the corner. Why don't we celebrate together?"

Oh yes, it was already March, Tatiana realised. International Women's Day was that week.

"OK, maybe. What are you thinking?" She tried to sound casual.

"You like the theatre, don't you?" he asked. "I have a treat for you, if you're in."

How very grown-up and sophisticated. "What play are we going to see?" she asked.

"Leave it to me, Sunny. You won't be disappointed, I promise." And with that, Oleg hung up.

Oh, him and his surprises! That's how he got me hooked in the first place!

Tatiana pushed away the throw and the book. She pressed the play button on her cassette recorder and began dancing frantically to an upbeat song. *He called! He must be still interested in me!*

"Tatiana! Keep the volume down! I am trying to work!" her mother shouted from the living room.

On the evening of 8 March, Tatiana was ready and waiting for Oleg. She wore her mother's best silk blouse, which was olive green and felt cool against her skin. It was a little big, but that was easily fixed with a pair of squishy shoulder pads pinned under her bra straps.

In the dim light of the hallway, Tatiana looked at herself in the mirror. With her mother's green eyeshadow, a hint of pink on her cheeks, and a touch of lip gloss, she was satisfied with what she saw.

At five past six, the doorbell rang. Tatiana jumped up and pressed the entrance buzzer. She just had a few minutes before Oleg would make it to her apartment door. Suddenly she found herself in a panic. *What's happening? He's been here many times before!*

Usually, she happily and calmly anticipated his arrival, but today it felt different somehow. She started rushing around the small apartment. "Mother, have you seen my hairbrush?"

"Check in the bathroom."

"Oh, it's already in my bag."

When Tatiana heard Oleg's footsteps outside the door, she just froze, trying to control her erratic breathing. "The door is open," she squeaked. Oleg burst in with his usual gusto.

"Happy Women's Day, Sunny!" He was carrying a huge bouquet of red carnations, maybe twenty-five of them. They looked so perfect that Tatiana had the urge to touch them to check if they were real.

"Sorry, Sunny, these are not for you. Viktoria Andreevna," he called out, "can we borrow you for a minute?"

Tatiana's mother appeared at the kitchen door. The warm odours of fried onions and chocolate cake followed her into the hall.

"Happy Women's Day!" Oleg beamed with charm. "I'm very sorry that I have to steal your daughter away from your family celebration. And these are for you." He held out the flowers. "I hope they keep long enough for you to forgive me for commandeering Tatiana tonight, maybe even long enough for you to start liking me?" He winked.

Tatiana noticed in dismay that her mother's face flushed like a teenage girl's and that she gave Oleg a huge smile, big and warm—the kind that made her eyes look narrow from the wrinkles. It was the smile she never gave for photographs—wide cheeks and a glimpse of golden molars. But at that moment, Tatiana's mother completely lost control over her facial muscles. Tatiana watched her falling under Oleg's spell.

Viktoria Andreevna Dobrova was a woman of imposing stature. She possessed a commanding tone that immediately gave her authority. A professor of criminal law at the best law school in the nation, she was used to people being subordinate and respectful in her presence. Her students were petrified of her and would hang onto her every word.

Tatiana grew up not seeing Viktoria Andreevna very often. Her mother was usually at work. She remembered the dark winter mornings when she was wakened by the sounds of her mother bustling in the hallway as she got ready to leave, dressed in her usual cream blouse and striped brown suit with the jasper brooch on the lapel.

Being a large woman, Viktoria Andreevna loved oversized pieces of jewellery. She had a collection of brooches and rings fashioned with semi-precious stones. The stones had been presents from her late father. Grandpa Andrey used to work for the Ministry of Trade and Industry and had spent years in North Africa. He had been responsible for importing fruits. Tatiana was still very proud of this.

When little Tatiana had seen boxes of sunny-coloured oranges being unloaded at the grocer's on the white wintry streets, she liked to address the quickly gathering queue, saying, "My grandpa sent you those. They're all the way from Morocco."

Her mother would tug her collar, saying, "Come on, chatterbox. Let's get going before your feet freeze." Tatiana was five or six then. She thought her granddad had the greatest job in the world.

But then Grandpa Andrey got sick and died very quickly thereafter, leaving Tatiana with just a vague memory of him. Even now, all grown up, she smiled at the sight of oranges in their boxes, all bright and waxy with the small black diamond-shaped stickers. *Thank you, Grandpa Andrey.*

Tatiana's mother's jewellery box was another reminder of her grandfather. She loved looking through it. A beautiful black-lacquered creation from Palekh, it was the size of a book. On the lid was a red and gold painting of dancing girls in old-fashioned traditional clothes and crowns. Inside it, Viktoria Andreevna kept her treasured gems, all carefully laid out on the lacquered crimson interior. There were pieces featuring jasper, black onyx, and gold and brown tiger's eye. She also had simple beaded necklaces, rings, and brooches all the way from Africa. Tatiana's mother wore her stones like medals.

On weekdays, Tatiana woke up to the clunk of her mother's

curling tongs. Viktoria Andreevna was out the door while her daughter was still rubbing her eyes and stretching in bed. It was only at the weekends that they managed to have breakfast together, Viktoria pottering around in her blue flowery dressing gown, her face bare and relaxed.

The woman greeting Oleg from the kitchen door that night was the cosy, homely version. Dressed in a relaxed flannel skirt and oversized T-shirt, Viktoria Andreevna didn't look like she could intimidate anyone, law school student or otherwise.

She was clearly taken by Oleg's gesture. "Carnations are my favourite! Thank you!" she gushed. "I'll have to look for a large vase to hold these beauties! You two better get going, though—we can celebrate together another time." She turned to Tatiana. "Are you coming back tonight?"

"I don't know yet, Mother." Tatiana hesitated. Both women looked at Oleg.

"Viktoria Andreevna, please don't worry about your daughter's safety. I give you the word of a gentleman that I will look after her tonight—and always." Tatiana blushed at the last word. Her mother was still smiling with approval.

Tatiana didn't mind at all that Oleg sounded like he'd just stepped out of a nineteenth-century novel. "I care about her" was what she had heard in his words—and that made her happy.

"Where are we going?" she asked him once they were in the taxi.

"Patience, Sunny. You'll see soon."

Their taxi turned the opposite way from the city centre.

"I thought you said something about a theatre?" Tatiana imagined that all the theatres were in the central part of Moscow.

"We are going to the theatre. Just wait and see."

They drove through a residential area in the outskirts of the city. Tatiana saw endless blocks of the exact same building, as if the city planners had no imagination at all. Those structures had been put together in different patterns to fit the landscape.

The streets were named after prominent scientists, communist leaders, or war heroes. The trouble was that all those blocks, all over Moscow, looked exactly the same. She could never tell where she was—on the south, west, north, or east. Tatiana and Oleg, too, lived in blocks like these.

Driving through these areas, Tatiana recalled a popular Russian film, a romantic comedy where the two main characters live in identical apartments on streets of the same name, except that the man lives in Moscow and the woman in Leningrad. After a drunken night with friends, the man, unconscious, ends up on a flight from Moscow and awakes in the woman's apartment in Leningrad.

"You remember *The Irony of Fate*?" Oleg asked, referring to the movie Tatiana had just been thinking of. "They filmed it here. This same building."

Tatiana couldn't believe the coincidence. *Can he read minds, too?*

"Let's go. We're here," Oleg said.

Tatiana noticed a queue of people at one of the entrances. *How strange. What are they queuing for outside a residential building?*

"This is the theatre door, Sunny. But don't worry, we don't have to wait. I don't do queues," he said, surprising her again.

Yes, I can't picture you standing in line either.

She realised that he had brought her to the underground theatre known simply as The Studio. It was small, mysterious, and well-known in the circles of young intellectuals and culture connoisseurs. It was impossible to get tickets to a show there, as they were never sold through traditional means. At one point, Tatiana had thought that The Studio was an urban myth. She had never met anyone who had seen a play there.

Now she couldn't believe her eyes. The place really existed, and she was going to see a play there. "This is the best present ever!" Failing to contain her excitement, she kissed Oleg on the cheek and clapped her hands.

"My pleasure, Sunny. I knew you'd like it," he answered, looking flushed by her outburst.

A tall guy with unruly curly hair called from the door, "Oleg! Come in!" He was checking invitations and letting people through.

"Do you want a hand with it?" Oleg shouted over the crowd, gently pushing Tatiana forwards. The tall guy looked down at both of them and smiled.

"Don't worry, I've got it. It's your day off! Come in—enjoy the show." He then nodded at Tatiana. "They are members of staff!" he called loudly to silence the disapproving cries from the queue.

"Since when are we members of staff?" Tatiana asked as she and Oleg walked into a small, dark foyer. "And who was the guy?"

"I'll introduce you later. And he was telling the truth. I do work here, part-time. I help them out at the door."

"You do?" Tatiana struggled to picture Oleg crossing names off a guest list.

"This is an amateur theatre," Oleg continued as they were checking their coats at the cloakroom. "So volunteering is the only way for them to avoid official censorship—to have their repertoire not dictated by the Ministry of Culture," he explained. "But make no mistake: this is the real deal. The creative director is very demanding and serious about his work. All the actors must have day jobs, with acting listed as their hobby. So sometimes I help them find 'official employment' through the people I know. We've registered many of them as street cleaners or night guards for grocery shops."

"But I've never seen any night guards at a grocery store!" Tatiana exclaimed.

"Exactly! There is no need for them, yet these positions exist on payroll. So it all looks proper on paper, but, in fact, these people work here in the theatre, rehearsing, performing, and making sets and costumes. I'm sort of proud to be a part of it." Oleg finished with his usual self-commendation.

"Any other hidden talents? Is there anything you can't do?" Tatiana mocked.

He looked at her seriously.

"I can't act," he said, sighing. "Let's go in, Sunny." Tatiana let him lead her inside the auditorium.

What was all that about? Him and acting? He was almost sad when he said it.

Inside, the venue was very dark. There were black stage curtains, black walls, and black benches.

This auditorium can probably hold around one hundred or two hundred people, Tatiana thought, struggling to judge. She had never been in a theatre like this one before.

From their seats at the back, she could still see every fold and crease on the curtains. It felt strangely intimate.

"What play are we going to see?" she asked Oleg.

"*The Master and Margarita.*"

"Are you serious? That's my favourite book!"

"I kind of guessed it," he said. "And it is by far the most popular play here. Impossible to get in. Some female Bulgakov fans have even been known to offer sexual favours to the actors in exchange for a ticket."

Tatiana blushed. "Don't exaggerate!"

"I swear it's true!" Oleg smiled a provocative smile. It was the first time he had mentioned the *s* word.

"I thought it was my Women's Day present?" she said bravely. "You didn't warn me about the price I'm expected to pay for the honour."

"Hold that thought, Sunny. We will discuss it after the show. I really like wherever this conversation is going." Oleg had lowered his voice to a whisper, his lips brushing her ear.

Oh my God! I'm not going home tonight! Tatiana felt a hot flush washing all over her, making her tingle inside. She wriggled on her seat. The intimate promise in his voice was new. *How am I supposed to concentrate on the play now?*

Once the curtains parted, Tatiana was able to get lost in her favourite tale of the Devil visiting Moscow and stirring chaos among the citizens, helping the doomed lovers along the way. As the scenes unfolded, she was entranced.

On Tatiana's sixteenth birthday, her parents had left a present by her bed. It was a book, *The Master and Margarita*. Once she read the title, she jumped up with joy. The book had just been published for the first time in forty years, to commemorate Bulgakov's death. And the simple black hardback, printed on cheap recycled paper, was an absolute treasure, very hard to come by. The demand almost exceeded the legendary status of the novel. At the time, Tatiana couldn't believe her eyes.

"Enjoy!" her mother had said. "In our time we had to read it as a censored magazine copy."

Tatiana devoured the novel. She read it three times in a row. Sitting on a park bench and biting her cuticles, she memorised her favourite parts. She envied Margarita and her magic cream that turned her into a witch and made her fly.

Woland fascinated Tatiana. He wasn't the one-dimensional evil Antichrist from her grandmother's old religious tales. He was a mesmerising and powerful patron of the hopeless lovers. The actor who played Woland that night wore dark glasses and a long black coat on stage. He spoke in a husky voice with German accent. Tatiana watched him, spellbound.

Oh, choose me! she almost cried out loud. *I would sell my soul to you for a jar of that cream!* She had to remind herself that it was just a play and that the people on the stage were just Oleg's friends, not Satan with his entourage.

She glanced at Oleg sitting next to her, his face animated, his mouth moving as he silently spoke the lines. *Oh, that's what he meant! He really wants to be on that stage.*

Tatiana realised just then that Oleg had his own regrets and insecurities. He wasn't all that mighty and brilliant at everything. She felt pity for him. She liked him showing his human side.

She shifted closer to him on the bench and put her head on

his shoulder. He reached out his arm and wrapped it around her waist. They sat in this close embrace until the end of the play.

The loud applause and bravos returned Tatiana to reality.

"That was wonderful!" She raised her head to face Oleg. "Thank you. The best surprise ever!"

"My pleasure, Sunny." Oleg gently squeezed her elbow. "We have to discuss those payment terms now, remember?"

"Oh yes. I'm open to your suggestions." Tatiana's voice came out low and sexy.

"I know a place we can go." Oleg winked and helped her to her feet.

Tatiana heard a voice ask, "Are you going to introduce me?" The foyer was crowded, but she immediately knew that the question was addressed to Oleg. She recognised the tall guy from the entrance. He towered over their heads with his broad shoulders and mop of brown hair.

"Of course. Alex, meet Tatiana. Tatiana, this is Alex, my old friend."

Ah, this must be the mad card-playing genius. "Oh, yes. I think I've heard about you," she said. "Unless of course Oleg has several friends named Alex."

"So, he's told you about me?" Alex smirked. "Either way, it's not true."

"What isn't?"

"Whatever he told you about me. It's not true."

"What do you mean?"

"I mean, no one, not even me, knows the truth about me. Don't look so confused now. I'm just teasing you!"

Finally, Alex turned to Oleg. "I'm glad to see you with a proper woman—sophisticated and cultured. Not like those leather-wearing, loudmouthed Bolshevik types you've brought here before."

Tatiana couldn't believe her ears. Alex was openly discussing her as if she weren't there. But she agreed with him about those "scary" women. It seemed that Alex didn't like them either.

"Congratulations. She's perfect!" Alex concluded. "And what are you doing with this old goat?" he asked Tatiana. His voice was warm and friendly. Tatiana could tell immediately that Alex was very fond of his friend.

"I happen to like him, I guess." It was the first time Tatiana had admitted that, but she had thought it was quite obvious.

"Stick with him—he's a nine."

"Nine out of ten, you mean?" she mocked.

"No, just nine. All headstrong. In Chinese numerology, nine means the long way. He will be a ninety-nine one day. And that means eternity."

He's mad but amusing. "What number am I then?" Tatiana was intrigued.

"You are a twenty-three, Tatiana, the way I see you."

"Why twenty-three?"

"Twenty-three is a magical number—for me, anyway. Two is a swan. Look at you, long neck, all graceful. But you hold your head down, unsure about your own beauty. Three is the Holy Trinity—you know, the Father, the Son, and the Holy Spirit. Three is the ultimate number for them—Christians, I mean. Martyrs. They love the martyrs. Tatiana—St Tatiana." Alex was mumbling now.

"How I would like to be that lion at your feet—the one who knew who you were, the one who didn't harm you. Maybe I was that lion—who knows?"

"Sorry, I don't quite follow," she said, trying to interrupt him politely. *What is he talking about? He really is crazy!*

"OK, let's go back to numbers," Alex went on. "Twenty-three—two plus three makes five. That's your sum. Nine plus five makes fourteen. That together is your sum with Oleg. And in fourteen, one plus four makes five again. It works." Alex looked exasperated, as if he had to explain something that was absolutely obvious.

"My friend, can you try not to scare off my girlfriend on our date?" Oleg interrupted.

He called me his girlfriend. Tatiana rejoiced inside.

"Thank you, Alex." Tatiana flashed him a grateful smile.

"OK, kids, I'll let you go," said Alex. "I need to start cleaning. Look at this tip." He gestured with a hand, turned around, and walked back to the auditorium. Tatiana scanned the foyer. It all looked just as clean as it had before the show.

"That's just Alex." Oleg shrugged his shoulders. "You'll get used to him once you get to know him better. Are you ready? Let's go."

Chapter 3

As if by magic, a yellow taxi with a green light was waiting for Tatiana and Oleg outside the theatre.

"How did you do that?" Tatiana couldn't hide the admiration in her voice.

"Years of practice, Sunny. Get inside. Kropotkinskaya, chief. Can we smoke in here?"

The driver nodded.

The address was one Tatiana didn't recognise. "It's my grandfather's place," explained Oleg. "It's empty. He died last year."

"Sorry to hear that."

"Yup. He was fun, Grandpa Ilya. He taught me to play cards. We had a laugh or two."

"My grandfather is dead too. I miss him. He used to send us oranges." Tatiana sighed.

"I want to hear that story one day," Oleg whispered into her ear as he pulled her closer to him.

After a while, the taxi stopped outside a low grey brick building on a quiet side street in central Moscow. The area was a far cry from the newly built blocks where Oleg and Tatiana both lived. This was a secluded corner of Moscow's old residential centre that had managed to stay unchanged for centuries.

The buildings around were mansions with ornate façades,

the former homes of wealthy Muscovites from a bygone era. Pretty old churches, lucky survivors of the communist cultural invasion, nestled between mansions, still intact with their brightly painted walls and golden onion domes. Here and there, small shops with old-fashioned windows had signs above their doors that read "Bread", "Milk", or "Gifts". Tatiana instantly loved this charming corner of the real Moscow.

In the dark entrance hall, the smell of cats and litter greeted them and made her feel at home. Inside, Oleg's grandpa's building was more modern than its neighbours. It had a lift and a waste-disposal chute, luxuries from the 1950s.

Grandfather Ilya's apartment was a studio on the fifth floor. The flat's two windows—one in the kitchen, the other in the main room—overlooked a small inner courtyard. There was a tall tree in the middle of the courtyard with a couple of benches underneath, and a small playground.

The apartment smelled like an old person's home, the distinctive odour of ancient upholstery and curtains mixed with valerian drops. Tatiana could recognise that scent anywhere. She associated the sweet fragrance of the medicine with her own grandmother, who wouldn't go to be bed without first slipping a few drops into a shot glass. She'd slam the elixir down quickly, muttering, "Ah, that's relaxed my heart."

Faded dusky-pink wallpaper covered the walls, and a dining table stood in the centre of six chairs. There was also an antique looking display cabinet full of china and glasses. Against the wall stood a large green sofa with wooden armrests. There were no beds in the room. Tatiana thought that maybe there was a sofa bed.

The couple sat down to smoke in the tiny kitchen. They were dwarfed by the chunky 1950s fridge, which had probably been a tractor in its former life, judging by the noise it was making.

"Are you hungry?" Oleg asked.

Tatiana realised that, apart from that very first evening in Oleg's apartment, this was the first time they had actually sat together in a kitchen. It was peculiar to see Oleg in a domestic environment.

"I think we have some sausages in here somewhere," he continued.

"Great, I can make us something then." Tatiana rose from her seat. She felt more comfortable moving around, opening the fridge door, and filling a pan with water.

"I love watching you here. It suits you, this place, this kitchen. You look like a natural hostess." Oleg had used that soft, sensual tone again.

She posed by the hob. "Are you still hungry, my dear guest? The food will be ready shortly."

"I'm famished!"

They ate steaming sausages with pickles that Tatiana had found at the bottom of the fridge, and they sipped Armenian brandy. Oleg had fetched the bottle from the old cabinet. Tatiana suspected it had been sitting there for a long time and that it must have belonged to Grandfather Ilya.

"Grandpa wasn't a big drinker," Oleg said, noticing her studying the bottle. "It was a birthday present a few years back."

"Why open it now? Didn't you want to keep it for a special occasion?"

"He would have offered it to us, believe me. I was his favourite grandson—his only grandson, in fact. He would have loved you! He would have approved of my choice—just like my parents."

"Your parents? I only met them for a minute." Tatiana recalled that brief meeting at Oleg's place on the morning after the Tatiana's Day party. It was still early. Everyone else had left. Tatiana had stayed behind to help Oleg clear up. He'd called her a taxi. After a while, a dispatch manager had phoned to say that it was outside.

Tatiana was already in her coat when the front door opened and Oleg's parents walked in. They had spent the night in Grandpa Ilya's apartment.

“Mum, Dad, this is Tatiana,” Oleg had said, introducing them. “We’re at university together.”

“Very nice to meet you.” They both smiled. Mr Isaev reached for Tatiana’s hand and kissed it old-fashioned style. Tatiana felt very self-conscious—she didn’t look her best after a sleepless night of smoking and drinking. She just smiled back, trying not to breathe on them, and then hurried out.

“Well, it was enough for them, I guess,” said Oleg. “They didn’t stop talking about you after that—what a lovely girl you were and how it was obvious that you came from a good family. They said I’d be a fool to let you get away.”

Tatiana couldn’t believe her ears. She was used to feeling uncertain about her place in Oleg’s world, but it turned out that even his parents approved of her. What’s more, he actually cared about his parents’ opinion.

He must have read the look of disbelief on her face. “What? We’re a very close family. You’ll see. I’d like you to meet my parents properly soon. Let’s have a toast to us and our families.” Oleg poured more brandy into their glasses. Tatiana, feeling the warmth flowing down the back of her throat, closed her eyes.

“It’s officially time for bed, sunny one. I’ll show you where everything is.” Oleg took the glass from her hand. Together they pulled open the old green sofa and took out the bedding from the drawer underneath. The sight of the bed made her feel uneasy.

“Um, I’d like to take a shower first,” said Tatiana, “but I don’t have a change of clothes with me.”

“Will this do?” Oleg casually pulled out a T-shirt from the cupboard. The worn-out cotton was soft to the touch. It must have been red in its early days, but it had faded to a girlie pink. Tatiana rushed to the bathroom.

Don’t overthink it.

When she came back wearing only the T-shirt, Oleg was already under the covers. “Jump in, Sunny.” His voice sounded strange. “Flick the switch by the door.”

In the dark, under the covers, they embraced and began to kiss. Tatiana couldn't help but think that the fuzzy excitement she had felt when sitting next to Oleg at the theatre was now gone. She felt distant somehow, as if it was someone else making these mechanical actions. She let out a quiet sigh, wanting to show him that she was enjoying what was happening.

Sex had never played a big part in Tatiana's life. Having had sex with only two boys before, she had never really come to like it. She thought that sex was something men enjoyed much more than women did, for their pleasure was clear and self-manifested. For her part, Tatiana found the whole thing a little painful, slightly uncomfortable, and repetitive. She felt she ought to do it because she was expected to.

What gave her satisfaction was the power that she felt when she saw that look of strain and wonder on a young man's at the end. She always got more excited by anticipating the act than by actually doing it. And she knew she wasn't the only one who felt this way. Once, Tatiana had overheard an older student talking to her friend in the Smoking Square.

"I'm a free woman for the next six days."

"Free from what?"

"You know. It was Wednesday yesterday, the day to fulfil my marital duties. I'm done for the whole week now. My husband was happy yesterday, and I am a free and happy woman today."

A duty. That was exactly what Tatiana felt about having sex. She was eager to get it out of the way and then do something more enjoyable, like chatting or smoking. Lucky for her, this time it was all over very quickly.

A few minutes later, Tatiana and Oleg sat up in bed, each holding a lit cigarettes. She relished that first intake of warming smoke. She watched in the dark as two amber lights did a little dance of their own. It felt intimate and cosy sitting like this, side by side. It was the perfect time for sharing stories and secrets.

"You know," she began in a mysterious tone, "I am one year

older than most of my class. When I was six I nearly died of pneumonia. Mother pulled some strings and I was sent me to a children's health resort in Yevpatoria, on the Black Sea. My grandmother came with me. I spent a few months there, having treatments and sunbathing—getting stronger. In the end, I missed a whole year of prep school. Instead of starting at seven, I started at eight."

"That's terrible," Oleg said, sounding serious. "Why didn't you warn me I was sleeping with an old-timer?"

They both laughed. Tatiana was getting used to his humour. "Sorry. I forgot to present my papers upon entry, Comrade Major." Tatiana continued giggling, her little amber light shaking in the darkness.

"Comrade Sergeant Major to you, Comrade Dobrova. And if I showed you my papers, you'd see that I wasn't even born in Moscow. My parents moved here when I was fourteen."

Tatiana sensed the beginning of a story.

My life is slightly pathetic compared to his. I just told him about the main event in mine, and it only took me a minute.

"So where did you live before then?" she asked quietly.

"I was born in Akademgorodok, near Novosibirsk." Oleg pressed his cigarette into the ashtray on the floor and then reached for another. "It's a scientific haven in the middle of Siberia. Both my dad and grandfather were physicists—a family tradition, they used to joke. My mum taught English and French at the university there.

"It was a very strange place to live, very isolated—privileged, if you will. Just research professors and students. We didn't even have to shop for groceries! Grandfather got home deliveries.

"And then Dad got a transfer to Moscow. Grandpa Ilya applied for a position too, and we all ended up moving here. It was a big shock. Huge city: life moves fast, lots of people everywhere."

Oleg pulled Tatiana closer in a tight embrace. She held her breath, afraid of interrupting him.

"I had a tough time settling into school. I was just a provincial kid with a funny accent. I couldn't understand the other kids' slang or fashion. I was different. 'Siberian Teddy Bear' they called me. I was a bit overweight back then.

"So I had to work hard to fit in. Playing guitar helped a lot. I learned the songs my classmates were listening to and played them at parties and school discos. I dropped my accent and began talking like them, making jokes they would find funny. I got accepted. They didn't laugh at me anymore, but they still called me names. Am I boring you?" He paused and kissed her hair.

"No, not at all. Please carry on." Tatiana tickled his chest reassuringly.

"I made only one good friend—Alex," Oleg went on. "He was an outsider, like me, because of his mental issues. Truth be told, he wanted everybody to believe he was crazy. He just wanted to be different. It takes courage. That's why I've always respected him.

"After we graduated, me and Alex decided to take a break from studying. My parents weren't happy, of course, but I told them I was going to 'fulfil my patriotic duty' and do military service for two years. I'd go to university later.

"I just wanted to stand my ground. With their connections in education, I could have easily gotten accepted to university and missed the army altogether, but I just wanted to prove myself to them. You know, youthful maximalism." Oleg waved his hand.

"What, you volunteered? Really?" Tatiana was astonished. "You could have been killed or injured in Afghanistan!" She reached for the cigarette packet.

"Yeah, that's where I *wanted* to go, believe it or not," said Oleg, striking the lighter for her. "Alex was smarter. He just got his mental disability papers in order. 'I'm not going to go anywhere with no central heating or plumbing,' he said. 'I'm not sure who's the crazy one here, but good luck.' That was his blessing."

"So, did you end up in Afghanistan?" Tatiana recalled the university rumours.

"Not even close. I think my grandfather interfered. Called some of his old army friends. He was a war veteran, you know." Oleg blew out smoke.

"At first they sent me to a quiet, civilised garrison outside Leningrad, close to the Finnish border. My musical talents were quickly discovered there, and they put me in charge of the radio station. For many it would have been a dream post, but I felt it was not 'real' enough. I was bored." He chuckled. "And then I ended up guarding an old tank-division outpost in Turkmenistan, by the Amu Darya."

"But how?" Tatiana remembered the name of the river from geography lessons. It sounded so exotic and distant. She also recalled the Karakum Desert; *Karakum* means "Black Sand" in the local language. The desert covered most of Turkmenistan. She closed her eyes for a second and imagined a caravan of old, tired camels gently stepping with their huge suede hooves onto the burning sand, crossing the endless sands in hope of reaching the cooling waters of the mighty Amu Darya.

Tatiana could have sworn she felt the dry heat of the desert sun on her skin. Then she remembered where the image had come from—the camels walking among sand dunes that were pictured on the chocolate wrapper from her childhood. The candy was called Karakum. It was a piece of dark chocolate with hard fudge inside—too bitter for a child's taste buds.

"How on earth did you end up there?" The picture was still vivid in her mind.

"Well, I called our commander a moron, so they transferred me. Well, he was! He was an uneducated, drunk, red-faced idiot. He only knew how to bark orders and how to speak direct quotations from 'The Regulations for the Servicemen of the Soviet Army'. Everybody thought those things about him; I am just the one who said it out loud."

Tatiana giggled. "And you call yourself intelligent, Comrade Isaev?"

"I know, I know. It was stupid. Childish. I came up to him and saluted, saying, 'Comrade Major, you are a moron.' Then I marched off.

"The next thing I know, they're preparing my transfer papers to the 1st Light Mortar Division, near Tashauz on the border with Uzbekistan. Not even close to the Afghan border."

"The post was to guard tanks and other military equipment. When I arrived there in the middle of the summer, the temperature was about 40°C. I quickly discovered that I was the only Russian speaker—among the soldiers, at least," he continued. "They called themselves *esger*, warriors."

Oleg went on, saying, "Military laws, subordination—all that army stuff doesn't matter to them. Those guys live under their own rules in the land of their ancestors. Most of them were local boys—farmers, cotton pickers."

"Wasn't Russian taught at school?" Tatiana asked finally.

"I'm sure it was, but I don't think they cared enough about going to school regularly. They had been working in the cotton fields since they were kids. It was a different world, Sunny." Oleg let out a sigh. "They were brutal. They beat me black and blue every single day. They must have had specific orders, but I never complained to the officers. I thought they'd kill me if I did.

"My nose was broken three times. My whole body was one giant bruise. Then I finally got a lucky break. One of them completely lost it one day and stabbed me in the leg with a bayonet.

"I ended up in the military hospital a few kilometres away. That was like heaven—the most luxurious break I've ever had. Clean sheets, spotless ward. I was the only patient."

"Oh, Oleg, that's terrible!" Tatiana started to run her fingers through his hair.

"For some reason, they didn't send the wounded from

Afghanistan there. I'm telling you, Paradise smells of chlorine bleach and slightly burnt porridge. There was an angel there, a half-Russian nurse called Zoya. I shall never forget her gentle hands."

"So it was that bad, huh? I mean, back in the barracks."

"Pretty horrible. Needless to say, I was petrified to go back. I knew I couldn't complain about the beatings, so I was just lying there on the hospital bed figuring out what to do next. I was even praying that the wound wouldn't heal too quickly.

"Zoya brought me a guitar. I killed time playing for her and the doctor. And then one day I had a visitor from my post. His name was Azat. He was like the leader of them—tall, dark, reserved. He grabbed my guitar and sat on my bed.

"'Oleg.' He said to me in Russian, 'You're OK. Sorry about that beating. It won't happen again. Come back as a friend.'

"'But I thought you all hated me. What changed?' I asked.

"He said, 'You took it like a man. You never complained. So you have our respect.' Then he reached over and gave me my guitar. And that was it.

"My leg got better and I went back. I played 'Yesterday' for them every day. Turned out to be their favourite song! They never got tired of it—even learned the words."

"And you just forgave them all?" Tatiana noticed that her cigarette had burned down to the filter. She stubbed it out in the ashtray.

"I did. Seriously. The first few nights in hospital I was dreaming about bloody revenge, but then I simply, I don't know, changed my mind. I didn't want to hurt them; I just wanted to make them like me, respect me. That's all.

"I was, in the end, smarter than them—more educated and more ambitious than them too. And don't forget, I could play 'Yesterday' on that guitar!" He smirked and paused.

"Why are you so quiet, Sunny?" he asked.

"I'm thinking about your story. It's not what I expected," she replied quietly. She'd been taken aback by his honesty.

"Sorry to disappoint you. I'm not a war hero. But at least you know how I got all these scars. I can show you the one on my leg later. You are the first person I have told the whole story to."

"What, not even your parents?"

"What? You think I would admit to them that I nearly got myself killed for being stupid? In their version of events, I got beaten up by some local thugs while on leave."

"Why are you telling me this now?"

"Because I trust you. Listen. Since I got back from the army and started university, my life has changed. On that hospital bed I was able to think about my future—a lot. Everything came into focus. I realised that I am a survivor. I am in control. I will succeed. How do it know it? Simple.

"Back then, I made myself a promise, which I'm going to keep. I said to myself, 'I will never be poor. Never.'"

Tatiana heard steel notes in Oleg's voice.

"That means, Sunny, that I will work hard and think hard every day because I don't have a backup plan. I don't have a millionaire uncle passing on his fortune to me. Nor am I going to find a pirate's treasure. I have only me.

"For my parents, money was not a priority. A different generation, as you know. But I believe this is our time, Sunny. Anybody can become somebody. We are likely to live through all these changes going on in the country. Are you with me?"

"I'm still here, sure," Tatiana said teasingly.

"No. I mean, will you go on this journey with me?"

"What do you mean by that? I don't follow." She was refusing to believe the significance of the moment.

"OK. I'll explain another way. Tell me, what's the best thing about the Moscow metro?"

"Oh I don't know. The fact that it always runs on time? Or the fact that it has the most beautiful underground palaces for stations?"

"No, Sunny. Neither of these. The answer is that it will always be missing me. I am not going underground ever again. Those bronze statues and marble walls will never see me down there. I will always take taxis. Eventually, I will own my own car, a big American limousine. I refuse to be part of the crowd. Understand?"

And before she'd even had a chance to answer, Oleg switched on a dim table lamp at the side of the sofa.

"Oh, Sunny, I almost forgot. Happy Women's Day." He stretched out his arm, pulled a small blue box from his jeans pocket, and placed it in her hand.

Tatiana blinked. Her eyes were still adjusting to the light. The fabric of the box was smooth and silky to the touch.

"Open it," Oleg said, gently nudging her.

Inside there was a delicate golden chain with a double pendant—a miniature sun and half-moon. "Oleg, thank you. It's beautiful!" Tatiana took it out of the box and brought it closer to her face.

"Well, you know you are like the sunshine to me. But I want to spend my life with you—under the moonlight, too. How would you feel about that?"

"You mean you want me to stay with you? But where?"

She just wanted him to say it.

"Right here, Sunshine. In this very apartment. It is mine now. We can live here."

"Just like that?" Tatiana tried to dilute his seriousness.

"No, not like that. The proper way. The official way. We can get married. What do you think?"

This time Tatiana didn't reply with a question. His tone was compelling, completely earnest. The answer hit her like lightning. It was very clear and simple.

This building with its homey smell of cats, this old bare tree outside the window, and this man with his steely eyes and his drive and talent: she wanted it all. More than anything in the world, Tatiana wanted to stay here with Oleg on this sagging sofa, in this room with the faded wallpaper.

"Yes. I'd say yes. Let's do it!" She heard an approving rattle from the kitchen fridge. "But shouldn't we tell our parents?"

"Of course we'll tell them. They will be happy for us, I'm sure. They've stayed married for all these years. It worked for them; it will work for us."

"What about kids? Do you want to have kids?" Tatiana hadn't thought about asking this question until now.

"Of course. In time though. We're still young and you need to finish your studies. You're so good at studying. I love that clever head of yours." Oleg planted a soft kiss on her forehead.

Tatiana blushed. It was the best compliment he had given her so far. She felt shy and proud at the same time.

"Hold on a minute," she said, something suddenly occurring to her. "Why are you saying that *I* should finish my studies? What about you? Are you dropping out of uni?"

"No, I'm not going to stop, but I won't go there quite as often. I was hoping you'd keep me updated with work—hand in what you can on my behalf. I've spoken to some of the teachers already, and our dean is a reasonable man. I've promised to pay for the end-of-year faculty party and the renovation of the library next summer—"

"How are you going to pay for that? That must cost loads of money." An alarming thought crossed her mind. *What kind of hustle is he planning?*

"Don't worry, everything is legal. I've got a job," Oleg said. "I was going to tell you. It's a new project—very promising. I have a new partner now. His name is Vlad. We met through the Préférence set.

"Alex and I tried our usual trick on him, but he was just too good. He pretended to be a beginner, but then he showed us his true colours. He's almost a pro, you know. A good actor, too. And no wonder—he has worked in show business for many years. But I'm getting ahead of myself." Oleg paused.

"So, when he figured out our game and we began to lose big time, Vlad put his cards on the table and offered us a proposition. 'We can continue playing until I walk away with all your money, or we can stop now and you can come and work for me,' he said. 'You're just the kind of people I need on my team—smart and resourceful.'

"He told us that he worked in television as the producer of entertainment programmes, but big changes and restructuring meant that more chances were being created and a whole new industry was starting: advertising on the TV. There is a lot of money to be made there, but you have to be well connected. You have to know the system. So Vlad's our guy." Oleg paused again.

"He's been around for fifteen years. He knows everybody, and everybody knows him. He wants to grow the business, get into the advertising scene. He's also planning to open some nightclubs and all kinds of things, Sunny!" Oleg's face beamed with excitement. He seemed to have completely ignored the fact that he was now standing in the middle of the room wearing only his underwear. He was gesticulating enthusiastically.

His passion was contagious. Tatiana found herself climbing up on to the sofa. It was very late at night, but the little girl inside her was fully awake—and, as if hit by a sudden sugar rush, she began to jump up and down. Grandfather Ilya's sofa screeched in protest, the old wooden legs scraping against the floorboards with each bounce.

"I can't believe I'm to be the bride of a future advertising king!" The little girl was out of control now, squealing with delight.

"I'm flattered, really, but let's not jump the gun here. The future king is Vlad, OK? I'm just the pageboy." Oleg's head was nodding up and down as he tried to follow Tatiana with his gaze.

"Oh no, baby!" she protested. "You will be a king one day. I can feel it!" And then suddenly they heard a horrible, echoing bang coming from a large radiator under the window.

"Oops, Sunny! We woke up the neighbours! Calm down."

Tatiana froze, standing on the sofa, her heart racing from the vigorous jumping. "Will they call the police? What do you think? It's not wise to upset the neighbours on the first day—especially if we're going to live here."

“Yup, they might! Anyway, we should treat Grandfather Ilya’s sofa with more respect.” Oleg went to the kitchen and quickly returned with a cup of water. “Have a sip and sit down, Citizen Isaeva; otherwise, you and that husband of yours will spend the night in a cell at the local militia branch.” Oleg switched off the side lamp, and the room plunged into darkness.

Citizen Isaeva. Before falling asleep, Tatiana repeated those two words in her head. *I better start getting used to that name!*

Her happiness felt almost surreal.

Chapter 4

Tatiana was making her way from the metro station to the Olympic Stadium. It was unusually warm for late March. She always loved the beginning of spring, what with the warmth of the sun on her face and the gentle music made by water droplets falling from buildings.

Tatiana walked with her head up, looking for the icicles. There were usually long rows of them attached to guttering. Water dripped from their pointy ends, falling into small pools on the ground. It was a cheerful soundtrack for the changing season. The icicles shone under the bright light like crystals. They looked like elaborate decorations from the Snow Queen's palace, nature's works of art. But they were dangerous too. They hung in large clusters and had sharp ends.

Many buildings got roped off with warning signs under them reading, "Beware of falling ice". The icicles often came down unexpectedly, killing or injuring unlucky passers-by.

There were lots of workmen standing on roofs at this time of year, breaking big pieces off with ice picks and shouting at people below, saying, "Watch out! Move out the way!" There would be a loud crashing sound as heavy lumps smashed to the ground.

Tatiana had to navigate her way very carefully among the paths and alleys of the Olympic Park, avoiding the deep puddles of melted snow. She stopped on a dry patch near a bench, under a street light.

The sun, reflecting off the snow, was unbearably bright. It started to hurt her eyes. She squinted and looked around. Was it the same alley? She couldn't be sure. They all looked so similar around here. Yet the direction was right.

I can't believe it was only a few weeks ago! Me running away from him like a silly little child, then us kissing under a light like this one. It was freezing back then, and the snow was deep and fresh. But look at it now—it's on its way out: lumpy, heavy, watery. Go, snow! Go away!

Still, she knew it only too well—this was just a thaw. The wintry weather would soon return with a vengeance. But who cared? Spring was on the way! She could smell it in the air. Tatiana closed her eyes and inhaled deeply. O the overpowering, unmistakable scent! It was a mixture of wet trees, melting snow, and above all, the warm, earthy tang of moist soil. There were just a few patches of it, showing here and there in the warmest spots, usually wherever hot-water pipes ran underground. But even these small patches could produce the indisputable, heady aroma of the approaching spring.

Tatiana recalled the old poem she'd read in school about the eternal battle between Winter as an old witch, all dressed in white, her hair long and silver, and Spring as a young, barefoot freckled-faced girl in a green dress. The redhead was always a bit disrespectful. She danced around and laughed at the old lady. So to punish the naughty child just before departing, the old witch would blow the very last blizzard.

Tatiana took another deep breath and continued walking down the path.

The open area just outside the stadium gates had been built up with temporary single-storey pavilions. They housed the newest, and largest, market in the city.

These days, the shelves of Moscow's shops were empty, so every weekend Muscovites made their way to markets just like this one. Here, everything could be found, from all kinds of food and provisions to clothes, shoes, and electronics. Everything was available—for double or even triple the official price.

Tatiana had gotten used to shopping this way. At least there was never a queue, and the stallholders were friendlier than the grumpy shop assistants. There were also cute cafes selling tea and coffee in proper cups, with a big variety of her favourite cakes and sweets. Plus, music was played everywhere through large speakers.

Today, Tatiana came to the market to see her friend Lena, who was working at a stall selling very good fakes of branded trainers. They were made in China and Vietnam. Apart for the fact that they all came in unmarked white boxes, no one could really spot the difference between them and the real thing.

The shoes were selling at a much cheaper price than the real ones, so business was good. Since the pavilion was usually full of customers at weekends, Tatiana had chosen a quiet midweek day to visit her friend.

She had met Lena at the university interviews the summer before. They had sat next to each other in the long corridor, waiting their turn to be quizzed by scary-looking grey-haired professors.

Tatiana had only glanced at the pretty slender brunette in front of her. The young woman in the faded denim skirt and bright Hawaiian shirt leisurely crossed her long legs at the ankles as she leaned against the wall. She looked too cool and too trendy for the occasion. Tatiana straightened her own long and frumpy over-the-knee dress and prayed that not all of the female applicants would be so fashionable. She spent a few more minutes avoiding looking at the young woman, but then their glances met. Lena's large hazel eyes sparkled warmly. She gave Tatiana a strange lopsided smile that made her face look almost tragic.

"Do I look nervous?" she asked, speaking first. "I'm petrified."

"Well, you're hiding it well then," Tatiana replied with a giggle. "I even thought you were in the wrong queue."

"Phew!" The young woman mopped invisible sweat from her forehead. "And I should know better. I already tried last year and failed completely."

"You're joking!" Tatiana's heart sank. "I thought the interview was just a formality before the exam."

"It is in this department," Lena replied with an assuring gesture. "I tried journalism before, but I didn't have enough articles published."

"Oh." It was Tatiana's turn to sigh with relief. "I heard that the competition for that one was insane."

"Yup!" Lena said, making a serious face. "So now you've established the state of my mental health!"

"Oh no. I didn't mean—" Tatiana tried to protest.

"Ha! I'm just messing with you." Lena winked and jumped to her feet. She crossed over the space between them and sat next to Tatiana on the bench. "I'm Lena," she said, pressing Tatiana's hand for a handshake.

"Tatiana Dobrova," Tatiana replied, squeezing Lena's hand.

"Nice to meet you. So, Dobrova, what's your story?" Lena completely ignored her first name.

Tatiana shrugged her shoulders. "I don't know," she said. "Just trying to get some higher education?" Both of them giggled. Tatiana immediately felt at ease with the strange young woman.

After the interview—which wasn't as bad as they had thought it would be—Lena Petrova invited Tatiana back to her family home. She lived within walking distance of the university, in an old apartment block on the edge of a leafy square. Inside the small flat, Tatiana found herself being greeted by a tired-looking mother and a small pale girl in a wheelchair: twelve-year-old Vera.

"Mum, I think I've passed this time," Lena reported cheerfully. "Oh, this is my new friend, Tatiana Dobrova. We'll sit in the kitchen for a bit, OK?"

"Thank goodness!" said Mrs Petrova, sighing. "It's nice to meet you, Tatiana." She quietly returned to the living room.

"Hey, Verunya." Lena turned to her sister and bent to give her a hug. "I'll read you a story before I go to work today, OK? I'll just have some tea with my friend first. Say hi to Tatiana."

The girl nodded her head and said, "Hello."

Lena carefully pushed the wheelchair into the living room, shouting, "Dobrova, go through to the kitchen. Make yourself at home."

Tatiana was almost frozen with astonishment. Lena hadn't mentioned her family when they'd chatted. She'd only said that she had a job. And now Tatiana saw why. Not in a million years had she imagined that Lena had sister with a disability—someone she had to support.

Lena seemed very confident and effortless, and yet, unlike Tatiana and most others their age, she made sacrifices for her family on a daily basis. Tatiana felt almost ashamed of her own carefree life.

In the kitchen, over a pot of raspberry tea and oat biscuits, Lena told her the full story.

When Vera had been born prematurely, it quickly became obvious that there was something wrong with her. The doctors and nurses at the maternity hospital, and even Lena's own father, tried to persuade her mother to give Vera up and turn her over to the care of the state. This was the choice often made by parents of babies with severe disabilities. But Lena's mother was absolutely determined to take her daughter home.

"What are you all talking about?" she'd said. "She's my child; I love her no matter what. She is my responsibility." Her husband gave her an ultimatum—either him or the baby.

Lena's mother was firm in her decision. Once, she brought Vera home, the girls' father walked away. "And I haven't seen the bastard since. Pathetic little man." This was the first and only time Lena mentioned her father to Tatiana.

After Vera's birth, Lena's family life changed completely.

The government's pension for disability was not enough for the three of them to live on. And since Mrs Petrova was too busy taking care of Vera to hold down a day job, she worked during the night, from home, as a typist. The girls got used to sleeping to the sound of their mother's old typewriter.

Lena had been working since the age of sixteen, first as a post girl and then at a farmers' market selling vegetables. There, she met a man called Armen who took her situation to heart and offered her work on his stall at the new Olympic Park market. His own estranged family lived in Yerevan.

"Armen is the father I should have had," said Lena.

Her mother insisted that Lena's working shouldn't interfere with her education, so she urged her daughter to apply to university. And that's how Lena ended up in that corridor of the Russian department. It was Tatiana's luckiest day. She had met her best friend.

But despite the fact that both young women had been accepted to university, they didn't end up in the same class. Lena's family needed money more than ever, so she had to transfer to the evening course. This is why she now spent her days at the market selling trainers—and her evenings in the classrooms. Lena continued to scribble articles, though, whatever else she was doing. Journalism was her passion.

Tatiana found her friend inside the pavilion, sitting at one side of a long table covered with brand new superwhite trainers with neon-coloured stripes and logos. A strong smell of plastic and faux leather filled her nostrils.

There were no other customers. The silence was broken only by distant music coming from the outside speakers, and the low humming of a fan heater that Lena had by her side. She was ferociously writing something on a large pad of paper, a few magazine clippings scattered in front of her.

Lena was wearing fingerless gloves. From time to time she stretched her hands towards the heater to warm them up. It was still quite cold inside the glass structure.

Tatiana watched her friend for a few seconds. Lena was so consumed by writing that she didn't notice Tatiana standing next to her.

Tatiana finally broke the silence. "Well, hello, friend."

"Oh, Dobrova! Hi!" Lena looked up with a smile as if she'd been expecting to see Tatiana. "How's your young life treating you?"

"Not bad, I guess. What are you up to?" Tatiana decided to bide her time before breaking her big news.

"Ah, just an article for a student paper, about the history of Russian public toilets."

"Really? Fascinating subject."

"I hear your sarcasm, but it's interesting, believe it or not. Besides, what do you want me to write about? That after the monetary devaluation Vera's disability pay has become ludicrous? Or maybe I shall write about your grandmother, the war veteran, who still needs a ration card after forty-five years of peace if she wants to buy flour or macaroni?"

Lena's voice grew louder. "Or do you want me to expose the biggest magic trick of our time—the disappearance of goods and groceries from the shops and their miraculous reappearance on the market stalls? That's all boring stuff, my friend. Our everyday life—who wants to read about that?"

"But public toilets. Why?" Tatiana was puzzled.

"Why not? What do you think about them?"

"I don't like to think about them. They're disgusting."

"Exactly! I've been studying articles on the subject and have found that not much has even been said. But maybe if we improve our horrible public lavatories, some other positive changes will follow!"

"Your political views never fail to amaze me!" Tatiana was in awe of her pal's strong-mindedness.

"What politics? I'm just amusing myself." Lena made a dismissive gesture. "So, what brings you here? Need a pair of new trainers to run away from that control freak Isaev? Or maybe you are after some matching 'his' and 'hers', so you can jog together holding hands into the sunset?"

Tatiana giggled nervously. "You should say a pair of matching rings, his and hers."

"Are you kidding me? How long have you known each other, like, three and a half days?

"Yeah, I know. It's been two months actually. Seems like a short time, but we decided to get married."

"Don't tell me it was your idea. I won't believe it anyway."

"No, you're not wrong. Oleg suggested it, and I sort of agreed."

"Sort of? But why? What's the rush? You don't know each other that well."

Tatiana drew in a sigh. She had expected an interrogation. "I know. It might look like a rushed decision to you, but I think I love him and I really want to live with him in his grandfather's apartment. I want to have my own home, my own family."

"So, is it all about you finding your independence, you growing up?"

"Call it what you wish. I've made a decision. Can you just be happy for me?" Tatiana implored.

"Dobrova, you are my dear friend and I really care about you. Of course I want you to be happy, and I totally understand what you see in him. He is not a handsome devil, that's for sure, but you can't deny his charm and talent. He is just so overbearing. It sometimes feels like there's too much of him in a room. Are you sure you can handle it?"

"I think I've done a good job so far," said Tatiana. "He is different when he is with me. Besides, people change, you know."

"OK, you go for it, girl." Lena shrugged her shoulders." You have a steel backbone. I just don't think he deserves you, that's all."

“Why would you say that?” Tatiana was still convinced that it was the other way around.

“You are so pure, and he is not.”

“I am not pure!” Tatiana shouted. “I am not a virgin!”

“That’s not what I meant.” Lena paused. “You look at the world, at the people around you, with those bright eyes of yours wide open. You just see goodness and positivity in everything and everyone. It even shows in your smile.”

“Oh, you make me sound so naive!” Tatiana was getting annoyed now.

“Not naive, but overly optimistic sometimes.”

“And you are overly cynical, you know.”

“I’ll agree with that. But I have good reason to be. You know I don’t think much of men anyway.” Lena’s face darkened. Tatiana understood she was referring to her father. “Anyhow,” Lena said, tapping the table, “Isaev better treat you well. Otherwise I’ll run him down. I have all the gear for it.” Lena nodded towards the display of trainers. They both giggled.

“What did your parents say about it?”

“Er, I haven’t told them yet. Actually, you’re the first to know.”

“Hmm, I wonder how Madame Justice will take it?”

“Mother?” Tatiana shrugged her shoulders. “I’m more worried about telling my dad.”

“Oh, Daddy’s-girl syndrome. I understand. I’m sure he’ll be all right as long as you are happy. Actually, I have some news too.” Lena took a business card out of her bag. The company logo and the name on it were foreign, possibly English. Tatiana couldn’t tell.

“What’s this? Got yourself an international admirer?”

“It so happens this is the business card of a British modelling agent. A few days ago, this foreign couple came in. I thought they were interested in trainers, but the woman tried to say—her Russian was terrible—that they thought I’d make a good model. They said I should call them to arrange an interview, and then they invited me to a casting next month. They didn't look fake either. Armen's secretary called the number. It really is an agency in London."

"Really? That's amazing!" Tatiana clapped her hands. "Congrats, my friend!"

"But, Dobrova, be serious. Do I look like a model to you?"

Tatiana stepped back to give her friend an estimating look. Even with her fingernails bitten short (Lena couldn't control the habit when she was immersed in writing) and her hair twisted into a tight bun and needing a good wash, Lena looked impressive. Her slender legs, always in black leggings, stretched far in front of her. At university these were the legs that were envied by all the young women and admired by all the young men.

"I'd kill to have pins like yours," Tatiana said with conviction.

"Oh, really? I can't find a single pair of jeans or trousers—they're all too short for me. I'll be buried in capri pants. Besides, these two poles come as a set with albatross wings." Lena stretched her slim arms to her sides. "Check out the span on that! If you give me two more, I can make a human helicopter! I can only wear men's sweaters. People always called me Beanpole at school."

"Nice try, but you'll get no pity from me." Tatiana shook her head. "Let's go outside for a smoke."

The blinding sunshine reflected off the tin roofs and the snow on the ground made them both scrunch their eyes. "I can smell it today!" Tatiana exclaimed. "The spring. It's coming."

"Yeah, along with cold puddles, wet feet, and flu." Lena turned away from the sun, sticking a cigarette between her lips.

"Always glass-half-full, but I still love you! So, what have you decided about modelling? You going? What did your mum say?" Tatiana clicked the lighter.

"She doesn't know yet. I'm still not sure about it. I've told Armen though. He took me to dinner, toasted my beauty and all that. Said he always knew he wouldn't be able to have me to himself for long. He even offered to pay for my portfolio. He knows this fashion photographer who can do it for me."

"But you were never *his* in the first place." Even as Tatiana said it, realisation sank in.

Lena looked Tatiana right in the eye. "Don't you judge me! I keep him company sometimes. He is a very lonely man. Armen's been so generous to us all. Last summer he paid for Vera to go to this mineral spa—and Mum too. It was the first time in eleven years she'd travelled anywhere other than the shops."

Tatiana was speechless for a bit. "But ... isn't he a bit old?" she finally managed.

"I am not going to marry him! I am extremely grateful for all he's done for us. That's all," Lena added with the force of a slamming door.

Tatiana knew it was the end of that discussion. "I think you should do it," she said quietly.

"I don't know about that." Lena looked hesitant. "Mum will be very upset if I leave the course. She's said it many times: 'You need a diploma to be somebody in life.' She doesn't want a sacrifice from me, but we need money. I can't keep seeing her like this—black circles under her eyes. She hardly ever sleeps between Vera and working nights. I dream about buying Vera a new wheelchair, too—a light one, modern. Not like the heavy, prehistoric one she has now. My mum has a bad back from pushing it." Lena's voice was determined and serious.

"So take this chance then," said Tatiana. "I will come with you to see the dean. We'll ask for you to be transferred over to the distance learning faculty or something, and I can always keep you up to date with work." As she was talking, Tatiana saw Lena's eyes well up with tears.

"You're such a good friend, Dobrova! Thank you!" Lena flicked away her unfinished cigarette and embraced Tatiana.

Balancing on her tiptoes, for the difference in their height was significant, Tatiana whispered into Lena's ear, "Will you come to my wedding? It's in July."

"I wouldn't miss it for the world! So, when are you breaking the news to your parents?" Lena asked, wiping her nose with the back of her hand and regaining her composure.

"Well, not for two weeks! It's Oleg's birthday, so we've arranged for the families to meet then."

"Good luck with that! Hey, I've got to get back to work. Customers! At last!" Lena nodded towards two women entering the pavilion. "So long, my young friend. Say hi to your charming Isaev." She went back to the pavilion.

Tatiana walked towards the metro station. *Young friend? We're the same age!* Sometimes she felt like she had a neon sign over her head reading, "Feel free to patronise!"

Chapter 5

Tatiana's fingers were playing with the double pendant on the chain around her neck, tracing the shapes of the sun and the half-moon. For his birthday, Oleg had booked a private dining room in an old, grand hotel. Tatiana was first to arrive. She was standing by the floor-to-ceiling window, mesmerised by the view outside. It was perfect, like a very detailed painting set in a massive oak frame.

The April sky was turning lilac as the sun set over the city. In sharp contrast to the pastels above, there stood the Kremlin in all its earthy red glory. The dark terracotta building housing the State Historical Museum was on the left, the tall Arsenal Tower was on the right, and the elaborate multicoloured cupola of St Basil's was just beyond. Despite the gloomy history of the cathedral's blinded architects, Tatiana always pictured St Basil's as a gigantic child's toy. The bold and random colours of its onion domes reminded her of the wooden pyramid puzzles from her happy kindergarten days.

Now she was watching the black clock face of the Spasskaya Tower. The brass minute hand was coming up to the 12, and Tatiana was anticipating the long solemn chime. For her, like all Russians, that tune was associated with the beginning of a new year.

Looking through the thick double glass, Tatiana realised

that she wouldn't be able to hear the chime anyway. Even the noise of the rush-hour traffic below was hardly audible.

"Hello, Stripey! Have you been waiting for a long time?"

"Daddy!" Tatiana smiled. Without turning back, she saw the reflection of a familiar figure in a grey shapeless suit standing right behind her. "It's not even seven yet. I was early." She pointed at the clock outside. Then she turned around to face Nikolay Ivanovich Dobrov.

"Mum went to pick up your grandmother. They're on their way. I came straight from work. You nervous, Stripey?" He gave her a warm smile.

"No. Not anymore. I felt better after I told you and Mother about the real reason for this party. What about Grandma? Did you tell her?" Tatiana asked anxiously.

"Your mum will brief her on the way. Sorry, I had to delegate that task to the lawyer. I'm sure Grandma will still have her comments!" Tatiana's father winked at her.

"I guess I'm ready for those," said Tatiana, and they both laughed. "Dad, one more thing." She paused.

"Sure, what is it?" Nikolay Ivanovich made a serious face.

"Please don't call me Stripey in front of everyone."

"Of course. It is our secret, Stripey." He mouthed the last word.

When Tatiana was four or five, her father had taken her to the zoo. She had been very impressed. As a true city child, she was seeing many of the animals for the first time. But it was a small tiger cub that captured her little heart.

She stood outside the enclosure refusing to move, watching him playing with his brother and sister while their mother lay beside them. She decided that the object of her affection couldn't stay anonymous, so she quickly gave him the most obvious name for a tiger—Stripey.

Nikolay Ivanovich had tried to pull her away, had tried the bribe her with her favourite waffle cone ice cream, but it was all in vain. Tatiana begged him to write a letter to—or, better still, to go in person to see—the director of the zoo and demand to buy Stripey. Tatiana pleaded, saying that she was more than capable of looking after the cub and would teach him tricks.

She had just watched *The Jungle Book* and was convinced that if Mowgli could talk to the animals, then Stripey could easily learn to speak, too. The parenting skills and patience of Nikolay Ivanovich were well tested that day. Eventually father and daughter made it home, but Tatiana didn't give up.

Viktoria Andreevna came up with a practical solution. She told her husband to take Tatiana to the pet market on a Sunday. Once there, they came across stalls selling kittens of all kinds and colours. "Look!" Nikolay Ivanovich was adamant that they were going to finish their ordeal here. "There's Stripey!" He pointed to a ginger kitten with orange streaks.

But Tatiana began to weep. "No, Daddy, no! That's just a kitten. I want a tiger! Do they sell tigers here?" she asked with hope in her voice.

"Wrong country, little girl," replied the stallholder.

The solution to this impossible problem came as suddenly as the apple that had fallen on Newton's head. Nikolay Ivanovich and Tatiana were at the local supermarket one Saturday, filling their basket according to Viktoria Andreevna's shopping list—their usual weekend chore. Afterwards, they would stop at the playground on the way home.

It was while standing in line to pay that Tatiana saw him. "Stripey!" she shouted from the top of her lungs, pointing at the shelf high above the cashier's head. There, among the bottles of unpopular syrupy liquor, dusty plastic flowers, and other things that nobody ever bought, sat a toy tiger. And he was even better-looking than the one from the zoo. His plastic green eyes sparkled and his whiskers stood up as if he was happy to greet Tatiana. "Daddy, it's him! It's Stripey!" Tatiana screamed with excitement. Nikolay nodded to the cashier, who rose from her seat to fetch the toy.

Close up, the tiger was even bigger and softer than Tatiana had imagined. When she wrapped her arms around him in a tight embrace, Nikolay had no choice but to say, "I'll take it." The cashier glared at him disapprovingly. The price tag on Stripey showed that he cost more than all the contents of the basket put together.

Tatiana spent the next year of her life talking to Stripey, putting him to bed every night, and teaching him all the tricks she could think of. And after that phase of Tatiana's young life was over, Stripey had taken a proud place on her bookshelf.

"Don't you think it's time to declutter your room?" Mother had asked recently. "That stuffed thing has been sitting there for years."

"Leave it, Mum. It's my room."

Viktoria Andreevna had always been good at organising herself and others, but she had never thought to ask about the story behind her daughter's nickname.

Thinking of her mother Tatiana let out a sigh. When she was younger, she used to think that for mother work came first, always ahead of her family. During their arguments she used it as her main accusation. But lately Tatiana has become more accepting of mother's ways. It was as if she stepped back a little and finally saw Viktoria Andreevna as a whole person, a woman, with her own aspirations, faults and attempts to balance all of her duties, to be a good wife and mother. After that realisation Tatiana's relationship with her mother had improved naturally. She no longer dreaded family gatherings, usually presided by the articulate Law professor.

Now Tatiana's reverie was broken by a tall man in a formal white jacket. He was offering drinks. "No, thank you. We'll wait for the others. They should be here soon," Tatiana said, refusing politely. The waiter nodded and hurried out.

It feels so strange, being in charge at this place. But he seemed in no doubt, so I must look the part. It doesn't feel too bad, ordering people around. Tatiana smiled with satisfaction.

"So, Dad, how's work been?" she asked as they sat down, side by side, at the large round table in the middle of the room.

"Lots of excitement lately. We're on the verge of a breakthrough which can change everything!" Nikolay's face lit up. The tone of his voice changed as he spoke with urgency and conviction about his work, just like always.

Oh, what have I done? I shouldn't have started him on that. Now he'll bore me to death about genes and molecular biology.

Nikolay Ivanovich was a scientist in the most complete sense of the word, as he was obsessive, stubborn, and meticulous. He worked in research at a microbiology institute specialising in genetic engineering. For the past few years, he had been working on applying genetic engineering to oncology. He truly believed that the process of growing and modifying human cells would produce a cure for cancer. Some of his colleagues were not so optimistic, tending to share a dark joke among themselves about how everyone dies of cancer if they live long enough. Despite this, Nikolay Ivanovich stayed focused. The disease—that plague of the twentieth century—had already claimed the lives of his wife's parents. For him, it was personal, Dr Dobrov versus cancer: game on.

Nikolay Dobrov had arrived in Moscow from a quiet village near Tula in the mid 1960s. A bright and determined provincial boy, he was accepted to study biology at Moscow University, where he embraced student life wholeheartedly.

He was part of a group who called themselves the generation of physicists and lyricists. And they studied hard, spending every holiday camping in the country. Often unshaven and dishevelled, in matching anoraks of faded khaki, they would sit around big campfires while singing along as someone played the guitar. Sometimes they would debate about the big questions, like the beginning of the universe or humankind's purpose in life. They cared very little about material things. Even the females among them were fine with living in a tent.

On one of these camping expeditions, Nikolay met Viktoria Andreevna. She was called Vika back then. A tall, serious law student who wore her long brown hair in two plaits, Vika was good at leading the young women in their cooking duties while the young men chopped wood.

Because of his rural upbringing, Nikolay was an outstanding lumberjack. He couldn't play guitar, but he could croon the well-loved song about skis drying by the stove. He sang it with so much soul and passion that he managed to catch Vika's eye.

As Nikolay Ivanovich talked about the results of his latest research, Tatiana daydreamed about her parents' whirlwind romance and long marriage. She had always hoped to find her perfect match. Now she had found him.

Where is he? she wondered.

Tatiana missed Oleg. She hadn't seen him since that morning, when she'd kissed him and given him a present—a CD of a band he liked.

Suddenly, there was a commotion outside the room. By the sound of the voices, Tatiana could tell that Oleg and his parents had arrived at the same time as her mother and grandmother.

Tatiana's father stopped talking abruptly as they both stood to greet the families. "Congratulations, Stripey," Nikolay quickly whispered into his daughter's ear. "I knew you wouldn't settle for a kitten. You've found your own Siberian tiger."

"Dad!" Tatiana gave him a little punch in the ribs.

"Just be happy, my girl."

With her father's blessing, Tatiana felt more confident and relaxed. She was pleased when, as everyone was talking at once, Oleg stepped forwards to kiss her.

"Hi, Sunny! Sorry I'm late. I picked up my parents, and the traffic was bad. Hey, thanks again for the CD. I've been listening to it all day at the office."

Everyone sat down. After the traditional toast to the health of the birthday boy, and the second toast to the health of his parents, they all felt more at ease.

After a few minutes, both sets of parents got wrapped up in talking about the future of science—clever stuff. Tatiana could see that they were well matched, these two academic couples.

Meanwhile, Grandma started telling embarrassing stories from Tatiana's childhood. Oleg seemed amused. He was laughing wholeheartedly while gently squeezing Tatiana's hand under the table. Still half-listening to Grandma's tales and preparing to interfere if they became too cringe-worthy, Tatiana studied Oleg's parents, who sat opposite her.

Boris Ilyich and Natalya Naumovna looked smart and formal in their starched white shirts. They both wore glasses with thin gold frames and sat close to each other. As the waiters were rushing in and out, clearing the starter platters of smoked sturgeon, Tatiana noticed a tense look on Oleg's mother's face. Natalya Naumovna seemed uneasy being served by the waiters. When the artfully assembled plates of golden-crusted chicken Kiev were brought, Tatiana concluded that Oleg didn't take his parents to places like this very often.

The realisation made her feel special. She turned to her fiancé and gave him a grateful smile. Oleg saw it as his cue. He stood up, glass in hand, and cleared his throat. "Dear parents. Dearest Maria Petrovna," he said, bowing to Tatiana's grandmother. "Tatiana and I have an announcement. We're glad you're getting on so well because you'll be seeing each other more often from now on, we hope. In other words, we have decided to follow your footsteps ... and get married!"

By the genuine surprise on Oleg's parents' faces, Tatiana guessed that he had kept them entirely in the dark.

"Isn't it a little bit sudden?" Natalya Naumovna muttered quietly.

"Congratulations!" burst forth Viktoria Andreevna, who quickly found her teaching voice. "We are so happy for you!" She stood up with a push, the china tinkling as the table in front of her shook. "Let's toast our wonderful children Oleg and Tatiana, and wish them a life of health and happiness together!" Everyone cheered and clinked their glasses together.

Tatiana was grateful to her mother for thwarting the awkward moment. It wasn't that bad to have a mum who could take charge and save the day. "Thanks, Mum," she whispered to Viktoria Andreevna.

"Be happy," her mother mouthed back.

"You see! Everything turned out fine, Sunny," said Oleg after cake was served.

"Is that what he calls you, Tanechka?" Grandmother interrupted. "Sunny is your name, you know."

"What do you mean, Grandma?" asked Tatiana.

"I know what I am saying," Maria Petrovna continued. "In the old times, on the day of the great martyr Saint Tatiana, the peasant women used to bake a special bread in the shape of a sun. They called it a sunshine loaf. So, Tanechka, he is right, your groom. You are our Sunny."

"That's a beautiful story, Maria Petrovna," said Oleg. "You see, listen to your grandmother. She's the matriarch of the family!" He reached out to take Tatiana's grandmother's hand in his and then brought it to his lips. Maria Petrovna blushed like a schoolgirl.

"Young man, you are very gallant," said Tatiana's grandmother. "You remind me of my late Ivan Ivanovich, God rest his soul. He was a charmer, you know, and the best accordion player in the whole of Tula! He died from his wounds ten years after the war, leaving me with my two boys. No one could ever measure up to my Ivan."

Maria Petrovna's eyes began to water. "Please treat my Tanechka well. She is such a good girl."

"I will do my best, Maria Petrovna," promised Oleg, taking a theatrical bow to lighten the mood.

Now it was Tatiana's turn to flush. "He will, Grandma, don't worry." Tatiana put her head on her grandmother's shoulder, like she used to do as a child. The soft yarn of the hand-knitted shawl still tickled her cheek as Tatiana inhaled the warm scent of her childhood—Red Moscow, the only perfume her grandmother ever wore, mixed with the sourness of goat's wool.

"Our taxi is coming soon," said Tatiana. "Let's go, Grandma. We'll take you home."

Chapter 6

Their wedding was a cheerful, if slightly chaotic, affair. It began with Oleg's morning appearance at Tatiana's apartment. She could hear him and Alex pleading with her grandmother to let them in. According to tradition, Maria Petrovna had insisted that Tatiana be locked in her own bedroom until Oleg paid a ransom for his bride.

Tatiana and Lena giggled like schoolgirls as they listened to the young men playing their parts. They could also hear the excited voices of the Dobrovs' neighbours and their children, who came out of their apartments to participate.

The groom and his best man bought their way in with money and sweets, but the final settlement was made with sparkling wine and chocolates. The bedroom door was opened, corks were popped, and glasses were filled with frothing Abrau-Dyurso.

After a toast to the health of the bride and groom, the party headed downstairs. The heat of the stuffy July day and the bubbles of the almost-warm wine made Tatiana's head go light and fuzzy. She began to titter. Alex and Lena wore matching red satin sashes with the words "Honorary Witness" embossed in gold. As the four of them squeezed inside the black Volga, decorated with white ribbons for the occasion, they all began to laugh and frolic like kids.

"There will be a limit to what I am prepared to witness

today," Alex joked, pointing at his sash. "Let's just say I won't be escorting you to your wedding-night venue. *She* made me wear this ridiculous piece of Soviet paraphernalia." He pointed at Lena.

"And you should shut up and feel honoured!" Lena was quick to reply.

Inside the Central Moscow Registry Office, they joined the queue of other couples and their witnesses in the vast, mirrored waiting room. "You have to queue for everything in this country," deadpanned Alex. "Hopefully for you guys there's a shorter one to get a divorce." Tatiana, Oleg, and Lena couldn't contain themselves. The others in the room looked at them disapprovingly.

They posed for the formal photograph in front of an oversized flower arrangement. It took them some effort to hold themselves still with respectable smiles on their faces. Tatiana had never liked posing for photographers because, she thought, people in photographs ended up looking unnatural and stiff. That picture of the four of them was no exception. Lena and Alex were both dressed unsuitably in dark-coloured clothes on the swelteringly hot day. They stood on either side of the bride and groom like a pair of prison guards at a court hearing. And Oleg, in his light beige suit and blue tie, seemed unusually tense.

Tatiana wore a simple long white lace dress, with her hair up in a sophisticated 'do, artfully decorated with white silk flowers and pearls. She decided not to wear a veil. In fact, she looked more like a coming-of-age heroine from a nineteenth-century classic than a modern-day bride who was minutes from being married.

The four continued to cackle inside the large, empty reception hall, where they were greeted by the registrar, a voluptuous woman in a lilac skirt suit two sizes too small.

Like a strict headmistress, she advised them to take the ceremony very seriously, which obviously had the opposite effect on the party. Ignoring their behaviour, she began her speech with the well-rehearsed articulation of an amateur actress.

Tatiana wasn't listening anyway. As she tried not to laugh every time the woman said "newly wedded", her gaze was drawn to the tightly stretched jacket that was struggling to contain an enormous bosom. Tatiana was hoping the woman would get to the end before it burst apart, making the pearl buttons ricochet off the walls.

Finally, the new husband and wife were told to sign the big registry book. That was a relief to everyone. For the first time, Tatiana got to practise her new signature. She scribbled down, "T. Isaeva". A new chapter of her life began with a giggle.

The group continued on to a small Georgian restaurant that they had recently discovered, just a few blocks away from Grandpa Ilya's apartment. They were joined by family and about thirty friends. There, for the first time, Tatiana met Vlad and his lovely wife, Mariana. She smiled kindly at Tatiana, showing little dimples on her soft, round face. Tatiana liked her immediately. Oleg ushered the important couple to their places with the four parents—far away from the noisy students. Along with the bride and groom's families, Vlad and Mariana were the only people at the wedding who behaved like grown-ups.

The party began with Maria Petrovna filling Tatiana's shoe with vodka and offering it to Oleg: "Bottoms up! Drink to the health of your beautiful bride!" Tatiana didn't even notice that one of her shoes had gone missing. She must have kicked them off the minute she sat down next to Oleg at the head of the table. Her feet felt sore and swollen. The outside temperature that afternoon was more suited to wearing flip-flops.

Tatiana watched, fascinated, as Oleg took her shoe from her grandmother's hand, held it as if it were a sacred chalice, and slowly drank from it, turning it upside down at the end to show that there was nothing left. The guests roared with appreciation.

"Kiss the bride!" someone shouted. Tatiana stood up readily. She had anticipated the traditional humiliation, as she'd seen it at other weddings. The bride and groom were commanded to kiss in front of guests quite a lot.

Luckily for them, at that moment the food arrived—a huge Georgian feast—and everyone forgot about Oleg and Tatiana as they tucked into salads, *lobio, khachapuri*, and a whole spit-roasted lamb. Once the Georgian band began to play, the sound of traditional music with mellow singing from the soloist drowned out the excited voices at the tables. The party was in full swing.

The hired cameraman, who held a heavy camcorder on his shoulder, was hijacked by Oleg's actor friends from The Studio. They began fooling around, impersonating TV presenters and giving each other mock interviews. It turned the wedding video into a comedy short, in which Tatiana and Oleg were featured only periodically.

Eventually, there was a lot of sweaty dancing in front of tables. When Tatiana finally sat down to cool off with some water, she saw Oleg, his white shirt unbuttoned and his sleeves rolled up, attempting some bold dance move in front of a pretty wasted Rocket.

Rocket was towering over him, her red lipstick smudged across her face and her miniskirt riding dangerously high, as she flapped her arms in some kind of energetic jig. When the band started playing the soulful "Suliko", a favourite folk song of Comrade Stalin, the two of them embraced and began to move in a leisurely slow dance.

Even though Tatiana was tired and tipsy, it wasn't lost on her that Oleg didn't even glance in her direction before resting his head on the Rocket's chest. An unpleasant feeling brushed against her insides.

Realising that she was desperate to go home, she was relieved when she and Oleg finally did, leaving their drunk guests behind. They strode down the street hand in hand,

Tatiana carrying her shoes and holding up the hem of her dress. Oleg was unusually quiet as he struggled to walk in a straight line. The black Volga, carrying flowers and presents, followed behind them slowly.

For their honeymoon, Oleg and Tatiana had chosen to visit Crimea. It was a bright, sunny morning when they walked down a long platform at Moscow's Simferopol station. All of their train's twenty-something green carriages were quickly filling up with animated passengers, kids, bags, boxes, pushchairs, and even cot beds. Tatiana welcomed the magical smell of long-distance train journeys, a heady mix of tar, oil, and burned wood.

"It smells of creosote, Stripey," Nikolay Ivanovich had explained to his daughter years before. She had been boarding a train just like this one, en route to the resort of Yevpatoria, where she was due to mend her weakened lungs.

Oh, Dad! Always the scientist talking. It smells of adventure!

Tatiana smiled to herself. She was carrying a bag of provisions and other travel necessities. Oleg was steadily walking in front of her, their suitcases in his hands and his guitar on his back. Suddenly, he stopped in front of the first-class carriage and turned to face Tatiana. She saw her own surprised reflection in his sunglasses.

Before she opened her mouth to say that this was definitely the wrong car (their tickets were for a shared compartment), Oleg whispered, "Be quiet, Sun. Don't say a word. Show that woman your best smile, and leave the rest to me."

Tatiana glanced over his shoulder at a plump train attendant. She was standing on the threshold of the carriage door, blocking the way in, and wore a uniform along with her impenetrable formal expression. Her round face was framed by short, neatly permed hair.

Oleg stepped forwards. After a quick exchange between him and the attendant, Tatiana watched in disbelief as the woman nodded and stepped to the side to let them through.

“Take No. 2,” she said and followed them into the compartment. Oleg put their bags down and unzipped his waist bag. He produced their original tickets and a few banknotes. Tatiana looked away.

“Can I get you anything else, young man?” the attendant said in a sickeningly sweet voice, choosing to ignore Tatiana’s presence.

“Some tea when you make it,” answered Oleg. “We will keep our door locked. We don’t want to be disturbed. Just wake us up when we arrive in Simferopol.” He then lifted his sunglasses and smiled at the woman.

“I’ll knock when the tea is ready.” She hurried out as they heard voices of other passengers entering the car. Tatiana shook her head. Yet again Oleg’s ability to have his way had left her speechless.

“Not too shabby, huh, Sunny?” Oleg waved his hand around, pointing at the luxurious interior of the private cabin. Two soft bench seats were already made into beds with fresh linen and red bedspreads. There were three red carnations in a small glass vase, and starched white curtains at the windows, stamped with the “First Class” logo.

“I refuse to smell other people’s unwashed socks in close quarters,” Oleg continued. “My brand new wife and I deserve much better.” He playfully grabbed Tatiana by the neck and gave her a peck on the cheek.

“Your persuasion skills continue to amaze me,” Tatiana said.

“Persuasion skills and cash, Sunny. It’s a powerful combination. Right, then. What shall we do for the next twenty-four hours and thirty minutes?” Oleg winked at her.

“I have a bunch of crosswords and other brainteasers.” Tatiana winked back, ignoring the innuendo. At that moment, the train jerked and the platform outside the window began gliding sideways, taking away from her sight the station benches, the lights, the departure boards, and dozens of people waving their goodbyes.

As their train began to pick up speed as it headed towards the south, the newlyweds settled into the unhurried routine of long-distance passengers. After changing into their loose tracksuits and T-shirts, they sat opposite each other by the window as Oleg strummed his guitar. Tatiana just watched the passing landscape outside.

She felt warm and cosy. It was a moment of pure bliss, just the two of them in that small space, with him lost in his music and her lost in her daydreams. Suddenly Oleg strummed the strings hard and pushed the guitar away. "This is torture, Sunny. Another twenty-two hours of this! We're taking a plane next time. I'm bored as hell. Let's do something. Let's eat."

Tatiana readily jumped to her feet like a good wife. "Sure. I'm starving too." She began taking out wrapped packages from their travel bag, all scrupulously labelled in Maria Petrovna's neat handwriting.

Grandma had thought of everything. There were even tiny salt and pepper containers, plastic plates, and cutlery. Soon the compartment was filled with the aroma of a railway feast: cold roasted chicken, jacket potatoes, hard-boiled eggs, mini cucumbers from Grandma's vegetable garden, and a jar of homemade pickles.

For Tatiana it had always been the highlight of a long journey, this special meal that somehow made the ordinary food of which it consisted very mouth-watering and delicious. And as if deliberately timed, at that moment the train attendant knocked on their door carrying steaming, strong tea in two clear glasses with aluminium holders that bore the Soviet stamp of the Ministry of Railways. Each sugar cube on the tray was wrapped in paper with the same symbol.

"Freshly brewed tea, especially for you!" She beamed a syrupy smile, looking only at Oleg. "Can I get you anything else?"

"No, that's all. Thank you. We've got everything we need now." Oleg stood up, forcing the woman out of the narrow space. He locked the sliding door behind her.

"She's a bit sticky, isn't she?" he muttered.

"I think you've charmed the wits out of her. The way she looks at you, I'm sure she just wants me dead," Tatiana observed.

"We better keep the door locked then. I don't want to wake up next to your cold body tomorrow morning and become a suspect in a murder enquiry." Oleg cracked a hard-boiled egg on the tabletop dramatically. They both laughed.

As they were finishing their meal, the train came to a halt. They heard the familiar voice from the corridor say, "Tula! Stopover for five minutes!"

"Let's go for a smoke," Oleg said, reaching for the packet.

Tatiana stepped out onto a familiar platform. She had been here many times before when Tula was her final destination. She often came to visit Grandma's old house in summer, or else she went to see Uncle Sergey. It felt strange now to be a passing passenger. She often complained how long the journey from Moscow was, but this time it just flew by in an instant. Tula was only their first stop on the way to Simferopol.

Tatiana thought, *Time is a peculiar thing. We'll never fully understand it. It's definitely made of something spongy and stretchy, and all the significant dates of our lives are just little red dots on top of it.*

Then she imagined her grandfather who had lived and died here in Tula. She had never known him. Her grandparents met just after the war in a military hospital on Defence Road, where Ivan Ivanovich was convalescing from his wounds and where Maria Petrovna was working as a nurse.

For Tatiana, it was very long ago, but Grandma used to say, "When I close my eyes, Tanechka, I can see him, my Ivan. He is so handsome, sitting on his hospital bed with an accordion on his lap and all the patients and nurses gathered around him. He played so beautifully, and his fingers were so quick on those keys. I remember it just like yesterday."

And Tatiana could see it now, that those red dots on the sponge of time were never lined up in order but appeared to be in random clusters, groups, and constellations. She also thought that one day she would close her eyes and see this train and this platform, smell the roast chicken, and hear the oily voice shouting, “The train is departing!”

“Come on, Sun. You heard the woman; we need to get back.” Oleg threw his cigarette into the gap between the carriage and the platform. “Let’s get in. Did you fall asleep with your eyes open?” He gently nudged Tatiana towards the door.

After leaving Tula behind, the train reached full speed. Tatiana loved the sensation and the fact that she had to balance herself every time she stood up or walked down the corridor towards the toilet. Even the water in the small sink was splashing around to the jerking rhythm. The rumble of the steel wheels crashing over the joints of the track was deafening.

She enjoyed lying down on the bench bed with a book in her hands, letting her body rock synchronously with the rhythm. Soothed and relaxed, she drifted into a gentle slumber. Oleg, having made the acquaintance of a man from the next compartment, stood together with him in the corridor. Holding onto the metal rails under the windows, he was lost in conversation.

I’m not sure my company will ever be enough for him.

Tatiana’s eyes felt heavy. Even her thoughts slowed down.

Oleg woke her when the sun was settling over the endless steppe outside the window. “Are you planning to sleep all the way to Crimea? You’ve missed Kharkov, our longest stop. I tried to wake you up, but you were completely out.” On the table in front of them, Oleg placed newspaper-wrapped packages containing a warm Ukrainian loaf, shiny black cherries, and purple plums.

“Oh no! Sorry! I don’t know what happened to me. Must have been all the rocking.” Tatiana sat up, yawning and stretching. “Let’s have dinner.” She took out the bag with the leftover food. After the meal, she and Oleg played cards, completed a crossword, and went to smoke in a vestibule, a small, dark space filled with tobacco fumes.

It was after midnight when they finally turned off the lights. They tried to make love on Tatiana's side, but the train was moving so vigorously, and Oleg was trying to keep up with the rhythm so desperately, that Tatiana found it all a bit comical and could only concentrate on suppressing her giggles.

She tried to hold the edge of the table with one hand and Oleg's back with the other, but then she hit her head hard on the wall. After hearing the loud thud of her skull, Tatiana let out a laugh. "I think now even your admirer knows what we're up to. I hope she sleeps on the other side!" Tatiana pointed to the thin wall separating the compartments.

"Sunny, what the hell. It's not fair!" Oleg's voice was tense and rigid. Then luckily the train slowed down and gradually came to a stop. The bright neon lights from the platform filled the cabin with a cold glow. The station's radio echoed through many speakers. A woman's voice announced their arrival. Oleg swiftly seized the moment of motionless calm and, in a few confident thrusts, managed to finish what had seemed like a completely lost cause only a few minutes before. They both lay there, quietly relieved for different reasons, compressed tightly against each other on the narrow bed.

"That's enough excitement for the day, don't you think?" said Oleg. "Is your head OK?" He was first to break the embrace.

Tatiana giggled again, remembering their comic romp. "I'll live. It sounded much worse than it felt. What's this station?"

"It must be Zaporozhye. We only have five minutes or so here. Let's go for a puff." Oleg, naked from the waist down and gloriously visible against the brightly lit window, rose to his feet. Tatiana looked away. She was still not comfortable with nudity. She preferred to get dressed in the bathroom and didn't like to see her husband in his birthday suit.

The couple dressed quickly. Tatiana tried in vain to smooth down her dishevelled hair.

Once they were on the platform outside, they noticed that they were the only ones there. The large station clock showed five minutes past two. Tatiana, feeling the light chill of the night air, shivered. Her body wasn't used to being awake at this hour.

They lit up. "So, Zaporozhye." Tatiana exhaled. "The home of a cheap and unpopular car."

"And also of DniproHES, don't forget." Oleg was quick to show off his knowledge, mentioning the Soviet equivalent of the Hoover Dam.

"It was built with the help of the Americans, by the way, at a time when we were still friends—in the 1920s."

"How would you know that stuff?" Tatiana, yet again, was impressed by her husband's erudition.

"I just read a lot. Always loved reading. I used to get sick often as a child, just like you. Spent my days reading random pages of the *Great Soviet Encyclopedia*. Knowledge is power, as they say, Sunny. Let's get in. As interesting as this city might be, I want to make it to the seaside."

Oleg fell asleep almost immediately. Tatiana was left to listen to the contented snoring of a satisfied man. She tossed and turned for a while, cursing herself for having had a nap earlier, and eventually dozed off towards dawn.

They were both wakened by loud banging on the door and a piercing voice from outside yelling, "Simferopol! Get up!"

"Damn it, Sunny! We've overslept!" Oleg jumped up as Tatiana was still struggling to find her bearings. She had been dreaming just moments before and couldn't even remember where they were.

Oleg slid the door open. The carriage seemed deserted. Even the screaming attendant was gone. There was a commotion on the platform outside as the last passengers left, pulling their bags towards the station building.

"Old harpy!" Oleg fumed. "She didn't wake us up in time."

"I'm sure she did it on purpose," said Tatiana, quickly pulling on shorts and a tank top. "She must have heard us last night."

By the time they stepped onto the sunlit platform, they could only see the backs of the last few passengers far ahead of them.

Outside the station, they found themselves on a vast square framed by white columns and a tall clock tower. A queue of people at the taxi rank was still growing.

"Right. We need to do something about this. Sunny, wait here." Oleg was in full determination mode. He put the suitcases and guitar down by Tatiana's side and walked away, scanning the square in search of potential transportation.

Tatiana's mood was completely the opposite. The minute she'd stepped out onto Crimean soil, or the pavement, to be correct, she relaxed. An enchanted smile played on her lips as she began to take in her surroundings, seen through the lenses of her new sunglasses.

She noticed two farmers selling melons from an open cart and walked in their direction, forgetting she was in charge of the luggage.

The melons were big and yellow. They lay there like a huge heap of party balloons. The sweet, nutty smell of the cut fruit filled the air.

"Try a piece, pretty girl!" one of the tan-faced farmers offered. He held out a juicy segment. "Sweet as honey," he declared in a strong southern Russian accent. "Where are you heading to?"

"Yalta," Tatiana replied after a pause, indulging in the sublime taste of summer. "Do you know where we can get a taxi around here? My husband went to look for one."

"Pah! Don't pay all that money for a taxi! Take a trolleybus." The farmer pointed to a stop on the opposite side of the square. "You'll get there in two hours, and you'll have the best views and the best breeze."

"I didn't know trolleybuses could travel so far." Tatiana was genuinely surprised.

"In Crimea they can. The bends on the mountain road are so steep that no car could get you there quicker anyhow."

"Oh, thank you!" Tatiana beamed, anticipating the adventure.

"Have a good holiday, pretty Moscow girl." The farmer then turned to another customer.

"Sunny! What are you doing?" Oleg's voice made her jump. "You can't leave our bags like that. Can't I trust you with the simplest task?" The look on his face told her he had been unsuccessful in his quest.

"Sorry, Oleg. I promise to concentrate now. Let's take a trolleybus!" She whispered the last words right into his ear, using her most seductive tone.

"I'm not using public transport on my honeymoon," he protested, but his voice softened a little.

"Even if your new wife begged you? Please!" She pressed her palms together in a plea. "Besides, it takes the same time as a taxi. That local man told me." That reasoning seemed to work on Oleg.

"OK, Sunny, no need for a scene. Where does that thing stop?"

"Thank you!" Tatiana gave him an excited peck on the cheek. "I know where the stop is. Follow me!" she said confidently, surprising herself.

Wow, this is the first time I'm the one leading him.

Chapter 7

Tatiana spent the journey drinking in the magnificent Crimean landscape, which was framed in the window. The old, kind-faced yellow trolleybus with "Yalta" written in red on its side was taking them on a journey. Surprisingly, there weren't many passengers on board—perhaps because the trolleybuses ran quite regularly.

Oleg wasn't sitting next to her. He had opted for the window seat in front. "I don't want to block your view, Sunny. Enjoy your adventure," he had said with just a touch of sarcasm. He was using his folded jacket as a pillow and was resting his head against the windowpane. He had fallen asleep minutes after they left the city. His motionless back seemed to radiate annoyance.

But Tatiana didn't care. The beautiful panorama took her breath away—an endless stream of green valleys, vineyards, and villages with the Crimean mountains on the horizon, dark jade against azure skies.

Growing up on the flat terrains between Moscow and Tula, Tatiana had only seen this kind of landscape on TV or in photographs. And she had spent most of her summer holidays at Grandma's house in Krapivna, near Tula, swimming in the river and gathering wild raspberries, blueberries, and mushrooms in the woods.

The sweep of mighty folds and cracks on the earth's surface made Tatiana suddenly strangely emotional. She pressed her forehead against the cool glass and felt her eyes well up with tears. She felt a sudden pang of self-pity.

I haven't seen much in my life. At least I've got my shades on. How embarrassing—a white-faced Muscovite crying at the sight of the hills! Better if they think it's because we've had an argument.

She briefly turned around to check, with relief, that no one was looking in her direction. The few passengers were perfectly occupied with their own business.

The trolleybus slowly climbed up the narrow serpentine road towards the mountain pass. As she looked back, Tatiana saw a long queue of cars behind them. She remembered the farmer's words about the trolleybus taking the same amount of time as a taxi. Only a madman would attempt overtaking a trolleybus on this road.

Tatiana looked down the steep, rocky slope covered with trees and shrubs. From Alushta, the road ran along the coast. She could see the dark blue of the sea. The warmth and saltiness of the water came back to her from a vivid childhood memory. She felt the inexplicable urge to run towards the shore and throw herself into the gentle waves, greeting the water with, "Good morning, Black Sea! And so we meet again!"

Impatiently, she looked at her watch. It was another hour to Yalta. "Oleg, Oleg, wake up!" She shook him by the shoulder. "You can't miss this view!" She was too restless in her excitement to spend the rest of the journey alone.

The plan was that in Yalta they would rent a room in an apartment not far from the seafront. Oleg had a neatly folded piece of paper with the address and phone number of the owner—an elderly lady with whom Vlad and Mariana had stayed a few years back. But as they finally stepped off the trolleybus in Yalta, Tatiana could sense that Oleg had something up his sleeve. He looked towards the taxi rank.

"I want to try something, Sunny. Just play along, OK, and

I'll do the talking. If it doesn't work, we can still go to that old lady's place."

"Where are we going?" Tatiana was getting used to Oleg's game changes.

"It's a place I've heard about. 'Who doesn't take a risk will not drink champagne,' as they say!"

Oleg said something to the driver and began putting their luggage into the boot. After a short drive, they arrived at a large white gate. There was a sign that read, "Sanatorium of the Union of Soviet Composers".

"Are you kidding!" blurted Tatiana instantly. "They'll throw us out in an instant! We don't even know any member of the Union." She anticipated inevitable humiliation.

"Sunny, are you suffering from short-term memory loss? A bit early in life, I'd say. I've told you to be quiet," Oleg barked.

A sleepy guard—a heavy middle-aged man with a moustache—approached the car. "Whom are you visiting?" he asked.

Oleg produced a picture ID card with many official stamps and watermarks, which Tatiana didn't recognise. He flashed it quickly from the open passenger's window and said in a tone of unquestionable authority, "We are from the Department of Hygiene in Moscow. We are here for a surprise sanitation inspection. We are to see your head nurse. You can stay where you are. We will find our own way."

It all happened quickly. Oleg sounded so convincing that, for a second, Tatiana thought that what he had said was true, as if she somehow hadn't been aware of her husband's post at the Ministry.

The guard instinctively stepped back. As the taxi slowly drove by, Tatiana watched his expression—mouth slightly open—as his lethargic brain tried to process the information.

"Poor guy," Oleg commented, nodding his head towards the guard. "He's still trying to figure out what would have gotten him into less trouble—letting us in, or stopping us there and then. OK, Sunny, first hurdle down. There's still hope for us! Thanks for keeping quiet!"

Oleg continued in an upbeat mood as they disembarked in front of the main building, which was white and airy with arched windows and doors.

"What did you show him?" asked Tatiana.

"Just my work ID," said Oleg. "The security head at Vlad's building is a bit paranoid. He insisted we all have one." Tatiana knew that Vlad's company occupied rooms at a substantially guarded television centre.

"Just continue with a straight face, Sunny," added Oleg as he strolled confidently into the foyer. Inside, at the large reception desk, sat a middle-aged woman in a white blouse. Her bulletproof expression made Tatiana feel crestfallen. Their hopes were ridiculous.

The woman's auburn hair was an architectural wonder. It proudly towered above her, doubling the height of her head and resembling a perfectly formed sandcastle. Not a single string was out of place. Tatiana wondered how long it took her to construct this masterpiece—and how much she spent on hairspray each month. The lady's shiny metal badge was engraved to read, "Zotova Z. P.—Administrator".

"Whom are you visiting? You will need to sign the visitors' book," she said.

"Ahem. Ahem." Oleg cleared his throat and sat on a chair in front of the desk. With his eyes, he told Tatiana to take a seat on the chair next to him. She quickly obeyed, stretching her face to a big friendly smile.

"Does 'Z. P.' stand for 'Zinaida Petrovna'?" Oleg guessed.

"Zinaida Pavlovna, actually. How can I help you?" Her tone was mildly threatening.

Tatiana thought, *This won't end well. She is going to throw us out!* But she continued to smile like a Soviet poster girl saluting party leaders at a May Day demonstration.

"Dear Zinaida Pavlovna," Oleg said, remaining absolutely

impassive, "my name is Oleg Borisovich Isaev. This is my wife, Tatiana Nikolaevna. We are on our honeymoon, having arrived today from Moscow. We are wondering if you can be so kind as to assist us in renting a room in this famous establishment?"

"Young man—" The administrator raised her perfectly shaped eyebrows.

"Oleg Borisovich, please." Oleg gave her a confident smile.

"Oleg Borisovich, let me explain something to you. Firstly, this is a specialised health resort for the members of the Union of Soviet Composers only. You need to have your membership card. And secondly, you must have a consultant's letter prescribing your treatment programme for the attention of our doctor, because"—and here she posed with her index finger, its neatly manicured pink nail pointing upwards—"this is not a hotel but a recreational facility, where our distinguished musicians restore their health and creative abilities. In other words, even if I wanted to, I couldn't accommodate you." Zinaida Pavlovna finished her speech on a more sympathetic note.

"We totally understand—you are doing your job." Oleg turned his chair to face the woman directly and then leaned forwards, lowering his voice to a confidential murmur. He took his business card out of his jeans pocket and put it down on the desk.

"We are all professionals here, Zinaida Pavlovna," he said. "By the way, can I trouble you for an empty envelope?" Zinaida Pavlovna nodded and took out an envelope from her desk drawer as he continued. "As you can see, I work in television. I am also as an administrator—like you—of Moscow's most prestigious new theatre. If you are ever in Moscow, please don't hesitate to call me. It would be my pleasure to provide you with tickets. Besides, I play instruments and compose music myself, so technically speaking I am a composer."

Tatiana noted in surprise that, as he was talking, Oleg had opened his waist bag under the desk and, with his deft card sharp's fingers, was counting out banknotes. He swiftly took the envelope and put a considerable pile inside it, still out of the woman's view. Tatiana shifted in her chair uncomfortably. *This could go so wrong.*

Oleg placed the envelope, plus their passports, on top of the desk in front of the administrator. She glanced down quickly, not a muscle moving on her well-groomed face.

"Zinaida Pavlovna." Oleg rushed in, before she could speak. "I should have mentioned that they are lucky to have you here. A woman with your grace and figure, with such beautiful skin and hair, belongs on the cinema screen. Sophia Loren has nothing on you." Oleg beamed her one of his special smiles.

Surely he's gone too far now. Tatiana just managed to keep a nervous grin from appearing on her face, anticipating their inevitably embarrassing exit. She was shocked to see that Zinaida Pavlovna was now flushing like a girl. She opened the drawer of her desk again and promptly swept their passports and the envelope inside, closing the drawer tightly.

"Young man, this kind of flattery won't get you far," she said, but her expression indicated the exact opposite. "However, I will make an exception for you, as we do happen to have a single room free. I hope you don't mind a small bed." For the first time, she looked at Tatiana.

"One of our older guests was taken ill. He needed surgery, and it looks like he won't be joining us for the rest of his stay. I will need the room back in two weeks' time.

"But you are on probation here. It means that if I hear a single complaint about your behaviour, or of noise or excessive alcohol consumption, I will throw you out immediately."

Zinaida Pavlovna stood up and reached for the cabinet that held the keys. Tatiana and Oleg scrambled to their feet.

"Thank you very much," Tatiana managed to squeak in disbelief. Oleg frowned.

"Thank you, Zinaida Pavlovna. It's been a pleasure doing business with you," he said with dignity.

"Breakfast is at eight, lunch at one, and dinner at seven. If you miss the times, you have to cater for yourselves. Make your way to the Beach House, Room 16." She handed them the key, indicating that the conversation was over.

There were only sixteen single rooms in the Beach House, the closest of all the buildings to the seafront. It was raised directly above the pebbly private beach and the small promenade that was dotted with a few plastic tables, a blue parasol in the centre of each. The boundary was outlined by a pier, which was topped by a scattering of white sunloungers. This was the most popular sunbathing space among the guests.

Tatiana quickly noticed that all the sunloungers were occupied. Also, the pier was high enough to provide shelter and privacy from the public beaches of Yalta beyond it.

Their room was small but bright and airy, with a single bed, a small television, a fridge, and a tiny bathroom that was impeccably clean and shiny with white tiles on the walls. There were no windows, only double doors leading out to a narrow balcony.

Tatiana leaned against the metal rails to soak up the breeze, the sunshine, and the uninterrupted view of the Black Sea. "Oleg, this is perfect! You're a genius! You had her in your pocket! How did you do it?"

"Years of practice, sunny one! Watch and learn!" Pleased with himself and encouraged by Tatiana's admiration, Oleg was busy unpacking, trying to squeeze their belongings into a slim wardrobe made for one. Eventually he gave up and pushed the suitcases under the bed instead. "That'll do. Let's go and explore!"

The path outside the front door led them up into the dense parkland. Tatiana had never seen such an exotic variety of trees and bushes before. It was as if they had travelled into the magical jungle of her childhood book. In fact, there wasn't a single familiar plant in that forest. She saw palm trees growing next to blue cedars, magnolias, and yews, and the ground was covered in flowers of all colours and sizes. The smells in the air were so strange and overpowering that Tatiana felt light-headed.

They eventually came across a tall rotunda—round white columns cupped with a domed roof. It was perched high above the sea, the top of the Beach House just visible among the trees. They sat side by side on a bench in the middle of a circular observation platform. Tatiana couldn't take her eyes off the Black Sea and its coastline with its green slopes, silver rocks, and white buildings.

The soft peaks and smooth contours of the Crimean Mountains resembled the body and limbs of the mythical green giant who came ashore after bathing in the warm waters, lay down to rest, and fell into an eternal slumber. Centuries later, people came and populated the fertile terrain, protected by the giant's motionless body.

"I can't believe we are actually here. I'm scared I'm going to wake up. Please tell me I'm not dreaming." Tatiana gasped.

"It's all real, Sun. Unfortunately, I've left our camera back in the room. So let's just take a mental picture and go search for the feeding place. My hunger is tangible, I can tell you." Oleg rose to his feet.

They found a large dining room inside the main building. A unfriendly grey-haired woman in a white apron asked for their names and room number and then showed them to a table by the window. The table was for four. Soon they were joined by an odd-looking pair—a middle-aged mother and her daughter, a girl of Tatiana's age. They looked like they didn't belong in the place full of old distinguished composers and their privileged families.

Everything about their lunch companions, from their clothes to their accents, betrayed their background as being far removed from concert halls and recording studios. Still, the mother was friendly enough.

"Oh, hello. You must be new! I'm Nina, and this is my daughter Mila. Don't have the cutlets here! They're disgusting—fatty and overcooked." The woman said all this without pausing for breath, her gold teeth glinting in the sun.

Oleg made a quick introduction. Tatiana watched as Mila, dressed in a baby-pink cropped top which was tightly stretched over her not-so-babyish bosom, tore pieces off her grilled chicken leg with her fingers and guzzled them down. The young woman had one lazy eye, so it was hard to tell which direction she was looking.

Tatiana decided she disliked the two women immediately.

However, Oleg was his usual sociable self, making conversation with the mother, who was notably flattered by a young man's attention. She openly told them that she was an administrator at a large furniture shop in Minsk and that, in these times of total deficit, she had supplied a Belorussian composer with furnishings for his dacha. In return, he had offered a three-week holiday here as his special guests. Besides, he preferred Crimea in September, Nina said, because of the smaller crowds and cooler weather.

Tatiana learned that the table allocation was final, and that meant that she and Oleg would have to see Nina and Mila three times a day. But it was a small price to pay for such a magical location.

It's a minor inconvenience. I can live with it. I will ignore them as much as I can.

"There are not that many young people around here," Nina said when they stood up to leave. "You two wouldn't mind if Mila tagged along with you sometime, would you? She gets fed up with me!"

"Of course, no problem." Tatiana almost hated herself as she faked a polite smile.

The newlyweds spent lazy days on the quaint pebble beach, sunbathing and swimming in the sea. At night they slept awkwardly, almost on top of each other on the old narrow bed, managing to test the rusty springs a few times with vigorous lovemaking. But that felt hot, sticky, and dull, and it didn't even come close to Tatiana's favourite pastime, reading.

She discovered a big library in the main building, quiet and old-fashioned with catalogues and neat shelves organised in strict alphabetical order. In addition to the biographies of all the composers, there were encyclopaedias of all Russian classics, and also some sought-after new works—books that were only available on black market stalls for crazy prices. Tatiana, unable to believe her luck, was determined to get through as many of them as she could in the two weeks she would be here—a plan that came to fruition. Over the two weeks, she would gulp the books down feverishly, page by page. Sometimes she would be so consumed by reading that she wouldn't even notice Oleg disappearing from the sunlounger by her side.

Restless as ever, Oleg had gotten bored with the beach routine after just two days. He managed to track down two Préférence enthusiasts—two friends, students from Moscow, called Dima and Slavik. One of them—Tatiana didn't pay enough attention to tell which one—was the son of a prominent composer whose surname was well known.

Both young men were impeccably groomed. They sported matching fashionable haircuts and always wore white to enhance their tans. They even showed up for dinner in pristine white jeans and shirts, flashing their pearly teeth at everyone. In fact, they smiled so often that they could have easily passed for foreigners.

Tatiana suspected that it was all a deliberate act. She overheard them once talking about going to a disco at the bar of the nearby Intourist hotel, where only foreigners were allowed and where the drinks were sold for US dollars.

Oleg displayed no jealousy towards the glossy pair. Tatiana admired him for that. Somehow he had established his authority with them very quickly and adopted a slightly patronising tone. Dima and Slavik didn't seem to mind. They enjoyed his company, his unquestionable expertise in Préférence and poker, and also his mastery at billiards. The three spent hours together in the resort's billiards room, smoking, playing loud music, and laughing. The composer's son's VIP status protected them from complaints from the other guests.

Tatiana discovered that even here, in this paradise of a resort, a certain unspoken hierarchy existed. It helped to be related to somebody famous. She also realised that Mila was helplessly in love with one of the young men from Moscow. Still struggling to tell them apart, Tatiana wasn't sure which one. Sometimes the young woman with the lazy eye took Oleg's empty sunlounger next to Tatiana and made meaningless small talk that always turned to gossip about the young men in white—their whereabouts, their clothes, and so on. Tatiana was hardly ever listening; she just nodded politely, gave Mila monosyllabic answers, and waited for her to go away so that she could continue her reading.

Mila finally got the message and disappeared one day. Tatiana was surprised when she later saw her, dressed up with full warpaint-like make-up on her childish face, hanging around the billiards room where the young men were playing. She also spotted Mila hovering by the object of her desire when Oleg played guitar at the promenade table.

His passionate performance that day quickly turned into an impromptu concert. A small crowd gathered around, cheering and clapping. Mila's voice could be heard over the others, shouting, "Bravo!" Oleg was on a roll after that. He continued on, playing and singing beautifully, encouraged by the warm reception.

Tatiana sat at a distance, quietly beaming with pride at her husband.

From then on, Oleg's status at the resort changed. People came over to him to shake hands, pat him on the shoulder, or make conversation. Everyone seemed to know his name. Oleg was clearly enjoying his new celebrity; he was in his element. Tatiana was happy for him, but for her, being in the spotlight had never been important. She was glad to take a back seat among his audience.

Mila enjoyed her association with the man of the moment. She readily told the other guests how talented Oleg was, that he worked in a famous theatre, and lots of other bits of information she had managed to glean while lingering around the billiards room. She even told people that Oleg was there on honeymoon with his lovely wife, Tatiana, who happened to be her best friend.

Tatiana found it all innocently entertaining. Plus, she would be able to report to Nina that her daughter was no longer bored.

In the evenings, the honeymooners watched old films in the improvised open-air cinema. The staff stretched the screen, made of thick white cloth, across the end of the promenade and then arranged the chairs and sunloungers in rows in front of it. Tatiana found it incredibly romantic to watch the black-and-white classics under the starry Crimean sky, she and her husband wrapped in woollen throws to protect them against the chilly sea breeze. The actors' voices coming from the old speakers were muffled by the sounds of lapping waves on one side and the tireless chirping of the crickets on the other.

To her annoyance, Tatiana noticed that Mila had once again sat down next to Oleg, who didn't seem to mind her presence. Tatiana once tried to fish his reaction to the irritating girl, saying, "She is a bit tiring, isn't she?"

"She doesn't mean any harm, Sunny. Besides, I find her unspoken passion for Dima very amusing. The way she gapes at him is almost heartbreaking. She couldn't be more obvious if she tried, don't you think?"

On their last day, Tatiana wanted to visit Chekhov's house-cum-museum in town. She returned the last book to the library and asked Oleg to join her on her outing. "Oh, Sunny, I'm sorry. I've agreed to play our last game of Préférence with the guys," he told her. "Do you mind going without me? You can take Mila for company!"

"Very funny! I've seen enough of that child to last me a lifetime. It's OK, I'll just go solo."

Oleg pulled a few banknotes from the stash in his waist bag as he said, "Here. I've almost made back what we paid for our stay, playing with these rich boys. The wife of Oleg Isaev deserves to have a great time. Go by the market and treat yourself to something nice. I'll see you on the promenade later—I'll be on one of the tables there."

So off Tatiana went, eventually finding the modest white dacha—Chekhov's beloved home in Yalta—on one of the quiet streets in the old part of town. On that scorching afternoon, she was the only visitor. It seemed that all the tourists had given up on culture in favour of cooling waves.

A leafy, mature garden at the back of the house provided some much-needed shade. Tatiana walked down the narrow rocky paths winding around eclectic gatherings of trees and shrubs. She read all the memorial plaques under them. Many of the trees had been planted there by the writer himself. Northern silver birches grew in harmony with cypress trees, straight and slim, like candles on a birthday cake.

Tatiana found roses and Chekhov's favourite azaleas in all shades of pink and red, and dozens of other plants that she laboured to name. She imagined the author resting on his spade in the shade, wheezing, coughing, and cursing the illness that had loomed over his last years, consuming him slowly and steadily. Here, he had planted his own cherry orchard, leaving his legacy not only on paper but also on this fertile piece of land.

Inside the house, with its fading wallpaper, the rooms were small and personal with many of Chekhov's belongings still on display. Tatiana was happy to wander there alone. It felt very intimate, the yellow pages of letters and manuscripts, the writer's leather coat still hanging on a cupboard door, and even the desk on which he had written many of his plays and stories.

Chekhov's single bed with a simple metal frame took up most of his tiny bedroom, wherein there was a bunch of dried palm leaves wrapped in red satin, with the words "To the artful interpreter of Russian reality" inscribed on the satin.

Tatiana sensed the immense sadness of Chekhov's short life, musing on the irony of his life—the brilliant doctor who had cured many patients but couldn't help himself. A sudden realisation dawned on her. Perhaps the reason he favoured the literary forms of short stories and plays was because, knowing his prognosis for years, he simply wasn't sure if he'd have enough time to finish a novel.

Tatiana looked out of the bedroom window over the tranquil garden and felt a pang of sorrow for the talented writer who had lived here on borrowed time. She tears sting her eyes. Leaving Chekhov's house behind, she decided the Central Market would cheer her up.

Many stalls were already empty when she got there. She bought a ceramic blue dolphin with "Yalta" written underneath—just as a reminder of their honeymoon. She bargained for a small bracelet made of local seashells and then put on her wrist. After that, she saw a woman selling the most perfect-looking peaches. The seller had beautifully arranged the large yellow and pink fruits into symmetrical piles on top of her newspaper-covered stall. Tatiana couldn't resist. She was sure they would taste even better than they looked.

She paid for a wicker basket at the next stall and bought all of those velvety perfections. Together with the woman, she carefully packed the peaches into the basket, protecting each layer with strips of newspaper.

"Do you think they'll make it to Moscow with me?" Tatiana asked.

"Of course they will! Look, not a single bruise on them. I picked them from the tree today—didn't let any fall to the ground." The woman was happy to close the deal.

Back at the composers' sanatorium, Tatiana rushed to the promenade to show Oleg her treasures, but it was empty. It seemed the scorching sun had chased the guests away to their rooms.

Tatiana walked to the Beach House and found that the door to their room was locked from the inside. Then she heard muffled voices. "Oleg! Open up! It's me!" She knocked loudly in case he was outside on the balcony. She heard a commotion and more muffled conversation, but the door stayed closed.

She picked up that one of the voices was female.

"Oleg! It's me!" she repeated with urgency. Finally the door opened. It was Mila who let her in, and then she quickly returned to her seat on top of the crumpled bed. Oleg sat on a chair with his guitar in his hands. They both looked slightly dishevelled and out of breath.

"Sorry, Sunny." Oleg gazed at her. "We really didn't hear you. Mila asked me to teach her some chords. She wants to take up guitar when she gets home."

Tatiana froze where she stood, her mind trying to process the scene in front of her. She suddenly lost control over her muscles and released her grip on the basket handle. It fell down with a dull thump, and her perfect peaches rolled out of it, covering the floor.

"Hi, Tania. Nice fruits," said Mila, standing up again. A smile of a naughty child caught stealing sweets made her face look more obtuse than usual.

Mila tiptoed across the room, avoiding the fallen peaches, and muttered, "I better go. It's nearly dinner time," as she squeezed past Tatiana.

"Don't call me that. It's Tatiana, not Tania," Tatiana snarled at her, surprised to get her voice back. She didn't look in Oleg's direction but turned on her heel and marched out, noticing that Mila had already disappeared down the stairs.

In a few quick steps, Tatiana had reached the beach beyond the promenade. A sharp pain, as if from a mighty punch under her ribs, made her bend forwards. The pain was so real and sudden that she panicked. She couldn't breathe. It seemed her body had forgotten how to inhale.

I'm going to die.

She tried taking a few shallow breaths through her nose. Like a helpless rag doll, Tatiana dropped onto warm pebbles. After a few seconds, she sat up, hugging her knees tightly, and watched the pink sun setting over the metallic surface of the sea.

How ironic. The sunset is so pretty and romantic. The world goes on. It doesn't care about my shattered heart. What shall I do? What to do? How could he? And on our honeymoon!

Her thoughts were scattered. The pain in her chest was sharp, all-consuming.

She began gently rocking herself back and forth, feeling the questions pulsating in her head. Betrayal. She sensed that something big, dark, and ugly, like a blurry character from her nightmares, had just entered her life. It was there, standing behind her, reaching out its sticky paws and putting them on her shoulders.

"Get away from me! Get away from me!" Tatiana wailed.

"Hey, Sunny, it's only me. Why are you crying?" Oleg took his hands off her shoulders and sat down on the pebbles next to her. His voice was artificially calm.

"Why, Oleg? Why? And why her?" Tatiana whimpered.

"What do you mean, why? Why what, Sunny? What do you think happened? I'll tell you what went on. After you left, I played cards with the guys, as I told you I would.

"Mila came round looking for you. She was upset that you went off without her. She really likes you, you know. Then the four of us went to our room to hide from the heat and listen to some music. You only missed the boys by a few minutes."

Oleg continued with conviction. "Mila stayed behind because I promised to show her some basic guitar chords. Had you returned ten minutes earlier, you would have found Dima and Slavik in our room too. Does that answer your question?"

As he spoke, he looked her straight in the eye. She watched his face closely, hoping in vain to find a sign, a hint, a trace, of a lie. His cool gaze betrayed nothing. It lost none of its penetrating power.

Tatiana could only stare, lost for words.

"Is that what really happened? Please, just tell me the truth!" she finally managed with the hope of a terminally ill patient.

"That's all, I swear." He nodded, not missing a beat.

Then he shook his head with disapproval. "I thought you were smarter than that, Sunny. Me and that little simpleton? Give me a break! This kind of jealousy doesn't become you. Let's go—we need to pack."

Oleg stood up. He didn't offer her a hand but just turned and walked towards the building. Tatiana followed him with slow, robotic steps.

The honeymoon was over.

PART 2

Chapter 8

1992

Tatiana rushed towards the grand steps of the State Library, a monumental greystone building framed by soaring rectangular columns. She could feel her toes ache from the merciless bite of January frost. Cursing the thin soles of her fashionable boots, she increased her pace. She counted the usual twelve steps to the top and said her customary hello to the statue of Dostoevsky, slouched uncomfortably on the edge of the bronze bench and half covered in snow.

Tatiana headed through the double glass doors. Inside, at the reception, she showed her library card. After checking her coat, she negotiated even more steps in the palatial hall, which was lit from above by enormous cast-iron chandeliers.

She paused for a second in front of the massive oak doors leading to the central reading room, which lately had become Tatiana's favourite place. It was a huge solemn room with an impossibly high ornate ceiling and endless rows of wooden desks with old-fashioned bureaus with green glass lamps above them. The room was divided down the middle by a wide aisle covered in ceremonial-looking carpet leading to a wooden balcony at the end of the room. The back wall was adorned with life-affirming murals depicting old Soviet scientists and proletarians working side by side.

On the top of the balcony sat a bronze Lenin. He looked much more relaxed than the writer outside the building. The sculptor had kindly placed him in a nice comfortable armchair, with a book on his lap. By the angle of his head, Tatiana had always suspected that the statue had been sneaking a nap.

Oh well, even great leaders have to take a break.

And this serene hall with the giant windows, mint-green walls, and improvised altar of communist relics was just the ideal place to escape from the crazy city that lay beyond its walls.

The absurdity of life outside on the streets of the capital wasn't lost on Tatiana. Her passport, her treasured library pass, and all of her other documents still bore the famous sickle and hammer—the emblem of a country that had ceased to exist. The mighty USSR, like a biblical colossus on clay feet, had toppled over and broken into pieces in no time at all. Now, there was a new three-coloured flag flying over the Grand Kremlin Palace.

When the Soviet Union was dissolved, Tatiana was disappointed that she no longer lived in the largest country in the world, but later she was relieved to find out that the Russian Federation was at least still bigger than China. Somehow, for Tatiana, that knowledge made the raging political and economic chaos in the country and especially in the capital, more acceptable. She didn't feel the urge to join the demonstrations. She preferred to watch the unfolding history-changing bedlam from a distance, preferably on a TV screen.

Oleg viewed the daily news from a different perspective. "We need to seize the moment, Sun!" He would switch off the volume after watching just a few minutes of headlines. He would turn it back on only during the adverts, checking the airing times for his biggest clients. His business, like many others, was conducted only in cash US Dollars, and it wasn't affected by the falling rouble and political turmoil.

A lot of Muscovites really thrived in the spirit of uncertainty and anarchy. There were spontaneous marches and demonstrations disrupting traffic in the centre of Moscow. The groups of old communists, carrying red flags and portraits of Stalin and Lenin, clashed with the supporters of the new Russia, who would be waving white, blue, and red flags and chanting, "Democracy!" In everyday life, this translated into two things. First, the rouble was falling. Second, organised crime was rising day by day.

Since life in Moscow had become increasingly dangerous—and more exciting—Tatiana loved coming to her library refuge all the more. She suspected the other readers here felt exactly the same.

When Tatiana entered the reading room this time, a strict-looking librarian rose from her desk and informed her, in a highly audible professional whisper, that the book that Tatiana had pre-ordered was on its way from the archives and would become available in forty-five minutes' time.

Tatiana decided to sit and wait rather than go to the busy cafeteria. Thinking that she'd catch up on the rest of her revision, she spotted an empty chair at the end of the middle row, right by the bookshelves that covered the walls. *My lucky day! I only have one neighbour on my right, and he won't even notice I'm here.*

She glanced at the desperate-looking young man in the next chair. Engrossed in the open reference books which entirely covered his desk, he was clutching his head as if trying to squeeze the information right into it. *He's either on the brink of a discovery or trying to cram the whole term's coursework into one day. Poor boy.*

Unhurriedly, Tatiana arranged her notebooks and pens and then positioned the green lamp over her workspace. She glanced at the bookshelves to her side and noticed a small black-and-white photograph of a familiar face with a goatee and pince-nez. *Oh, hello, Doctor! I came to visit your home in Yalta last year. Not sure if you remember me. I'm doing a thesis on your plays, you know.*

The memory of the last day of her honeymoon made Tatiana

suddenly shudder. Mila's high-pitched voice and childish smile sprang unwillingly to her mind. Tatiana quickly blocked the image. After Crimea, Oleg had acted like nothing had happened. Tatiana had had to work hard to convince herself of the same.

Even before the summer was over, Oleg had plunged himself into his work. He seemed inspired. Together with Alex, he stayed up working and talking late into the night in his late grandpa's small kitchen.

Tatiana could hear their voices as she struggled to fall asleep on the sofa bed. Often in the grey light of dawn, she found them sitting at the kitchen table over a large ashtray overflowing with squashed cigarette butts, still discussing work. It seemed the boys' card-playing days were over. They both spoke of Vlad with great respect. Meetings with "the boss" were equal to sacred rituals. If Tatiana happened to call Oleg during one of these meetings, the office secretary would say politely, "He's in Vlad's office and is unavailable at the moment. Can I take a message?"

Tatiana was proud that her husband wasn't like their classmates—beer-drinking, carefree, philosophising students. She liked that Oleg had a job which earned good money and was completely dedicated to it. Seeing herself as his comrade-in-arms, a kind of Nadezhda Krupskaya to his Vladimir Lenin, she tirelessly completed his college work for him so he could remain on the course while working.

She also helped him pass his oral exams, although that was more of a group effort, and quite the complex plot. After taking his question paper from the teacher's desk, he would pass it to a fellow plotter on the way back to his seat. The two, in turn, would rush out for a toilet break—where the paper would be given to Tatiana outside the auditorium.

She was well-prepared with her neatly handwritten answers. She had less than a minute to pull out the relevant sheet and carefully place it into the special sewn pocket inside the collaborator's jacket.

The next step was to deliver the answer to Oleg. Sometimes,

more people needed to be involved to pass it to him under the desk. Oleg would have enough time to study the answer, memorise it, and then deliver it brilliantly. The only thing he'd struggle with was the additional random question asked by a professor.

Tatiana was sure the staff suspected what was going on but that they chose to turn a blind eye, perhaps advised to do so by the dean.

Eventually, Oleg would leave the exam room with a big smile, having passed. "Thanks, Sunny," he'd say, trying to play it down as Tatiana hugged him, bouncing on her toes like they'd just won a relay race together. This was her moment of shining glory. She had been instrumental in the victory. It was good to feel one of the crew.

Studying was what she did best, and she particularly loved doing it in this grand reading room at the library. Here, Tatiana felt truly at home.

She now looked over rows of faces in serious concentration, people's eyes fixed on the pages in front of them. She could hear a soft rustle of turning pages. Tatiana closed her eyes and felt a light touch of wind on her face. She imagined that it was the spirit of learning, descending from above. But the fresh breeze was so tangible that Tatiana opened her eyes to check. She saw a woman in a staff uniform opening an upper part of the huge window above the gallery, skilfully using a hook on a long wooden pole and trying not to make a sound.

Ah, it must be an "aeration time".

Tatiana remembered the plaque on the door with the exact hours the windows had to be opened to let in fresh air. This was an essential ritual in all public places from the early days of the Soviet Union. It must have been one of the first directives from the Department of Hygiene. Tatiana chuckled, remembering how Oleg had negotiated their way into the composers' sanatorium by pretending to represent that institution. It was one of his best stunts. Tatiana let out a small sigh. Their honeymoon was the longest time they had spent together in the same room.

Oleg's been so busy since then.

On rare occasions, the couple managed to breakfast together before he would fly out the door, shouting, "I'll be back late, so don't wait up." She knew that the meetings, dealing with clients, would extend into the small hours of the next day. And that was the usual lifestyle of the new breed of Russian businessman. High-achieving and wildly ambitious, they were tirelessly seizing the moment of economic instability and general confusion.

Oleg gave Tatiana a convincing speech about it once, concluding with a personal plea: "I need your full support and understanding, Sunny. This is our time to make it. We'll be very rich one day. We'll travel the world, but it all comes at a price. You won't see me often, I'm afraid. I'm not going to be your typical husband, with slippers and a newspaper in front of the TV at 7 p.m."

"Oh no! I'd hoped you'd be exactly one of those—add a beer belly and a cat on your lap. My dream spouse," she teased him.

"Joking apart, Sunny, it means I have to work even on weekends. That's when all the promotional events and concerts happen. On the plus side, you get to come along as a VIP! Are you ready for all this?" He pressed her for an answer.

"Oleg, I fell in love with you because you're not like anyone else I know. I guessed that my life with you wouldn't be ordinary. It's fine. You go and do what you have to do. I'll be here, waiting for you with a bowl of home-made chicken noodle soup."

"Thank you, my Sun. You're the greatest wife in the world." He'd hugged her tightly and kissed her hair. "OK, I have to run." She heard the slamming of the front door before she could say anything else.

Since that talk, she had never questioned where he'd been when he came home in the middle of the night. It was much simpler if she assumed he was working.

At the library, she looked at her watch again. Seeing that

she had another twenty minutes to kill before her book arrived from the archives, she opened her notebook and wrote out the date on a new page. Then she thought, *It is 23 January, two days before Tatiana's Day—our unofficial anniversary.*

She smiled, remembering the surprise Oleg had prepared for her last year. He didn't have exams that day and she hadn't expected to see him at the university. She was standing there among their friends in the Smoking Square, happily chatting with relief after passing her last exam. When a sporty red Lada swerved in front of them, she instantly recognised Oleg's favourite new toy. It was not quite an American limousine, but it was still the first brand new car in the university's very modest car park, a place that consisted mainly of a few rusty antiques belonging to some lucky teachers and a couple of students. Only the dean himself and a handful of privileged kids arrived in a chauffeur-driven Volga.

Oleg climbed out, making his grand entrance: "Hi, guys! Did you miss me?"

"Oh wow, Isaev, nice set of wheels. Do they come in hopeful yellow and sunset orange as well?" Tatiana heard the excited voices of the boys who were eager to show their approval and expertise in the world of motoring.

Oleg took out two packets of branded American cigarettes and generously offered them around to everyone. "Thanks, man. Climbing high on the world's ladder! It's a wonder that you're still talking to us!" And the guests began a friendly banter as they opened the packets.

Oleg finished his cigarette and looked around. "Oh, there you are, Sunny," he exclaimed when his eyes finally found her, as she was hiding as usual on the sidelines. "I'm here to pick you up! Happy Tatiana's Day! I've got a surprise for you, but we need to hurry. Come on," he shouted over the heads. Everyone turned to look at her.

"OK, give me a minute. I just need to fetch my bag." Tatiana hurried, embarrassed by the attention.

"Be quick—we have a plane to catch!" Oleg continued in a loud voice, making sure everyone could hear him. Tatiana was mortified, anticipating the jealous inquisition upon her return.

He doesn't care. He appears here rarely, like a magical wizard from a faraway kingdom, showcasing his powers and wealth. And I have to deal with all the teasing and smirking.

But while she was manically packing an overnight bag, her anxiety was quickly forgotten (Oleg still refused to tell her where they were going). And before long, she found herself on board her first ever aeroplane, bound for Prague. They spent the night and the whole next day in the enchanted medieval city. Even on a grey winter's day, it looked like it belonged in Tatiana's favourite fairy tales.

They both got unexpectedly drunk on a dark, aromatic local ale that tasted of herbal medicine. Then they chased each other over the quaint Charles Bridge. Oleg stopped abruptly in the middle and began to star jump, half shouting and half singing, "We're going to be rich! We're going to be rich!"

A gentle snow had begun to fall, covering the ground below as well as the red-tiled rooftops and ornate towers. A few tourists, brave enough to embrace sightseeing in freezing temperatures, walked past, obviously trying to avoid the two odd-behaving Russians. Even the silent statues of the saints lining the bridge seemed to glare down in disapproval.

But Oleg and Tatiana were completely lost in this moment of careless, drunken joy. They finished crossing the bridge by waltzing in a tight embrace, trying to hum one of Strauss's Viennese waltzes and laughing.

Tatiana smiled at the memory.

That was the best surprise so far. What a magical city. I'd go back to Prague in a heartbeat.

She checked her watch again. It was time. She rose from her seat and made her way to the collection point. As she predicted, the guy next to her didn't move a muscle, keeping his eyes fixed on a page.

Chapter 9

"Happy Tatiana's Day, Sunny!"

Still out of breath, Oleg lifted himself on his elbows and stretched beside her. The old springs inside the sofa bed groaned one more time as if begging for mercy.

Tatiana was still basking in the warmth and intimacy between them after making love. The room was filled with the darkness of an early winter's morning. For a change, neither of them seemed in a hurry to start their day.

"Was this my present then?" Tatiana smiled at Oleg innocently. "I really appreciated it. Thank you. It looked like you enjoyed giving it, too."

"Glad you liked it." Oleg smirked back at her. "I always knew you weren't materialistic. Now, let's get up. Be a good wife and make us breakfast? Your husband needs to replenish his protein reserves."

Still in their pyjamas, they ate fried eggs and sausages and drank sweet milky coffee in the kitchen. "Thank you, my Sun. That was delicious," Oleg said, standing up to clear his plate. "But of course, I have to run now."

"It's Saturday, Oleg! I was hoping to spend the day with you. I'm completely free since my last exam yesterday." Tatiana struggled to hide her disappointment.

"Sorry, Sunny. I've got a few meetings to get through. But

I can give you a task for the day, which might make you feel better about it. Go and buy something nice to wear. I'm taking you out somewhere special tonight." Oleg left the kitchen and returned with a few hundred-dollar bills. "I'll pick you up at seven. Be ready."

"Where are we going? I need to know what to wear."

Tatiana was excited, but she was not relishing the idea of going shopping, as she didn't like doing it on her own. Her only shopping partner, Lena, was far away now, having disappeared into the cold English fog. She'd finally gotten her visa after the long months of applying and appealing. Just when it seemed all hope had been lost, she'd called the previous winter with something important to discuss.

"Isaeva, we need to talk. I'll come to you after work tonight, OK?"

Tatiana had bought Lena's favourite cake and a small bottle of liquor for the occasion, thinking that her friend had fallen in love and wanted a heart-to-heart. "I'm off. I'm out of here," were Lena's first words after she'd managed to tuck her long legs under the narrow kitchen table, sitting opposite Tatiana. Her eyes were dancing with excitement, her cheeks pink from the frost. She looked different somehow, radiant and upbeat.

"What do you mean?" Tatiana hadn't understood at first. The subject of the pending visa had become almost taboo between them. And since it had been such a long time, Tatiana had completely forgotten about it.

"I've got the visa!" Lena exclaimed enthusiastically. "They called me from the British Consulate yesterday. They gave me a multiple-entry student visa. It means I can study there as well as work some hours."

"Congratulations! That's amazing! I'm so happy for you." Tatiana couldn't believe that her best friend was actually leaving her.

"But you'll come and visit of course, won't you, Isaeva?" said Lena, picking up on her friend's sadness. "You're a respectable married woman now, so they won't suspect you preying on a potential British husband. You shouldn't have problems with getting your visa."

"Of course, of course, I'll come. London is not that far anyway. Thank goodness that those fashion scouts weren't from Australia." She smiled at her friend cheerfully. "Come on, we need to drink to your new modelling career. And this could be the last piece of chocolate cake for a long time. Go and kill them with your looks, Russian beauty!" Tatiana raised her glass in a half-mock salute.

"I'll kill them if they put me on a diet." Lena mirrored Tatiana's gesture. "You know me. I don't handle hunger well."

So now Tatiana had to face a trip to the boutiques on her own.

"What's the dress code, Oleg? What kind of place is it? Who's going to be there?" Tatiana fired questions at her husband.

"Oh, slow down, Sunny. Don't worry, you look lovely in everything. Buy something black. That's all I can tell you. I thought you liked surprises?" Oleg was moving quickly around the room, putting on his clothes and filing out his pockets with various things—keys, cigarettes, wallet, business cards. "If you need a second opinion, you can always take Marina with you—you know, the office secretary. She's got good fashion sense. She's a nice, serious girl—a single mother. You might enjoy her company. Shall I give her a call?"

"No, thanks, Oleg. I don't need a chaperone, especially not your secretary. Let her have a day off with her family," Tatiana hissed at him with irritation. She had met the very efficient and always polite Marina before—a petite, cold-looking brunette with an ever-serious expression on her pretty face. And although she couldn't imagine anything inappropriate happening between Marina and Oleg, she still felt annoyed at his suggestion.

"What time is your first meeting?" She took out a shoe-polishing brush and worked on his shoes in the corridor. Tatiana had developed the habit of judging a man by his footwear. Somehow she couldn't forgive scuff marks and dirt. It told her a lot about a person's character.

She remembered her father stepping outside every morning into the communal corridor with shoes, wax, and brushes in hand, not wanting the musky smell of turpentine to linger in the apartment. Naturally, Tatiana expected all men to be this meticulous, but she discovered early on in their relationship that Oleg took a more relaxed approach to the shininess of his shoes. Without pointing it out to him, Tatiana took the matter into her own hands, making sure that her husband always left for work in perfectly polished footwear.

"Are you kicking me out, Sunny?" Oleg raised an eyebrow.

"No, baby. I just don't want you to be late," Tatiana replied with a touch of frost in her voice.

"OK, then." Oleg hesitated by the door. "I'll see you at seven." He said it softly and then kissed her on the cheek. Tatiana realised that this was his way of apologising for upsetting her. She smiled back at him. "Go on then. Enjoy your meetings, workaholic."

An hour later, Tatiana walked into a long marble lobby. The five-star hotel had only recently opened in Moscow.

It was still early on a Saturday morning, so the place was quiet, the vast leather couches and armchairs in the middle of the foyer all empty. The small, brightly lit shops lining the lobby hadn't a single customer. The hotel had become a new gathering place for some of Moscow's elite. In addition to the boutiques selling everything from designer clothing to expensive jewellery and watches, there was a beauty salon, an American cinema, a casino, and several exotic restaurants. The modern concept of indulging all the senses by spending big money under one roof was new and thrilling to the emerging nouveau riche.

Usually, the foyer was filled with smart-looking men in expensive jackets and heavy gold watches. They would sit on the sofas smoking long Cuban cigars while their tall, beautiful girlfriends, in mink coats and high-heeled boots, walked leisurely from shop to shop.

Serious-looking bodyguards—unmistakable square giants in formal blazers with handguns bulging at their sides—waited for their clients outside these boutiques, scanning everyone around them. When on the street, they walked a few meters behind their masters. The boss's importance, and ability to upset his competitors, was directly proportionate to the number of bodyguards required. Tatiana had seen some members of the elite walking around with not two but six intimidating bodybuilders. They drove through the city in odd-looking clusters of bulletproof limousines sandwiched between huge off-roaders. All their cars were black with tinted windows, and with a blue police siren on top. They zoomed through the city traffic, using only the middle lanes and never stopping at junctions. The alarming sound of the siren had become a constant soundtrack to the life of Moscow.

Watching the black cavalcades flying through the busy streets made Tatiana think of dark forces of the underworld. They had come to the surface and materialised as the latest models of prestigious automobiles. And although she was curious about the mysterious powers of these new masters, she didn't think she'd like to be driven around like this, seeing her beloved city through tinted windows. She knew Oleg was very eager to become a part of this new club. Indeed, he was well on his way to joining it.

At the end of the lobby, Tatiana reached the Italian fashion boutique. The two young and immaculately groomed salesgirls openly looked her up and down. She even saw their pretty heads nodding. After a second, they turned to each other to continue their conversation. Tatiana obviously hadn't passed the test of "worthy customer".

She held her breath, feeling small and humiliated, but at the same time she was relieved to be left to browse alone.

She decided to be as quick as possible. After a brief look

around, she picked a pair of wide, high-waisted black trousers, a simple black and white top, and a pair of black shiny shoes with dangerously high heels. Both salesgirls looked at Tatiana in surprise when she stepped out of the fitting room and approached the cash desk. "I'll take all of these, please," she said, trying to sound casual.

"Can we offer you anything else?" one of the girls managed to say, smiling professionally.

"No, thank you. That will be all."

Tatiana noticed with satisfaction that there was a look of regret and confusion on the girl's face. A large carrier bag with the boutique's logo added to her confidence. With a new spring in her step, she walked to the cosmetics store next door. There, she bought a lipstick in a bold shade of red before heading back to the entrance. Looking down at her bag, the doorman nodded politely and then asked, "Would you like a taxi, young lady?"

"Yes, please," answered Tatiana, realising that it would look completely inappropriate for her to use the metro now. Once inside the cab, she let out a sigh of relief.

By the time she heard Oleg turning the key in the door, Tatiana was ready. Her hair was tucked in a tight ponytail, and her fringe hung over her forehead in a straight line. The new clothes fitted her perfectly. Although she felt slightly wobbly on her heels, she was satisfied with her new look. She had even braved the red lipstick.

"Wow, Sunny, you look great! Like a sexy French sailor," said Oleg, smiling with appreciation.

"What do you mean, Oleg? What French sailor? So I look like a boy?" Tatiana was not impressed by the comment. It had put a dent in her already shaky confidence.

"Oh no, that's not what I meant. It's just that I expected you to be in a black dress, that's all." Oleg raised his hands in protest.

"Oleg, you said wear black," answered Tatiana, not feeling very reassured. "You didn't say anything about a dress."

"Sunny, you look absolutely fine. I love the *rouge fatale* too. I'll just change my shirt and then we can leave. The taxi's waiting," he said, stopping in front of the wardrobe.

"You've not driving tonight?" Tatiana reached for her coat.

"No, we're going with Vlad and Mariana. We'll swing by for them."

Tatiana felt a stab of disappointment. She had hoped it was going to be just the two of them, but lately it never was. She realised that the last time they were together on their own was on that short trip to Prague exactly one year ago. Since then, whenever going out, they had always been a part of a group of "useful" people, new business associates, investors, sponsors—all newly rich and powerful men and their glamorous wives.

And that wasn't the only thing these men had in common; they all talked about women as if they were part of their collection of luxury accessories, together with their expensive cars, watches, and designer clothes. They showed little regard for their partners and for all women in general.

Once, when Oleg and Tatiana were at the billiards club, Tatiana had found herself suffering with a splitting headache—no doubt not helped by the thick tobacco smoke that permeated everything. She had managed to wait until Oleg finished his game before approaching: "Oleg, can we go home now? I'm not feeling well."

But before Oleg had even opened his mouth, his billiards partner, a tall, dark-haired man named Roman—head of security at Vlad's company—cut in loudly, saying, "Isaev, control your woman. She should know better than to interrupt her man's business. She can wait a bit."

And although he had said it in a mocking tone, grinning and chuckling, he had deliberately failed to acknowledge Tatiana. He had not even glanced in her direction, as if she weren't even there.

"Really, Sunny, wait a bit," answered Oleg. "I'll have a drink with my friend Roman here, and then we can go." He seemed to be slightly embarrassed by her. Tatiana felt belittled and betrayed. That leather-clad, utterly unpleasant self-proclaimed mafia boss was more important to her husband than she was.

"Oleg, it's OK. You stay. I'll call a taxi," she said, not wanting to admit defeat.

"Listen, girlie, it's not safe out there." This time, at least Roman was talking directly to her. "Too late at night to go by taxi. They'll know where you live. Stay put and wait for your man like a good wife should." He ended with a condescending smile.

"He's right, Sunny. It's not safe," said Oleg. "I won't be long," he said, trying to soften the impact. Tatiana had returned to her armchair in the corner and ordered a pot of tea, resigned to the idea that it would be a very long night.

Despite the initial disappointment tonight, Tatiana was relieved to know that at least they were going with Vlad and Mariana. Apart from Alex, these were the only people inside Oleg's circle whom she liked.

Vlad and Mariana lived with their two daughters and a nanny. The nanny was Vlad's distant cousin from a village in the Rostov region. They shared a large three-bedroom apartment on the top floor of an uninspiring-looking block outside a metro station, on the Moscow Garden Ring. Tatiana had been there before. She loved the atmosphere of calm, warmth, and old-fashioned family life.

Vlad opened the door to them, smiled kindly, and showed them in. "Come on in, guys! Do you mind waiting a few minutes in the living room? Mariana is just reading a bedtime story to the girls. Would you like a drink?" He opened the polished cabinet containing an impressive collection of all kinds of bottles.

"Vlad, thanks, man. I'll have what you're having," Oleg answered politely, his voice softening. The two men didn't look like boss and apprentice, but more like a respectful student and his favourite teacher.

Vlad turned to Tatiana. "What about you, young lady? Will you join us?"

"Oh no, thank you. I'm fine," answered Tatiana, who was already sitting comfortably in an armchair with a large art book on her lap. Vlad poured whisky into two crystal tumblers and then sat opposite Oleg on the sofa. Inevitably, they began talking about work.

Tatiana noticed that at home Vlad looked different from his office persona. He smiled more often here and tried to keep his voice low. He sat with his back relaxed against a cushion, his legs crossed and stretched out in front. Instead of formal office shoes, he was wearing a pair of old man's tartan slippers.

"Hi, everyone!" said Mariana suddenly, breezing into the room, followed by a gentle whiff of floral perfume. "Drinking already? I thought we agreed," she said, addressing her husband with motherly affection.

"Sorry, sweetheart. I'll have one less in the club." Vlad looked almost guilty. Tatiana could sense the loving bond between the couple.

"Did my husband forget to offer you anything?" Mariana turned to Tatiana, displaying her charming dimples.

"Oh no, I just didn't want anything," Tatiana replied, rushing to Vlad's rescue.

"You look lovely, Tatiana," Mariana continued. "The red lipstick really suits you."

"Thank you!" Tatiana blushed. She wasn't used to getting compliments.

"Perhaps we should go now, if you don't mind. You boys can continue talking in the club," Mariana said firmly. Everyone stood up in obedience.

Mariana was the head of a department at a neurosurgical hospital. Her ability to make quick decisions and take charge continued to save many lives. She was clearly in control at home, too. For Tatiana, it was surprising to see that even the powerful and authoritative Vlad was happy to take a back seat when it came to his wife.

They were a rare couple in their social group, treating each other with great respect. Mariana wasn't a glamorous trophy wife, and Vlad wasn't a chauvinistic, power-chasing husband.

Downstairs, outside the building, Vlad's loyal driver, Ivan, opened the door of their family jeep. "I hope you don't mind," Vlad said to his guests. "It's a bit of squeeze in the back seat, but we'll be there in a few minutes."

"I don't even know where we're going! Oleg wouldn't tell me," Tatiana whispered in Mariana's ear.

"Oh, don't worry. I haven't been there myself, but apparently it's a new club just opened by one of Vlad's old acquaintances," said Mariana, who then pulled out a small mirror from her bag to check her make-up. Tatiana turned her attention to the snow-fringed streets. In no time, the jeep stopped in front of a white building on one of the quiet side lanes leading down to the Moskva River.

Written on a large Soviet-style plaque over the double doors was, "Beam—Culture and Recreation Club of the Workers of Moscow Lamp Factory No. 1". Underneath, a new but smaller black-and-white sign had been erected. It read, "Black Cat—members only".

The narrow street was busy with traffic at this hour. Black limousines were queuing up to let their passengers out in front of the club, or trying to find a parking spot close by. Most of the cars were exactly the same model and were all black, as if other colours and makes didn't exist. Vlad's silver off-roader looked refreshingly original next to them. Tatiana now realised why Oleg hadn't driven. He would have been embarrassed by his modest Lada.

A young man, dressed in an old-style militia overcoat, crossed their names out on the guest list and then directed them through the doors. In a large dimly lit foyer, a small band of musicians in old-fashioned tuxedos played Soviet jazz from the 1950s. The staff, young men styled like American gangsters in black fedoras and white shirts with braces, were helping guests check in their coats and showing them to the various rooms.

Tatiana guessed that the Black Cat was named after the infamous criminal group that had operated in Moscow during the fifties. The members of Black Cat were responsible for many a bloody raid on banks and jewellery shops. The mob shot anyone who happened to be unlucky enough to be in the wrong place at the wrong time. Passers-by, personnel, security guards, and militiamen, if they tried to stop them, were all were gunned down in cold blood. The gang's deeds had been immortalised in Russian books and films.

Tatiana thought, *How fitting. These days mafia connections are in vogue. In fact, they are the only guarantee for success in business.*

The two couples were directed to a table in one of the rooms. The walls were burgundy red, and each round table was lit by an antique bronze candlestick. The menu card, made to look like a retro-style booklet, was printed on yellow paper.

"You have to guide me!" Tatiana addressed Mariana. "I have never tried most of these dishes. Where are they even from?"

"Don't worry. I'll try to help." She nodded at Tatiana. "The club's owner studied in Europe and got a taste for fine cuisine in France and Belgium. Now he's trying to educate Moscow's beau monde. We've only been to Paris once, so I'm not an expert either," she said, glancing fondly at her husband. Oleg and Vlad were still immersed in conversation. "Let's live dangerously!" Mariana exclaimed, addressing the whole table. "Let's all order frogs' legs and snails."

"Why not," Vlad agreed. "And some champagne for the ladies to help with their digestion. Oleg and I will stay on the single malt."

Tatiana noticed that Mariana quickly glanced at her husband and shook her head. "He's not supposed to drink," she told Tatiana in a low, confidential voice. "He's got a stomach ulcer. He's so careless and so obsessed with work. I have to call him from the hospital every day to remind him to eat his lunch! I even ask Marina to bring him something if he's in a meeting. This company of his, it's his third child. He'd work there for free, I'll tell you." Mariana paused to take a sip of champagne.

Tatiana had been listening attentively. She asked, "Where did you two meet?"

"Oh, it was years ago. We met at a party—mutual friends. I was just a junior doctor then, and Vlad was working as a lighting engineer at a TV studio. We are both southerners, you know. I think that's why our friends decided to introduce us in the first place. Vlad's family are from Rostov-on-Don, and I'm from Kiev."

That explains Marina's soft, dark looks. It's like she came out of one of Gogol's Dikanka tales. She's a beautiful, wholesome Ukrainian girl.

For the first time, Tatiana picked up on Mariana's slight accent. Mariana continued: "We clicked instantly, as they say. Vlad was so funny, trying to impress me by taking me to the studio during filming and introducing me to TV stars.

"I was so tired back then, though, working long shifts at the hospital. Once, I fell asleep in a chair in the corner and dropped to the ground in the middle of filming. I think Vlad got into trouble for that, although he never told me." Mariana smiled at the memory.

"I think you make a very harmonious pair. Your girls are very sweet, too. In fact, I'd like to propose a toast to you and your family," said Tatiana, raising her champagne flute.

"Marriage is a work in progress, Tatiana. Nothing is a given," said Mariana, suddenly serious as she lifted her glass to Tatiana's. "Vlad is a great father, I agree. The girls adore him. I just wish we had more family time together. Both our work schedules are insane.

"I worry about him," Mariana added in a whisper. "How would he manage if something happened to me?"

"Don't say that. What's going to happen to you?" said Tatiana, trying to lighten the mood. "You're young and energetic. You are a brilliant doctor and the best mother I know!" she explained with sincere admiration. “I think it’s the boys who should be more careful. They work long hours and drink more often than they eat.”

“You’re right.” Mariana nodded. Her soft brown curls danced around her rounded cheeks. “No need for doom and gloom. Let’s eat and be happy!” She gestured at the foreign food that had just arrived at the table.

When they had finished dinner, Vlad stood up. “Ladies, the concert is about to begin,” he said. “May I show you to your seats?”

“Concert? There is even more entertainment tonight?”

“What kind of concert?” Mariana and Tatiana spoke at the same time as they rose to their feet.

“Follow us,” Oleg chimed in. “You’ve got the best seats in the house. Bread and circuses, as the Romans used to say.”

He just can’t help showing off, Tatiana thought, feeling slightly embarrassed by her husband’s ability to take credit for everything. If the club’s owner was a friend of Vlad, then it must have been Vlad’s invitation after all.

They walked up a grand staircase leading to a large hall, where they saw large doors open to reveal a vast auditorium with a stage. In the glory days of the lamp factory, the space must have housed amateur dramatic productions, worker lectures, and even party meetings. But now, the rows of seats had been removed and the room was filled with small round tables, surrounded by chairs and impossibly beautiful waitresses in French maid outfits, complete with fishnet stockings. These waitresses graciously circled the tables, wafting trays of glasses and clean ashtrays held aloft.

Vlad led the group to a table right by the stage. There were only two chairs. “Aren’t you going to stay for the concert then?” Mariana asked her husband.

“Sorry, girls,” said Vlad. “We have a meeting with a potential investor over at the bar. You can come and find us when it’s finished.” He signalled to one of the waitresses: “Young lady, can we have two of your special cocktails for this table?" And with that, the two men made their way out.

Tatiana and Mariana looked around. The room was quickly filling with representatives from Moscow's new high society. Russian actors, film directors, and musicians nestled alongside bankers, businessmen (with the obligatory belle on their arm), and modern-day gangsters. The gangsters were young men of imposing sizes, all with wide necks, close-shaven heads, thick gold chains over black jumpers, and trademark burgundy blazers. They looked happy and relaxed after a long day of blackmailing, racketeering, and contract killing.

At the table next to them, Tatiana noticed a well-known TV presenter from her childhood. The woman in question was accompanied by a youth who could have easily been her son, had she any children. She still looked fabulous now, this glamorous woman with her complicated hairstyle and impeccable make-up. However, the boy next to her was far too young in contrast. And it was odd to hear the voice that Tatiana once associated with comforting bedtime children's programmes coming out with, "Get me a vodka Martini, darling."

Finally, the light went out and the male announcer spoke into a microphone: "Ladies and gentlemen, tonight, on our stage, at this exclusive concert, we are privileged to have—" And then he said the name of a very well-known underground musician whose songs were popular even during the years of tight Soviet censorship.

The Bard, as everyone called him, had made one or two official records back then, but it was his black-market albums that had made him famous. People copied these songs on their home tape recorders and then passed them on to friends and family. No one had expected to see a star of this calibre tonight. The resulting gasp and applause from the audience echoed throughout the room.

"I can't believe it!" said Tatiana. "I have all his records! My classmate made copies for me and didn't even charge me for them." The realisation suddenly hit Tatiana: "He must have been in love with me!"

"I bet he was!" Mariana agreed. "I met the Bard once before at Vlad's studio. He's a real ladies' man and a bit of a drunk, but I do love his music."

The heavy velvet curtains parted, and a tall figure in a long navy-officer-style coat appeared on stage. Perching on the high stool in front of the microphone, the Bard strummed a few chords on his guitar and mumbled, "Good evening." Then he began. One ballad led to another.

Tatiana closed her eyes and found herself sitting in her family living room with her tape recorder on her lap. She listened to every chord and word, wondering why such talent had been so offensive to the official cultural perspective. Perhaps it had simply been a case of jealousy? The censors didn't like the Bard's influence on the nation?

Tatiana found herself overwhelmed by the singer's corporeal voice and guitar in the intimate space. She sat there immersed in the music until she heard him address the audience. "Ladies and gentleman," he began. "Today is Tatiana's Day, and this next song is dedicated to Tatiana Nikolaevna Isaeva, by her husband. Where are you, Tatiana Nikolaevna?" He looked out across the audience.

Tatiana's eyes shot open. Her cheeks blazing, she timidly raised her hand. She glanced at Mariana, who also had surprise written over her face.

"Ah, there you are, pretty one," barked the Bard. "You're a bit young to be married, aren't you? I was hoping to buy you a drink later. What a disappointment."

There was light laughter and a few approving claps as he then began to sing one of Tatiana's favourite ballads, "Winter Song". She could hardly believe that her childhood idol was actually singing to her! He had even given her a clumsy compliment.

When the song was over, the Bard stood up abruptly, bowed his head, and mumbled, "That's all I've got for tonight, good people. I'm off for a drink now, so thanks for listening—and good night." He walked off the stage to applause and whistles.

"Did that really just happen?" Tatiana exclaimed. Mariana didn't reply. It seemed she hadn't even heard her and was busy searching for something inside her handbag.

"Ah, there it is," mumbled Mariana, pulling out a small pillbox. She threw back a few tablets, chasing them down with a gulp of water from a crystal glass. "Sorry. I've got a terrible headache. Do you mind if I go home?" She gave Tatiana a guilty smile. They both started moving towards the doors.

In the marble foyer, they noticed a small, excited gathering. Some of the guests were pointing at something and making animated comments. Tatiana could have sworn there had been nothing of interest there before the concert.

She let a pale and weary-looking Mariana go ahead to find Vlad and Oleg while she craned her neck to see what was causing the commotion. Moving through the crowd, Tatiana could finally see what the fuss was all about.

In the middle of a red Persian rug sat a beautiful black panther with a sparkly diamanté collar, chained to a shiny metal pole. The animal's yellow eyes were half closed. It looked distant and indifferent to its surroundings. Tatiana was reminded of the Egyptian sphinx.

One of the leggy waitresses in fishnet tights was explaining to the admiring public, "Simona is our lucky charm and only comes out at night to greet our special guests. We saved her from a circus that could not afford to keep her, and now she gets only the best of everything. She has her own personal trainer and a chef who provides her with the best cuts of beef."

Simona did indeed look brimming with health. Her short and silky black fur gleamed under the shimmering lights. Suddenly Tatiana felt tears pricking the corner of her eyes. She turned away and quickly started walking.

She remembered Stripey, the lively tiger club from the zoo. She had been happy to settle for a soft toy, but it seemed that the owner of the Black Cat hadn't wanted to let go of his own childhood dream. He was making a statement: "I bought this club. I bought this panther. Why? Simply because I can."

Slightly confused and caught off guard by mixed emotions, Tatiana caught sight of the bar, where Oleg and Vlad were smoking cigars with a grey-haired man she had never seen before. Oleg saw her approaching and hurried over. Tatiana realised he wanted to cut her off, to avoid having to make an introduction.

"Sunny, Mariana's gone home—she wasn't well. Ivan's coming back to get you soon, OK? I need to stay here a bit longer though. We're in the middle of something important." Oleg gestured towards Vlad and the stranger.

Nodding in acceptance, Tatiana mumbled, "Oleg, there is a real black panther upstairs."

"I know, I saw it—the real 'black cat'. How cool is that?" He couldn't read her mood.

"It's a beautiful wild animal, Oleg, born to roam free in the jungle." She was playing nervously with the clasp on her handbag.

"You're too impressionable, Sunny. Relax. It's just a cat. A big one. Besides, think of all the juicy steak it gets."

He stroked her shoulder and she sniffed.

"Did you enjoy your song?" Oleg began to look annoyed, glancing impatiently towards the bar counter.

"Oh yes. Sorry, I meant to thank you," said Tatiana, suddenly feeling guilty. "How immature of me. Here I am going on about a cat when you were trying to make my day special." She kissed Oleg gently on the cheek. "It's been a very memorable Tatiana's Day. Thank you. I would prefer to go home with you together, that's all."

"Why are you doing this, Sunny?" Oleg stepped back, looking cross. "You know very well I can't go. I've got very important business to discuss. It affects our whole future. You promised to be understanding, remember?"

Before she could say anything else, he turned and walked away, radiating exasperation. Tatiana sighed.

How come I'm always wrong? I have to hand it to him: he's seriously gifted in making people regret their words and actions.

She recovered herself, collected her coat from the cloakroom, and then walked outside. The ever-silent Ivan had been waiting for her. He opened the back door of the jeep.

Chapter 10

Lena returned unexpectedly in April.

Tatiana was walking back from the metro station one evening, the pavements wet from a passing shower and the air fresh and moist. She always loved Moscow after the rain. The city looked renewed and clean somehow, like a more focused picture of itself.

In a small park outside the station, Tatiana paused for a second and inhaled deeply. The smell of wet tarmac was mixed with the freshness of new grass and damp tree branches swelling with the buds of future leaves. On the fresh grass she noticed a few bright yellow blossoms. Dandelions. Tiny pieces of summer sun.

Tatiana smiled, remembering her happiness at discovering a whole field of dandelions outside her grandma's village once a few years ago. She had run towards the sunny yellow clusters and then dove into them, the small petals tickling her nose. Then she sat on the ground and made the longest dandelion chain in the world.

Her thumbs had turned black from the sticky white juice that had trickled from the long hollow stems. She wrinkled her nose. She could almost taste the sharp bitterness of the dandelion milk.

Tatiana adjusted the strap on her heavy messenger bag,

which was full of books and papers, and continued on her way. In addition, she was carrying a plastic bag of groceries and a bunch of red tulips and pussy willow. Shopping for everyday goods had become very easy. There was no need to go to the stalls or supermarkets anymore. The whole city had become one giant open-air market, and it had happened almost overnight.

Since the government had brought in a new law about the freedom of trade, anyone could sell or buy whatever they wanted, whenever they wanted. Improvised street markets had formed outside every metro station and along every busy street. The city's pensioners had found a new source of income.

Old ladies no longer had time to sit on painted benches outside their apartment buildings and gossip. Now, early in the morning when everyone else was rushing to work, the retired sector of society would form an orderly queue outside the local shops. Once inside, they bought everything they could afford: butter, cheese, milk, sausages, soap, shampoo, toothpaste. Later in the day, they lined the pavements, displaying their goods on overturned cardboard boxes. They sold these for a profit to the working half of the population.

Some of the pensioners invested a bit more time and effort in their new venture, selling hand-knitted woollen hats, socks, and gloves—traditional home-made goodies that had previously only been made for family members.

Tatiana didn't mind innovations like these. She was happy that her elderly neighbours now had more to do than sit around bad-mouthing the youth, or worse—giving her advice on life and marriage, if she was foolish enough to stop and ask about their health.

Besides, she had always hated shop queues, inevitably finding herself standing alongside a hostile Muscovite who had a compulsion to argue about politics with any stranger at hand. Often, a debate would end in a physical fight. Everyone seemed to know best and was prepared to take a beating for it.

That day, Tatiana had finished her weekly shopping in a

matter of minutes. She hadn't even bothered with haggling, making a few old ladies very happy indeed.

The spring bouquet had been impossible to resist. She loved the shape of tulips with their pale green leaves, and the furry buds on the branches of the pussy willows were like tiny cuddly creatures from the land of Thumbelina.

From a distance, Tatiana noticed a lonely figure sitting on the bench outside her door. The stranger was facing away, but by the full mane of long brown hair, Tatiana could tell it wasn't one of her gossipy neighbours. She let out a sigh of relief and continued on without a second thought. It was only as she came closer that a familiar face turned to greet her.

"Isaeva! It's about time! What took you so long? I've been sitting here for an hour. I know what time your lecture finished, remember!" Lena had jumped to her feet and thrown her arms forwards for an embrace.

"Lena! I can't believe it. Why didn't you call? You look so different!" Tatiana, overcome with emotion, hugged her friend tightly.

"Why, I thought you liked surprises! Or has married life banished your romantic nature?" Lena stepped back, giving her friend an estimating glance. "You look great. The fringe is cool. Have you lost weight?"

"Oh, thanks, but I don't think so. You look well, too. So foreign!"

Tatiana studied Lena's face. Her eyebrows were shaped thinly, arching in perfect curves over her big brown eyes. But that wasn't the only change. Lena's smile was much wider. It had lost its sarcastic asymmetry. She wore a black leather biker's jacket over a floral dress, and black ankle boots with yellow soles and fluorescent pink laces. Tatiana knew not a single person who dressed like this in Moscow.

Lena looked the exact opposite of Tatiana and her set, who wore very grown-up designer clothes. Lena seemed to be dressed according to her age, and she looked very comfortable doing it. With not a hint of make-up on, her bare skin was glowing.

"Come on, let's go upstairs. I'll show you something foreign!" Lena pointed to a large carrier bag on the bench. Tatiana could just make out the shape of a bottle inside it.

For the next few days, the two friends were inseparable. Tatiana would rush from lectures to meet up with Lena. Being reunited with her friend reminded her of how much she'd missed her wit and openness.

Once, she had even stopped by Lena's apartment, where a proud little Vera had showed off her new wheelchair, lightweight and shiny. Tatiana and Lena sat for hours on a park bench around the corner, smoking and chatting. The late April sun was shining, the birds were chirping, and the two girls enjoyed the strong bond that continued to blossom.

Lena told Tatiana stories about life in London and her modelling work, which turned out to be not as easy as it had sounded. "We're only allowed to show the emotion required for the photo shoot," she said. "Can you imagine me in that puppet show? That's why I smile so much now—my professional camouflage, you know. They don't know what a volcano I'm taming inside. Believe me, it's not easy to play dumb all the time."

With her usual self-irony, Lena told Tatiana that she didn't feel like the other women in her agency, who seemed to take their careers too seriously. She was also doing a course in English and dreamed about having a proper job one day. "But they pay us good money," she continued, "and it feels great to see Mum and Vera looking happy.

"I like the people there, too," Lena added. "Now that my English has improved, I'm able to converse with them better. I'm fond of the Brits—they're very professional, very polite, and always in control of their temper. They're curious about me, too, as if I'm an exotic animal who happened to make it to the other side of the Wall.

"They ask about life in Russia—you know, politics. Some of them have even read Tolstoy and Dostoevsky, so they don't ask silly questions like whether there are brown bears in Red Square or if it's −30°C all year round.

"They adore their own traditions—love their afternoon tea," she continued. "But they unquestionably believe everything that's printed in their newspapers. Imagine that!"

Tatiana looked at her friend in surprise. "So, a good place to be a journalist then!"

"I'm telling you," Lena carried on. "On the one hand, the British are very advanced and trend-setting, especially with their fashion and design. But on the other hand, their hygiene standards are prehistoric."

"What do you mean?" asked Tatiana, pulling another cigarette from a slim white packet brought by Lena.

"I mean, in the apartment where we stay, there is no shower, only a bath with separate hot and cold taps. And there is a fitted carpet on the floor of the toilet."

"What!" Tatiana raised her eyebrows in surprise. "But what if—"

"Exactly!" said Lena, interrupting her. "Let's just say I'm glad there are no men sharing the flat."

"Sounds like you've got plenty of new material for your favourite subject!" They both giggled, remembering Lena's article on public lavatories.

Oleg seemed genuinely happy for his wife, glad that she had her best friend back. But while Tatiana was immersing herself in her renewed friendship, she hardly saw her husband, who continued to come home late each night. As he'd explained, it was necessary to put this much effort in at this stage of a potential new venture. Together with Vlad and Alex, he had regular meetings with Maks Polonskiy, the grey-haired man from the night at the Black Cat.

Maks represented the first generation of Russian investment bankers. A son of a diplomat, he was well educated and polished, and had studied Western financial systems and investment programs in detail. He had previously worked for the International Export Import Bank, dealing with the Eastern Bloc. Now, in Russia's chaotic days of privatising the industry, he was building a banking system to support the country's new industrialists. However, he was also interested in the media, and had already bought a newspaper and launched a magazine. He wanted to invest in TV advertising time, with a view to buying one of the official Russian channels.

It was no wonder that Maks found Vlad, with all his connections, very appealing. He had already proposed a joint venture, but Vlad was cautious about a potential partnership.

In contrast, Oleg seemed to be taken by the new, powerful, flamboyant player in their game. The gambler in him welcomed a fresh opportunity to raise the stakes.

One evening, when Oleg was still at work, Tatiana and Lena sat at Tatiana's kitchen table, blowing smoke into the open window that overlooked the little courtyard outside. The maple tree's branches had already turned pale green with swelling buds, which were ready to burst into large velvety leaves, each one resembling a human palm. Tatiana had gotten used to watching the change of seasons through the old maple.

Usually, the silence of the flat was broken only by the rattling of the old fridge that Tatiana refused to swap for a new one. But today she was happily chatting to her friend. Even after a few days together, they still had a lot to say to each other.

It was a surprise when they heard a noise at the front door. Oleg had returned home early.

"Hi, girls," he said, bursting into the kitchen.

"Hi, Oleg. Good to see you." Lena crushed her cigarette butt into an ashtray and stood up. "I must get off now, so I'll leave the two of you in peace."

"Oh no, stay for a minute," Oleg quickly interjected. "I have a proposal for the both of you."

He pulled up a chair. "Listen, girls, we have this new

client—the owner of the first Russian luxury travel agency. He wants to advertise through us, but more importantly, he wants to spread the news about his business in our circles. In his line of work, a personal recommendation is everything."

Oleg lit up a cigarette. "So, the May holidays are next week. What would you say to a quick trip to the Seychelles?"

"What do you mean, a 'quick trip'? Where are the Seychelles, and who else is going?" Tatiana had her questions.

"Hold on, Sunny, let me explain." Oleg took out a cigarette. "The Seychelles are somewhere in the Indian Ocean, off the Kenyan coast. Not far from Madagascar, I think. And we would like to commission you two, Comrades Isaeva and Petrova, to help the budding Russian tourism industry.

"Imagine! You will be like two beacons, leading the way for your countrymen and countrywomen to explore unknown tropical shores." Oleg finished with a smirk.

Tatiana already knew what was coming. "What about you, Oleg? Aren't you going to join us?"

"Sorry, Sunny. I really can't afford to take a week off. You know our situation right now." He hinted at the negotiations with Maks. "What about you, Lena?" he asked, turning to their guest. "Can you step in and accompany my wife on this mission? I'm sure your writing skills would be useful to my client, too. Perhaps you can put together an article for his brochure on your return?"

"Isaev, you're full of surprises, as always." Lena tried to play things down and hide her excitement. "I'm here until mid- May, so yes, I'll go, but only if your wife agrees. I'd love to have a holiday with my best friend. How much will it cost?"

"Oh, don't worry. All expenses are taken care of," said Oleg. "You are helping *me* out, if anything." The two of them looked at Tatiana, waiting for her reaction.

"OK then," said Tatiana. She smiled. Suddenly, a week with Lena on an exotic island didn't seem like a bad idea. She said to Oleg, "I still can't believe you have to work during public holidays, when everybody else is relaxing at their dachas." She had a job hiding the doubt in her voice.

"Some of us do have to work, believe it or not, Sunny," said Oleg patronisingly. "OK, that's agreed then. I'll need your passports for the bookings. You two can start shopping for bikinis!"

Tatiana jumped to her feet, crossed the floor space between them in a few steps, and draped her arms around her husband's neck. "Thank you, baby," she crooned, leaning over to kiss his stubbly cheek.

"OK, that's it!" Lena stood up in feigned exasperation. "Looks like you kids need to get a room. This time, I'm really leaving."

"I'll show you out," said Tatiana, giving Oleg a luscious smile.

Chapter 11

The Aeroflot flight bound for Mauritius, with stops in Dubai and the Seychelles, was almost empty. Tatiana and Lena were able to stretch out over whole rows of seats, lifting armrests to make beds. A friendly stewardess brought some pillows and blankets to make them comfortable.

The young women were still flying over the endless waters of the Indian Ocean when the plane began descending. Tatiana was glued to the window. Under the low grey clouds she could see a scattering of dark green islands. The captain announced that they were preparing to land at Seychelles International Airport.

Thick clouds lay steaming over green mountain peaks, like heavy chimney smoke. But Tatiana could still see sparse groups of low buildings peeping through the dense tropical forest. Apart from the narrow stretch of white sand that fringed the coastline, green seemed to cover everything.

The plane was flying so low now that Tatiana could make out individual palm trees hanging over the sand, their trunks like giant, slithering snakes hovering just above the ground. The view was richly exotic yet slightly alien and gloomy at the same time.

"It is still early morning in the Republic of Seychelles," said the captain into the microphone. "Those passengers disembarking here will have a hot, sunny day ahead." The cabin intercom gave his voice an official ring. "But lavish greenery like this needs a lot of water, as you can imagine," he added, pleased with his own quip.

Tatiana and Lena's hotel on Mahé looked almost deserted. A tall white building with arched windows, balconies that overlooked tropical gardens, and a small sheltered cove, it had been built in the 1980s by an international hotel chain. Tatiana immediately felt the dissonance between the man-made structure and its beautiful surroundings—especially as it bore signs of deterioration. It reminded her more of a hospital than a luxury resort.

There were no windows or doors in the vast lobby, and the large arches opened onto a courtyard with a swimming pool in the middle. Tatiana and Lena were greeted by a fresh breeze blowing in from the ocean, filling the space with the unfamiliar smells. The two young women walked over to the reception desk, where a beautiful Creole, with a plump frangipani flower tucked into her black curls, spoke to them with a dutiful smile.

"Welcome to the Paradise," she said, offering freshly cut coconuts with cocktail straws sticking out of the holes. Lena stepped forwards and began talking in perfect English. Tatiana gawped at her in awe. She had never heard anybody speaking so fluently in a foreign language before.

Minutes later, the young women were shown to their room. It was very simple, with white painted walls, plain furniture, and a small shower room. The TV set on top of a chest of drawers looked ancient. Two double beds were covered by faded bedspreads, and matching faded curtains hung by the French doors leading to the balcony.

Tatiana and Lena didn't care about their room or its lack of luxuries. Excitedly, they rushed onto the balcony and then stopped, stunned by the incredible view. The perfect secluded beach lay beneath the gardens, protected by huge grey granite boulders on either side. The boulders' contours had been altered by thousands of years of splashes and licks from the ocean, creating strange lines and dents.

The sand of the empty beach was an impossible shade of white, looking more like a baking ingredient. This scenery was so extraordinary that Tatiana and Lena held their breaths in awe. Then, as one, they began jumping up and down with childish joy, hugging each other and shouting, "We are in paradise! A whole six days!"

I just wish Oleg could see it. Tatiana thought about her husband with regret, but she decided not to say anything, because she didn't want to hear a smart retort from Lena.

The two friends settled easily into a holiday routine. They were surprised to discover that the other hotel residents—retired French or English couples, plus a loud German family with young kids—preferred the pool to the gorgeous beach. In the following days, Tatiana and Lena took full advantage of this fact, turning the little cove into their private sanctuary.

They stretched out on the hot white sand after swimming in the warm turquoise water. The sea was so clear that they could see right through it to the abundant multicoloured fish and seashells on the bottom.

Looking at the snow-white sand was impossible without sunglasses, and after midday it was always too hot to walk on it with bare feet. These new sensations overwhelmed Tatiana and Lena. They lived each day in bliss.

When they tired of the beach, the friends ventured to nearby markets in the capital of Victoria, and hired a hotel boat for a deep-sea fishing expedition. This was where they caught a frightening big-mouthed fish that turned out to be absolutely delicious after being grilled over an open fire on the beach by their cheerful French captain.

One day, they visited the island of Praslin, the home of the coconut famously shaped like a female bottom. According to local legend, Praslin was the original Garden of Eden. Tatiana had her doubts. This botanical oasis looked more like a dense jungle than a garden with an apple tree in the middle of it.

Their guide had argued that this must have been the place, because despite all the lavish and diverse flora, there were no poisonous snakes or nasty beasties on the island, only multiple breeds of beautiful birds. Tatiana at least agreed that perhaps it wasn't the apple but the immodestly shaped coconut that had sealed the fate of humankind.

Their deserted and draughty "infirmary", as Tatiana and Lena had nicknamed the hotel, came to life three times a day, when meals were served. The guests would come out to dine on the local offerings. Even then, the atmosphere would remain serene. Only the energetic German family injected some liveliness into the place. Their children skipped and hopped into the restaurant, talking loudly and moving their chairs.

The long buffet was plentiful, but the trouble was—as the young women discovered after just two days—that the menu stayed exactly the same for every meal. One night, Lena lost her patience. "That's it. One can only have so much octopus curry in four days. I want meat!" she said to Tatiana, who was busy filing her plate with rice.

"So, what can you do about it?" Tatiana reached for a piece of grilled fish.

"I'm going to talk to them. Watch." Lena walked confidently towards the chef, who was posed outside the kitchen door. She returned to the table after a few minutes, carrying a plate of grilled fish.

"Would you believe it!" she exclaimed. "They said they've run out of steak. The next shipment from Kenya only arrives next week. 'Sorry, madam, no space for cows on our island.' He offered me the local speciality—flying fox stew."

Tatiana looked horrified. "Maybe he was joking?" She remembered a picture of a giant bat with orange fur from their guidebook.

"No, he's not joking, mate. The chef showed me the

saucepan. Apparently he's treating the staff to it later." They both agreed that stewed bat was a step too far, even for them, the adventurous travellers.

The young women spent their evenings in the hotel's only bar sipping pina coladas and comparing tans after a day of sunbathing. The Seychelles' close proximity to the equator meant that the sun set very rapidly here. By 7 p.m. it was pitch-black.

One night, they braved a walk to the dark beach. The black skies bore myriads of stars, which seemed breathtakingly close. The white smudge of the Milky Way was so clearly visible that Tatiana gasped. "I've only ever seen this kind of sky inside the planetarium. I thought they just made it look closer so the lecturers could point out constellations."

"Amazing!" Lena nodded. "Imagine, you and me, two Russian girls, on this tiny island in the middle of the Indian Ocean. There is no big city with bright neon lights for thousands of kilometres."

Suddenly, they heard a loud rustling by their feet, as if someone was turning over large heaps of old dry leaves. "What's that?" Tatiana couldn't place the sound.

"We shall find out," said Lena, pulling out a small torch from her pocket.

"You've had that all this time and didn't use it? We could have fallen down and broken our necks!"

"Relax. I didn't want it to spoil our stargazing." Lena pressed the on button and directed the beam of light in front of her. They were standing on a patch of sand that looked silvery grey under the bleak glint of stars. But beyond the small semicircle, the entire beach was black and seemed to be moving.

"Do you see that?" Tatiana jumped back, terrified, and they heard the rustling noise again. The cove was coved in crabs, thousands of them, scuttling away from under the young women's feet in waves.

"That's impressive." Lena was the first to collect herself. "Don't worry, Isaeva. I think they're harmless. They look scared of us. I'm surprised there's no crab salad on the menu. Maybe these little guys are more difficult to catch than flying foxes?" She pulled Tatiana, still stunned and motionless, by her hand. "Let's go back. They're probably all gossiping in the bar about the two crazy Russians taking a walk at night."

Tatiana followed her friend back to the hotel, stepping carefully.

On a different night at dinner, Lena confessed that she was "a little bit in love". Strangely, she had not even touched on her love life until now.

The two friends had been tucking into their octopus curry when a waiter came over to their table and said, "Miss Petrova, there is a phone call for you, from London."

Lena flushed and quickly followed the man. She picked up an old-fashioned phone from the counter. Tatiana watched from afar as her friend stood there talking animatedly, the whole time cupping her mouth with her hand.

"I can't believe he found me here!" Lena was almost out of breath when she finally came back to the table.

"Talk to me, Petrova! How could you not have told me about *him*?!" Tatiana couldn't hide her annoyance.

"Don't be mad," said Lena. "Listen, I sort of forgot all about him in this paradise. Bedsides, I'm on holiday with my favourite person."

"Ha. Very flattering. Now go on, spill the beans!"

"OK, hear me out, but don't judge. He's not boyfriend material. He's just my ... lover." Lena looked Tatiana straight in the eye, waiting for her reaction.

"Lena, I'm so upset with you. You've been having sex with someone and haven't even mentioned it!" Tatiana said encouragingly.

"I'm afraid I'll disappoint you, mate. The truth is, I value your opinion of me." Lena pushed her plate away, signalling to the waiter that they'd finished their meal. "Can we move to the bar? I need to fuel my courage."

They sat on tall bamboo armchairs at their favourite table in the corner. Lena told Tatiana all about Roberto, the Italian photographer who had taken her under his wing in her early days in London. When she had still been homesick and couldn't speak much English, Roberto had tried to cheer her up with his enthusiasm and Italian charm.

He dragged Lena around London—a city he loved and knew very well—showing her the sights, art galleries, flea markets, and quirky little pubs in dark narrow alleys. Roberto introduced her to his artistic friends—fashion and interior designers, cinematographers, and journalists. His positivity and passion for beauty in all of its forms was contagious and irresistible. The two quickly became more than friends.

Of course, things that seem too good to be true usually are. One day Lena discovered that Roberto was married. He had a wife in Milan, his second favourite city.

Roberto spent all his holidays and some weekends in Milan, being an exemplary husband, as he adored his wife, Francesca. Lena even suspected that she knew about her husband's weaknesses but was prepared to tolerate them for the sake of their marriage.

"As I said, I'm surprised he called me here. I thought he would have replaced me with someone new by now. That's why I didn't want to tell you, Isaeva. I'm not a homewrecker. I would never let him leave his wife for me. I'm just a fallen woman." Lena's mouth formed into her old lopsided smile.

Tatiana took a big gulp of her margarita. "You're not a fallen woman, Lena. You're my best friend, and I love you no matter what. You'll make the right decision about this, I'm sure. You're so good at making those." Tatiana reached for Lena's hand and gently squeezed her palm.

"OK, enough about me. I've confessed my sins. What about you? You haven't said much about life with Isaev since I've been back. Is it a taboo subject now it's all official?" Lena looked searchingly into her friend's eyes.

"No, not a taboo. There is just not much to say. I can't complain, as you can see." Tatiana waved her hand around. "My life is pretty amazing, thanks to Oleg, and I feel very lucky. My parents could only dream about travelling to places like this.

"Oleg still surprises me with his generosity, his gestures. He asked the Bard—you know, the real, actual Bard!—to sing my favourite song for me one night. Did I tell you that?" Tatiana smiled at the memory.

"OK, so you found your Prince Charming. I get it. But I'd still like to hear the gory details. You seem different since we last saw each other. Even with me, you're more reserved than you used to be. Isaeva, let your guard down, please. Talk to me." Lena kept pressing.

"I think we need another drink for that," answered Tatiana, trying to divert the conversation and turning her head to search for a waiter. Tatiana was always uncomfortable with heart-to-hearts. She didn't see the point of them and had always been much better as a listener than as a talker.

A displeased-looking waitress from the restaurant approached their table. Lena beamed a smile at her and said, "Can we order more cocktails, please?"

"Sorry, madam, the bar is closed," the waitress replied, seemingly offended by the request. "The barman has finished for the day."

Lena raised her voice in protest. "But it's only nine o'clock. And we're still sitting here."

"The barman's gone home. He needs to rest." With that, the waitress stalked off, swinging her full hips. Tatiana and Lena looked at each other and began to laugh. They'd already noticed the lacklustre approach to service among the locals. It was as if the staff thought they were doing a huge favour when serving the annoying tourists.

"I bet what she really wanted to say was, 'Go and make your drinks yourselves, you lazy cows!'" Lena snorted. "This country is proof that socialism doesn't work in a tropical paradise.

Surely Marx and Engels didn't travel this far before writing their manifesto. They only had countries with colder climates in mind."

"Yes, it's just like back home," said Tatiana, giggling. "'All labourers have a right to rest,'" she quoted. She was relieved that the conversation had taken a safe turn. By now, she began to realise that the true reason she hadn't quizzed Lena about her love life before was that she was trying to avoid Lena's questions about her own in return.

Tatiana sensed that there were problems in her marriage, but she wasn't ready to admit them, not even to herself, let alone to her best friend. She also felt that she would be betraying Oleg by talking about it.

Since they'd arrived at the hotel, Tatiana had tried to telephone her husband, but there had been no answer, not at home or at the office. She made sure she phoned at different times of the day and night, but it was all in vain. Eventually, she managed to speak to her parents and ask them to pass a message on to him, asking him to call her back. Late last night, when Tatiana and Lena were fast asleep, their telephone started ringing.

Oleg sounded overly cheerful: "Hello, Sunny! I miss you!" By his voice, Tatiana could tell that he'd been drinking. "Where is Lena? What are you up to now?"

"Oleg, we're sleeping. It's really late here," she whispered in reply. "Where have you been? I tried to call you, but I couldn't find you." She hoped Lena wasn't listening.

"Sorry, I didn't mean to wake you. What time is it there?" Oleg slurred.

"The same time as it is in Moscow, silly. And why are you still up?" Tatiana softened her tone, realising how much she missed her husband.

"Oh, it's a long story, Sunny. We finally reached an agreement with Maks tonight, so we're all out celebrating. We're going to make it big, really big, and I need your support. I can't wait for you to come back, Sunny." He sounded very candid, a little helpless even.

"I miss you too, baby. I love you." Tatiana sniffed. "It's so beautiful here. I wish you were here with me."

"We'll come again together soon. I promise. You can be my personal guide to the Seychelles." Oleg's voice began to fail.

"I can't hear you very well, Oleg. The line is bad." Tatiana raised her voice. "I'll see you in two days. Goodnight." She put the receiver down. Still whimpering softly, she crawled back to bed. With thousands of kilometres between them, it was the closest she had ever felt to Oleg.

The following morning, Lena acted like she hadn't witnessed the night-time drama. Tatiana tried to sound casual as she mentioned how Oleg had phoned. "He had some good news about the business. They've made a deal with a new partner. Looks like he didn't stay behind for nothing. He said to say hello to you."

"Was that all that he said?" Lena smiled, raising a perfectly shaped eyebrow.

"No. He also said he missed me." Tatiana blushed as if she had just shared something very intimate.

"That's better. Not all hope is lost for Isaev, then. He better treat you well or I'll come and get him!" Lena did a pretend karate chop. That was the end of their morning conversation.

This time, Tatiana was saved from further interrogation by a rude waitress.

"Let's go to bed," she said, standing up and inviting Lena to follow. "It's our last day tomorrow, so let's get up early and spend as much time as possible on the beach."

"Good idea," said Lena. "There's no point in us sitting around here when even the barman is observing his 'right to rest'."

Two days later, on the plane which was about to take off, Tatiana decided on a distraction in the form of a heavy novel that she still hadn't finished on holiday—she'd been too busy chatting with Lena. Her friend seemed serious and focused as she took a notebook and pen from her bag. "OK, let's get started on that article. I've got so much to say about the Seychelles. Let's hope your husband's client approves."

"Just don't put people off with your sarcasm!" Tatiana fastened her seat belt.

"I'll try," Lena muttered, looking at the blank page in front of her and already biting on the cuticle of her little finger.

On the runway, the aeroplane began to gather speed.

Chapter 12

The first thing that Tatiana spotted in the arrivals hall of Moscow's international airport was Alex's mop of dark hair flying above the heads of the crowd. Then she noticed Oleg beside him, barely detectable among the tight mass of jackets and shoulders. He was hiding his eyes behind his favourite sunglasses. Tatiana couldn't tell if he was looking in her direction.

Lena insisted on pushing their luggage trolley and was now skilfully manoeuvring her way among the hesitant passengers. Alex waved at them first, and then Oleg joined him, his mouth stretching into a big smile.

The two young men made an odd-looking pair. The tall, towering Alex with his messy hair, looked casual in his customary jeans and American rock T-shirt; and Oleg, almost petite in comparison, was all neatly groomed in a formal white shirt and a well-fitting jacket. It was hard to imagine that these two had been inseparable for years and now worked for the same company.

While Lena and Alex exchanged hellos, Tatiana threw herself at Oleg, kissed him full on the lips, and removed his glasses.

"Hey, Sunny! You look fantastic! The tan really suits you. You even smell different." He tickled her neck with his nose.

"And you look tired!" Tatiana noticed the dark circles under his eyes that he had been hiding behind the sunglasses. "Are you OK?"

"Yeah, I'm fine. It's just been a crazy week, that's all. I'll tell you all about it later. Let's get you girls home first." Oleg spoke this last sentence louder. He began to walk in the direction of the car park.

"Let's move it," agreed Alex. "Hey, Twenty-Three, you look divine with that tan. And you, of course, our international model," Alex quickly added for Lena while flashing her a smile. "Needless to say, you look stunning. The male population of the Seychelles must still be mourning your departure, girls."

"Smooth as usual, Alex," Lena said, acknowledging his compliment. "Now be a good boy and push that trolley a bit faster. I'm dying to get home and go to sleep.

"I was writing during the whole flight," she said, catching up with Oleg, who had been walking in front of them. "Isaev, thank you again tor the unforgettable holiday. You can tell your client that the article will be with him on Monday."

Tatiana looked at their group and the bulging suitcases, drawing a sigh as she thought of the lack of space inside the Lada. But in the car park, instead of the usual red car, Oleg stopped in front of a large black jeep, the kind Tatiana had seen being used by NATO troops on the television.

After Oleg pressed a button on a key holder, the door locks popped up with a welcoming ping. "Whose car is this, Oleg?" Tatiana asked, puzzled.

"Oh. For now it is still one of Maks's," Oleg said, loading the bags into the spacious boot. "He's got a huge car collection, of course, and he got this one for his dad to use, but Grandpa Polonskiy refuses to use 'the enemy's army vehicle'. Still prefers his old-school Volga.

"I'm just testing it, Sunny. But it can be ours, if you want it."

"Can we afford it, Oleg?" Tatiana asked carefully. By now they were speeding down a half-empty motorway, leaving the airport building behind. Tatiana was annoyed by the easiness of Oleg's decision making. He made it sound like borrowing someone else's expensive car wasn't a big deal.

"Sure, we can afford it, Sunny. We made a lot of money this week, didn't we, Alex?" He nudged his friend, who was in the passenger seat next to him.

"We certainly did," Alex confirmed absent-mindedly.

"Do you mind me asking, how much did you make on the deal, Isaev?" Lena butted in. "Just out of curiosity."

"Why not," said Oleg. "I'll tell you exactly. Last week a client wanted a TV advertising spot for his brand of vodka. He said his budget was US$200,000, but we managed to do it through Vlad's contacts on the prime channel for only US$20,000 cash. The rest is pure profit."

"You made 180 grand!" Lena said, calculating quickly. "Not bad!" She was clearly impressed.

"That's right. Sixty grand each way, since there are three of us who closed the deal." Oleg nodded to Alex, who had his eyes closed and didn't seem to be listening.

"Right, Alex, wake up!" Lena tapped him on the shoulder. "Tell us what you did with yours? I demand to know! That's a lot of rock T-shirts."

Alex jumped in his seat. "Er, I gave mine to my mum." He had been listening after all. "I kept a bit for myself and went to a casino. I was winning at first, but I lost it all in Blackjack by the end of the night. How do they do that? Why does the house always win?" he asked in childlike wonder. "It doesn't have to be that way. I'll have to do something about that. We'll see." He continued murmuring to himself. No one was listening to him anymore.

"Oh, I almost forgot, Sunny. For you—a celebration present," said Oleg. They were waiting at a traffic light when Oleg pulled a slim navy box out of his inner pocket. He twisted around and gave it to Tatiana.

"Oh, thank you, baby!" She studied the box in her hands.

"Open it, my sunny one," Oleg said, returning his gaze to the road and pressing on the gas pedal. Tatiana lifted the lid. Inside, on a blue velvet cushion, lay a gold heart-shaped pendant on a gold chain. It had a clear crystal window. Inside the tiny space were three diamonds, which were moving freely as the car swerved. It looked very expensive.

"It's beautiful, Oleg. Thank you," said Tatiana. She then passed the box to Lena, who wanted to see the necklace.

"That's a serious piece of jewellery, Isaev!" said Lena in an appraising tone. "You are one lucky girl, Tatiana." Instantly, Tatiana felt a familiar urge to disappear. As always, she found her husband's need to show off painfully embarrassing. His big gestures were always performed in public—it was as if the more he spent on a gift, the bigger he wanted the audience to be.

"It looks very costly, Oleg." Tatiana tried to hide her uneasiness. "But I still love my old one." She tenderly pulled the golden half-moon and sun from under her collar. She treasured it more than ever now. It had been Oleg's first and only gift presented to her in private.

"Oh, you're still wearing that old thing?" he said. "From now on, I will buy you only diamonds." Tatiana didn't know what to say to that. With relief, she noticed that he was pulling up in front of Lena's place.

Later, back at the apartment she shared with her husband, Tatiana was greeted by a waft of stale tobacco as she opened the front door. "Oleg, you didn't open the windows," she said, rushing in to find that the curtains weren't even drawn. The morning sun was peeping through a crack between them, and a thousand specks of dust were swaying in the column of light. She opened a window and welcomed a surge of fresh air, accompanied by cheery sounds from the street below. "That's better!"

In the kitchen, Oleg took out some containers of food from a plastic bag that he had brought up with him. "I met with my mum on the way to the airport. She said to say hello. Look at all this food. You don't have to cook today."

He opened the fridge. "There wouldn't have been much to cook with anyway," he muttered.

Tatiana looked over his shoulder. "That's an understatement!" The fridge was empty. "What did you eat while I was gone?"

"Er, I wasn't home much," he answered hesitantly. "I spent a few days at Maks's dacha. He has a big place twenty kilometres away."

It was then that Tatiana spotted two crystal glasses in the sink. One of them had a visible lipstick mark on the rim. "But you've clearly been here—and had a female guest too," she said, pointing at the sink.

"Oh, yes." Oleg followed her gaze. "That was just after you left. Alex came over with a girl. What was her name, Alex?" Oleg raised his voice. Only now did Tatiana notice their friend standing in the hallway. He had brought up her suitcase.

"Where shall I put this?" he said. "Sorry, Number Nine, did you ask me something?" He looked quizzically at Oleg.

"Just put the bag down, Alex," Oleg answered before Tatiana had a chance to say anything. "I asked you the name of the girl who came here with you a few days ago." Oleg's voice was loud and clear, as if he were a teacher talking to a slow-thinking student. He nodded towards the kitchen sink.

Still looking confused, Alex stared at the glasses. "Ah," he finally said. "That time. It was a while ago. I can't even remember her name. Dasha? Or maybe Masha? I'm not very good with names. I find them pretty meaningless anyway." As he was talking, he avoided Tatiana's gaze. She knew they were both lying.

"You were a great host, Oleg," Tatiana continued. She refused to take it lying down. "It seems you even forgot to pour a glass for yourself. There are only two glasses."

"Oh, no, that would be me—I had to take my medication, so I couldn't drink," Alex said quickly, his eyes searching for Oleg's.

"Are you satisfied now, Detective Isaeva?" Oleg tried to turn the awkward conversation into a joke. "But look, unfortunately

Alex and I have to dash off for a bit now. We're seeing Vlad at his home to talk through a few things. He's a lonely man right now. Mariana has stopped working. She's back in Kiev with the girls.

"They're not separating—don't worry," Oleg said quickly, reading a silent question in Tatiana's eyes. "Mariana's just been overworked this past year and needs a break. Every weekend, Vlad joins them at her family's place, but not this time. We need to go through a few details."

"It's true. Vlad is waiting for us!" Alex exclaimed loudly. Tatiana could hear relief in his voice.

"OK, don't be late, Oleg, and please don't let Vlad drink too much," she said, remembering Mariana's concern about her husband's ulcer. "And you, Oleg, you look like you could do with cutting down a bit on the alcohol, too." Tatiana tried to sound calm and casual, but she was suppressing the urge to shout and make a scene.

He's so smart. He brought Alex with him as a safety buffer. He's given his friend the main part in his alibi.

Tatiana felt exhaustion wash through her. The long journey had taken its toll. She suddenly wanted to be left alone. *Let him think he got away with it. I can confront him later, without witnesses.*

"I'll try to come back from the meeting early, OK? We can go food shopping together," Oleg said, interrupting her thoughts.

In the hallway, he gave her a kiss on the cheek. He looked relaxed and relieved, like a captain who had just managed to steer his boat clear of a storm.

"OK, we can do that. Don't be late, baby," Tatiana replied mechanically.

"Take care of yourself, Twenty-Three," said Alex. For the first time that day, he didn't avoid her eyes. He paused and raised his arm in a small salute.

Tatiana knew that he was saying more than the usual goodbye. She had gotten to know his signals well. The two of them shared a connection unknown to Oleg or anyone else in their circle. It had all started after the honeymoon.

One late August evening, Tatiana had been trying not to fall asleep before her husband got home. He had a habit of returning just when she was in her deepest slumber. She was frustrated that she never heard him come in, take his shower, or crawl into bed. She had even asked Oleg to wake her. "But I do sometimes, Sunny. You even say hello," was his reply, but Tatiana doubted this really happened. So that night she finished cooking later than usual. The potato and meatball soup was gently simmering on the hob when Tatiana decided to take a cigarette break from watching the ever-unsettling news on the TV.

The doorbell rang. Initially she thought that Oleg had come home early and had forgotten his key. She was surprised to find Alex standing there instead. "Hello, Twenty-Three. Is Oleg at home?"

"Alex, come in," said Tatiana, automatically tightening the belt of her slightly revealing dressing gown. "I thought he was with you."

She gestured to Alex to follow her into the kitchen, drawing the flaps of her robe tighter on her way.

"We were together a few hours ago, but I had to leave. He stayed behind with Vlad. I thought he'd be home by now." Alex spoke quickly, as if he wanted to finish his explanation as soon as possible.

Tatiana sat down at the kitchen table opposite and looked closely at his face. She could tell he was lying, covering for his friend. Alex lowered his eyes and let out a sigh. He must have realised that she could see through it.

The likely explanation was that Oleg had asked Alex to come over for a meeting but had completely forgotten about it himself.

"Are you hungry?" Tatiana was the first to break the silence. At this moment she felt sorry for Alex, who was slouched over her small kitchen table. "I've made soup with meatballs. I can boil some pelmeni for the main course. I've managed to buy a tub of fresh sour cream to go with them."

"Oh, thank you. Sounds like a feast fit for king." Alex seemed grateful that they'd dispensed with the uncomfortable part. He ate quickly and greedily, wolfing down the food and then smacking his lips in appreciation.

Tatiana watched him with fascination, as if he were an actor in a strange slapstick comedy. She was so engrossed that she almost forgot about her own soup, which was getting cold in front of her.

"Delicious," he muttered. "You are a goddess. Isaev is so lucky."

Alex's sincere compliment flattered her, so she forgave his table manners. "Don't get carried away, Alex." She laughed. "I didn't make the pelmeni. They come from a packet. I can only take credit for the soup."

"Well, this is all divine. It's the most delicious pelmeni I've ever had, Twenty-Three."

"When will you stop calling me Twenty-Three?" Tatiana asked, trying to divert the conversation away from her cooking. "My name is Tatiana."

"I know that," Alex replied, still chewing vigorously. "But there are thousands of Tatianas out there, and only one of them is Twenty-Three." Tatiana couldn't argue with the logic.

After dinner, they sat in front of the open window, smoking in silence, feeling strangely at ease in each other's company.

"I often don't know where he is or who he's with," said Tatiana suddenly. "And I don't even know if he's telling me the truth. He often makes me question my sanity." She paused, shocked at her own unexpected outpouring. *What on earth possessed me to say that?*

For a few long seconds, Alex remained silent. His voice sounded almost eerie when he finally spoke. "'Shall I tell you what true knowledge is? When you know, to know that you know; and when you do not know, to know that you do not know—that is true knowledge.'" Alex paused.

"What's that supposed to mean?" Tatiana felt slightly offended. "Are you mocking me?"

"Never," Alex said, looking serious. "Listen again." He repeated the passage. "So said Confucius, the famous Chinese philosopher. He lived five hundred years before Christ. And he spoke in simple truths.

"This one is my favourite. 'In his errors a man is true to type. Observe the errors and you will know the man.'" Alex let out a thick puff of smoke. "I love Chinese philosophy. It makes sense of everything. And it calms me.

"Oleg loves you, you know. He is a man of many errors, like all of us. But he loves you," Alex added, looking out of the dark window, appearing to be talking to himself.

"Well, he has a strange way of showing it," Tatiana protested. Weeks after the scene in Crimea, she could still feel the dull ache in her chest.

"It's getting late. I better go." Alex stood up. "Thank you for the delicious dinner. I'll come along again sometime if you don't mind. I won't be able to stay away from this culinary paradise. Take care, Twenty-Three. Stay where you are. I know my way out."

"Bye, Alex. Pop back anytime. There aren't many fans of my cooking." Tatiana smiled back.

She didn't see Oleg that night. She was fast asleep before he got back, but strangely after that conversation with Alex, she felt like she was finally ready to put the honeymoon memory behind her.

Alex had kept visiting her from time to time, always with a legitimate excuse, but always in Oleg's absence. He brought her philosophy books, jazz records, Western magazines. He never declined her invitation to stay for a meal and was always full of praise for her food.

When she would casually mention to Oleg that Alex had stopped by to lend them a book or a video, she was always surprised by his reaction. Instead of showing any jealousy, he seemed content, like he was giving his friend a nudge of approval. And so Tatiana trusted Alex completely.

Just a few days before her departure for the Seychelles with Lena, Alex had come by again. She had been in a great mood. The sun was shining, and her bikinis and shorts were scattered all over the floor. She hadn't cooked anything, as she was still packing, but she offered to make Alex a cheese sandwich.

"Don't worry, Twenty-Three, I've just had lunch. I'll take some coffee though. I need to tell you something." Alex seemed excited. When they sat at the kitchen table, he offered Tatiana a cigarette from an open pack and simply said, "I'm leaving soon."

"Where are you off to? On holiday?" Tatiana was still smiling.

"No, I'm leaving for good—emigrating." Alex lit Tatiana's cigarette and then took out one for himself.

"What? Really?" Tatiana couldn't believe it. "That's huge news. But you've never mentioned it before. Does Oleg know?"

"No. Only you and my mum. Can I ask you to keep it a secret? I'm not ready to announce it at work yet. We can't even tell your husband."

"Sure, Alex. Of course. But emigration. It's so unexpected. It sounds so permanent and irreversible. Have you thought this through?" Tatiana wasn't convinced it was the right decision.

"I'm ready to go for good," said Alex. He seemed nervous. "You know that I'm Jewish, don't you?" Tatiana nodded. "My parents got divorced when I was four. My dad remarried soon after and emigrated to Israel. I have two half-sisters there.

"Mum wasn't so lucky. Stepfather No. 1 didn't stick around for long. I guess he didn't sign up for raising a lunatic stepson." Alex grinned bitterly. "But I love my mum. She's always been on my side. Men came and went, but I've always been her favourite boy."

His smiled changed as he mentioned his mother. "Anyway, my dad's still in touch. He's always pressed me to come and live in Israel, and finally I've agreed. Mum is single again, so she'll join me soon. Only I don't want to stay in Tel Aviv for long. My final destination will be America. I've got an uncle in New York. I'd like to end up there." Alex paused.

"But why, Alex?" Tatiana wanted to understand. "Why now? The timing is strange. You've got so much going for you here. Business is good and life is exciting. You can travel anywhere you want. Why don't you just *visit* your uncle?"

"Look, I'll tell you why I've decided to go. When it all started," Alex said, waving his hand towards the window, "all these changes in the country, it seemed so promising at first. I was happy to be a part of it. But I don't like where it's going anymore. Sometimes I don't even recognise the people around me." He stopped. Tatiana knew he meant Oleg.

"We broke the old stale system, but we're still not free. They've started worshipping a new idol. Now it's money. They want lots of money. For them it equals power. I understand that, but it's just not for me."

"What's for you then, Alex? And why America?" Tatiana still wanted answers.

"I don't know. I just have the impression that there I can be myself; no one will judge me. Besides," Alex said, his eyes lighting up with mischief, "I want to know how their casinos work. I'd like to check out Las Vegas and places like that. The Chinese wisdom didn't rub off on me, I guess. I'm shallow!"

"Alex, I understand. This parade of vanities isn't for you. Sometimes it's not for me either." Tatiana sighed. "But I'll miss our talks when you're gone. Call us, and we'll come and visit you, OK?"

"I will, Twenty-Three. I guess I'll miss you too." Alex looked down, avoiding any eye contact.

Tatiana kept her promise not to say anything to Oleg. And now as she and Alex were saying goodbye in the hallway, she looked at him with his arm raised in a salute. She understood that he was waving goodbye for the last time. He held her gaze now. She saw a deep sadness in his eyes—and something else.

Suddenly, a women's intuition told her the true reason for

his departure. There, in the dimly lit corridor, she saw love. *It can't be. I'm married to his best friend. It's my imagination.*

She closed the door and shrugged her shoulders, trying to brush the idea away. She diverted her attention by switching on the radio and beginning to unpack from her holiday. In the bathroom she emptied her wash bag and then opened the mirrored cabinet.

Right there, in the middle shelf, stood a jar of face cream. There was nothing particularly extraordinary about it, only it wasn't hers.

She took out the glass container—an expensive brand, half full—and realised that whoever had left it there had wanted her to find it. Tatiana carried the jar, holding it as far away from her as she could, as if it were poison, into the kitchen, where she put it on the table. Then, after opening the bottle of coconut liquor that she'd bought back from the Seychelles for Oleg, she took out a clean glass. She poured in the sweet, sticky liquid and then topped it off with some Coke.. She drank it down quickly. Then she made another one.

This time, she sat down, lit a cigarette, and sipped the sugary drink between puffs. Her eyes were fixed on the jar as the alcohol began spreading warm waves through her body. Tatiana stood up, stubbed out her cigarette, and began washing up the two glasses in the sink, meticulously scrubbing off all traces of lipstick.

Her head was spinning and filling up with a pleasant fuzz. She opened the window fully, slumped back into her chair, and slurred at her favourite maple tree. "Can you believe it? I was only gone a week, and it seems my husband has started using lipstick and moisturiser! Imagine that!" She snorted. With unsteady hands, Tatiana pulled out another cigarette. "I'm so stupid," she mumbled. "What on earth am I going to do now?"

Chapter 13

When Oleg finally came home, it was after midnight. Tatiana was drunk and ready to fight. From her chair, she pointed at the lonely jar of face cream that looked out of place atop the floral oilcloth on the kitchen table.

"What's this, Oleg?" she hissed. In her alcohol-infused mind, it was the strongest piece of evidence she'd obtained so far.

Oleg regarded Tatiana and the cream in front of her with a puzzled look. "What's this all about, Sunny? Have you been drinking?"

A hot wave of anger hit Tatiana. She jumped to her feet, unable to control herself. "You bastard!" she screamed in a high-pitched voice. "Did you bring a woman here while I was away? Did she stay the night? What's this cream doing in my bathroom cabinet?"

Oleg's expression instantly changed from relaxed and tired to cold and determined. He put his arm out, as if ordering her to stop. His reaction almost scared her. She had never seen him this angry before. She kept quiet, trying to catch her breath.

When he spoke, he looked disgusted. "You finished now?" he rasped." You disappoint me, Sunny. That thing was left by that Dasha or Masha character that Alex brought with him. But that's beside the point. You choose to have a fight now, when you're just home from an exotic holiday I arranged for you and your friend? You spoiled bitch!"

That last word hit her like a slap across her face. He had never called her that before.

"What did you just call me?" She choked with outrage.

"You heard me," he confirmed coldly.

She couldn't find the words. Angry tears rolled down her cheeks as she stood before him, shaking on her unsteady feet. His voice sounded ice-cold and detached.

"You know very well how much pressure I've been under lately. I'm doing this all for us. That includes you! But instead of showing me your gratitude, or at least your understanding, you give me a half-witted rant about nothing!

"I can't stay here. I'm out!" Oleg stormed from the kitchen. Tatiana heard him opening the wardrobe door next door. Her anger was quickly giving way to a fear that he might leave and never come back. That wasn't what she wanted. She had only wished for his honesty.

"Oleg! Wait! Don't go! Maybe I have overreacted." She ran after him, sobbing. Oleg was hurriedly packing his overnight bag.

"I'm going to stay with Maks at his guest house for a while," he said without looking at her. "I suggest you sober up and think about your behaviour."

"Page me if you need anything." He softened his voice slightly. Then he wrote something on a small piece of paper and placed it on the side table. "That's my new number." Only now did Tatiana notice a small black device clipped to his belt. He picked up his bag.

"Oleg, don't go!" she repeated timidly. His answer was a loud bang of the front door.

Chapter 14

Tatiana awoke the next morning on the sofa. She was still in her robe, her body covered by the itchy throw. She couldn't remember how she got there. She had a burning headache, and her mouth was filled with the synthetic aftertaste of rum and cola. She shuffled into the bathroom in search of painkillers, carefully avoiding her own reflection, as she felt that her eyes had been reduced to little cracks under puffy eyelids.

After an hour spent reviving herself, Tatiana was ready to face the day. She read the numbers on the piece of paper that Oleg had left for her. In order to reach him, she would have to phone an operator and dictate a message. She wasn't ready for that, so she called Lena instead. Remembering that her friend was soon going back to London, she decided to miss a few lectures and spend time with Lena.

The two friends sat in their favourite open-air cafe, chatting, smoking, and eating cake as the gentle May sunshine played on their tanned faces. Tatiana never mentioned the argument with Oleg, and she never asked Lena what she was going to do about Roberto.

The next day, she felt ready to phone Oleg at work. The ever-polite Marina told her that "Oleg Borisovich" was out at a meeting all day and that Tatiana could leave a message for him, either through her or on his pager.

At the subtle shift in Marina's tone, Tatiana could tell that something had changed in the office. Marina's special intonations had been reserved exclusively for Vlad before. "Oleg Borisovich", with the subtle enunciation, signified that Oleg had a new status at the company. Tatiana marvelled at Marina's ability to change her secretarial loyalties so quickly, making her understand the office hierarchy simply by pronouncing the boss's name.

"It's OK, Marina, I'll page him. Thank you," said Tatiana before she hung up. She couldn't wait another day before making contact with her husband. She began feeling guilty for starting an argument with him. She just wanted to make up with Oleg and have him accept her apology.

He was probably right for calling me spoilt; he did pay for our holiday. That cream could've been there for a while, even before I had left. I must have looked ridiculous to him, she thought, trying to persuade herself. The jar in question was now long thrown into the rubbish bin.

That night, Tatiana said goodbye to Lena. "Isaeva, I don't want any tears and sloppy goodbye kisses!" Lena shouted over the phone. "I'm off to the airport now, and I don't want you there. But I am not leaving before you promise me that you will get your butt to the consulate and apply for the damn British visa!"

"I will, I promise," Tatiana agreed. "I'll see you soon, pushy friend! Safe flight!"

Tatiana was quite relieved that Lena was leaving now. She could not have kept her problems a secret for much longer.

The next day, Oleg came home early without warning. Tatiana was doing her coursework and had papers scattered all over the kitchen table when she heard the lock of the front door turning. *That could only be him!* She promptly decided to play it cool.

"Oleg! Is that you?" she called casually. He stood in the threshold, looking pale and lost.

"Mariana's dead." He breathed out. "Vlad phoned. From Kiev."

"What? When?" Tatiana dropped her pen. "Was it an accident?" Tatiana struggled to make sense of the news.

"Last night. It wasn't an accident." Oleg sunk heavily into the chair in front of her. "She had a brain tumour. No one knew except her close family. It's why she stopped working and went back home.

"I think Vlad was hopeful until the end," he continued. "But he got a call two days ago and rushed off to the airport. We didn't think much about it—family issues, we assumed. And he didn't explain at the time."

Oleg pulled out his cigarettes and offered one to Tatiana.

"A neurosurgeon dying of a brain tumour. It couldn't get more ironic," he added. His hands were shaking as he tried to light the cigarette's end.

"Vlad sounded so calm on the phone," said Oleg with a timbre of disbelief, "like a newsreader—as if what he was saying didn't concern his own wife. He even started asking about work."

"He must be in shock," Tatiana muttered. Her mind was refusing to accept the information. Suddenly, the memory of their night at the Black Cat came back to her. She remembered Mariana's sudden sadness and concern for Vlad, and the rushed search for her pills.

"Oleg, she knew. She must have known for some time," said Tatiana, who then told him about the episode. "I think Mariana went to Kiev to make her final arrangements."

They sat in silence for a while. For the first time in her life, Tatiana became acutely aware of human fragility. She'd never experienced the death of someone so young, and so close to her, before. She felt pity for Vlad and their orphaned daughters, but at the same time she felt strangely embarrassed on Mariana's behalf, as if her friend had somehow failed her family by dying so early and putting them through this unpleasant ordeal with the funeral and all those archaic rituals, and the uncertainty of their future life without her. Tatiana's arguments with Oleg seemed completely insignificant in comparison.

After a while, Oleg stood up and grabbed a bottle of vodka from the fridge. He half-filled two glasses and put them on the table between them. "To Mariana," he said. Still standing, he emptied his glass in one gulp. Tatiana stood up and mirrored his gesture.

Mariana was buried in Kiev. According to her wishes, the funeral was very small and private, with only her family and a couple of her childhood friends present. Tatiana and Oleg stayed behind. Vlad returned to Moscow three days later, leaving his daughters in the care of Mariana's sister.

Oleg drove to the airport to meet him. He told Tatiana that evening, "Vlad wanted to talk only about work. He went straight to the office and asked Marina to bring him all the correspondence for the days he was absent. He looks like a robot. I'm worried about him. He seems in denial."

Since Mariana's death, Oleg had changed his pattern, coming home for dinner every night. He looked drained and weary. Tatiana and Oleg would sit together quietly in the kitchen, eating, smoking, and talking softly. Tatiana saw more of him in that week than ever before.

The immense sadness of Mariana's fate couldn't stop her from treasuring these intimate moments with her husband. But it made her feel a little guilty too, when she thought of the once warm and beautiful Mariana who was now laid forever under the greasy earth of the cemetery. It seemed that in her death, Mariana had brought Oleg back to Tatiana.

Oleg would sit opposite his wife and talk, and Tatiana would listen without interrupting. He told her how Vlad was still not convinced about their venture with Maks. He was afraid that the company would lose its identity and that Maks was leading it in the wrong direction.

"He just doesn't like Maks," said Oleg one evening. "It's as simple as that. He won't agree with anything Maks proposes, but to me it's clear that we need him. We need his money and his connections if we want to grow."

"It sounds like you've got a serious problem there, Oleg," Tatiana answered as she cleared the dishes and put on the kettle. "What are you going to do?"

"I don't know, Sun. I'm right in the middle of it. Sometimes I feel like a referee in a boxing ring. Of course it's been quieter since—" Here Oleg's voice trailed off, as if he couldn't say Mariana's name out loud. "But a few days ago they had a massive row over company security. You know that Roman oversees it." Tatiana nodded, pursing her lips at the sound of her nemesis's name. Roman's arrogant grin and leather jacket popped into her head.

"Roman is connected to one of the groups in the south of Moscow," Oleg continued, and Tatiana understood that he meant one of the mafia gangs that traditionally offered their protection to all Moscow businesses. For their services, they charged either a fixed fee or a percentage of the company's profits. These protectors called themselves "roofs", referring to their structural importance. Every entrepreneur in Moscow and beyond had to have a reliable roof.

"Maks wants us to use *his* people," Oleg said as he lit up a cigarette. "He's using some very serious Chechen boys." Oleg blew thick smoke out of his nostrils. "Roman is not very happy about it, although he's willing to lead negotiations between the two groups. But Vlad is furious. He says that Maks only needs the Chechens to cover up some shady money transfers between Moscow and Grozny. Our business is based in Moscow, so we should only use local guys, like we do already.

"It all got out of control very quickly, Sunny. I've never seen Vlad lose his temper before. He even started accusing Maks of helping the Chechen separatists! 'Are you blind?' he was shouting. 'They will use our money in the war against us!'

"It took me and Roman ages to calm him down. Maks stormed off. I don't think they've spoken since."

Tatiana could tell that Oleg was trying to play down the significance of the conflict. "Oleg, I'm not sure I like the sound of Maks. It looks like he's involved in something big and dangerous. I think I prefer boorish Roman to the scary Chechens."

"Then I shall tell Roman that my wife chooses him!" said Oleg. "I'm sure he'll be flattered." He squeezed her hand gently. "Don't worry, Sunny, we'll resolve it. Let's have tea. What's for dessert?"

On another night when they sat down to dinner, Oleg said casually, "Alex left for Israel today. He brought in his letter of resignation and then went straight to the airport." As he spoke, Tatiana felt he was watching for her reaction. She managed a look of complete surprise.

"Are you serious? What's he going to do in Israel?" She sounded genuinely astonished.

"Don't tell me you didn't know, Sunny. You two have been thick as thieves lately."

"No, Oleg, he really didn't say a thing. I did know his father lived in Israel though. Would you like your main course now?" She stood up, turning her back to him.

This is the first time I've ever lied to him and gotten away with it. I can play this game too. It's actually quite fun.

"How strange. I really thought you knew. But that's Alex. He's always been full of surprises." Oleg shook his head. "I didn't see that one coming. Although he did seem to lose interest in work lately."

"Is he not coming back? Is he going to get a job there?" Tatiana thought it was more natural to ask questions.

"Apparently the States is his final destination. He's got an uncle there. Or perhaps he was lying and has gone to the great plains of China to trace his spiritual teachers. He just chose the long way round." Oleg's voice suddenly dripped sarcasm.

"He thinks he's above all of us with all his Chinese wisdom! That's his problem. He'll be back once the money runs out, I guarantee you that!" Oleg proclaimed, hitting the table with the side of his hand. The plates and glasses clattered. Tatiana realised that Oleg was hurt by his friend's departure, more than he was willing to admit.

"You're right, baby. I'm sure he'll be back soon. It's just one of his capricious ideas."

Tatiana put her hand reassuringly on Oleg's shoulder. She didn't believe it for a minute. She knew Alex was gone for good.

Chapter 15

The academic year now over, Tatiana got to enjoy the freedom of lazy summer days. She stayed in bed late until the insistent rays of the sun peeping through the curtains made the room uncomfortably hot. Then she would venture to the nearby park on the other side of the river, stopping at a shop on the way to buy a tub of salad and a small box of fresh strawberries. The latter would always be a little bit soft and soggy, oozing their bright red juice and the unmistakeable smell of summer—strong and tempting.

She would sit on the grass under a young birch tree, cross-legged and with the hem of her maxi skirt rolled up high. Her little picnic would be by her side, a book open on her lap as the gentle breeze tried to turn the pages for her.

One late afternoon, Tatiana was walking home from the park when she noticed Oleg's black jeep levelling with her along the pavement. The brakes screeched as it came to an abrupt stop. Oleg opened the passenger door from the driver's side. "Jump in, Sunny!"

"Oleg! Perfect timing! Where are we going?" Tatiana pulled the door shut, tucking in the bottom of her skirt. "That's a classy-looking bottle you've got there," she added, pointing at a clear plastic bag from an expensive shop. It contained a gift box of whisky.

“I’d like to pay Vlad a visit,” said Oleg. “We all thought he was in Kiev with his daughters, but he’s been back a whole week. Ivan told me.

“I’m a little worried. He hasn’t shown up in the office, and he doesn’t answer his phone. Can we check on him together? I’d like you to come with me.” Oleg’s eyes were fixed on the road.

They had to wait a while before they finally heard the faint shuffling of feet and the locks on the front door clicking open.

“Oh, hello, you two. Come on in. Nice of you to visit an old man.” Tatiana was shocked by Vlad’s appearance. Usually groomed and well dressed, he could have passed for a homeless man who was squatting in someone else’s apartment. He wore a faded blue tracksuit, and it was obvious that he hadn’t shaved or washed for a while. The air inside the flat was stale with the mixed odours of cigarette butts, rotting food, and body odour. There was hardly any light, as all the blinds at the windows were shut.

Oleg did not look surprised by Vlad’s transformation. With the usual spring in his step, he followed his boss, who wobbled on his feet, into the living room, pulling Tatiana along by her hand.

The entire contents of Vlad’s drinks cabinet seemed to be displayed on the coffee table. Many of the bottles were half full or empty. Squashed-up beer cans were scattered across the floor. Tatiana could even detect a sharp whiff of ammonia in the air. Instinctively, she pulled up the blind, twisted the handle, and threw the window wide open.

“Thank you for coming, kids,” Vlad said, busy clearing some space for them on the sofa. With trembling hands he removed pieces of crumpled newspaper and dirty clothes. Tatiana couldn’t bear to look directly at the dishevelled man in front of her, but Oleg was still acting as if everything was normal. He settled into the large leather armchair with the TV remote in his hand and began scrolling through the channels, putting the plastic bag with the whisky by his side.

"Vlad, shall I water these?" asked Tatiana, pointing at two large potted aloe vera plants on top of the windowsill.

"Oh yes, please, Tanyusha. Marianochka would be mad at me if they died." He was standing and swaying slightly. "She swears by aloe juice. Says you can heal practically everything with it." He chuckled and sniffled as he talked, wiping his eyes with the back of his hand.

Unable to watch, Tatiana wandered around in search of a watering can.

"Vlad, why didn't you stay in Kiev? You need to be with family," Oleg said. "How are the girls? Maybe you should go and visit your parents in Rostov. We've got it all under control here." He sounded calm and casual.

"My girls are fine, Olejhek. Marianochka's sister took them to the seaside for the summer. I rented a nice house for them in Odessa." With his eyes still tearing, Vlad smiled lovingly at the mention of his daughters. "So, I've got it under control as well," he said, slurring some of the words. "And you can go and tell that slithering python that I'll be back in the office tomorrow. I'm thinking to reverse our agreement. I haven't signed anything yet."

Vlad stumbled back onto the sofa and slapped his pocket. "Oleg, I'm out of smokes. Can I have one of yours?"

Oleg took out his packet of cigarettes and handed it to Vlad. "Keep it," he said. "But I don't think we should rush into making decisions now, Vlad. After all you've been through lately, you need to stop and rest. Sunny, don't you think Vlad should go and spend some time with his girls in Odessa?" Oleg raised his voice and turned to Tatiana, who was just about to leave the room with the watering can in her hand.

"Oleg's right, Vlad," she answered. "You need a break. You look terrible and," she said, taking a deep breath, "you need to sober up. Stop drinking. That's what Mariana would have wanted. I know about your ulcer. She told me."

Worried that she'd gone too far, she looked at Oleg for

approval. He nodded and turned to Vlad. "You see, the woman speaks the truth," Oleg said firmly. "You need to look after your health—and you need to be with your family."

"Thank you, Tanyusha." Vlad ignored Oleg's last comment. "You are a good girl, but I'm not going anywhere." He shifted himself on the sofa to face Oleg. "No way. It's still my company, remember?" Suddenly he sounded almost sober. "You tell Maks *that.*"

"Sunny, go down and wait for me in the car, will you?" Oleg said, tossing her the keys. "We need a few moments alone here." Tatiana heard icy notes in his tone.

"Take care of yourself, Vlad. I can call your housekeeper to come and clean this place up," she said.

"Thank you, Tanechka. I'll see you soon," Vlad replied.

With a heavy heart, Tatiana left the apartment. She sat in the passenger's seat of the jeep and listened to her favourite radio station, unable to make up her mind about what she'd just witnessed. Vlad was unfit to make decisions or run a business in his present state, but he seemed determined. And Oleg clearly wanted something from him.

She remembered Vlad's shaking hands and muffled sniffs. Mariana would have been horrified to see her husband in such a state! How the greats fall. Tatiana could barely recognise the man she had once seen here, charming and welcoming in his crisp white shirt and cosy tartan slippers.

There was also something alarming about Oleg's urgency to send Vlad away. Tatiana barely knew Maks, but she could sense his influence on her husband. "Slithering python," Vlad had said of him. She wanted to talk to Oleg about it.

At one point, Tatiana realised that she had been sitting in the car for an hour. There was still no sign of Oleg. She felt annoyed and abandoned. *Why did he bring me here today? Why do I always have to fit into his busy schedule? He never even asks if I have something else to do or somewhere else to be,* she fumed in irritation.

He sees me as just one of his belongings. It's so unfair. She closed her eyes and began counting, trying to supress the urge of lashing at him again.

Oleg appeared on a count of sixty-seven. She held her breath. "Stay calm!" she commanded in her head. Oleg climbed in with an unreadable expression. A faint smell of alcohol followed him. Tatiana noticed the absence of the plastic bag.

"You've been drinking," Tatiana blurted as Oleg started the engine. "And Vlad clearly didn't need that bottle. What's going on? I've been sitting here for an hour and a half."

"Sorry, Sunny, but you can surely see we have a big problem here. I'll have to drop you at home now. I need to go and speak with Maks. Don't wait up for me." He said this firmly. She instantly knew that there was no point in arguing.

Chapter 16

Tatiana decided to spend a week in her grandmother's house in the village of Krapivna, outside Tula. Oleg, immersed in work and trying to end the conflict between Vlad and Maks, readily agreed with her decision and even offered to drive her there on a weekend.

Tatiana packed a small overnight bag for him as well, anticipating that he would stay till the next morning and that she would be able to show him her favourite places. One of them was a wild meadow with grasses and flowers so tall that it had taken Tatiana many summers to grow tall enough to be able to peer above them. She used to love to free-fall backwards into the wild fragrant tangle where the stems were strong enough to break her fall. With her arms wide open, she plunged in and watched the clouds gliding by in the pale blue sky. They looked like ragged clusters of cotton wool.

Tatiana could already smell sweet clover and drying grass and hear the buzzing of bumblebees and the chirping of grasshoppers. She imagined herself and Oleg running together down the bendy path towards the high bank of the River Upa, diving straight into clear water the colour of weak tea. No stopping to test the temperature allowed!

In the car, Tatiana wriggled with excitement and sang along to the tape they'd gotten for the journey.

Oleg also seemed more relaxed as they drove. He tapped his fingers along to the rhythm on the steering wheel. By late afternoon, they pulled up outside Maria Petrovna's wooden house on the narrow, unpaved street. Opposite was the brick ruin of an old church. Everything was the just way Tatiana remembered it.

By the crooked old gate with its rusty ring of a handle, two speckled hens froze to give the new arrivals a suspicious look. A few seconds later, they lost interest and went back to pecking busily under a hedge of stinging nettles.

Time stood still in Krapivna. Tatiana imagined that this street and her grandmother's house had looked exactly the same a hundred years ago—all except for the church, which was used and cherished back then. It was hard to believe when looking at the crumbling wreck now. There was even a young birch tree growing through the top of the dome.

"Welcome! Welcome!" Maria Petrovna came rushing out of the house. A second later she was hugging them and kissing their cheeks. "Thank God I got your telegram yesterday, so I could prepare. The post has been so unreliable. Our new postman is a drinker. He only works on the rare days when he's sober!

"Tanechka, you've lost weight. Olejhek, you look tired. Come in, come in! Dinner is ready!" Maria Petrovna ushered them into the house, bustling excitedly like a mother hen.

"Slow down, Grandma! Stop fussing! We don't want to trouble you!" Tatiana smiled and hugged Maria Petrovna by her shoulders.

Inside the house, in the middle of the large front room, stood a wooden table covered with plates and bowls of all sizes. Between them, they held the season's entire haul from Maria Petrovna's vegetable garden, as well as treasures from nearby woods. Tatiana salivated at the sight of her grandmother's special pickled gherkins along with the steaming new potatoes and wild mushrooms.

"I'm starving, Grandma! I'll just wash my hands. Oleg, follow me!" Tatiana danced out of the door with childish glee.

"This is wonderful, Maria Petrovna," said Oleg. "How many guests are you expecting? Ten? Twenty?" He chuckled.

"Sergey will join us later," said Maria Petrovna, ignoring his little joke. "Tatiana's uncle, you know. It's not that much, Olejhek. These are only the appetisers.

"Go outside to the backyard. Your Sunny will show you the bathroom facilities," added Maria Petrovna, offering him a fresh towel.

They washed their hands and faces under the old-fashioned washstand, which was screwed to the trunk of a gnarled linden tree. "Water closet, if you need one," said Tatiana, nodding towards a small wooden hut at the far end of the garden.

"I think I'll pass," said Oleg. "Being a man has its advantages. I might use the shelter of this accommodating tree." He looked suspiciously at the withered cabin. "That convenience looks far too exotic for me."

"How ever did you manage in the desert, pampered city boy?" teased Tatiana, splashing him playfully with cold water from the basin.

"I told you that I can be very resourceful. You'll pay for that, Sunny!" Oleg wiped his face with the towel and then quickly splashed her back.

Tatiana let out a surprised squeal. "Isaev, you're doomed! Prepare for sweet torture by Grandma's dinner. Be warned—she takes no prisoners. You'll be crawling away from that table." For the first time in days, they let themselves giggle wholeheartedly.

Tatiana and Oleg were still negotiating the piled plates of starters when Maria Petrovna left the table and disappeared behind the enormous Russian stove that divided the room in two. Maria Petrovna's life was centred around that stove. She always started her day by making a fire. She cooked everything on it, ignoring the small gas burner that her son had bought her years before. She even washed her dishes using the ashes from the stove.

And behind the clay monster was Maria Petrovna's favourite sleeping space: a simple narrow bench with washed-out cotton bedding. Even though there was a spacious room in the back of the house, containing a comfortable double bed, Maria Petrovna remained faithful to her peasant roots, preferring to sleep there by the side of the stove, regardless of the season.

"I have a treat for you children," announced Maria Petrovna, returning with a heavy cast-iron pot. "Sergey got lucky yesterday and caught a nice big pike downstream from here. Just look at this fish stew!" She put the pot down in front of Oleg and lifted the lid. A blast of steam rose up high, filling the room with the delicate aroma of fresh fish, onions, and herbs.

"Grandma, that smells amazing, but I'll have to have it later. I'm fit to burst." Tatiana put her hand on her stomach to demonstrate.

"Olejhek, I'll rely on you, then. Tatiana was never a strong eater." Maria Petrovna shook her head and began piling the steaming stew into a bowl with a wooden ladle.

"Maria Petrovna, I—" Oleg looked panicked. But he was interrupted by two sharp beeps. The modern sound was so alien in the folk-tale setting that Tatiana and Maria Petrovna shuddered at its abruptness.

"Sorry, ladies. That's my pager." Oleg unclipped the black plastic box from his belt. His face turned serious as he read the message.

He put his fork down and stood up. "I'm so sorry, Sunny. I've got to go. Something needs taking care of, urgently.

"Maria Petrovna," he said, gently bowing his head, "thank you. It was fantastic, the best meal I've ever had. Now I know why my wife is such a good cook. It obviously runs in the family."

Tatiana stood speechless for a second. She had planned their weekend together in her childhood paradise. "But Oleg, we were going to swim after dinner, remember? And how will you drive back? You haven't even rested properly. It is two hundred and fifty kilometres to Moscow. Stay the night, please!

You can go first thing in the morning," she pleaded with hope in her voice.

"Oleg, dear boy. Sergey will be here any minute. You can sit together, have a drink. I've been saving my special hooch just for you!" Maria Petrovna looked concerned. "And what about my blueberry pie? It's Tanechka's favourite. And you haven't even touched your main course yet."

"Sorry again. Duty calls." By Oleg's expression and adamant tone, Tatiana knew he wasn't going to have his mind changed. "I have to be back in Moscow—today."

"What's happened, Oleg? Who was it, Vlad or Maks?" Tatiana asked, fighting the piercing pain of disappointment.

"Neither of them, actually," replied Oleg, "That was Roman. Something important has happened. I can't tell you any more right now, Sunny, but it's not all that bad," Oleg said, trying to reassure her.

"I'll send Ivan to pick you up from here next Saturday, OK?" He added, "Have a good time. Try to enjoy yourself without me.

"Maria Petrovna," Oleg said, addressing Grandma respectfully, "please look after my Sunny. And save your hooch for the next time I visit. I have to go." Turning to his wife, Oleg said, "Bye, baby." He gave Tatiana a peck on the cheek and then left the room.

After a bit, Tatiana and her grandmother heard the start of the car engine. Tatiana sighed and closed her eyes. Maria Petrovna hugged her gently by the shoulders.

"Why does it always have to be like this, Grandma? Why does he always leave me? His work always comes first!" Tatiana raised her head, looking searchingly into Maria Petrovna's eyes.

"I don't know, Tanyusha," her grandmother said gently. "All I can say is your Oleg is not one to sit around at home with you, attached to your skirt. But that's why you chose him, isn't it?" She tightened her embrace and began rocking Tatiana as if she were soothing a child. "Love and patience, it's all you need. Do you love him? Is he still your knight on a white horse?" she asked softly.

“A knight in a black jeep, more like it,” Tatiana replied, wiping her eyes.” Yes, I think I love him. That’s why he gets me every time. Bastard.”

They heard the knock on the door. “Let’s go, Grandma!” Tatiana was the first to react. “That must be Uncle Sergey!”

Chapter 17

Ivan arrived two days early, on a Thursday morning.

It was a grey, drizzly day. Tatiana had happily stayed in bed reading. She had an old volume of *War and Peace* in her hands, a novel by Krapivna's most famous resident—and her favourite writer—Lev Tolstoy. His family home of Yasnaya Polyana was just a few kilometres away. Tatiana had often visited the writer's simple grave in the serene parkland there. She was proud of her remarkable countryman and felt strangely obliged to revisit his works whenever she stayed at her grandmother's house.

But the soft raindrops were giving soothing, melancholy tap-taps on the wooden window frame, making her gently dozy. Even the blossoming romance between Prince Andrei and Natasha Rostova couldn't keep Tatiana awake.

She awoke to a loud bang of the rusty ring handle against the front gate, jolting at the urgency of the sound. By the time she had changed out of her pyjamas, Ivan was already standing in the front room politely rejecting Maria Petrovna's invitation to drink tea. "We have to leave right now," Tatiana heard him say.

"Tatiana Nikolaevna, good morning," he said, addressing her. "I have orders to bring you to Moscow. Can you get ready, please?" he added firmly but politely.

"Ivan, I wasn't expecting you today. Weren't you coming

on Saturday? Is Oleg OK?" She felt an unpleasant premonition forming in her chest.

"Oleg Borisovich is fine, but he needs you at home," said Ivan, laconic as ever. She noticed that his natural frown had deepened. "I can explain more on the way," he added. Then with a nod to Grandmother, he said, "Maria Petrovna, it was nice meeting you. I hope to see again," before walking out of the door.

"Tanechka, what's all this? He said he's 'got orders'. It sounds like we're back at war or, worse, in the 1930s!" Maria Petrovna looked uneasy.

"Don't worry, Grandma. They all talk that way," Tatiana said in an attempt to reassure her, relived that nothing had happened to Oleg. "I'm sure Ivan's exaggerating. There is probably some very important dinner party we have to attend!" she added, trying to sound cheery. "I better pack. But I'll be back to see you soon, I promise." With that, she darted off to collect her things.

Tatiana almost managed to convince herself that nothing bad had happened, that it was just Oleg snapping his fingers.

Ivan drove for some time in silence before he cleared his throat and said, "Vladislav Yegorovich was killed in a car accident yesterday. The funeral is tomorrow." His voice trembled and he clenched his jaw. His gaze stayed fixed on the road. Only now did Tatiana realise that they were in Oleg's black jeep and not Vlad's silver one. She sat speechless for a moment.

"How did it happen, Ivan? Was he alone?" Tatiana managed to whisper. The force of the double tragedy that had hit Vlad's once happy family was almost unimaginable. It was like an aftershock from a devastating earthquake that rips through ruins, claiming the lives of the survivors. She felt dizzy. "It's so stuffy here. I can't breathe! Open the windows, for God's sake!" she blurted. Ivan obliged by pushing down buttons next to him.

"He was driving alone, Tatiana Nikolaevna." Ivan said, his voice strangely devoid of emotion. "It was late at night. He crashed into a railway bridge on the Yauza embankment. You must know the place—the road is very narrow and winding there. "He lost control and drove head-on into the wall. He wasn't wearing a seat belt. He didn't stand a chance." It was the longest Tatiana had heard Ivan speak. She could see his shoulders tensing.

"Ivan, was he drunk?" Tatiana asked.

"He had had a drink that night, sure. But he wasn't wasted. I drove him home from the office. It was already after midnight. Then an ambulance was called two hours later. Vladislav Yegorovich was pronounced dead at the scene." Ivan's voice trembled for the first time.

"They had had some whisky at the office—Vladislav Yegorovich, Oleg Borisovich, and Mr Polonskiy." Tatiana detected steel notes in Ivan's voice when he mentioned Maks. "I saw the secretary clearing away the glasses when I was waiting at reception. But, Tatiana Nikolaevna!" Ivan turned around to look her in the eye. "He wasn't that drunk. I saw him.

"Vladislav Yegorovich sometimes drove under the influence—he said it made him more cautious on the road. I told the detective so yesterday. But they said he was way over the limit." Ivan rose a bit in his seat, unable to contain himself any longer.

"Where was he going so late at night, especially after he had another drink at home? Why didn't he call me? He always did if he had too much! It just doesn't make sense!" Ivan hit the steering wheel in anger.

"What are you saying, Ivan?" Tatiana gasped. She remembered an urgent message from Roman that made Oleg abandon her so suddenly. But then again, she couldn't be sure it was from Roman. She hadn't seen Oleg's pager's screen. The uncertainty made it suddenly hard for her to draw a breath. She needed to see Oleg urgently; she needed to speak to him! He must have more information than Ivan. *He will tell me the whole story.*

"I am sure, Ivan, it was an accident," she said, trying to

reassure herself. "Horrible timing for the family. So soon after Mariana—" She couldn't recognise her own voice. It sounded strangely hollow.

"Who am I to say anything?" Ivan grinned bitterly. "I'm just a driver, and I'm supposed to know nothing. But the whole thing stinks, Tatiana Nikolaevna. I've told Oleg Borisovich that today is my last day at work. My boss is dead and so is his wife, and I'm done working there," Ivan said with determination.

Could it be that he is right and that it wasn't an accident? Where was Vlad going so late at night? Did he kill himself? The questions were burning in Tatiana's mind. "Ivan, please drop me at the office. I want to see Oleg straightaway."

"No problem." Ivan nodded. They continued the journey in silence.

The company office occupied the entire ground floor of an unremarkable building near Novokuznetskaya metro station. The car park outside was completely full when they arrived. All drivers—usually behind the wheel reading newspapers or snoozing—were gathered in one spot, smoking, gesticulating, and animatedly discussing something. Tatiana knew they were talking about the accident.

"Tatiana Nikolaevna, do you mind waiting here for a minute?" Ivan spoke for the first time in hours. "I'll go and tell Marina that you're here. The police are inside." He pointed to an unmarked Lada with a lone driver, clearly not part of the debating group. Tatiana could see the policeman's blue uniform.

"Go ahead, Ivan." Tatiana began to wish she'd gone home instead. She sat with her eyes fixed on the entrance. After a few minutes, Oleg marched through the doors. He raced towards the car, his eyes blazing, his face paler than usual. Tatiana's heart sank.

She could sense his anger even before he'd swung open the driver's door. "Sunny, why are you here? I told Ivan to take you home. Can you for once follow simple instructions and do what you're told?" He jumped in and started the engine. "I'm taking you home. It's a madhouse in there," he said, nodding towards the office.

Tatiana blurted, "Oleg, how did it happen? Where was Vlad going? Did you call his parents? And what about the girls?" She couldn't stop herself. The unanswered questions kept falling out of her mouth, her mind still refusing to accept what had happened.

"Shut up!" Oleg screamed, his voice reaching an odd high pitch. "Listen, Vlad is gone. Dead. He was drunk and he crashed into a wall. End of story."

Tatiana could see that Oleg was fighting his emotions. His voice was quivering. "Oleg, I'm so sorry. I can see it's hard for you—you were close to him," she said with a jolt of compassion. "But do you know where he was heading to in the middle of the night?"

"I don't know, Sunny. I wasn't his babysitter. If you remember, I tried to persuade him to take a holiday, and so did you. You remember that, don't you?" Oleg pressed her for an answer.

"Yes, of course we did. We went to see Vlad together and he didn't look good. That was the last time I saw him alive." Tatiana pressed her hand against her mouth, unable to say any more. Her shoulders began shaking with silent sobs.

"What are you going to do?" she managed to ask after a few moments. "Are you under suspicion?"

"Suspicion of what? Are you crazy?" he shouted with anger.

"I don't know. You tell me. What's the police detective doing in your office?" she screamed back. "Wasn't Vlad standing in your and Maks's way lately?"

"Shut your mouth, you stupid woman!" Oleg blared. "You don't know what you're talking about! It's none of your business!"

"What did you just call me?" Tatiana choked with anger. "Let me out here! Go back to the police in your office, smart-arse. Surely you can outwit them all!"

Oleg pulled over on the side of the road. "Sorry, Sunny," he said quietly after a pause. "I don't know what came over me. It's been a hell. I still can't believe he's gone. It's like a bad prank or something. I haven't been to the morgue yet. Haven't seen him. I think that's what I need to do now." Oleg hid his face in his hands.

Tatiana could see he was in pain. She put her hand on his shoulder.

"I think he was going to see his girlfriend," Oleg, lifting his head, said abruptly.

"What girlfriend? But Mariana just—" Tatiana didn't finish.

"I don't know which girlfriend, Sunny. He was a man. He had needs. He had girlfriends." Oleg seemed to have regained his composure. Tatiana remembered Vlad's trembling voice when he had mentioned his Marianochka.

"Are you sure about that?" she asked in disbelief.

"Nobody is sure of anything, but that's the latest version. They are checking his phone records as we speak. Let's go. I'll drop you off at home. They need me there." Oleg swerved back into flowing traffic.

As they pulled up outside their home, Tatiana kissed him goodbye and asked the burning question: "Oleg, are you in danger?" It was her deepest worry.

He held her gaze. "No, I'm not. What happened to Vlad was an accident." He spoke slowly, as if explaining something to a child. "Besides, we have excellent security, remember? Roman is looking after us." He gave her a faint smile and a wink.

"Bye, baby." Tatiana climbed out of the car feeling vaguely reassured.

Chapter 18

Vlad's funeral was held the next day at Moscow crematorium. His parents wanted to take his ashes to Kiev and bury them in Mariana's grave. "That's what Vladik would have wished for, to lie next to his Marianochka," Tatiana overheard Vlad's mother, a small grey-haired woman in a coal-black shawl, saying to one of the female relatives.

The crematorium was a long, white-panelled modern building in the middle of a large memorial park. Vlad's funeral party was by far the largest of the day. The long queue of cars, buses, and people had assembled outside Door No. 3.

On this breezy midsummer morning, everyone was dressed in black and hid their eyes behind oversized sunglasses. Half of Moscow's business and artistic elite were present. Tatiana recognised a few actors, musicians, and newsreaders alongside the obligatory glamorous women in heels. These women, dressed in expensive frocks, their perfect hairdos adorned with black lace, towered over their companions.

Tatiana could identify everyone who worked in the office, from the accountants to the chauffeurs and security guards. Once Oleg quickly disappeared from her side, she found herself standing alone and peering at the tall monument across the lawn. A pair of white pillars were joined at the top. On the far side of the park, she noticed three colossal chimneys. The sight of them made her shudder. She turned her gaze back to the pillars, suddenly comprehending their macabre symbolism.

She was reunited with Oleg inside the large marble hall, where they were led by the master of ceremonies. In the middle of it, placed on the tall podium, stood Vlad's simple wooden coffin. Because of the injuries to his face and head, the lid was closed.

People were filtering in slowly and silently, letting out loud sighs on seeing the coffin, with Vlad's large black-and-white photo on a stand next to it.

Undertakers were carrying in endless wreaths and flowers and placing them by the walls. The base of the podium was already completely covered in arrangements of red carnations and roses, all with even numbers of blooms tied with red and black ribbons. Some of the women began to weep. A string quartet in the corner of the hall played softly—something classic and immensely sad.

Tatiana, feeling her eyes filling with tears, reached for her handkerchief. Oleg gently squeezed her hand. He stood closely by her side, his eyes still invisible behind his mirrored shades. Next to him stood the tall, athletic Maks. Tatiana noticed that he was the only man wearing a light grey suit. He was also the only one in an open-collar shirt without a tie. Maks briefly glanced at Tatiana and gave her a nod. It was the first time he had directly acknowledged her existence.

Maks's piercing eyes, the colour of frosted glass, had met Tatiana's just for a split second. His clean-shaven and tanned face expressed nothing.

Tatiana realised now that Maks was younger than she thought. His silver-grey hair added years to his looks. His upright posture radiated self-importance.

"Slithering python." Tatiana heard Vlad's words in her head.

The musicians stopped playing. Amid the silence, a heavy middle-aged man began his speech. He introduced himself as Vlad's close friend and ex-colleague before saying a few formal sentences about Vlad's life. Struggling to compose himself, he could hold back his grief no longer. He put his hand on the coffin's lid and sobbed, saying, "Sleep tight, friend. I'll miss you."

The master of ceremonies asked if anyone else wished to speak about the deceased. Tatiana quickly glanced at Oleg. He shook his head in response.

The quartet began playing Chopin's Funeral March.

Mourners lined up to give their final farewells.

A small, slender woman in front of Tatiana and Oleg turned out to be Marina. Tatiana recognised her usual tailored office suit. Marina stopped at the coffin, put two scarlet carnations on top, and made the sign of the cross. Her cheeks turned paper-white as she swayed on her feet and sank heavily to the floor. Two men quickly stepped forwards to carry her slumped body outside.

Tatiana couldn't shake the sense of the surreal as she approached the coffin for her turn. She touched the smooth polished wood with her fingers. Vlad's presence was so tangible that she even glanced to the other side of the podium, expecting to see him standing there, smiling his usual warm smile.

A few minutes later, the casket disappeared slowly down the shaft beneath the platform.

Back in the jeep, Tatiana caught sight of Oleg's ashen face. The reality of their friend's death dawned on her all over again.

"Marina took it badly," she said for the sake of breaking the silence.

"Of course she took it badly. Who do you think was the father of her little son?" Oleg's voice sounded remote.

"What are you saying, Oleg, that Marina was Vlad's mistress? Did Mariana know about it?" Tatiana felt disbelief.

"Listen, Sunny, grow up already. Give up your silly idealism, will you? Vlad was just a man, a very good one, but still only human. None of us is without sin. But what matters is what we do with our lives, whether or not we change the landscape around us. Vlad managed that. He was a pioneer, and that's how he will be remembered." Oleg's tone was cold and firm.

"Why didn't you want to speak there, Oleg? You could have put Vlad's life into perspective." Tatiana tried to hide a bitter sarcasm.

"Perhaps I will still do that. We have a long wake party ahead." Oleg nodded.

Vlad's friends had hired the whole of the Black Cat for the occasion. When Tatiana and Oleg arrived, the place was crowded with people who had not made it to the crematorium. Upstairs, in the theatre, the long tables had been arranged in rows. The tables were already covered with dishes of traditional wake fare, including stacks of blini with caviar and smoked sturgeon. Countless bottles of chilled vodka stood between the plates of food.

At the head of one of the tables was a place reserved for the deceased. Vlad's empty plate held a glass of vodka covered with a piece of rye bread.

People were quickly filling the room, taking their seats along the tables. Once again, Tatiana lost sight of Oleg. Looking for him, she wandered into the bar downstairs. It was full of men, all talking and holding shot glasses in their hands.

A young waiter approached with a tray of single vodka shots. She took one and gulped it straight down. She swapped the empty glass for another shot. The room began to spin a little. Tatiana remembered that she had had nothing to eat since the night before. She took a third glass from the tray and looked around in search for Oleg.

He wasn't there. She decided to go back upstairs when a conversation grabbed her attention. Two men she recognised from the office were talking loudly to a third.

"I'm telling you, there's something odd about the whole thing. Our mechanics had orders to take the wrecked car from the police pound to see if any parts were salvageable. They were supposed to deliver the rest to the scrapyard."

"How do you know that?" the stranger asked.

"They told us so," explained the man. "And guess what? Our

guys checked the car and said that someone had played with the brakes. It looked that way."

"Are you kidding?" The stranger raised his voice in disbelief. "Did they tell the police?"

"Course not. They just reported it to Security. The police wouldn't have cared anyway—they wanted to close the case as soon as possible. In their books, it's a drunk-driving accident, especially after the detective had a long lunch with our bosses."

"Then what happened? What did Roman say?" the third man insisted.

"He said, 'Thank you, guys.' Then he gave them a big cash bonus and asked them to scrap the car immediately."

"Do you think Polonskiy and Isaev know about this? Has anyone told them?"

Tatiana felt dizzy. She frantically tried to get out, not wanting to hear the reply. She already knew it.

"What do you think? They're Roman's bosses—it's their company."

Tatiana didn't stay to listen to the rest of the conversation. She ran out of the bar, hoping to make it to the toilet. There she was violently sick.

PART 3

Chapter 19

1994

"Tatiana Nikolaevna, sorry to disturb you. You said you wanted to go to town in the morning. It's eleven o'clock." Vasily's insistent voice pounded inside Tatiana's half-awake head. Her new driver was obsessed with timekeeping.

I should complain about him to Oleg.

"I've got to go to the airport later to pick up Oleg Borisovich." Vasily was still there.

"Thank you, Vasily. I'll be ready in half an hour," Tatiana managed, her eyes still closed. She tried to speak loudly, but her voice came out all dull and croaky.

"Ask Natasha to prepare my breakfast. The usual," she added, before finally opening her eyes. The bright light of the January morning reflecting the snow outside the window made her squint.

Why didn't I shut my bedroom door and curtains last night? Irritated, she reached out to grab her new wristwatch from the side table. The solid-gold bracelet felt cool and heavy in her hand.

She brought the dial close to her eyes. Under the full glare of the sparkling winter sunshine, the tightly packed diamonds on the watch face lost their expensive dazzle, being no match for the might of Mother Nature.

Five past eleven. I've never slept this late before.

Tatiana noticed a crystal tumbler next to her bedside lamp and remembered the reason for her heavy head. She had felt lonely last night and wanted to celebrate the end of her exams. Oleg was in Geneva. She had fetched a bottle of his treasured cognac from the bar and opened it, along with a fresh jar of caviar—a lavish party for one.

I must have drunk a lot of it.

Thoughts rotated slowly in Tatiana's brain as the smell of freshly brewed coffee and the scent of Natasha's signature curd-cheese pancakes filled her nose. She carefully climbed out of bed, trying not to shake her head, and pulled a hooded robe from the armchair.

Downstairs in the kitchen, Natasha had already laid everything out on the counter. Tatiana muttered a "good morning" and began sipping a glass of freshly squeezed orange juice like it was the elixir of life.

Natasha nodded her greeting before discreetly disappearing into the living room. The surge of vitamin-packed liquid began to work. Tatiana started to feel better as she reached for the TV remote. She switched on the news and started her breakfast, accompanied by the monosyllabic murmur of a newsreader and the distant hum of Natasha's vacuum cleaner.

Oleg and Tatiana had been renting this brand new, Canadian-style cottage since the previous summer, shortly after Oleg and Maks had bought plots of land next door to each other's in this prestigious area of woodland on the high bank of the Moskva River. The building of Oleg and Tatiana's new country residence nearby was now well under way, and Oleg dedicated all his free time to it.

Erecting the house of his dreams had become Oleg's latest obsession. Living close to the site allowed him to keep an eye on the construction. Summer and autumn had flown by in a frenzy, with every moment Oleg could spare spent on checking the suppliers of bricks, roof tiles, and paving stones.

Oleg had swapped his wife's company for that of a clever German architect. The two of them would spend hours on the outside terrace discussing the minutiae of the future Isaev mansion while they sipped pricey cognac and smoked extravagant cigars.

When the weather eventually turned breezy and wet, they had decamped to the living room, where they covered the entire floor with drawings, catalogues, and blueprints, driving Natasha insane.

That was the summer of obsession. Oleg was obsessed with the house; the architect was obsessed with his ever-growing budget; and Natasha was obsessed with the cleaning. As for Tatiana, she just felt left out. Since Vlad's death more than a year ago, everything was different. At first she tried to find out what had really happened to him, so she confronted Oleg.

His reply was, "So you've heard already the office rumour about the tampered brakes?" "I swear I'll find the idiot who started it, and then I will sack them!"

"So it's not true then?" Tatiana wanted a confirmation.

"Of course it's not! They watch too many American gangster movies! They have too much free time on their hands, the lazy bastards!"

Tatiana wanted to argue that Oleg himself wasn't impartial to that film genre, but she said nothing.

"Hollywood is opium to masses, I tell you!" Oleg continued.

"I thought Karl Marx said it about religion," she answered.

"Whatever, Sunny. I'm sure had he lived long enough, he would've changed his tune."

And so it was the end of that. The rumours had died out, no one had been sacked, and everyone in the company seemed to have moved on. Even Marina reappeared at her desk outside Oleg's office after a two-week leave. She was thin and pale, but still in her perfectly tailored suit. Even if she did share a big secret with Vlad, she was going to keep her half of it, while he had taken his to the other side—forever.

With Maks's investment, the business was doing well. The share profit and salaries were growing by the day, and everyone seemed happy, everyone except Tatiana. Oleg had changed. He was now completely under Maks's spell. He started to dress like Maks, talk like Maks, and smoke the Cuban cigars that Maks liked to smoked. Maks was his new idol. He had replaced Vlad in Oleg's life, and Tatiana didn't like it. Maks continued ignoring her, but Oleg didn't seem to mind. They never went out together as couples with Maks and his wife, but Oleg was prepared to abandon Tatiana at any hour of the night or day if Maks called him to a meeting. The money was rolling in, so Oleg lavished his wife with expensive gifts, diamonds, watches, fur coats, and designer dresses. He was generous, as always, but it wasn't what she wanted. She wished she could spend more time with him. She dreamt of becoming his first priority. But she had to keep it to herself, for she was very aware that many women were envious of her position. In the eyes of the outsiders, she had it all. She didn't dare to complain. She had no right to demand more. She resigned herself to simple pleasures, like reading, sleeping, drinking, and walking alone.

Tatiana liked exploring her peaceful new surroundings. The white wood-clad house stood amid tall pine trees. She often ventured outside the perimeter fence to enjoy a walk in the wild.

This forest was her favourite kind, the ground crisp and sandy and covered in dried needles, which made gentle crackling sounds under her feet. These woods were never menacing. The tall trunks let sunshine right through, making it a happy, friendly place. Tatiana would march, humming cheerful songs she had learned during her time in the Young Pioneers Choir.

Occasionally on her strolls, she would bump into some of their neighbours who lived in the wooden dachas from the 1950s and 1960s that dotted the forest. These dachas had been built for the party bosses and for distinguished artists of the time.

The Soviet elite had loved this secluded area, only a stone's throw from the city, with its purifying air filled with the aroma of pine. Here, the fresh waters of the river were wide and clear enough for both swimming and fishing.

To make their journey from the centre of Moscow even quicker, the lords of the Kremlin had removed all the traffic lights from the avenue on the way. The legacy of one of them, who often insisted on driving himself—to the horror of his security team—was a very wide bend on a road in a nearby village.

A sharp left turn had been made incredibly broad. According to locals, the Marshal was one day driving himself to his dacha, having had a few drinks at the Kremlin reception, and didn't quite make the turn, narrowly avoiding a crash. Shaken and ashen-faced, he was promptly replaced at the wheel by his driver. The Marshal's only reaction to the incident was, "This is a very bad turn." His words were taken as a command by his loyal entourage. In no time at all, the infamous bend was widened to its current breadth.

The neighbours Tatiana had come across on her summer walks were mostly surviving family members of these once-powerful leaders. Conveniently forgetting that their dachas were the property of the state, they had tried to live there undetected, quietly, and modestly. The ones who did manage to privatise their summer homes began to sell them off—at a price—to members of the newly emerging business nobility.

These young men, contemporaries of Oleg and Maks, had no sentiment for the wooden pieces of Soviet memorabilia. Confidently dealing with them like the merchant Lopakhin in *The Cherry Orchard*, their demolition trucks would arrive promptly, sometimes while the previous owners were still gathering the last fragments of their clutter—books, chessboards, jam jars.

As usual with the history of Russia, the old class of elites was giving way to the new class, who were more assertive and more desirous. So among the pines Tatiana had also spotted newly erected construction fences. The quiet was often disrupted by loud banging, hammering, and sawing.

Only when the winter arrived and a thick, fluffy blanket of snow claimed everything did the work have to stop. Once more, the woods reclaimed their silence.

The usual dacha residents retired to their heated city homes. Tatiana wanted to go back to Grandpa's warm and cosy apartment, which was only a short distance from the university, but Oleg had other ideas.

"No way, Sunny. It's not going to happen. That apartment building is not secure. We have to stay here." Oleg was adamant. He had become paranoid about security since Vlad's death, and even more so since the blunt murder of his main competitor later that year.

Tatiana had never liked Arkadiy, who'd owned a rival advertising company. She had met him a couple of times and found him to be tiny and cocky. He always wore a black trench coat that ended just above his boots. He marched into a room, clutching his messenger bag as if his life depended on it.

He had been shot at close range outside his front door. A few witnesses heard two shots and saw a tall man running towards an old Lada, which was apparently waiting for him around the corner. It all happened so quickly that bystanders couldn't even agree on the colour of the Lada.

Arkadiy was pronounced dead at the scene with one bullet hole in his chest and another through his temple. The precision of the execution meant that Arkadiy's killer was a professional.

So Tatiana had to brace herself for a long and lonely winter in the woods. And with building work put on hold until spring, Oleg went back to his usual routine of long hours at the office and coming home in the dead of night.

It seemed that Oleg only ever needed a few hours of rest, and very often he was gone in the morning before Tatiana had even awakened. She had gotten used to finding traces of her husband's presence: the dimple on his pillow left by his head, wet patches on the bathroom floor where he'd stepped out of the shower, a lingering whiff of cologne.

On her lecture days, Tatiana would have to get up early, so on these mornings she and Oleg would share a quick breakfast together, get dressed, and then both climb into the back of their black American car.

The luxury sedan would be heated to tropical temperatures by Vasily. The hot air was heavily scented by cheap aftershave. Sasha, their bodyguard, was already on the front seat.

Looking at Oleg and Tatiana in the rear-view mirror, Sasha would give them a nod. "Morning," would be the first and last word to come out of his mouth. He would say nothing else throughout the entire journey.

In truth, Oleg had hired two bodyguards, who worked in shifts. But by some bizarre coincidence, they were both called Sasha. Also, they both had closely shaven heads on thick necks. Their square shoulders were draped in burgundy blazers. Apparently the Sashas were friends, but Tatiana had never heard them speak to each other. When she saw them together in the security lodge, they would both sit in silence in front of the small TV. Mostly, they watched badly dubbed American action films.

The Sashas communicated with Tatiana and Oleg in two- and three-word sentences. One of them was slightly taller, but Tatiana could only tell them apart if they stood side by side. She had secretly named them Chip and Dale.

All the way to Moscow, the four of them drove in silence. Vasily watching the road, Sasha watching the passing cars, Tatiana glancing through her coursework, and Oleg reading his paperwork—contracts, letters, faxes, or whatever was in his designer briefcase. Occasionally, the quiet would be broken by the beeping of his pager.

Their first stop was the university. Tatiana had gotten used to the excited whistles and shouted greetings from the crowd of smokers as their car arrived in front. After a few quick hellos, she would wave goodbye to Oleg and rush into the building. She knew that the brief show of her husband's power and aplomb would come next.

Closely followed by Sasha, Oleg would climb out of the car, generously give away dozens of branded cigarettes, and tell an admiring congregation a few jokes before making his way inside, shaking hands and waving salutes on the way like a celebrity greeting fans.

Oleg would make his way into the dean's office and then emerge a few minutes later, still shadowed by Sasha.

The limo would drive off, its mighty engine rumbling softly like the gut of a powerful beast.

Tatiana always anticipated the aftershock of Oleg's visit, which would play out all day long. She knew that the animated discussion in the ladies' toilets would stop dead as soon as she walked in, and she could bet that they had been gossiping about her—Oleg Isaev's lucky wife.

I wish one of those designers would come up with an invisibility cloak next season. I'd buy two.

Since Lena's departure, Tatiana had not made any other friends at university. With Oleg rising in the world, she had to avoid anyone who asked questions about him—and there were plenty of those, especially ones accompanied by sarcastic comments.

I am just here to study and get my diploma at the end of the year. In a few months I'll be out of here. She repeated this mantra to herself every time she made her way through the entrance.

Tatiana really missed Lena and her no-nonsense attitude, free spirit, and ability to see right through people regardless of their social status. Lena appeared twice a year now, just to pass her tests and exams, and then she dived right back into her life in London. Tatiana hadn't fulfilled her promise yet. She still had to get her British visa.

Lately, Tatiana's confidant had been her beauty therapist, Nika. During the hours spent in Nika's welcoming white room, which was tucked at the back of a hair salon, Tatiana could relax to the soothing scent of lavender and open up her heart to the warm Ukrainian who had come to the capital straight out of school at the age of seventeen. Strong-minded and ambitious, Nika had left the industrial town of Mariupol in a bid to make it in the big city.

Making women feel pretty was Nika's true calling. She had become the queen of the Moscow beauty world. Her phone number was hot property in high circles, and women of all ages vied to be on her client list. Everyone wanted to experience her legendary hands.

Nika was excellent at everything she did—from filing and painting nails to giving rejuvenating face massages and body wraps. She made her own creams and masques, cooking them up in her tiny kitchen at home. Only her most loyal clients were offered small brown glass jars to take with them after a treatment.

Anticipating Nika's soothing touch, Tatiana got up from the kitchen stool and made her way back upstairs to dress. The dizziness and dull headache were almost gone.

"Tatiana Nikolaevna," a voice said, interrupting her thoughts. "Roman Viktorovich is expecting you on the shooting range at three o'clock today. Will you finish with your appointment by then?" Vasily was standing by the front door, shifting rigidly on his feet and clasping his rabbit-fur hat in his hands. The dedicated driver looked almost pitiful. Tatiana gave him a reassuring smile.

"Please don't worry, Vasily. We won't be late for anything. But call Roman and tell him that I'm not feeling well today. I won't go shooting."

Tatiana hated this latest trend of teaching the boss's wife lessons in self-defence, including handling a firearm. She saw no point to it. It was Roman's brilliant idea that the ladies should come and practise with him at the indoor shooting range. Tatiana was convinced that Roman had his own perverse agenda, but she kept her thoughts to herself.

Oleg had recently bought a small handgun and placed it inside a tin container with the word "Cake" written on it. "For you, Sunny," he'd said. "I'll feel safer leaving you here alone." He smirked. "Oh, and your favourite man will teach you how to use it."

"Oleg, I'm never alone here. I've got Natasha and the Sashas outside in the lodge. It's enough that both Chip and Dale wear these things under their jackets. Aren't they supposed to be our own Rescue Rangers?" Tatiana tried to joke. "I hate guns."

"I know you do, but these are crazy times. Please, won't you try to use it? For me?"

She had known by his tone that the matter wasn't up for discussion. But today she decided to give the shooting lesson a miss. Oleg had mentioned a concert they were going to in the evening. She wanted to look her best for it. *I hope it's one of his Tatiana's Day surprises,* she thought.

Tatiana slept all the way to Nika's salon.

"Darling Tanyusha! How are you, sweet girl?" Nika gave her usual broad smile. "Aw, your face looks all puffed up," she said, inspecting Tatiana with a sharp professionalism. "Top off. Jump on the bed," she commanded.

"How have you been? Any news from the ex?" Tatiana asked politely.

"Lie under the blanket, and then we can talk." Nika was adamant.

"No news of him, Tanyusha. I'm not taking him back. I need to find a respectable businessman, like your Oleg. I've already been on a date with one, you know?"

"You kept that quiet! Where did you meet him? How was it?" Tatiana shifted under the cover.

"OK, you are my friend and I'll tell you. He's a client. He's come to me a few times for a manicure. I love a man who takes pride in his appearance, don't you? He's well groomed and well dressed, and he smells so nice." Nika grinned widely.

"He's a bit older. Forty, I think. We talk about everything," she said while massaging Tatiana's face with her special strokes.

"So what happened? He asked you on a date?" Tatiana felt her facial muscles relaxing.

"OK, here comes the worst bit." Nika paused. "He's married, Tanyusha. He told me that before we started anything, which is very honourable, don't you think?" She continued without waiting for an answer. "His wife lives in Cyprus. She hates the weather here. I don't blame her. They have no kids and not much in common."

"So why did he invite you for dinner? And where did you go afterwards?" Tatiana asked.

"I went home. I didn't sleep with him, if that's what you mean," Nika replied. "It's not like that. He just wanted someone to talk to."

"How convenient. A wife in Cyprus and an understanding girlfriend in Moscow!" Tatiana tried to say, but her words came out all garbled as Nika intensified her strokes.

"I know. Not ideal. But he says he's not happy and wants a divorce," Nika said, trying to justify herself.

"Sorry, but I don't buy it, Nika. He should get divorced first and then start dating again." As Tatiana spoke the words, an unpleasant thought, like a sudden bolt of heartburn, invaded her mind: *Is this what Oleg tells his other women?*

The thought was too upsetting. She tried to push the idea away, concentrating on the warm sensation on her skin instead.

"I agree. But he's such a gentleman and makes me feel like a princess. You're lucky. You've found your Prince Charming. He buys you all these beautiful things. He's even building a palace for you. I bet he never hits you, does he?"

"No, of course not." Tatiana shook her head.

"You see," Nika confirmed. "You have to hold onto your man. They are in short supply."

"I'm trying, Nika. Sometimes it feels as if he's slipping through my fingers." Tatiana poured out her inner anguish and immediately regretted her honesty. Could Nika possibly understand what she meant?

“I know how to fix it, Tanyusha. I’ve been around for a while, so I know many stories. Men like Oleg enjoy winning. They need to see the shiny medal—not inside their cabinet, but in public view.” Nika chuckled.

“I’m not a medal, Nika. I’m a person.”

“Of course you’re not a medal. You’re better than that. You’re a woman. We have powers over men. So, when you are in the public eye, you always have to look your best for your husband, for his pride. And I’m here to help you with that. Do you know what you’re wearing tonight?” Nika changed tack, getting back to business.

“Uh-huh.” Tatiana nodded. At that moment there was a soft knock on the door.

“Sorry. I won’t be a second.” Nika glided quickly around the bed and stepped outside.

Tatiana wasn’t sure she was supposed to, but she could hear the muffled conversation. “Nadyusha, darling! I haven’t seen you for a while. How are you, my dear?”

Tatiana picked up on the familiar sweet notes in Nika’s voice. She couldn’t hear the woman’s reply. “I’m sorry, but I’m fully booked today. But for you I’ll make an exception. Come at 7.30 p.m. and you can tell me all about your trip.”

A minute later Nika returned to the room.

“Sorry, Tanyusha. What can I do? They can’t live without me!” Nika sighed. “Now I have to stay late listening to her problems with the new boyfriend.”

Tatiana thought, *I’m so silly. I thought I was her friend, but we’re all the same to her.* The embarrassing revelation was like a slap across her cheek. An unwelcome childhood memory popped into her head. She recalled her excitement when, one day, her pretty, older neighbour had wanted to be friends. After a few days, Tatiana discovered that the girl’s only interest was in Tatiana’s birthday present from Grandpa—her exotic and highly prized Barbie doll. After all these years, Tatiana could still feel the sting of her embarrassment.

Nika's sweet voice interrupted her reverie. "All finished here now, Tanyusha darling. Describe your dress for tonight, and I'll draw you a face to go with it."

Chapter 20

Tatiana briskly walked across the old bridge over the now non-existent Neglinnaya River that had once flowed along the Kremlin walls. After leaving the pregnant white belly of the Kutafya barbican behind, she strolled towards the entrance at the base of the imposing Troitskaya Tower.

She stepped carefully, trying to avoid the deep grooves between the paving stones with the thin heels of her boots. The air was cold and crisp. She could hear the heavy shuffle of her bodyguard's stride just behind her.

Chip is struggling to keep up. Too much TV and too many sausage sandwiches. I should mention it to Oleg. The Sashas' sedentary lifestyle can put our lives in danger.

She paused for a second in the middle of the bridge and looked up. The red star on top of the tower shone brightly against the black winter sky. Tatiana had always been mesmerised by the ruby stars of the Kremlin, with their exposed gilded spines and majestic red glimmer. Years ago she'd asked her dad to take her to see the Kremlin panorama after dark, from a special spot across the river. There, she had a view of the imposing brick citadel stretching along the embankment, with its red and green pyramids of towers linked by impenetrable walls that had been built to protect the white palaces and churches behind them. The tallest four towers were each topped with a glowing star.

Tatiana absorbed the scenery with her eyes wide open and her little heart filled with pride. The Kremlin was real and more impressive than all the magic castles from her fairy tales. "Stripey, we should go now. It's cold," Nikolay Ivanovich had said, pulling her by the sleeve. "They're not really made of rubies, you know?" He pointed at one of the stars.

"Yes they are, Daddy. They are called ruby stars. We read about them at school," she'd protested.

"They're made from ruby-coloured glass. It's different," explained Nikolay Ivanovich, who then stopped in his tracks because he saw the look of disappointment on her face. He added, "But don't worry. It's a very rare kind of glass, and very precious, too. They achieved the colour by adding gold to the hot molten glass. But, shh, it's our secret, Stripey. The evil wizards might hear us and want to steal the stars if they know they're made of gold."

"Don't worry, Daddy, I won't tell a soul," Tatiana had promised, pressing a finger to her lips. She'd always suspected that the stars of the Kremlin were very special. And in a magic kingdom, gold was just as useful as rubies.

"Ahem. Oleg Borisovich is waiting." Tatiana heard the voice behind her. She'd forgotten about the Rescue Ranger.

"Thank you, Sasha. Let's go."

She adjusted her fur-lined gloves, smoothed an invisible hair behind her ear, and resumed her walk. Outside the glass entrance of the State Kremlin Palace, a small crowd of expensively dressed people was gathering.

"Excuse me," Sasha barked over Tatiana's head, like the words were an insult. But they did the trick: the crowd parted.

A young militia officer was standing in front of the door. "Ticket or guest list?" he asked seriously but politely, scanning the impressive physique of the bodyguard.

"This is Mrs Isaeva," Chip replied before Tatiana could open her mouth.

When the officer gave her a quick glance, Tatiana saw a

hint of curiosity in his eyes. "Go on through," he said in a bland official manner, stepping aside.

"I hate cops," Sasha muttered over the echoing clanking of their heels on the polished marble. Tatiana could detect rare emotion in his remark, so she immediately decided not to ask him why. These kinds of personal stories were better left unknown to the employers.

The bright vastness of the central foyer, with its white marble columns, stairs, and escalators, was just the same as Tatiana remembered it. She had been in the palace before, years ago. Viktoria Andreevna had managed to get her daughter a ticket to see the famous Christmas tree. Tatiana had been six or seven then.

She vaguely recalled dancing in circles with the other lucky children in front of an enormous fir tree in this very hall. Then, they were led by the county's leading Ded Moroz, towering over them like the tallest basketball player, into the auditorium, which was rectangular and airy with honey-coloured wooden walls and endless rows of wide, velvet seats. Tatiana couldn't concentrate on the New Year pantomime because in her hand she held the most-wanted present of all Soviet children.

In exchange for a slip from her ticket, the lady in the foyer had given her a red plastic box in the shape of the Spasskaya Tower. Before the lights went off, Tatiana had already checked its contents, opening a small plug at the bottom and glimpsing a kaleidoscope of beautiful wrappers. She saw chocolates and hard-boiled sweets in the box. They were the best kinds—the kinds rarely available in shops.

After taking the peek, Tatiana glanced around her. All the other children were doing exactly the same, gasping with delight after inspecting their treasures. These were sweets not for immediate consumption. They were for admiring and counting out on tabletops back at home.

Tatiana was sure that the plastic red tower was still around, gathering dust in the storage cabinet on her parent's balcony, along with the empty jars that Viktoria Andreevna kept for jam making. No one would dare throw away this piece of history, this souvenir from the country that no longer existed.

Feeling a pang of hunger, Tatiana looked around the almost empty hall. Oleg had said there would be food before the concert. Chip pulled out a walkie-talkie. "One moment, Tatiana Nikoloevna. I'll find out where we're supposed to go."

Oleg is in the building!

Tatiana was excited to see her husband. He had been gone for three days, and she'd really missed him. "What kind of concert is this going to be?" she had asked, but, of course, Oleg liked his surprises.

"You'll like it. I promise," he'd said. "Wear something nice. There'll be a reception before and after. It's the Kremlin, you know."

Tatiana wasn't surprised by the choice of venue. The palace could now be hired out for commercial projects, and Maks had connections in high places. The company had been granted permits to stage two concerts there in the near future, with some of the world's megastars on the bill.

But who is going to sing tonight?

"Would you care for a program?" a soft voice asked her. A middle-aged woman with a metal palace badge was standing nearby.

"How much?" Tatiana opened her clutch bag.

"It's complimentary today." The woman offered Tatiana a dark red card from the pile in her hand and then walked towards another guest.

"OBI-TV Presents: A Night at the Kremlin", read Tatiana. She opened the card. 'Welcome, dear friends! Thank you for joining us at the launch of our new channel. OBI-TV: news, music, and more."

What? Is this is his launch party? He could have told me!

Tatiana was annoyed. This new channel was Oleg's brainchild, and its name bore his initials. He had attracted a few serious investors thanks to Maks. Among them were a couple of gas and oil magnates. With their money, OBI-TV had started broadcasting a few weeks before. It had just five hours a day during prime-time viewing, after six in the evening, but its popularity was growing rapidly. Tired of the political seriousness of all the state channels, the Muscovites were ready for light-hearted entertainment involving the newest Russian pop acts.

Domestic music videos were still a novelty. Many young talented directors were clambering over one another to express their artistic ambitions in the modern genre. Suddenly, the release of every song had to be accompanied by a video—a miniature film with its own storyline that usually involved exotic locations, cool cars, beautiful women, and rare animals.

Tatiana also often enjoyed watching today's TV adverts, not only because of Oleg's direct involvement but also because many of them were genuinely funny with recurring characters and developing plot lines. Some of them were visually beautiful, too.

The most popular program on OBI-TV was presented by a tall, enigmatic frontman called Mikko. Despite his ash-blond hair, square jaw, pale skin, and unusual name, Mikko spoke perfect Russian with no hint of a Baltic accent. On screen he wore large sunglasses and a biker jacket, and his shades were never removed, leaving his admirers to guess at how handsome he really was.

In the spacious cloakroom, Tatiana checked her coat, pulled off her shiny boots, and changed into a pair of black stilettos. She quickly glanced at herself in the full-length mirror. Looking back was a slender, platinum-blonde young woman with her hair tied back into a high ponytail. The straight line of her fringe covered her eyebrows. Her grey eyes were outlined in black, and her lips were painted in rose pink. Nika was certainly an expert at her craft.

The large diamond earrings caught the glimmer of the overhead lights and sparkled splendidly. *Snow Queen*, Tatiana thought of the woman in the mirror, giving her reflection an approving nod. She straightened the hemline of her long black dress, adjusting a high split in the middle of her skirt.

"Good evening. Can I leave this with you?"

Tatiana thought she recognised the voice. She glanced over her shoulder and saw a familiar figure clad in black leather. Mikko was talking to the cloakroom assistant, pointing at his large shoulder bag. Just like on TV, his voice was devoid of intonation.

"Yes, by all means. What about your jacket, young man? It's customary to leave your outerwear when you enter the palace." The old lady seemed completely unimpressed by the presenter.

"No, thanks. Just the bag, please," Mikko insisted coldly. He took the token and walked off.

"Young generation. Where does he think he's come to, a discotheque?" the old lady grumbled. She was now addressing Tatiana as if looking for her support. "They have no respect for anything. This is the Kremlin!"

Tatiana nodded. "I totally agree. Very disrespectful!"

"And those dark glasses. Can he see anything in them?" The lady kept on.

Tatiana shrugged her shoulders and smiled in agreement. She had wondered about the sunglasses too. Surely they would obstruct his vision in the dim winter light?

Tatiana looked around for Chip. The lady was still muttering to herself. Clearly she wasn't an OBI-TV viewer.

The bodyguard was standing at a professional distance, politely looking away.

"I'm ready, Sasha," Tatiana called.

"I'll take you upstairs, Tatiana Nikolaevna. Oleg Borisovich is waiting." Chip nodded towards the escalator at the end of the cloakroom. The enormous banquet hall occupied the entire top floor of the palace. The vast room with elaborate parquet floors and bright lighting was almost empty when Tatiana entered, followed by Chip, who walked three steps behind her.

Long tables, obviously set for a sumptuous buffet reception, displayed an array of hot and cold dishes. There were rows of champagne glasses, frosted bottles of ice-cold vodka, and crystal bowls filled to the brim with caviar. A dozen young men in red velvet waistcoats and white gloves stood behind the displays, ready to serve the guests.

At the far end, in the area behind the brass railings, stood a single long table with chairs all along one side—the VIP section. Almost all the seats were occupied. From a distance, Tatiana could already see that most of the VIPs were men. She could guess the degree of their importance by the large number of blazer-wearing bodyguards standing in front of the railings and all around the room's perimeter. Their expressionless faces were turned towards the entrance, their steel gazes examining the arriving guests.

She took a deep breath. *This is not how I imagined spending Tatiana's Day.*

Tatiana strode confidently towards the table, stretching her lips into a necessary smile. She had no teeth and no dimples on show, just a cold and polite countenance. She knew it was still too early in the evening for the moguls to have consumed enough alcohol to drop their masks of self-importance.

Straightaway, Tatiana singled out Maks, who was sitting at the middle of the table. He was speaking to a man on his right. The way he was nodding his coiffed silver head, and the way his shoulders were turned towards the object of his attention, indicated the significance of this man. *Gas or oil money,* Tatiana figured. The chair on the other side of Maks was empty.

It took Tatiana a few seconds to locate Oleg. He was standing at the end of the table, leaning against it and talking to a young brown-haired girl. She was sitting next to Maks's wife, Irina, who was easily identifiable from a distance thanks to her trademark blonde wavy bob—her tribute to a long-gone Hollywood icon.

Oleg, smiling broadly at the girl with the brown locks, was

hovering over his companion, almost touching her. Tatiana's feet gave way. For a split second, she thought she was going to skid clumsily across the beautiful parquet and fall down with a loud thump. She could picture everyone's faces, their mouths hanging open, their conversation halted. It would have been an entrance and a half.

But she didn't stumble. *Phew.*

Tatiana pulled her hem up a little and continued walking forwards, her smile now full-blown. She screamed at him inside her head, *OK, Oleg, look at me now! I don't want to say hello first!* Maybe he felt her silent plea, or maybe Irina gave him a little nudge after noticing her, but Oleg stopped talking and looked up in her direction. He straightened up with the salacious smile still playing on his lips.

"Hello, Sunny!" he said loudly, although Tatiana was almost standing by his side. "Well, you look nice," he continued with exaggerated cheeriness. "I love the earrings," he said, increasing the volume even more.

Seriously, Oleg? You can't even give me a compliment without a reference to yourself?

"Thank you, darling. I love them too," she said out loud. "I happen to be married to a very generous man."

I couldn't sound more pretentious if I tried.

"Oh, let me introduce you," continued her husband. "You know Irina of course." Tatiana nodded, returning Irina's acknowledging smile. "And this is Ksenia—rising star of OBI-TV and the whole of Russia in the not-too-distant future." Oleg beamed with pride.

Self-praising again. It's nothing to do with Ksenia's own talents, I'll bet.

By now, Tatiana recognised the brown-haired starlet. Ksenia had started out as a newsreader on Oleg's channel, but her true ambition was to be a pop star. She had a fresh, pretty face and a pleasant voice, and had convinced Oleg and his production team that she was the next big thing. Noticing the look of pure adoration that Ksenia gave Oleg during his introductions, Tatiana quickly sized up the situation.

I really don't want to know how you managed to persuade my husband. You'd better stay away from me, girl.

"It's nice to meet you, Ksenia. I'm Tatiana," she pronounced clearly.

"I know," she answered. "I'm so happy to meet you finally, Tatiana. Oleg always talks about you. Won't you sit down with us and toast our first meeting?" The honesty in Ksenia's big brown eyes made Tatiana suddenly doubt herself.

I've become far too cynical. Maybe there's nothing going on.

"Oh, I'd love to. What are you girls drinking?" Tatiana walked around and took a seat next to Irina.

"Sorry, Sunny." Oleg leaned down to give her a peck on the cheek. "I've got to talk to the guys over there," he said, pointing towards Maks and his companion. "After all, they're sponsoring all of this." Oleg waved his arm in a wide gesture. "I'll see you after the concert. Come back up here, OK?"

"Why after? I thought we'd be sitting together." Tatiana struggled to hide her disappointment. "Aren't you going to watch it?"

"Yes, of course, but I need to be backstage. It's work," he finished firmly. "You do understand, don't you? Happy Tatiana's Day, by the way!" With that he was off.

Tatiana looked down at her hands. Her husband had the ability to make her sound so unreasonably demanding.

"Hello, Mikhail Stepanovich! My dear friend!" Oleg's usual upbeat timbre could be heard from Tatiana's end of the table. "Why is your glass empty? Waiter!" he yelled. After that, his voice blended into the discussion that had taken over the middle of the table.

"He's a charmer, your husband," said Irina, taking a gulp from her champagne glass. "My Maks is very reserved. Not good for business. He doesn't know how to talk to people. He's lucky to have Oleg. They make a good team. To our husbands' success!" she added, raising her half-empty glass and inviting Tatiana to follow.

"To their success!" agreed Tatiana, mirroring Irina's salute. She brought the flute to her lips and took a careful sip. Yeasty bubbles tickled her tongue, making her nose wrinkle. She put the glass down politely. Champagne was not her drink of choice.

"To your husbands, ladies!" Ksenia intervened eagerly, holding her glass up high. Tatiana read a surprised expression on Irina's face, as if she had just only just noticed Ksenia's existence.

The pop star had yet to discover that Maks's wife had a very short attention span when it came to "unimportant" people. Irina's view was that once she'd finished talking to someone, they disappeared from her personal space forever. Tatiana felt a bit sorry for the wannabe just now. "Thank you, Ksenia," she said, picking up her full glass again.

"Oh, and I always wanted to tell you," Ksenia said quickly, as if running out of time, "that I think your husband is a visionary. He's amazing. Oleg always comes up with new ideas.

"Just look at it. His channel has the highest ratings—in just a few weeks. All of us—his production team, I mean—adore him." Ksenia paused to catch her breath. "He's like a big brother to us. And he's so funny, too," she added warmly.

"Lucky me!" Tatiana said playfully. "I'll tell Oleg tonight that he has a very supportive team. Are you going to sing for us tonight?" Tatiana made sure she stressed the "for us" part.

"Oh, yes. In fact, sorry, I haven't been watching the time. I've got to go and get ready backstage. See you later." Ksenia jumped to her feet and galloped gracefully out of the hall on long, tanned legs.

"She's very tall," remarked Irina. "How do you know her? What a strange girl."

They were taken into the auditorium by a serious young man in a cheap suit, one of the new managers of the palace. He ushered them to the best seats, right in the middle of the front row. The lights were already off; only the stage was softly lit. The theatre was almost full. Tatiana couldn't believe that almost six thousand people had arrived and taken their places in the time they were holding the reception upstairs.

The invisible orchestra began to play. The stage lighting turned yellow as Mikko sauntered leisurely towards the microphone. "Good evening, Kremlin!" he announced with his usual aloofness. The echoing applause muffled his next words. Mikko was an unquestionable star.

Once the concert was well under way, Tatiana couldn't believe how many famous singers and groups were taking part that night—all negotiated by Oleg. It seemed that Ksenia was right: people respected Tatiana's husband and believed in him.

The entire Russian musical beau monde was present, and all performers were congratulating OBI-TV on its successful launch. Many thanked Oleg personally. They said he was building a bridge between their music and their audience. A well-known aging diva whose career had taken off in the seventies said simply, after singing one of her most popular love songs, "Thank you, Olejek."

Tatiana could not hold back her proud tears.

The closing act was Ksenia. The "young and promising star", as Mikko described her, appeared on stage in a delicate white and silver dress. There must have been an invisible wind machine carefully positioned below her feet, as the long skirt made out of dozens of sheer ribbons was trying to fly away, flapping around her perfect legs.

Behind her stood a grand piano. After Ksenia sang the first verse, the orchestra began playing softly. She then announced in a deep, sensual voice, "Ladies and gentlemen, let me present to you the man whose many talents will never fail to surprise; the man who gathered us all here tonight; the man who wrote this song; the one, the only, Oleg Isaev."

Deafening applause drowned out Ksenia's words. Under the bright beam of the lighting, Oleg walked smoothly on stage, to a now thundering ovation.

Tatiana could tell he was nervous. He took a seat at the piano and gave a small nod to the conductor. Then he began to play, pensively at first, but then he managed to rein in his anxiety.

Tatiana saw his face had relaxed as he closed his eyes and gave in to the music. She couldn't see his hands, but she noticed his body moving up and down the stool. She remembered when she had seen him play like this for the first time. That was four years ago to the very day, in the smoky living room of his family apartment.

Ksenia continued to sing. The song was strange and moving, about an exotic firebird the colour of a sunrise. Tatiana had never heard it before.

I can't believe he wrote a song for her and never even hinted at it. They must have been rehearsing together for a while.

It seemed Oleg had taken betrayal to a new exquisite level. Suddenly, the air around Tatiana became thicker, heavier, making it difficult for her to breathe. Gasping and fighting back unwanted tears, she muttered something about not feeling well to Irina and then began moving towards the exit, bending awkwardly forwards and holding up the skirt of her stupidly long dress. She didn't want to see the adoring look on Ksenia's face when she turned to greet Oleg at the end of the performance. She didn't want to hear her sexy low voice murmuring, "Good night, everybody! And happy Tatiana's Day!"

Chapter 21

Tatiana covered her face with a pillow. The faint familiar smell of cheap Soviet washing powder filled her nostrils. *Where am I?*

She opened one eye to see the faded purple pansies of her favourite old bed sheets. *Damn, I must be late for school.* She sat up in confusion and looked around the room. Stripey was propped proudly at the foot of her bed, meeting her puzzled gaze with his shiny green plastic eyes. The memory of the night before was coming back to her.

After fleeing the concert hall, she had found Sasha in the foyer and ordered him to call Vasily. "I feel unwell and am going to my parents'. It's too far to drive to the dacha. I won't make it!"

"Understood, Tatiana Nikolaevna. What about Oleg Borisovich?"

"He is still busy here. Stay with him, and Vasily will return after dropping me off."

"No problem." Sasha pressed a button on his walkie-talkie. "Car to the entrance! Now!" he said, barking the order. Even if he was surprised by her request, he hid it well. Inside the perfumed warmth of the car, Tatiana curled up in the corner of the back seat like an injured furry animal.

Not since she'd moved in with Oleg had Tatiana come to her family's home so late at night—and unannounced.

To her surprise, Viktoria Andreevna and Nikolay Ivanovich, both in dressing gowns with their hair pushed flat on one side by their pillows, greeted her warmly and casually.

"Are you hungry, Tanyusha?" Viktoria Andreevna asked. She stepped forwards for a hug as if she had been expecting her daughter at this hour of the night.

"You look nice," said Nikolay Ivanovich, ever the gentleman, as he helped her out of her fur coat.

"Thanks, but I'm not hungry, Mum. Sorry to wake you up. Can we talk tomorrow? I have a splitting headache. Can I sleep here tonight?"

"Of course. This is still your home. You can stay here anytime. I'll get you a painkiller," Viktoria Andreevna said before leaving the hallway.

"You still have the keys, don't you, Stripey?" Nikolay Ivanovich smiled with an assuring wink.

"I do, but I've left them at home. Oleg has this big event at the Kremlin, but I felt ill and couldn't stay till the end."

Viktoria Andreevna, walking out of Tatiana's old bedroom, said, "Your bed is ready. I left the medicine on the desk for you. Do you need to go somewhere in the morning?"

"No. I think I'll just stay here for a while," Tatiana replied, looking down.

"Great!" Viktoria Andreevna sounded delighted. "I'm not teaching tomorrow either. I was planning to do some baking. Want to help me?"

"I'd love to. Thanks, Mum."

"Night, Stripey. We'll leave you to it," Nikolay Ivanovich said before he ushered his wife to their bedroom.

In the morning, Tatiana threw the duvet to the side and stretched on the bed. Then she forced herself up and walked to the window. The midday sky was grey and dim, spilling hard grains of snow. The rooftops, trees, cars, and pedestrians all looked subdued and pitiful. It was one of those dusky winter days that was best for spending indoors in old comfortable pyjamas, wishing for night to come sooner to bring back the warm glow of the lit windows and the magical glimmer of the snow under the street lamps.

Alluring smells of cooking food and the loud clunking of dishes led Tatiana to the kitchen. Viktoria Andreevna was embarking on one of her baking sprees.

The two of them spent the whole day side by side in the tight kitchen, their aprons and hair sprinkled with a light dusting of flour. They made pizzas, dried-fruit teacakes, and Viktoria Andreevna's speciality—small savoury pasties filled with cabbage, meat, and mushrooms. This generous supply of baked goods would feed the whole family, including Grandma and Uncle Sergey, who came to Moscow often during winter months.

As in her childhood, Tatiana sampled the fillings and the raw dough along the way. "Patience! They'll be ready soon. You'll get a tummy ache from eating uncooked things," Viktoria Andreevna said, admonishing her daughter as if she were still a little girl. Tatiana found herself giggling.

An incredible mix of aromas, rich and cosy, filled the apartment. It smelled of fried onions, cabbage, and boiled beef with a sprinkle of cinnamon and vanilla. And above all, there was the mouth-watering smell of freshly baked pastry.

Finally, they sat at the cleaned-up table over a pot of blackcurrant tea, a test batch of hot pasties on a plate between them. Tatiana leaned over the tablecloth, propping her flushed cheeks with her hands, and smiled widely for the first time that day.

"Mum, you were right," she said sheepishly. "I'm so full, I can't put another thing in my mouth."

"And who's to blame? I told you so!" Viktoria Andreevna looked almost insulted. "By the way, Oleg called earlier," she added.

"What? When?" Tatiana raised her eyebrows.

"You were still sleeping. He didn't want me to wake you."

"Oh, how nice of him," Tatiana said coldly, shrugging her shoulders.

"Do you want to tell me what's going on between you two?" Viktoria Andreevna had switched to her probing lawyer tone.

Tatiana thought, *I prefer it when you tell me off for eating raw pastry.* Out loud she said, "Not much. We've just had an argument, that's all."

"That's not what Oleg told me," Viktoria Andreevna said, pressing her. "He said you'd left without telling him where you were going. He'd had to find out from the driver—"

"OK, Mum. I got upset with him. Stop looking at me like that. Whose side are you on?" Tatiana's fingers had started rolling the edge of the tablecloth in small nervous movements, up and down.

"I'm not taking sides. You and Oleg are a unit now, remember. So you have to figure out your disagreements between you." Viktoria Andreevna picked up the teapot and poured steaming liquid into the cups. The strong summery smell of blackcurrant rose from them, but the usually soothing aroma didn't ease Tatiana's anxiety. She began to tense up under her mother's scrutinising gaze.

"That's easy for you to say! You and Dad never argue."

"How do you know?"

"Because I've never seen you arguing." Tatiana jerked up on the chair, nearly spilling her tea.

"Your dad and I sort out our differences before they get out of hand and become ugly arguments. But we don't agree on everything. That's impossible."

"Until Dad gives in and does what *you* think is right, you mean," Tatiana muttered.

"What did you say?" Viktoria Andreevna seemed unable to hear Tatiana's remark over the resounding power of her own voice.

"Nothing, Mum. Carry on. This is all very educational." Tatiana took a sip of her tea.

Now she's atop her favourite horse. I better be ready for the lecture.

"All I'm saying," continued Viktoria Andreevna, choosing to ignore her daughter's sarcasm, "is that Oleg seemed to be genuinely worried about you. He told me he'd been working long hours lately and regretted not spending more time with you. He also mentioned you've been drinking more than usual."

Ever the experienced teacher, Viktoria Andreevna stopped short of making judgemental comments. Instead, she looked directly into Tatiana's eyes with the unspoken question.

"Oh yes, how considerate of him to inform you. What else did our newly canonised saint have to say?" Tatiana felt hot flushes on her cheeks.

"It's not about your husband," Viktoria Andreevna protested. "As I said, you have to work on your marriage together. Besides, he's the one who's got the job—an aim in his life. And he seems to care about his wife. He's clearly a mature adult. Let's talk about you." Viktoria Andreevna softened her tone as she tried to sound more parental.

"What about me? I'm fine." Tatiana shifted uncomfortably in her seat and grabbed a pastry. "Mum, they're getting cold," she said, taking a bite.

"You're graduating in June, Tatiana. What are you going to do, become a highly educated housewife?" In her turn, Viktoria Andreevna also took a pastry and bit into it. "Mmm, mmm, these are a success. Well done, us."

"I don't know. I haven't decided yet. There's still time." Tatiana sat up straight. "Maybe I'll go and teach. I need to start working on my teaching tone: 'Good morning, class! Open your books and write as I dictate: (*A*) The teacher is always right; (*B*) If the teacher isn't right, see point A.'"

"I see," Viktoria Andreevna said and took a long sip from her cup. It was a masterful pause, just long enough for Tatiana to feel guilt.

"I think I'll continue with my studies," Tatiana said intently. "Apply for the postgrad course or something."

"That sounds a good idea, but you should probably get a job as well." Viktoria Andreevna put the last piece of pastry into her mouth. "Although you probably don't need to worry about making your own money right now. But you never know what might happen tomorrow."

"What do you mean, Mum?" The wave of disagreement was still rising inside Tatiana's chest, threatening to spill out and turn the conversation into a stormy quarrel. "That Oleg is going to throw me out on the street?" Fighting to keep her composure, Tatiana found herself rolling the tablecloth again.

"No, that's not what I'm saying at all." Once again Viktoria Andreevna used her categorical intonation. "Things can change quickly in this new country of ours, and the ones making it to the top so fast can easily lose it all one day. But some professions will remain no matter what. There will always be hospitals and schools."

"So you think I should teach schoolkids for a few roubles a month?" Tatiana raised her voice, instantly realising how arrogant she sounded.

"Tatiana, all I'm saying is that it's not good to have a lot of free time on your hands." Viktoria Andreevna seemed to ignore her daughter's outburst. "Time to sit in the living room or even a library, wondering when your husband is going to come home. If you have a profession, you respect yourself—and he will respect you too."

"Thank you for the valuable advice, Mum. Cicero would have been impressed."

Tatiana hated that her mother was always right. Oleg never mentioned that his wife should get a job. In fact, he probably wanted her to continue with the studies. The formula of "I'm a successful businessman, and this is my studious wife" had to be appealing to him, and although Tatiana could imagine the conversation between him and her mother behind her back, she was certain that the part about the independence, work, and self-respect was purely her mother's interpretation.

Strong-minded and outspoken, Viktoria Andreevna had never been a typical Russian wife, for whom caring for children, husband, and home would always come first, before work and other obligations.

"Let's clear up. Then we can watch your favourite game show—the one with the funny presenter." Viktoria Andreevna had completely ignored Tatiana's last remark. She stood up to reach for the cloth. By her stance, Tatiana could tell that her mother was pleased with herself.

"No, thanks. I think I'll lie down. I have a headache, and I haven't watched that programme in years. Besides, the presenter is vulgar and his jokes are flat." Tatiana walked out of the kitchen.

By the evening, Tatiana had calmed down. She and her mother both acted as if nothing had happened earlier. When Nikolay Ivanovich came back from work, the family sat down for dinner. Nikolay Ivanovich was in his usual upbeat mood. He didn't mention Oleg once, and acted as if Tatiana was seventeen again and still living at home. She giggled at his naive puns, helped him to clear the dishes, and went to bed early.

In her childhood bed, under the soft covers with faded pansies, Tatiana plunged into a deep night's sleep. The following morning she was wakened by a persistent buzz of the intercom.

"Mum? Dad?" she called helplessly, knowing very well that they'd both left for work. "There's no one home!" she shouted, as if the invisible visitor could hear her from downstairs. When the noise stopped, Tatiana let out a sigh of relief. Then the telephone started to ring. Her heart sunk in premonition. She didn't feel prepared to speak to him. After a few hesitant moments, she lifted the receiver.

"Sunny! Why don't you open the bloody door?" Oleg barked at her before she'd even said hello.

"Good morning, Oleg," she replied coldly. "Did it occur to you that I might not want to see you?" Tatiana tried to sound collected.

"Sorry, I don't know ... I don't live here ..." Oleg's voice was muffled as he was talking to someone else. "Wait a second ... Sunny, where is the nearest bakery around here? This lady is asking," he said loudly.

"Past the playground to the left. The corner building," she replied automatically. She couldn't make out the woman's response. "Where are you, Oleg? Are you calling me from a public phone?" Tatiana struggled to picture her expensively groomed and scented husband inside a smelly booth decorated with graffiti and swear words.

"I'm in my office, giving passers-by directions to the local shops!" he quipped sarcastically. "My car phone died. Vasily had to search the earth for a coin. We need to talk," Oleg continued. "Please let me in."

Even with the crackling line and background street noise, Tatiana could hear palpable remorse in his voice.

"Go back to the front door," she said after a pause. "I will let you in."

They sat opposite each other at the kitchen table, Tatiana trying to conceal her childish pyjamas under her mother's fleece robe. She felt conscious of her puffy, just-woke-up face and messy hair.

Oleg was dressed in his trademark well-fitted black suit and white shirt, the top button of which had been left undone. Between them, on a large formal plate, stood the elegant arrangement of pastries, left there by a provident Viktoria Andreevna.

Mother must have known that Oleg was coming here, Tatiana observed with dismay.

"Would you like some?" She nodded towards the pastries, feeling the need to begin somewhere.

"Are they your mum's? Of course! You don't need to ask!" Oleg grabbed a piece with exaggerated enthusiasm.

He's trying to act as if nothing happened. Please, God, let me stay strong.

"I'll make coffee. You want one?" she asked. *You're doing well so far. Just be cool and friendly—it's the only way.*

"Yes, please," Oleg replied, and Tatiana stood up to reach for the mugs. "When are you planning to come home?" he asked reluctantly.

"I don't know, Oleg. I think I'll stay here for a while." Tatiana was facing the cupboard, away from his eyes. "Besides, my mum's pastry diet can do me a lot of good," she added acidly.

"But I miss you, Sunny. I just love your dry wit. Please come home. I've been busy lately and we haven't spent much time together." His voice oozed sincerity.

What's that all about? He's changed his tune.

"Here, your belated Tatiana's Day present," he said, taking a square red box from his inside pocket. Slowly stirring sugar in her coffee cup, Tatiana watched her husband's face closely. His candid apologetic expression matched his words perfectly. And he said he couldn't act!

"What is this, Oleg?" She frowned. "You don't need to buy me a present every time you screw up. Why don't you give it to Ksenia instead?"

The sardonic question slipped past her lips before she could stop it. She regretted it immediately, but it was too late.

"Is that what this is all about? You think me and her—?" Oleg managed to look surprised and hurt at the same time. "For your information, she's got a boyfriend. Haven't you heard?" He dropped the name of a famous singer-songwriter, twice the age of Ksenia.

"That's convenient," hissed Tatiana. "Why doesn't he write a song for her, then? Why did you have to do it and then keep it a secret from me? I sat there at the concert feeling like a complete idiot!"

"I wanted to surprise everybody—especially you," protested Oleg. "I wasn't sure if the song was any good, not until we'd performed it on stage. You know that music is a big part of me, but I don't want to be judged as just another businessman with a fancy whim. I want to be taken seriously as a musician."

Oleg, after having raised his voice, hurriedly pulled out a cigarette pack from his pocket. "Can I smoke here, or should we go to the balcony?"

"Let's stay here." Tatiana didn't want to interrupt this rare moment of honesty. She watched his quick hands tearing open a plastic wrapper– those skilful fingers, so adept at dealing cards or gracefully running up and down a piano keyboard. Now there was a real Oleg, the complex and mysterious man she'd fallen in love with.

She stood up and opened the window. "Maybe Mum won't notice. The smell will fade by the evening," she muttered. "OK, give me one too," she said, putting an ashtray on the table.

"I would like to write music, sitting in that studio, playing out the melodies that warble in my head all day long and that are begging to come out, to be untangled, to be organised, to be completed. I think I have a solution. I can continue writing songs under a nickname—no one needs to know it's me." But Tatiana could hear doubt in this last remark.

"You don't need to use a pseudonym, Oleg," she said with encouragement. "If your music is good, it will speak for itself."

"Yes, sure. And the fact that I own a music channel and a magazine might also help to generate some positive reviews." Oleg smiled.

"Yup. That will come in handy, too." Tatiana giggled readily. She had missed their banter. They shared a sense of humour. Sarcasm was their thing.

"Please, don't think of Ksenia," said Oleg, suddenly serious again. "She is a good singer, a pretty face, but she has nothing on you. She is silly and shallow. And please take this. I bought it for you from Switzerland." He pushed the box across the table.

She opened the red lid. Underneath it, a thin diamond chain bracelet sparkled discreetly under the light, looking charmingly odd next to the plate of home-made pastries.

After the moon and sun necklace, this was the second of Oleg's gifts she loved at first sight. "Oleg! It's so delicate. Thank you." She gasped.

"Put it on! I knew it was made for you the moment I saw it. And you wanted to get rid of it!" Oleg was visibly flattered by her reaction.

Yes. I wanted to pass it on to that brown-haired siren, the one who is beautiful and stupid and has an old and accomplished musician for a boyfriend. Ksenia is just like Mila, who, according to Oleg, was just a silly girl in love with a handsome rich Dima, the son of a famous composer..

Both of those men had something that Oleg didn't—fame, looks, money. Suddenly a beam of realisation flashed brightly through Tatiana's head. It was one of those moments when things become clear, completely visible, and disturbingly simple.

Oleg wanted to claim his superiority the only way he could—by conquering those men's women. The thought was so new and significant that it made Tatiana stop and look at him.

"Why are you looking at me like this?" Suddenly he blushed like a smitten teenager. "Stop it, Sunny. Let me help you put on the bracelet."

He reached over to close the delicate clasp on her wrist. His hands were shaking. His touch felt different. It seemed she possessed some powers over him. For the first time, she felt desired. Her newfound wisdom was quickly evaporating from her head. "Oleg, I'm—" she began in a whisper as her voice started to abandon her.

He pulled her hand towards his lips and gently kissed a blue vein on her wrist.

"You have beautiful hands," he muttered, tracing little kisses inside her palm. "Oh, I've missed you."

His voice changed to a husky murmur. His stubble tickled her skin as she tried to pull her hand away, but Oleg strengthened his grip. He grabbed her other wrist and then buried his face in her open hands, kissing them and breathing erratically. "Such delicate hands."

Feeling his cheeks and sideburns under her fingertips, she tenderly clasped his head.

Hot and sticky desire began brewing inside her. She closed her eyes and let out a small moan. And as if he had been waiting for this cue, Oleg stood up from the chair, still holding her wrists, and pulled her into her bedroom.

His lovemaking was passionate and strangely skilful, as if he'd recently learned a new dance and was in a hurry to show off the moves. Tatiana was left puzzled and panting.

"What did you do to me, Sunny? I turned into a raging beast!" mused Oleg, propping himself up on his elbow by her side. He looked refreshed and contented.

"Mmm, that was different, Oleg. Athletic." Tatiana turned her face towards him.

"I'll report back to my personal trainer that my wife appreciates the result of his murderous circuit routine," Oleg bragged.

"Then tell him that I want to join his class myself."

"But for that, you have to come home. And that's the deal." Oleg looked her straight in the eye. Changing tack, he said, "You'll be pleased to know that you have been given the official title of Best Wife among all my friends and partners."

"I didn't realise there was a Best Wife contest. What are the criteria, and who was runner-up? Irina?" Tatiana purred.

"No, Sunny. There is no one in second place. You're the one and only winner," Oleg whispered softly, blowing on her cheek. "You want to know why?"

Tatiana nodded.

"Because you've never changed. You're the same smart and serious girl I met at university. You haven't turned bitter and demanding. I can afford so much now, but you don't seem to care. Having money hasn't altered you. Plus, I know you already fancied me when I was just a student with a guitar and a big dream.

"I trust you," Oleg said in a confiding, disarming voice.

"Oh, there you're wrong, Mr Isaev. I'm only with you for your money!" Tatiana tried to joke.

"Speaking of which," said Oleg, "let's go and spend some. We deserve a break." He touched her gently on the shoulder. "I've got another surprise for you."

"What? More diamonds?" Tatiana sat up, leaning back on the pillow.

"Just wait." Oleg climbed out of bed and reached for his designer jacket, which was crumpled on the floor. He returned with two passports in his hand. "Check inside. This one is yours."

Tatiana started looking through her passport, still wondering what the surprise was. Oleg pointed to a new visa stamp on one of the pages. "United Kingdom of Great Britain and Northern Ireland", Tatiana read.

"I asked our travel agent to help out. I know how much you miss Lena, so let's go and surprise her. We can leave on Friday and spend a whole weekend in London, just me, you, and Lena."

Tatiana was gobsmacked. Oleg was sitting on the edge of the bed naked. He looked helpless and boyish. His eyes were fixed on hers.

A warm wave of pity, mixed with excitement, blossomed in her heart.

"Oleg, thank you!" She leapt towards him and hugged him tight, pressing her bare skin against his.

Somewhere in her consciousness, the bright beam of realisation began to dim.

Chapter 22

The long, clear traces of raindrops distorted the picture outside the window. The straight row of bare plane trees divided the steady flow of traffic on Park Lane. Beyond that, the view was obstructed by the wet branchy mass of Hyde Park.

That was a very unexpected portrait of central London for Tatiana. On her first-ever trip to the Western metropolis, it seemed she would see more wood than brick. The strangest detail was the healthy and juicy green grass under the trees, mown to a perfect carpet in the late British January.

Most of the cars driving along the wet tarmac were taxicabs, their smooth black bodies glistening like lacquered Chinese boxes and their kind faces smiling apologetically.

Two hours earlier, Tatiana and Oleg's own taxi had been manned by a red-faced, grey-haired driver straight out of a Dickens novel.

"Welcome to London!" he'd greeted them as they climbed onto the spacious back seat at the airport taxi rank. "Sorry about the weather!" the cabby added as if it were his personal fault that England offered them low grey skies and cold, trickling rain.

"I'm nearly ready!" Oleg's call snapped Tatiana out of her reverie as he came out of the bathroom. His hair was wet and his face freshly pink, his small frame almost disappearing inside the plush white bathrobe with the hotel logo.

"OK, I've unpacked already," answered Tatiana. "Your clothes are all in that wardrobe, OK?" She closed the net curtain behind her.

"Or, on second thought, we could give this oversized monster a try." Oleg winked at her, pointing his chin towards the king-size bed adorned with a fancy arrangement of cushions and pillows in different sizes.

Matching curtains with a pattern of cream and beige roses were perfectly pleated and pulled back by satin ties in a noble shade of copper. A side table holding a beautiful circular arrangement of cream-coloured roses completed the understated English luxury.

The room was actually cosier than Tatiana had imagined after seeing the hotel's opulent marble lobby and long lounge framed by golden columns and palm trees in large wooden planters. The only odd detail in their room was the colour of the carpet. Deep blue and very masculine, it deviated from the whole soft English-garden theme as if nodding towards the British Empire's naval history.

"Can't we test it later tonight?" Tatiana shrugged her shoulders. "We only have two days here. I really want them to take these covers and pillows off, too. This bed, in fact the whole room, looks like it's from *Alice In Wonderland*, or a fragment of a giant doll's house.

"OK, sure." Oleg stepped closer and swatted Tatiana's backside playfully. "But don't think you can escape me, Alice!"

"Aw, don't be creepy, Oleg! She was just a girl!" She shook her finger at him. "I still can't find Lena." She sighed. "I called her number, but there's no answer. I should have warned her that we were coming."

"Sunny, it's only two o'clock. Maybe she's at work. We can try later, even pass by her place if you want." Oleg was pulling on a sock, dancing awkwardly on one foot.

Outside the hotel entrance, the tall doorman in a ceremonial black coat and top hat opened the door of another black cab for them.

"Trafalgar Square, please!" Even speaking English, Oleg sounded bossy, like he was giving orders to Vasily.

From the steps of the National Gallery, Trafalgar Square, bound in wet greystone with the famous column, lions, and fountains in the middle, looked smaller than Tatiana had imagined. She could easily see all the details on the surrounding buildings and read the time on the face of Big Ben beyond them. It all looked compact and perfectly in proportion, a bit like a theatre set. The small man with a funny hat and a sword on top of the soaring column had rudely turned his back on them.

He might as well. I wouldn't be able to see his face from this distance anyway. Let's hope he doesn't suffer from vertigo. Tatiana sympathised with poor lonely Nelson. Unlike the monumental colossi in Moscow—war heroes and party leaders carved in stone to dominate the crowds below them—this petite admiral seemed to be a mere decoration on top of an imposing pedestal. It was the column that was the architectural centrepiece of the square, not the man.

"This is a different take on the role of the hero in history." Tatiana touched Oleg's elbow and pointed at the admiral's back. Oleg was busy taking photos on his newest pocket-sized camera.

He paused for a second, as if thinking over Tatiana's remark, and then he grinned and kissed her cheek. "Well said, Sunny! I know exactly what you mean!"

Tatiana flushed proudly.

Leaving the rain behind, they walked hand in hand through the endless rooms of the National Gallery. Oleg, quick to show off his knowledge of European art, dragged Tatiana from painting to painting, explaining and gesticulating.

Tatiana smiled and nodded. She tried to listen at first, but then somewhere in the room with Italian paintings from the eighteenth century, her mind began to wander. She studied Oleg's lively, young face and his deep pink lips, and giggled inside when he furrowed his brow, trying to remember a historical fact or an anecdote.

It was obvious that her husband's understanding of art was more limited than he was prepared to admit—even to himself. But he did have a good knowledge of European history, and the improvised tour deviated more and more towards a narrative of the curious events that had taken place around that period.

Tatiana loved listening to his voice and feeling his close proximity. She felt warm and happy inside, just like on that night under the lamp post in the Olympic Park. Deep in her daydream, she couldn't even have said if the gallery was crowded or empty that afternoon.

"Why did you stop here? You like this one, Sunny?" Oleg's question brought her back to reality. Tatiana realised that she was standing opposite a large strange painting of a tiger in a dense jungle. The childlike style of the artist suggested that they had arrived at the hall of post-impressionism.

Tatiana briefly glanced around and spotted a few of Van Gogh's colourful masterpieces depicting crabs, sunflowers, and chairs. But there was something magnetic and odd about this botch of a jungle scene in front of her: the tiger, with his disproportionally long tail and his hind legs coiled under the belly, appeared to be balancing on top of giant tropical leaves.

Everything in the picture seemed to be leaning diagonally: the trees, the branches, the bushes, the grass, the long lines of rain, and the lightning in the stormy skies above. Even the tiger was swaying sideways, caught in the power of a tropical storm. Everything was swaying except for a dark green plant in the bottom corner. Its large, meaty leaves pointed straight up, as if it was just a potted lily from the artist's bedroom, added on provocatively perhaps, or to cover up an artistic mistake. The title of the picture was also strange: *Surprised!*

"What do you like about it, Sunny? Rousseau wasn't

as important as the other guys here. Come and look at this Gauguin." Oleg tried to pull her by her sleeve.

"I don't know, Oleg. There is something about this one. The colours are so crazy; the whole scene is bizarre. Or maybe it's because I sometimes feel like this odd plant in the corner—the skies are opening, the storm is raging around me, and everything is moving, but I'm just sitting there, motionless and ridiculous. You're the tiger, you see, and I'm just an add-on, an afterthought."

"C'mon! That's a little too deep for this eccentric feller. Let's stop now and go to the shop. We'll see if there's a print of this, if you like it that much." Oleg pointed to the door at the end of the hall.

"What, not the original? I thought you were going to make them an offer they couldn't refuse, just for me!" Tatiana giggled and followed him out.

When they finally left the gallery and stepped outside—Tatiana carefully holding a museum carrier bag with a rolled-up poster, and Oleg carrying a large umbrella with the hotel logo—the darkness had already swallowed up the gloomy sky.

The city had changed its character, from demure and distant to enticing and welcoming. The brightly lit signposts, street lamps, and windows, mixed with double-decker buses in festive red, looked playful and light-hearted, even against the cold vapour of January rain.

Before finding shelter under their oversized umbrella, Tatiana felt compelled to look up in the hope of seeing Mary Poppins descending on the square, holding onto her own brolly with the long wooden handle.

"Oleg, wait! Can you smell it?" She stopped as they walked down the grand steps, closed her eyes, and inhaled.

"What, Sunny? No, I can't smell anything. But I think we need to turn left here so we can smell food. I'm starving!" he declared, pulling her impatiently.

"No, stop for a second," Tatiana pleaded, inhaling again.

"The air here, it's so moist, so different. It's strange. We're in the middle of the city, but it's like we're at the seaside! It's nothing like Moscow air, don't you think?"

"Of course it's different. It's damp! You're probably smelling your soggy coat! Let's go; we have to find a restaurant."

They began walking, weaving their way through the crowds of Covent Garden. Tatiana noticed the narrowness of the pavements here. It was laborious trying not to bump into other people.

Once they finally found a cosy piano bar on the corner of a side street, they ordered Scotch on the rocks and a large pizza to share. As they ate, they listened to the soft tinkling of a grand piano, played by a blonde ageless woman in a black concert gown. She sat very composed, with her back gracefully straight and a hint of a smile on her narrow lips. This woman looked effortlessly professional with her strong fingers lovingly calling forth a selection of melodies from musicals and films. For Tatiana she was the perfect English lady: laconic in her gestures and expressions, a glint of mischief about her blue eyes.

After their third whisky, Oleg stood up, waited for the music to stop, and then clapped loudly, exclaiming, "Brava!" To Tatiana's astonishment and the delight of other customers, he then walked towards the piano and bowed to the lady. He reached for her hand and kissed it gallantly.

"You play beautifully! Thank you!" he said, taking a fifty-pound note from his pocket and stuffing it into the top of the piano.

"For you, miss!" he declared.

"Are you sure about that?" The pianist raised an eyebrow as she positioned her hands over the keys and prepared to play once more.

"Yes, I'm sure!" Oleg bowed his head again and prepared to return to his seat. There was sporadic applause from the other tables.

"Thank you, young man," said the pianist with a tinge of

derision as she began playing gently. "Then this one is for you and your lovely companion."

Tatiana almost sobered up; she was mortified.

"Oleg, you've insulted her! I don't think they have the same tipping culture as in Russia!"

"Nonsense! She would have been insulted if I'd given her a tenner!" Oleg shrugged his shoulders and furrowed his brow, but Tatiana could see that his mood had taken a hit.

"It's my money. I work hard for it. I can do whatever I like with it, and tip those I want to tip. Do you have a problem with that?" He glared at Tatiana.

"No. Of course not." Tatiana sighed. "Your money, your call. Can we go now, please? Call on Lena?"

As they were leaving, from the corner of her eye Tatiana caught the barman approaching the piano with a glass of red wine on a small silver tray. He placed the wine on top of the piano lid. As the piano player smiled and nodded to him, he ceremoniously put the banknote onto the tray and carried it off towards a door with a "Staff Only" sign.

Their taxi stopped outside a grand Mayfair apartment building. "Whom are you vising today?" asked a large dark-skinned man as he rose from his seat at the concierge desk. He looked displeased. Tatiana noticed a small TV set in front of him and a remote control in his big hand. As he talked, he pressed down on the volume button to silence the television. It definitely wasn't the remote for a security monitor.

The look of sheer annoyance on the guard's face translated perfectly in all languages. Tatiana and Oleg had unwillingly interrupted the sacred hour of the soap opera.

"We're here to see Miss Petrova," said Oleg, stepping forwards confidently. "She's expecting us."

"And your name is?" With an effort, the guard followed procedure.

"We are Mr and Mrs Isaev," Oleg replied, remaining calm.

"Wait a second, sir." With a heavy sigh, the man dialled a

number on the dirty white phone in front of him. “Mr and Mrs Isaev are here,” he said to someone on the other end of the line. “OK. Thank you.”

“You may go up. First floor, apartment three.” He gave Tatiana and Oleg a look of relief. His hand was already reaching for the remote.

Oleg looked as if he was going to say something else, but Tatiana softly pushed him towards the stairs. “We’ll find it. Let’s go.”

“Why are we climbing up if he said it was on the first floor?”

“Because this is England, Oleg. They call the first floor ‘ground’.” Tatiana was glad she could show off her knowledge of British eccentricities, which Lena had shared with her. And as if to confirm that, she stopped outside a door with the number 3, at the top of the first flight.

Oleg pressed the little white knob on the side of the door frame. Hearing loud music coming from inside the apartment, they looked at each other. Oleg chuckled. “Sounds like your friend is having a party.”

No one rushed to open the door for them.

“They can’t hear the doorbell.” Tatiana shifted impatiently. In her mind she was already hugging Lena.

“But the doorman spoke to someone in there!” Oleg reasoned, and started banging on the door with his fist.

That method worked. After a few seconds, the door flew wide open. Tatiana and Oleg were greeted by a tall, skinny, dark-haired girl in torn jeans and an oversized T-shirt. She had a half-empty plastic cup in her hand, and the long messy strands of her hair were covering half her face. Tatiana could picture her dancing and waving her head about just moments before. The girl’s feet were bare.

“You must be Lena’s friends,” the girl said as she smiled and moved out of the way. She didn’t sound English. “I’m Carlotta. We’re roommates. But she’s not here. She didn’t come back from that shoot today.”

"Did she go hunting?" Oleg raised an eyebrow.

"No!" The girl giggled. "I mean the photo shoot. She was in Scotland all week, and we were expecting her back tonight." Carlotta barked suddenly into the open door of the front room, "Guys, keep it down! I can't hear myself!"

Tatiana could hear male and female voices, loud and excited, chattering, trying to compete with the blaring music. Someone pushed the door shut.

"That's better." Carlotta turned to the visitors. "The agency called. Lena was staying there for the weekend, but she's left Edinburgh, so they couldn't reach her. She travelled up to the Highlands to take some pictures."

"Can we get a message to her? Can you help us?" Oleg stepped a little closer to Carlotta, glancing at her lean body. Tatiana could tell that he was impressed by the friendly, laid-back model.

"I wish I could," Carlotta replied. "There are no telephones where she's gone. I'm sure she'll be back by Sunday night though."

"But we're leaving on Sunday afternoon!" Tatiana exclaimed in frustration. She wasn't embarrassed about her English when she spoke to other foreigners.

"Give me your number where you're staying, and I'll pass it on to her if she calls here. Sorry I can't help you more. Would you like to come in and join us?" Carlotta said with a disarming smile.

Tatiana shook her head firmly. "No, thank you, Carlotta. We need to go." She turned towards the front door.

"Thank you. Maybe next time," added Oleg with disappointment.

Oleg had stopped outside the building to light his cigarette. "What's up with you, Sun? Since when did you become so boring? How often have *you* been invited to a cool London party?"

"Well, I didn't think it was your scene either, Oleg. Carlotta definitely wasn't drinking a fine cognac from that plastic glass," Tatiana hissed.

How can I explain to him that it is every woman's nightmare to be invited to a party where everyone but you is a model?

"But I admit Carlotta was pretty. Sorry I dragged you away."

"She was too skinny," Oleg remarked. "Sunny, you have to stop eyeing me suspiciously with every woman we meet. What's wrong with you? It's becoming tiring. I'm with you here, aren't I?" he asked with irritation.

"Because I see the way you look at them." Tatiana didn't give up. "When you're with me, please treat me with respect."

"I brought you to London. I came with you looking for Lena, the girl who doesn't even like me. And you dare to accuse me of treating you badly? Ungrateful woman," Oleg blared.

He threw his cigarette butt to the ground ferociously and then stomped on it. Then he walked away from her, nearly jogging down the narrow street.

Tatiana knew they were within walking distance of the hotel, but she wasn't good with directions. She suddenly felt abandoned and helpless, completely out of place in this cold and formal area.

"Oleg, wait!" Swallowing her pride, Tatiana trotted after him. He gave a quick glance over his shoulder but didn't slow down.

They didn't speak the rest of the evening. When Tatiana walked out of the bathroom, leaving a cloud of expensively scented steam behind her, he was standing by the front door, still fully dressed.

"I'm going down to smoke a cigar," he announced and then slammed the door behind him.

Tatiana couldn't fall asleep that night. She shifted and sighed. The day that had started out perfectly, with their tangible closeness at the gallery and their bonding walk through rain-soaked streets, had ended in a fight and her cowardly retreat.

The next morning they sat opposite each other for breakfast in the elegant dining room. Tatiana was conscious of her puffy eyes. On the contrary, Oleg looked composed and confident. His glance fixed on a page of the thick British newspaper he was pretending to read as he whistled softly to himself.

"Stop it, Sunny," he instructed abruptly, looking up at her with a hint of a grin and then folding the paper on to his lap.

"Stop what? I'm not doing anything." Tatiana's voice came out husky. She hadn't spoken in many hours.

"Stop sniffling, looking all cute and pitiful. Although I must admit I love it when you wrinkle your nose like that. You look like a stroppy child who's missed out on a special treat."

Before Tatiana could react to that, Oleg leaned over the table and cupped her chin with his palm. His hand was warm and comforting. She closed her eyes, wishing for her night-time worries to evaporate.

"I'm sorry," Oleg whispered, stroking her cheek gently. "I don't want to argue with you."

"Me neither. I'm sorry too," she whispered and then looked around. Thankfully the tables next to them were all empty. She didn't like public scenes.

"Waiter, can we have our breakfast upstairs, please? Room 284. In thirty minutes," Oleg commanded in English.

"Come on, we'll eat later." He was already standing by his wife's side, pulling her out of her chair. In his voice, she recognised the same urgency and desire that had taken her by surprise at her parents' apartment.

Feeling her whole body responding to his carnal call, Tatiana stood up. "I'm not hungry anymore," she said suggestively.

Two hours later, they stood hand in hand in the middle of the hotel's black and white marble hall deciding where to go. They were both giggling like a pair of kids.

Tatiana felt taller and looser, as if her limbs had become more supple and flexible. She saw herself like a graceful cat and even had to stop herself from purring. Sex could be a very pleasant exercise, she had just discovered. "And let's go shopping!" Oleg said.

“What about the Tower, Oleg?” Tatiana made a serious face at him. “What kind of tourist are you?”

“The kind that wants to treat his wife. The Tower can wait until the next time. It’s been there for nine hundred years; I don’t think it’s going anywhere anytime soon.” His tone eliminated any objection.

“Where can I go to buy my wife something nice?” he asked, addressing the concierge, a tall figure in a three-piece suit behind a dark wooden desk.

“That would be Bond Street, sir,” the man replied with a wide professional smile. “Do you need a taxi?” He signalled to the doorman.

At the counter, in the boutique of Tatiana’s favourite Italian designer, she watched the assistants, two girls in dark trouser suits, folding and packing her purchases—dresses, suits, jumpers, coats, and even a wide-brimmed felt hat. The girls were working in unison, wrestling with tissue paper and closing large silver-grey carrier bags, tying the handles with ribbons.

Tatiana’s initial excitement was giving way to shameful guilt. “I shouldn’t have bought so much,” she said quietly to Oleg, who was busy counting out cash, watched admiringly by a pretty cashier.

“Would you like us to deliver the bags to your hotel, sir?” the girl asked, still beaming at Oleg. She was trying to catch his eye.

“Yes, please,” Oleg replied with a smile, putting down a pile of fifty-pound notes in front of her. “Check it, please. I think I’ve counted it correctly. And we don’t need the change either. It’s for you ladies. You’ve all been extremely helpful.”

The assistants paused and raised their heads. “That’s very kind of you, sir. Thank you!” The girls were grinning wider than professional protocol required.

“What did you say, Sunny? I didn’t catch it.” Smiling and visibly pleased with himself, Oleg turned to her.

“I said, it’s too much for me. I didn’t really need all these things.” Tatiana let out a sigh.

"Listen. All these clothes looked lovely on you. I wanted to buy them, so I did. End of story. What's up with you? You get upset if I ignore you, and you sulk if I spoil you. Make up your mind. Turn around and appreciate the look on these girls' faces. I bet they would swap places with you in a heartbeat!" Oleg looked exasperated.

"You're right. I'm sorry. I don't know what came over me. Thank you for everything." Tatiana kissed him on the cheek. She envied the clarity and simplicity of Oleg's world of money.

"Ahem. Listen." Oleg suddenly paused by the door of the shop. "It turns out I have a meeting with a big advertising executive today. So, here, go and spoil yourself a bit more." He held out a thick envelope. "I think you may need to buy a new suitcase as well." He winked cheerfully.

Tatiana was stunned. Even for him, this was a low blow.

"I'm sorry. I got the confirmation fax only today. It could be big for us, Sunny. We're talking a potential merger here. I'm meeting the managing partner of the advertising house at his tennis club."

"You said nothing until now! And what about me, Oleg? Can I come with you?" Tatiana still couldn't believe he was leaving her all alone.

"No, sorry. No wives. Gentlemen only. He's playing a doubles match, and I'm meeting him there for 'tea'. I won't be long."

Oleg looked at his watch. "I've got to run now. I'll meet you back at the hotel." And with that, he sprang out of the door and leapt towards a black cab that a passenger was busy exiting.

In numb disbelief, Tatiana walked out onto the pavement, feeling lost in more ways than one. She didn't want to look back and face the stares of the salesgirls. "Lucky cow," she could almost hear them thinking.

Oleg didn't come back in time for dinner that night. Tatiana tried to drown her anger in a deep bathtub filled with hot water and frothing foam. After feeling a little calmer, she ordered room service for one.

Before the food arrived, she emptied the contents of two miniature whisky bottles into a crystal tumbler and topped it up with Coke. Then she dived underneath the silky-smooth bedcovers and turned on the TV.

Lying on the bed, she watched her favourite film, a modern Cinderella story about a wealthy grey-haired businessman and a young prostitute with a gregarious laugh. She ate fish and chips with her hands and had almost forgotten about her traitorous husband when the phone rang.

"Sorry, Sunny. Change of plan. Jeff's a great guy. We've ended up having dinner. I'll probably be back late, so don't wait up. I will make it up to you tomorrow, I promise."

"Oleg, you're drunk," she stated, slightly slurring through her own words. "And we're leaving tomorrow! But I'm not mad at you. You're always true to yourself. I feel a bit stupid for believing that this weekend was about us. You knew all along about this meeting. That's why you brought me here."

"Asshole," she concluded after putting down the receiver.

She awoke the next morning with a fishy smell floating up her nostrils. The remains of her lovely supper stared at her from the plate on her bedside table.

I must have fallen asleep with the tray still on the bed.

A low, sinister roar of snoring came from Oleg's side of the bed.

Before even turning over, Tatiana could tell he'd fallen asleep on his back, like a drunk, with his mouth wide open. She quietly climbed out of bed and darted towards the bathroom, glancing at her sleeping husband.

As she predicted, he had passed out with his head tilted unnaturally backwards over the pillow and his feet sticking out of the duvet. He still had one sock on.

Tatiana got dressed and went down for breakfast, choosing a discreet table in the corner of the room. She was halfway through her ham and cheese omelette when a slight commotion in the background caught her attention. "I'm looking for my friend," she heard a familiar voice say. "There she is!"

Lena was walking speedily towards her, her face ablaze. "You call that a surprise, Isaeva?! I've been waiting for your visit for three years, and this is how you do it?" Lena shouted at her in Russian.

"Um, will you be joining your friend for breakfast, madam?" The restaurant manager had appeared from behind Lena's back, looking concerned.

Still fuming, Lena said, "You bet I will." She turned towards him, regaining her composure. "Can you take my coat, please?" she added more softly, reading the flash of panic in the man's eyes. "I'd like some tea. Do you have English Breakfast?"

"Certainly, madam." After nodding with relief, the manager swiftly disappeared with Lena's wet raincoat.

"So, explain yourself!" Lena said, turning to Tatiana.

"I'm so sorry! It was Oleg's idea to surprise you. It was a last-minute thing, I swear," Tatiana began apologetically.

"That was a dumb thing to do." Lena was in no mood for apologies. "Only by chance I phoned home last night, and Carlotta told me that you came by. I rushed back like a lunatic to Edinburgh to get the first flight, and all the way I was just praying you hadn't left yet."

Tatiana could feel her friend's frustration.

"I'm sorry. It was completely stupid of me. But I'm so happy to see you. You look amazing with that hair!"

Only now did Tatiana realise that Lena's long brown locks had been replaced by a very short boyish cut that made her large almond eyes and delicate features stand out all the more. Her distinct beauty had become alien-like.

"Yeah, yeah. Keep talking," Lena grumbled. "So, where is the generator of these ingenious ideas? Did you finally dump Isaev somewhere?"

"He's upstairs, enjoying the last moments of sobering sleep before a flight home." Tatiana smirked, picking up on Lena's sarcastic humour.

"How come you've recovered? Didn't you drink with him?" Lena poured milk into a delicate cup.

“No, I did not. But that’s a long story, if you care to hear it.”

“I’m all ears.” Lena took a small graceful sip and asked the waiter, “Can I have a menu?”

“I haven’t had anything to eat since last night,” she explained to Tatiana. “So, I’ll be eating, and you, Isaeva, will be speaking.” As Lena was tucking into picture-perfect pancakes with berries and maple syrup, Tatiana began her story.

For the first time in their relationship, she didn’t hold back. Maybe because they lived in different worlds now, or maybe because she so clearly saw how much Lena valued her friendship, it felt as if floodgates had opened.

Tatiana poured out all her worries, doubts, and suspicions about Oleg, and her guilt about spending his money.

What she loved the most during her confession was that Lena didn’t stop chewing. She even ordered a fresh pot of tea. There was no pretentious, “Oh, you poor thing,” or dramatic rolling of the eyes. Nothing seemed to shock Lena enough to stop her from enjoying her food, or Tatiana from telling her tale.

Tatiana concluded with the events of the previous night. “But it’s not all bad, don’t you think?” she asked with a faint smile.

“Wow. I had no idea,” Lena said reflectively. “I’ve always known that Isaev played by his own rules in his game, but I sort of thought you had accepted that and obeyed his leadership. Now it doesn’t look that simple.”

“What shall I do, Lena? What would you do?” Tatiana pleaded.

“Oh, you don’t want to take relationship advice from me. Look at me! Two married ex-boyfriends and I’m currently single, pursuing a crazy, penniless career in nature photography. I’m thinking of turning my back on modelling and all its financial securities. I’ll probably still be dating the wrong man when you’re looking after your first grandchild. I think we just want different things in life.” Lena folded her napkin neatly on top of her plate.

"But at least you know what you want in life. I haven't a clue," Tatiana protested. "I thought I did. I've always wanted to be married, to have a family, but I'm not sure about anything anymore." Tatiana looked down at her fingers.

"Ah, there you are! Morning, girls." Oleg's chirpy voice made Tatiana jump.

"Lena, hi. I'm so glad she found you finally." He approached the table looking freshly shaven and bright-eyed, bringing in the zesty aroma of aftershave. He displayed no trace of hangover.

"Hello, Oleg." Lena turned her cheek for a kiss, raising slightly from her seat.

Oleg bent down to give a peck and said, "You look fantastic, Miss Petrova. Very sophisticated hairdo."

"Oh, thank you." Lena batted her eyelashes. Tatiana could see she wasn't impartial to his compliment. "Only it was me who found you here, not the other way around."

Lena stood up and waved at the manager, signalling for her coat. "Now, kids, I'm going to leave you. I understand you have a flight to catch. I'll be in Moscow in a few months. We'll get together then.

"Isaev, next time, think of a better way to surprise me," she said teasingly to Oleg. "And thanks for my breakfast."

"You're going so soon?" Tatiana couldn't hide her disappointment.

"Yeah, I have to. But you can walk me to the door." Lena threaded her long arms into the sleeves of the raincoat that the manager was now gallantly holding out for her.

"OK. I'll be back in a minute," Tatiana remarked to Oleg over her shoulder. He nodded without lifting his eyes from the breakfast menu.

The two women stood in front of each other by the revolving door. Rain gushed in diagonal bursts over the old gnarly trees and a display of expensive cars outside.

"Listen, Isaeva. I don't have any final words of wisdom for you." Lena lowered her head, looking trustingly into Tatiana's eyes. "You have to figure it out all by yourself. And I must admit, every time I see you two together, I get this feeling that, despite his ridiculous ways, he still loves you."

"You think so?" Tatiana's voice trembled. *Is there really still hope for me?*

"I do, my friend." Lena moved forwards for an embrace. The two young women stood still for a second in a close hug.

Lena breathed right into Tatiana's ear. "And you love him too, don't you?"

"I think I do." Tatiana nodded. She could faintly smell rose—Lena's perfume—and a hint of pancake, the sweet scent of her friend. Tatiana's eyes began to tear up. "I'll miss you," she whispered.

Lena stood back abruptly. "Isaeva, I'm not doing that," she quipped. "No soppy goodbyes. I'll come in two months and kick your butt if you don't stop drinking."

Lena looked briefly into Tatiana's eyes. Then she took two long strides towards the revolving doors and, without glancing back, disappeared into the London rain.

Chapter 23

Two soft beeps from Tatiana's handbag interrupted the silence of the reading room. She winced in surprise and looked around her. The long airy hall was almost empty, and the only other reader—a man at a window table by the far end—did not react to the sound. The way he was slouched over his desk told her he was absorbed in his work.

Tatiana reached inside her bag and took out a pager, Oleg's latest gift. "So I can still reach you in the depths of the archives and other obscure places, Sunny!"

Since their return from London, Oleg had plunged back into his usual routine of working late and entertaining "useful people", but Tatiana, after her heart-to-heart with Lena, decided to give him another chance. She started working on her dissertation at the Library of Foreign Languages. The spacious rooms of this unremarkable brick building on the Yauza embankment, not far from the spot where Vlad died, were always quiet and empty.

The library housed works published in more than a hundred foreign languages, which meant that readers would have to be fluent in at least one of them.

The pager had disturbed Tatiana's labours to translate a wordy article on a hard-going US novel. Rustling the pages of a massive English–Russian dictionary, Tatiana scribbled ferociously in her notebook, unconsciously playing with her hair. Messing up her expensive hairdo was a sign of extreme concentration.

She stared with annoyance at the small screen in her hand. *I should leave the damn thing at home next time.*

"I am outside," read the message. It was Vasily. Tatiana looked at her watch. Two o'clock. Of course! She had agreed to have lunch with her husband.

Oleg hadn't come home last night, blaming an "insane amount" of paperwork. "I'm crashing in the office tonight, Sun. I'll grab dinner with Maks and then come back here. Sorry. Come by tomorrow after the library and we'll have lunch together, OK?"

With that he hung up.

It wasn't the first time. Late in the evening before going to bed, Tatiana fixed her usual, whisky and Coke in a crystal glass, but somehow it didn't taste right. After the first sip, she felt strangely queasy. She dialled Oleg's office number. The clock showed five to midnight. No one picked up.

The dinner with Maks must have run late. She had become highly skilled at inventing excuses for her husband. She preferred not to ask questions, choosing instead to create her own explanations for his absences. But the clock was ticking on his second chance. She was getting fed up with all of it.

She returned the books to the librarian's desk and decided to confront her husband at lunch.

Tatiana was crossing the paved courtyard of the library when a sudden gust of late March wind blew into her face. A cluster of lined blank pages torn out of someone's notebook danced in jerky swirls in front of her. She felt a sudden bolt of anxiety.

Tatiana often felt unsettled on windy days, but somehow this time was different, as if all her senses had sharpened at once. A strong smell of fried onions and hot cooking oil hit her nostrils. She remembered seeing a kiosk selling pasties outside the library gates. The odour made her nauseous.

Stupid wind. It carries around everything it finds.

Vasily was waiting for her by the cast-iron gates. She sat on the front seat. "I'm feeling a bit dizzy today, Vasily. I'll sit here if you don't mind," she said, answering his silent question.

"I'm supposed to meet Oleg for lunch. Do you know what restaurant we're going to?" she continued, grateful that Chip and Dale were absent.

"I believe Oleg Borisovich is still in the office. Let me check." Vasily reached excitedly for the car phone.

"Marina? It's me, Vasily. Is the boss there? I have Tatiana Nikolaevna in the car."

"Understood," he confirmed after a brief pause. "We're on our way." He hung up.

"Oleg Borisovich is in his office. He's got someone with him. Marina said that I should bring you there. Is that OK?" Vasily's tone softened as he gave Tatiana a smile.

Tatiana shrugged her shoulders. "Yes, it's OK. Let's go."

A man whom Tatiana didn't recognise was exiting Oleg's office. She swiftly slipped past him through the heavy door, which was bulletproof and upholstered in black leather.

"I hope I'm your next appointment, Oleg!"

Sinking into the bulky leather sofa opposite his desk, she noticed the imprint of the visitor's large behind still visible on it.

"Sunny! You made it!" By his tone and satisfied smile, she knew the meeting with the owner of the big bottom had gone well.

"I thought we were having lunch together," Tatiana said with irritation. She got a sudden urge to dampen his mood. "Made tons of money, did you? I can tell by your glee."

"As a matter of fact, I did." He refused to take the bait of her sarcasm. "We're halfway to buying a mainstream TV channel. That man was an investor. Imagine all the advertising time that will be ours all day! Not just a few hours, like with OBI-TV. We're talking the really big bucks here! And by the way, the

Brits are interested in us, too. Remember Jeff? He called me. Our London trip came through." Oleg winked at her.

Tatiana sighed and felt a pang of annoyance. She really wanted to wipe the smug look off his face. She was preparing to challenge him about last night, but she didn't want to do it here. They needed to be on a neutral territory.

"So, where are we going for lunch? Shouldn't we book?" She shifted on her seat, crossing her legs.

"This is all good news, Sunny!" Oleg ignored her question. "We can finish the house this summer, and I can take you on the trip of your life!" he exclaimed euphorically.

"That's all great, Oleg. But I am hungry!" she quipped.

"I tell you what." Oleg got up from his chair. "Why don't we have a nice lunch here at the office, you and me? I'm sure Anna's cooked up something delicious today. I'm starving—haven't even eaten breakfast. It was an early start." He seemed pleased with this idea.

"I was hoping to go out. I am not a big fan of Anna's cooking. A bit heavy for me," Tatiana tried to insist.

"Ah! But I have a very special bottle of cognac here. I've been saving it to celebrate something big. Besides, I don't have much time left before my next meeting. What do you say, my lady?" Oleg pretended to waltz towards the sofa. He was wearing one of his irresistible smiles and reaching out his hand as if inviting her to dance.

Tatiana shook her head but gave him her hand nonetheless. It was clear that her questions had to wait for another time.

"Smooth operator. All right, you win. It better be a nice lunch."

A few minutes later, Anna—a large homely woman in a white starched apron and a maid's cap, which she wore proudly like a crown—converted the shiny mahogany boardroom table into a fancy-looking dining sit, complete with sparkling white tablecloth, fine china, and silver cutlery.

"I see why you like the office so much, Oleg. You don't need to leave—you have everything you need," Tatiana remarked.

“To us, Sunny. To success!” Oleg declared, raising his pre-warmed cognac glass in a salute.

“To us!” she repeated, pouring a different meaning into these words. A strong woody taste hit her palate unpleasantly. She spat the little sip she had taken back into the glass and then put the glass down on the table. Oleg didn’t seem to notice. *How strange. I usually like cognac.*

Anna appeared at the door, carrying a tray laden with bowls of soup and a platter of spring salad. She placed the plates in front of Oleg and Tatiana and then departed as quickly and quietly as she’d arrived. Despite her imposing size, Anna moved with a graceful ease.

“Look, Sunny. Anna has changed her ways. She cooks light now.” Oleg nodded at the table.

Tatiana peered at the orange liquid in front of her. Ever since their trip to England, Oleg had developed a strange obsession with carrot soup.

“I think she’s overdone it with the coriander,” began Tatiana, playing with the citrusy goo with her spoon. She didn’t fancy putting it in her mouth. They were interrupted by a gentle knock at the door.

“I told Marina not to let anyone in!” Oleg furrowed his brow. “Who is it?” he barked.

Marina smiled apologetically as she entered, wearing her coat. “Oleg Borisovich, Tatiana Nikolaevna, so sorry to interrupt. The bank closes in half an hour and I have these urgent payments to make. They require your signature.” She was waving some sheets of paper in front of herself.

“It’s OK, Marina. We won’t be mad, because it’s you.” Oleg got up and walked to his desk. Reaching for his silver fountain pen—Tatiana’s New Year’s gift—he asked, “What are they for?”

“The top one is for the office, and the other two are for the apartments on Tverskaya Street. You instructed me to bring them to you personally.”

Marina spoke quickly, her cheeks a little flushed.

"OK. There. Off you go." Oleg rushed to sign all three papers. "I don't see why it couldn't wait until tomorrow," he muttered through his teeth. His discomfort was palpable.

"Thank you. And sorry to disturb, again," Marina pronounced in her phone voice. She then breezed out of the room, making brief eye contact with Tatiana.

Tatiana understood that this little show had been for her benefit.

"What was that all about?" she mused out loud. "You never mentioned you were renting apartments in the centre. Is this something new?" She looked at Oleg directly.

He used a question to deflect hers. "What if I told you it's none of your business?" he started in a raised voice. "I sign dozens of invoices every day. Do I need to report every single one of them to you?"

Oleg stopped himself then and took a deep breath. "I was looking forward to this meal with you until that bitch spoilt it for us. It's time to sack her, anyway. I took pity on her when Vlad died, but she's outstayed her welcome." Oleg punched the tabletop. The glasses clinked and the orange soup wobbled from side to side. After a moment he regained his composure. "Yum, carrot soup!" Oleg changed the subject suddenly, overplaying the soup. "Pick up your spoon. Let's eat!"

Tatiana obeyed, although she was still in shock about Marina's apparent career suicide. *What is so important about those apartments? Why did Marina want me to know about them? What was she trying to say?*

The sickeningly sweet taste of carrot made her gag. Pressing both hands over her mouth, she jumped up and ran towards the toilets.

Chapter 24

Through the large window of the coffee house on the Garden Ring, Tatiana watched the black limousine pulling over. Chip jumped out and unfolded a large umbrella before opening the door for his boss. Oleg climbed out. Next to the towering bodyguard, he looked diminutive and somewhat vulnerable. As he came closer, Tatiana could see his tightly pressed lips.

"What was so urgent that it couldn't wait until tonight?" Oleg blared through the door of the coffee house. His voice reverberated off the walls. She was glad she had picked this quiet place for their meeting. It was the neutral ground.

The only other people were a student couple and a waitress. Tatiana registered a taint of silent panic among them.

The witnesses must have assessed the situation pretty quickly after spotting Chip with a walkie-talkie by the door. As one, they all looked down and away.

Probably wish they were somewhere else right now. Bad luck.

"Thank you for coming, Oleg. Please, sit down and have coffee with me. This couldn't wait. I wasn't sure I'd see you tonight." She managed to keep her voice calm.

"OK, one coffee. I'm on tight schedule today," Oleg agreed, pulling out a chair. "Waitress!" he said, raising his hand. "Double espresso and a glass of water!"

"Sure. One moment, sir." The girl behind the counter grinned at them as if she'd just heard she'd been given a promotion.

"I'm having a mad day, Sunny. Maks had an argument with the new investor and it might jeopardise the whole deal. I have to mediate—be a peacekeeper. It's all hanging by a thread."

Oleg unbuttoned his coat and took out cigarettes. "Sometimes, I get tired of all of this," he said, waving his hand. "I dream of locking myself in a studio and just composing, creating something, you know?" His voice trailed off.

"You probably should, Oleg. One day. It will make you happy." Tatiana looked down and sighed. *Why is it always about him?*

"What's up?" he continued. "Why are you looking sad?" He offered her a cigarette. Tatiana shook her head. She'd played the scenario in her head all morning, ever since paging him.

Tatiana looked at the wet street beyond the coffee house window with the wide stream of traffic flowing by. All those people in cars and buses were rushing to get somewhere, oblivious to her and to each other.

"Oleg, I'm pregnant," she said quietly, nonchalantly, still looking away.

"What? When? Are you sure?" he asked with a genuine shock.

She turned to face him. "I'm sure. I saw the doctor today. Seven weeks or so."

"But how?" Oleg looked puzzled. It wasn't often she could take him by surprise.

"London, I think," she whispered. She had figured it out. It wasn't difficult, as they hadn't slept together since that trip.

"Are you sure it's mine?"

A rush of blood to her head made her gasp. "What do you mean?" she nearly shouted. The couple in the corner fell silent again. "Who else's can it be?" she hissed before lowering her voice. "I'm married to you, the last time I checked. Not everyone behaves like you do."

"What did you say?" Oleg's voice radiated a heat to match hers. "Choose your words carefully, woman."

The smiling waitress appeared just in time.

"Your espresso, sir." She put the cup in front of him. After that she withdrew quickly back to her place behind the bar. Tatiana used the pause to catch her breath. She felt her pulse throbbing in her temples.

"I'm saying that I don't sleep around, Oleg. But that is not what we're discussing here," she said. "The question is: what do we do? Are you ready to become a father?" Tatiana looked straight at him.

"Sun, this is so unexpected." Oleg looked away for a moment .He paused and faced her again. " I understand you're emotional. Of course I want to have children, in principle, and I'm ready when you are, but it's your body. Your life will change. I'll do everything I can. Hire the best help for you. But the big question is, are *you* ready for this? Is it what you want right now?" His tone was probing. He seemed to have regained his composure.

"I don't know." Tatiana's voice trembled. Once again, she looked at the unconcerned Muscovites outside the window. Oleg was right. His life would not be affected. She had to make the decision.

"I don't know, Oleg," she repeated, feeling the tears trickling down her cheeks.

I don't want to have a child with you. Not now. Not like this.

"OK, then. You think it through. I need to get going. See you at home. We can talk then." He stood up and signalled to Chip. Then he walked out of the coffee shop without looking at her.

Chapter 25

Two days later Tatiana and Oleg pulled up outside the modern building on the outskirts of the city. Oleg seemed concerned. "Are you sure about this place?" The façade decorated in blue and beige tiles looked oddly frivolous next to the gloomy brick structures from Stalin's era.

"Family Planning Clinic", read the sign above the front door.

"I am sure," said Tatiana. "It came highly recommended by the Rocket, who is a bit of a regular here, apparently." She smiled bitterly. "Thanks for driving me. I really didn't want Vasily to know. It's none of his business."

Tatiana reached for her overnight bag on the back seat.

"You don't want me to go in with you?" Oleg asked.

"No, thanks. I'll see you tomorrow." She opened her door.

"It's your call, Sunny. I'll be here at ten. Good luck." She could detect relief in his voice.

"Bye." She marched to the entrance without looking back.

After Tatiana completed the necessary forms, she checked into her room and noticed someone's bag on the bed next to hers. A quick check-up followed, during which she had to confirm that her decision was final. Then she found herself sitting on a long bench by the wall in the waiting room.

Almost all the seats were taken by young women, just like her. It was a strange gathering, all of the women dressed in home robes and slippers. They looked like a large group of friends having a slumber party. But the mood in the room was far from merry.

The women avoided looking at each other, and a few were even sobbing quietly. Every few minutes a nurse appeared and called the name of the next patient. After walking through that white double door, patients didn't come back to the waiting room. New arrivals in their cosy gowns came in, looking timid and nervous, and took the recently vacated places.

Tatiana closed her eyes and leaned back against the wall inhaling the distinctive hospital smell of antiseptic. Even through her clothes she could feel the cold and shiny tiles.

She opened her eyes and glanced at white squares. Light reflecting off their polished surface gave the room a bright, almost unbearable glare.

Those white tiles. Our first date at the swimming pool. That dazzlingly bright changing room. A different kind of anticipation. How did it lead me to this place? Tatiana shook her head at the irony.

Tatiana heard a hushed voice near her say, "I already have two, both at kindergarten. My husband got fired two weeks ago and is still looking for a job. What am I to do?" She looked in the direction from which the voice had come. A plump older woman in her thirties was trying to engage with her strained, silent neighbour.

"I know it's a sin, but it's all on me. My husband doesn't even know that I'm here. I know what he's like. 'Let's keep it,' he would say. Fool." The woman chattered nervously. "Where can I put the third one? One-bedroom flat and only my salary to live on?"

"Shut up, will you?!" came a loud cry from the other side of the room. Tatiana wanted to see who had been brave enough to interrupt the uninvited confession, but at that moment the nurse came out from the white door and called, "Isaeva." Her voice was cold and tired.

The lighting in the operating theatre was even more blinding. Tatiana squinted.

In the middle of a large space, under beaming lamps that looked like upside-down cosmic mushrooms, lay an unconscious woman with her face turned away from Tatiana. Her legs were propped up, wide open, atop shiny metal supports.

Tatiana noticed a smear of fresh blood on her thigh—bright red against milky white. Then came the sound—a horrible frosty clang of metal instruments being dropped into a steel tray. "All done here. Next."

Only now did Tatiana notice the doctor sitting between the patient's legs. The doctor was a woman. She frowned, wrinkling her forehead—the only area of face visible between her white hat and surgical mask.

Tatiana tried hard not to look at the doctor's white robe stained with drops of blood. A soft male voice urged Tatiana, "Come, lie on this bed for me." He was a tall, masked man, also dressed in white, standing by a narrow surgical table on four wheels. "I'm going to administer the anaesthetic."

Tatiana tried to walk towards the trolley, but her legs began to shake. It was like someone had put a generous smear of glue onto the soles of her silly pink slippers. Her whole body was shivering now. Her teeth started to chatter so loudly that it seemed everyone in the room could hear it.

In her peripheral vision, she caught sight of two male nurses moving their unconscious ward to another trolley and pushing her out of the theatre.

"I don't have all day. Help her!" the female doctor quipped, nodding in Tatiana's direction.

One nurse was cleaning the table while another was bringing in a new set of utensils in a sterilised tray. The anaesthetist stepped forwards and reached out his hand. "It will all be over in a few minutes. Don't worry. I'll give you something very strong and you won't feel a thing." Tatiana could hear his reassuring tone.

"OK, thank you," she whispered as her legs finally gave way. Losing consciousness, she softly sank to the floor. The last thing she registered was a strong hand catching and lifting her body.

She was travelling through a narrow tunnel. The black walls and low ceiling were covered in glimmering stars—tiny flickering lights, like the ones on a Christmas tree, only brighter. A cold wind blew the hair off her face. She was going fast. The small lights started joining up in blurred neon lines.

The wind whistled in her ears as she sped up. Rocking from side to side, she could feel the twists and turns of the track. She might be on a roller coaster—American Hill, as they called it—in the amusement park.

"Stripey! Don't be a chicken! I bought you a ticket. You're going for a ride," called Daddy.

"I'm already on it, Dad. I'm not scared."

She wanted to scream, but she couldn't make a sound. Her voice was stuck in the bottom of her throat.

"No, wait, it's not a roller coaster. It's a train cart, inside our compartment. We're on the way to Yalta on our honeymoon, and Oleg is. Oleg is—" And then she saw it, the brightest, most spectacular light right in front of her, at the end of the tunnel.

She leapt forwards to welcome the rays and felt their warm glow on her face. Her heartbeat paused in anticipation. With a dull thump, Tatiana banged her elbow on something hard and woke up.

She was lying on her side, facing a pale beige wall. A heavy, dragging ache in her lower abdomen made her groan. "Where am I? What am I doing here?"

The vision of incredible light was still so vivid that she felt a pang of sadness at losing it. Then she felt like crying.

Tears, generous and quick, began falling from her eyes. They fell easily and readily, like when she was little.

Tatiana sobbed, shaking her shoulders and burying her face in the pillow. "What's wrong with me? What am I grieving about?" She took a breath in and remembered: the clinic, the cold tiles, the doctor's frowning forehead, the pain in her tummy—deep and low.

So it's done then. It really happened. But I was wrong. I don't feel relief. I feel ... sad.

She pulled the hospital cover-up over her head.

"Hello, girlie. Are you going to lie down here all day? Come on, up you get. There's dinner for you in the canteen." A friendly voice woke Tatiana. She opened her eyes. There was the same beige wall in front of her, but the light in the room had changed. It had become soft and comforting. It reminded her of her grandmother's house—the large low-hanging lampshade over the oval table gave out the same kind of glow. It was upholstered in dark red cloth, with tiny white dots resembling the head of a giant toadstool.

"Come on, precious, help me out here." Even the intonation was Grandma's. Tatiana turned and propped herself up on her pillow. That sudden movement sent a wave of pain through her body. She winced.

"I don't want food, thank you. Can I have a glass of water?"

"Are you sure, girlie? You must be hungry. I'll bring you water and a bowl of soup then." The elderly nurse smiled. She had a wrinkly, mellow face and thin grey hair tucked up into a small bun. She probably even used a little sponge cushion to shape it—just like Grandma did.

"My name is Yevdokia Savelievna, but everyone here calls me Auntie Dunia." The nurse leaned forwards and touched Tatiana's forehead.

"You're not feverish. Good. Tell me if you want to go to the toilet. And you'll be needing one of these too." She pointed at a large sanitary pad on a side table. "You might be bleeding."

The nurse's presence was comforting. Tatiana didn't want her to leave.

"What happened to her?" Tatiana nodded towards an empty bed by the window.

"Ah, she's gone. Don't ask." Auntie Dunia shook her head in disapproval. "Good girls like you don't need to know," she said as she tucked in Tatiana's covers. "That one, she checks in every three months or so. 'Vacuum cleanse', she calls it. She must be one of those, you know, professionals. She had a mini-procedure. Not like you.

"She catches them early," she added, unable to hide the disgust in her voice.

"I'm not a good girl." Tatiana felt her eyes fill with tears again. "What did they give me?" She shook her head. "I can't stop crying. And I had the weirdest dream just before you came in."

"Ah, that would be your anaesthetic. Dr Popov is very inventive. He's handsome too," Auntie Dunia added with admiration. "He doesn't believe in heavy sedation. You are asleep but not completely unconscious. And of course you're a good girl," she said, reverting to the earlier topic. "I see so many women here every day. I can tell. We're all human and we slip sometimes. Anyway, you'll meet a nice man and you'll get married."

"I'm already married," Tatiana said quietly and looked away.

"Oh, that happens, too. It wasn't the right time. But you're so young—practically a child." Auntie Dunia's words were soft and non-judgemental.

"It's not just the wrong time. I think it might be the wrong man." Tatiana's voice lowered to a husky whisper. She suddenly gulped for air. A hot flush hit her. "I'm boiling!" She tried to kick off her covers. "Can you open the window?"

"Oh, your temperature is climbing up," said Auntie Dunia, checking Tatiana's head again and reaching into her pocket for a thermometer.

While Tatiana was waiting with the cold glass tube pressed under her armpit, the older lady sat on the edge of the bed and smiled another of her grandmotherly smiles. "Listen, girlie. I was young once. I understand. Very often, pretty little things like you fall for the wrong man. We just love the bastards. You can't dictate to your heart, as they say. But you're clever, I can tell. You'll work it out. And one day, you will become a very good mother. You'll have healthy babies. You'll love them and they will love you back."

"You think so?" Tatiana sniffled again.

"I know so." Auntie Dunia nodded. She pulled the thermometer out. "Thirty-nine point six. You have a fever. I will be back with a pill and a drink," she announced before leaving the room. "You need to rest."

The next morning, Tatiana sat in the cool, spacious doctor's office. She could still feel a dull ache, but she wasn't feverish anymore and she seemed to have regained control of her emotions.

"Bottoms off. And climb up onto that table, please," the doctor instructed. Tatiana recognised the voice and the lines on the high forehead. Without the mask and hat, in a different setting, the doctor wasn't so frightening. She was just a very tired, normal-looking middle-aged woman. Tatiana shivered when icy metal touched her flesh. She winced at the sharp pull of pain, but it was over quickly.

"Was this your first pregnancy?" the doctor asked coolly.

"Yes."

"All looks perfect here," she confirmed. "You will be able to have children in future."

"Thank you." Tatiana rolled off the table and got dressed.

"You can go now," the woman concluded formally.

"Bye." Tatiana tried to make eye contact with the doctor, but the latter was scribbling something on a sheet of paper and didn't raise her head. Tatiana hurried to the door.

"Tatiana Nikolaevna," the doctor's voice called after her as she reached for the handle, "I sincerely hope not to see you here again for the same reason. Ever."

Outside the clinic door, Oleg was waiting for his wife. He looked nervous. He rushed towards Tatiana the second he saw her coming out.

"How did it go? How are you feeling?"

"I'm OK. Let's just get out of here," she said, passing her bag to him and ignoring his open arms.

"You look pale," said Oleg inside the car. He seemed concerned.

"Of course, Oleg, I look like crap. I've had surgery, but I don't want to talk about it," she snapped.

"I understand. I'm sorry," he said softly. "Oh, I forgot. These are for you." He reached behind and pulled out a big arrangement of red carnations in a fancy wicker basket.

"They're lovely. Thank you. Very thoughtful of you," Tatiana said with an artificial smile. "Can we please go home now? I need to rest."

"Of course. I'll get you there as quick as I can." He started the ignition.

The image of Vlad's coffin covered in the same scarlet buds floated out of Tatiana's memory. *Of all the flowers, Oleg had chosen these.*

Blood and death. How fitting.

Chapter 26

"One for the road and I'm out of here." Mikko kneeled down in front of the glass coffee table and inhaled noisily. After that he jumped up to his feet and pushed a rolled-up hundred-dollar bill into his breast pocket.

"My lucky one," he said, tapping his chest playfully. "Right over my heart." He glanced at his watch. "Damn, I must shoot. I'm on air in less than two hours. Thanks for the fix, mate." Mikko patted Tatiana on the head cheerfully. "Did you want a chaser yourself?"

"No, thanks. I'm good." Tatiana sat cross-legged atop Grandpa Ilya's green sofa. Her eyes were closed and her right hand was beating an energetic rhythm on the half-empty whisky glass she held in her left.

"Yeah, I'd say you're properly wasted." Mikko gave her a surveying look. "You've had enough of that, too." He took the glass from her hand. "Whisky and cocaine is a heady cocktail." He chuckled. "Say hi to your cute husband from me." He picked up his trusty shoulder bag.

"In your dreams!" Tatiana swung her legs off the sofa and stood up. She began pacing up and down the room, opening the curtains and moving the chairs around. "Besides, there is a chance you'll see him first, anyway. I never know when he's going to grace me with his presence."

"That makes two of us!" Mikko let out a theatrical sigh. "Oleg Isaev. So near and yet so far."

"Get out of here, diva!" Tatiana threw a small cushion in Mikko's direction. "Don't make your fans wait."

She had uncovered Mikko's secret unexpectedly, about two weeks earlier.

After Tatiana had recovered from the operation, Oleg suggested that she busy herself with a project besides her dissertation. He gave her the green light to revamp Grandfather's apartment, make it more her own. She'd hired a decorator. Within a week, the place was transformed. The walls and ceilings were painted, the kitchen and bathroom remodelled.

Tatiana hadn't had the heart to throw out the furniture, although Oleg hadn't felt quite so sentimental. He'd said, "You can scrap the lot of it—pile of old junk." But Tatiana had only banished the bulky dining table, replacing it with a fashionable glass one. In the kitchen, too, she had kept the faithful old fridge. She could swear it grumbled gratefully every time she walked in. The newest large-screen TV and music system were the last things installed.

"Hmm, Soviet retro. I like it," Mikko had declared on his first visit.

They had bumped into each other earlier that day at Moscow's newest "in" bar. Part of a well-known theatre in the city centre, its enterprising director had decided to keep the bar open all day long to bring in some extra cash for his productions. The bar had quickly become the latest place to hang. Thanks to regular live jazz, it attracted a wide spectrum of clientele—performing arts connoisseurs, businessmen from nearby offices, production teams from a neighbouring TV station, students of all kinds, and a few bored rich housewives. In other words, anyone who felt more comfortable about consuming alcohol at inappropriate hours of the day within the walls of a cultural institution patronised the bar.

Tatiana warmed up to the place. It resonated perfectly with

her current mood. The dark interiors and blackened windows provided her with shelter from the ridiculously joyful April sun. That day, she was quietly enjoying her second vodka Martini at the tiny round table inside an alcove when she heard a familiar monotonous voice.

"Oh, there you are, chick! Why are you hiding in that corner?" Tatiana glanced around in search of whomever that question was addressed to. There was no one else sitting nearby. She turned and looked over her shoulder. Mikko stood behind her wearing his customary dark shades. She couldn't tell if he was looking at her.

It must be a mistake. He doesn't even know me.

She turned back and lifted her glass to take another sip.

Mikko slid into the chair in front of her. "Hi," he said, his black shades staring right at her face. "I don't think we've been formerly introduced. I'm Mikko. I work for your husband, technically speaking."

"Hi." Tatiana eyed him suspiciously. "Tatiana. Nice to meet you."

"Do you mind if I join you? I'm here for a drink before I go on air."

"Sure." Tatiana nodded, still puzzled. They chatted for a while. In real life, Mikko turned out to be just as witty and amusing as he was on stage and screen. His facial expressions changed very little, making his dry deadpan humour all the more funny.

"Listen, chick, I've got a bit of time left. What do you say we go to your place and continue with our impromptu party?" With that, Mikko pulled out a tiny paper packet from his wallet. He held it out between his two fingers and gave Tatiana a meaningful nod. The three vodka Martinis and engaging conversation had given her a buzz. Although she had never taken drugs before, this seemed like the perfect moment to give it a try. Mikko was the ideal partner for it.

He's so tall and well groomed and smart. I'd like to kiss him. Tatiana licked her lips dreamily.

Once inside Grandpa's apartment, and still basking in Mikko's compliments on her decorating efforts, Tatiana had to face a double disappointment. First, cocaine gave her an immediate nosebleed and made her feel very jittery. Instead of falling into a tranquil, forgetful state as she'd hoped, her brain had tried frantically to focus on many things at once.

Second, when she'd expected Mikko to try and make a move on her, he had struck her with a startling confession—he fancied her husband, and had done so for months.

Even intoxicated, Tatiana struggled with that revelation. Reserved and cool, Mikko didn't even slightly resemble the many homosexual men she'd met in her life—flamboyant fashion designers, popular hairstylists, famous pop singers. They were all very glitzy and slightly, well, feminine.

"Yup, it's not public knowledge." Mikko sighed. "And let's keep it this way, shall we? It won't do my career any favours."

"But why did you tell me?" Tatiana asked. "Did I need to know?"

"There is something about you, chick. I've been watching you. You seem like the right person to open my heart to. And you happen to be married to the man of my dreams," Mikko replied.

"I got married to the man of my dreams," she said bitterly. "But it seems that I live with someone else. Dreams should stay just that: dreams."

"Oh, a bit deep for this hour of the day." He flicked the tip of her nose. "See you soon, chick. Ciao!" Tatiana heard the energetic slam of her front door.

Since then, Mikko had appeared regularly at Grandpa's apartment on his way to the TV station, always armed with a little white package.

Tatiana began to suspect that he just used her company to share a line or two or to openly declare his love for Oleg, but she didn't mind.

Lusting after a gay man! Oh well, I might as well, as pathetic as I am.

After the visit to the clinic, Tatiana had changed. On the surface, she appeared just the same—young, pretty, smart. But that was not how she felt inside. Her self-loathing had reached a new level.

Worthless baby killer. You deserve a cheating husband. You deserve to be alone.

Oleg, as usual, was too busy with his eventful life to take any notice of his wife. Whisky and Mikko's white packages made Tatiana's life slightly more bearable. Now he was gone to face the cameras while she was still sitting on the sofa, tuning in to the emptiness inside her chest.

The low grumble of a telephone ringing made her jump. She had completely forgotten that there was one in the flat, so seldom had anyone called there. Even the vintage green phone with a chip in the dialling disk seemed surprised to discover it had a voice.

"Hello?" Tatiana concentrated hard on sounding sober.

"Isaeva, where've you been? I've been trying all your numbers—your dacha, your parents. Finally I find you here!" Lena shouted.

"Oh, hi there! Sorry, I've been working on my dissertation. How's yours going?" Tatiana replied in a cheery voice.

"Isaeva, cut the crap. You're drunk. I can hear it."

"Sorry, what did you say? The line is so bad. Can I call you back?" Tatiana tried to wrap up what was an unpleasant interrogation. She hadn't spoken to Lena in a while and had resolved not to tell her about the operation.

"What's happened? Don't hide from me. I know something's up."

Tatiana could hear concern in her friend's voice. "No, seriously, I'm fine, Lena. Let's talk in person. You said you were coming soon?"

"I did, but I got stuck here with a new contract and a new course. I'm flying over in two weeks' time. I'll only have three days though. I need to meet with my tutor. I've managed to almost finish my thesis. I hope to spend all the evenings with you. You better be ready for me!"

"Yes, sure. That would be great! Got to go now. Bye!" Tatiana hurried to slam the receiver down. The old phone tinkled resentfully.

Chapter 27

"Sunny, you look terrible!" Oleg stated, tucking a starched napkin inside the collar of his polo shirt. "This is a divine-looking plate of pasta. Just smell these morels! They're in season, I'm told."

"Thanks for the compliment, Oleg." Tatiana pursed her lips and picked up her fork. "Smells good, but these are really ugly-looking mushrooms."

Tatiana and Oleg were sitting on the terrace of a newly opened restaurant in the middle of a pretty glade near their almost-finished house. It was a rare Sunday afternoon when Oleg wasn't dashing to some emergency talk in Moscow or to meet their two pretentious interior designers. Instead, he graciously treated Tatiana to a tête-à-tête lunch at this new local spot.

"You're very pale and you've lost weight," he continued, studying Tatiana from behind his mirrored glasses. "Eat up!"

"I'm not hungry." Tatiana played with a few strings of pasta on her plate. Her lips began trembling.

"A glass of good red wine, that's what you need." Oleg seemed impartial to her obvious state. "Wine list, please." He clicked his fingers, addressing the waiter." I know, you need a break!" he continued merrily. "A nice little trip will do the trick. You've been working so hard, and your health—" He waved his hand instead of finishing the sentence. "I want to treat you to one," he concluded.

"A trip? Where?" Instantly, Tatiana was reminded of Lena's arrival in a few days' time. Perhaps getting away from an inevitable inquisition was a good idea.

"New York, Sunny. The city that never sleeps." Oleg's voice got louder. Other people on the terrace paused over their plates, pretending not to listen.

This part of the show is for the audience, not for me.

"Sounds great," she said enthusiastically, choosing to play along. "I've never been to New York. But what about an American visa—they're hard to get, aren't they?"

"Not to worry, Sun. It's all been arranged. It will be ready in a couple of days," Oleg concluded boastfully.

Tatiana lowered her voice. "Are we going together? What about your visa?" The diners returned attention to their food.

"Of course I have a visa, but I can't go this time." Oleg sent a forkful of pasta into his mouth.

"Oh, a solo flight for me then." Tatiana took a sip of water.

"No, of course not. Irina will keep you company."

"Oh, please, not her! She struggles to remember my name half the time. Can't it be someone else?"

"You're missing the point." Oleg finished chewing and dropped his voice to a whisper. "I need you to go with her. Do some sightseeing, shopping, whatever. My ties with Maks will be even stronger. We're together in this for the long run. The future looks good, but we need to be as close as a family. It helps business. So, be friends with Irina. It's all I ask from you. Is it too much?"

"OK, Oleg, I'll do my best," she replied quietly.

I can certainly manage that arrogant harpy for a few days. I need to miss Lena's visit.

"Good girl. Now eat. At least half of it."

Chapter 28

After a few long beeps that seemed like an eternity, someone on the other end picked up the phone. "Hello," said a coarse male voice, as if the word wasn't a greeting but a hostile challenge.

"Good morning," Tatiana said politely in Russian. "I'm looking for Alex. Is this the right number for him?"

"And who are you?" the voice questioned.

"Just a friend from Moscow. Tatiana. I'm here in New York," she replied clearly.

"And how did you get my number, Tatiana from Moscow?" the old man continued. He spoke with a distinct Odessa accent.

"Actually, Alex gave it to me before he left for Israel. He said he wanted to end up in America. We've lost touch. I'm trying to track him down."

"Why are you here? Have you emigrated? Are you looking for help? A job?" Alex's uncle didn't give in.

"No. I'm just here on a short visit with my friend. I'm staying in a hotel in Manhattan."

"Oh, rich girl!" The old man chuckled and then coughed. "You must be Oleg's wife. Sorry. Alex didn't tell me your name." His tone had become friendlier.

He must get poor relatives looking for a favour all the time.

"Yes. I'm married to Oleg. So can you tell me where to find Alex?"

"Oh, my lovely girl, I wish I knew myself. He took off months ago. Last time we talked, it was New Year's Eve. He called me from the West Coast—Los Angeles, I think. He said he was travelling through there—Nevada, Utah ... God knows." The old man was wheezing now.

"OK. Thank you," Tatiana cut in politely. "If he calls you again, please say a big hello from me."

"I will, Tatiana," he rasped. "And come visit us in Brighton Beach sometime."

"I will one day. Goodbye." Tatiana put the receiver down.

It looks like I won't see Alex this time. It'll be impossible to trace him if he doesn't want to be found.

She turned off the tap of the sunken bath. Their suite may have been huge, but she hadn't wanted Irina to overhear her conversation with Alex's uncle.

Tatiana had never stayed in such luxury before. Before entering the lobby of the narrow tower opposite Central Park, she had mistakenly thought that the five-star hotels in London were opulent. But everything in this place was vivaciously over the top.

Their suite on the top floor had a lounge, a dining room, and two sumptuous bedrooms. The interiors were unashamedly decadent, with blue and pink silks and satins, silver-leaf-covered chairs, Murano glass mirrors, crystal chandeliers, and perfect-looking flowers. Oversized pink peonies and powder-blue hydrangeas in neat arrangements were dotted everywhere, while towers of multicoloured macaroons and exotic fruits on silver stands topped every single table, all in quantities that were simply unimaginable for two people to eat. Even Tatiana's en-suite marble bathroom had a big window that overlooked the famous park outside.

When Tatiana and Irina had first checked in, Tatiana heard the receptionist say to Irina, "Welcome back, Mrs Polonskaya!"

Then the receptionist, wearing a chocolate-coloured suit, had beamed them an American megawatt smile. Tatiana thought he was at risk of tearing his facial muscles. "Will Mr Polonksiy be joining you this time?"

"No, Rob, but Maks says hello." Irina had pinned a hundred-dollar bill to the polished countertop with her vampire-red nails. Pushing it towards the receptionist, she'd narrowed her eyes. "And he wants you to look after us." Irina's English was heavily burdened by her Russian accent.

"Always my pleasure, ma'am," replied the man, effortlessly sweeping the note into his pocket. Then he ceremoniously announced, "Ladies, as our very special guests, the hotel has the pleasure of upgrading you to our only Presidential Suite."

"Why, thank you. I hope it's better than the dark prison cell you tried to put us in last time!" Irina shook her finger at Rob.

Inside the small, old-fashioned elevator, Tatiana had been astonished to discover a plump, old black woman in a hotel uniform. "Which floor, ma'am?" she asked formally.

"Twenty-eight," replied Irina, handing out a folded green banknote.

"Thank you, ma'am," the woman said as she pressed the button.

"Do they think the guests are too dumb to use the lift on their own?" Tatiana had mused in Russian when all three of them were standing inside the claustrophobic cabin. "Is this her job, to ride up and down all day long?" she asked Irina.

"It's a tradition, I think, and another way of collecting tips." Irina had shrugged her shoulders dismissively.

Once inside the suite, Irina expressed her approval. "I like it!" she announced, nodding her head. She picked a giant purple grape from one of the fruit arrangements and popped it into her red mouth. "Check out this view, Kitty!"

Kitty? I bet she's already forgotten my name.

"It's incredible," said Tatiana. She was still in shock at the size of their accommodation. Tatiana could see the green mass of Central Park and, around it, the tall Manhattan buildings lined up on parallel and perpendicular streets.

She glanced at the jogging map she'd picked up at reception. It resembled a computer-generated spreadsheet with streets and avenues named by their numbers. It looked nothing like the maps of the old European cities she'd visited. Their layouts resembled spiderwebs, the roads crawling out around a focal point—a fortress or a cathedral—all of them having been woven over the centuries.

Irina knocked on Tatiana's bedroom door. "Let's go down. I'm starving."

They sat at a round table underneath a blue sky that was painted onto the domed ceiling. The walls of this grand, circular room were covered in Roman murals depicting columns, vines, and antique goddesses.

"Pretty, isn't it?" said Irina. Before Tatiana could reply, Irina waved her fingers. "We'll have your legendary afternoon tea!" she instructed a Hispanic-looking waiter who had materialised at their table in a split second.

"But, ma'am," he said, hesitating, "it's nine o'clock in the morning. Breakfast is being served right now."

"It may be nine o'clock to you, but it's five in the afternoon for us. Don't they call it five o'clock tea?" Irina raised her voice condescendingly.

"And we'll have a bottle of this with it." Irina pointed to the bottom of the page titled "Champagne". Tatiana could swear she saw four figures in the price column.

The waiter grinned and nodded. "Certainly, ma'am. I'll find out how long it will take to prepare your tea."

"You see? Easy," Irina said to Tatiana in Russian.

When they were brought a tiered tower of finger sandwiches and tiny cakes, Irina continued her solo performance. "Kitty, what's your plan for the immediate future?" Before Tatiana could answer, she continued. "I'm opening a modern art gallery back home. Maks thought it might keep me busy. He's bought me a nice space on the embankment.

"It used to be a furniture shop, but now it's called simply 'Irina'. I'm renovating it. Why don't you come and work with me?"

"Sounds wonderful, thanks. But I don't know the first thing about modern art," Tatiana replied, declining politely.

"Oh, silly thing. You don't need to know much. You learn on the job. Just imagine all the men! Young and promising artists. And all the art collectors—businessmen, bankers, Hollywood stars. Think of all the champagne receptions we can throw!" Irina took a large sip from her crystal flute, inviting Tatiana to join her.

Tatiana resisted the urge to wrinkle her nose at the hit of yeasty bubbles. "I think I need to talk to Oleg first," she mumbled.

"Surely he'd be happy for you to busy yourself. Maks can't wait to get me off his back."

"Oh, I don't know. Is it going to be good for our family life? We already don't see enough of each other." Tatiana picked a tiny lemon cake from the stand.

"Rubbish! You won't see any more of him anyway. The boys are busy. They like it that way—to play with their toys. So let's play with ours!" Irina was getting tipsy.

"I'm not sure I like it this way," Tatiana started to protest.

"Grow up. That's how it is. They're men. They can't help it. It's in their nature. They need to play around. I know Maks does. But as long as I don't see it, I couldn't care less. They're young now, but when this doesn't work anymore"—Irina made a lewd gesture—"they'll come back to us crawling. In the meantime, we can have our fun too." She winked.

"But I want to have children. How will that work? I'd like their father to be around!" blurted Tatiana.

"Who said you can't have children? I have a daughter. Sonechka. Beautiful girl. She's four. I'll show you a picture. I have one up in the room."

"I didn't know." Tatiana struggled to imagine Irina as a mother. "I've never seen her."

"Because she's too small to travel. She stays at home. She's got everything she needs—a Russian nanny who feeds and spoils her, and a strict Australian governess who teaches her English and other stuff. You see? Simple. And Maks is proud to have her."

Tatiana tried and failed to imagine ice-cold Maks cuddling his little girl.

"OK, Kitty," Irina concluded with one of her dazzling smiles, "let's go. We'll begin your art education now, starting with MoMA. Then later we can pay a visit to my dear jeweller on Park Avenue. He's got something pretty fabulous for us. Let's make the boys pay for their sins!" Irina signalled to the waiter: "Check, please!"

On their last night in the sleepless city, the two women sat in the smoky hotel bar. Tatiana's feet were aching from following Irina around as she trawled the boutiques and department stores on Fifth Avenue. Closing her eyes, she could still picture the steady flow of yellow streaming up and down the wide streets. It seemed the whole of Manhattan travelled by taxicab.

"Oh, these are torture," said Tatiana, looking down at the skyscraper heels Irina had made her buy. Despite the almost unbearable discomfort, she hated to admit that they did make her legs look pretty good. "And this is definitely too short," she complained, trying to pull down the stretchy black lace of the new cocktail dress. "Oleg would kill me if he saw me wearing this!" That last comment brought her a strange satisfaction. She smiled.

"You look fantastic, Kitty," said Irina, signalling to the waiter for another glass of pink champagne. Tatiana refused and ordered a whisky and Coke instead.

"You need to loosen up and be naughty sometimes," Irina declared. During the past three days, Tatiana had found Irina's company almost tolerable. She'd learned to handle her companion's outbursts of self-adoration and urge to spread her own brand of wisdom.

"Behind you. At the bar," Irina whispered, making round eyes. "Don't look now. There is a handsome guy in a tux checking us out."

Tatiana glanced over her shoulder. At the same time, a dark-haired man turned his head and caught her eye.

"Saw you! I told you not to look!" Irina sniggered. They both laughed. "Shh, he's coming over!" She shook her perfect platinum bob.

"Good evening, ladies." The stranger showed his white teeth. "Do you mind if I join you? It's completely lonely over there." He nodded towards the empty bar. "The bartender is OK company, but I'm sure yours will be so much better. But please tell me to get lost if I'm intruding. I'm Luc."

"Oh! Luc? Nice to meet you. Irina. And this is Tatiana." Irina waved her hand playfully before placing it under her chin. "Now tell us everything about you so we can decide whether to banish you or not."

"OK. That's fair, I guess. But if I stay, you have to tell me everything about your beautiful selves." Luc waved at the barman. "Another round of whatever the ladies are having, please, and put it on my bill."

"I'm from Zurich," Luc began. "I work for a large investment bank."

"But you speak like an American." Irina showed off her knowledge of the accents.

"Yes, that's true. I went to school over here. And I'm currently staying at this fine establishment in a small room on the tenth floor, unlike you ladies." Luc pointed at their room key on the table. "You probably have a royal suite stretching over an entire floor."

"Not royal. Presidential, actually." Irina sipped her champagne. "We may even show it to you if you behave."

She's already drunk. God help us.

Tatiana began to study the man on the chair next to her. He was so close that she could smell his fresh woody scent and feel the heat of his lean athletic body.

"I'm in New York for a charity event—one of my clients organised it. Hence the penguin suit. I had to supervise the auction." Reading puzzlement on the women's faces, Luc added, "It's basically a bunch of drunk wealthy people showing off to each other by bidding on things they don't need. All for a good cause." Luc shook his head.

Tatiana, finding him to be amusing, felt at ease in his company. This was a man who looked entirely different from any Russian businessman or banker. He wore a tiny silver stud in his ear and resembled a rock star or an actor with his black hair in a small ponytail. He had a habit of tucking the unruly shiny strings behind his ear and smoothing them down with his open palm.

Luc spoke like he hadn't a care in the world, and he laughed readily like a child, throwing his head back and showing two rows of pearly teeth. When he stretched his long legs to one side, Tatiana noticed his socks: bright purple with red dots.

After the third round of drinks, Luc carefully laid his large palm on Tatiana's knee. The warmth from his skin radiated through her body, making her tingle.

She didn't object.

"So, have I qualified to be taken upstairs?" His brown eyes shone earnestly.

"Hmm, I think you passed the test," Tatiana said teasingly, holding his stare. "What would you say, Irina?"

"I say, let's continue this party in our room." Irina stood up and wobbled on her heels. "Oops!" She laughed loudly.

Irina and Tatiana sat next to each other on the palatial silk settee in the living room of their suite, giggling like schoolgirls.

"Kitty, he's so hot!" Irina spoke in Russian in a loud, drunken whisper. "Swiss banker, and so handsome. No one will ever know. I'll take it with me to the grave!" She put her index finger to her lips.

"Don't get excited. Maybe he's not interested. Maybe we'll just sit here and chat." Tatiana shrugged her shoulders.

"Ladies, a nightcap." Luc walked towards them carrying

three rocks glasses. "I happened to spot this fine bourbon in your bar and took the liberty of pouring some for us. You have to try it—it's really smooth."

With her glass in hand, Irina tried to get up. "I'm going to my room. Leaving you two alone. I need to lie down."

"Only after you finish your drink!" Luc insisted. They sat for a few moments in awkward silence, sipping their bourbon.

"OK, now I'm off." Irina finally succeeded in standing up from the sofa. "You made me drunk, you scoundrel!" she proclaimed. "It was nice to meet you, handsome Luc." She sauntered towards the door, managing to sway her hips in exaggerated waves.

"Where are you off to, Russian Marilyn? Why don't you stay and join us, perhaps?" He gave her an ambiguous smile.

"Hmm, maybe. Later." Irina stopped and turned to face them. She wiggled her behind and blew them a kiss, closing one eye. Tatiana could tell that Luc's comparison had made Irina's day.

Just don't sing "Happy birthday, Mr President"!

When the door behind her closed, Luc shifted up the sofa, moving closer to Tatiana, and put an arm around her waist. "So, princess," he whispered passionately into her ear. "Now we're alone. What would you like me to do to you?" He planted a gentle kiss just above her lip.

"I don't know." Tatiana gasped, feeling electric currents zipping through her body. "I want to leave it up to you."

She moved closer to his chest. Luc started slowly caressing her inner thigh with his free hand. "As the princess wishes," he breathed into her ear. "God, you're beautiful."

His lips found hers. Tatiana opened her mouth, letting his tongue in. It felt so wrong, but at the same time so enticing and necessary, that she closed her eyes and leaned forwards, helping his fingers to find the zipper at her back.

Take this, Oleg. Taste your own medicine! Look what you made me do. I might regret it tomorrow, but I am curious: can I be like you? I need to go through with this.

I want to.

Chapter 29

"Tatiana, get up! Now! We've been robbed!" Irina's muffled scream reached Tatiana's ears from the far boundaries of her consciousness.

She used my name. Must be serious.

Her eyelids seemed to be laden with lead. She had to use her fingers to pry them open. She registered a dull headache and a strange metallic taste in her mouth.

Tatiana was lying on the hotel bed, fully dressed. The new shoes stood neatly arranged on the floor next to her.

Strange. I managed to put away my shoes nicely but not to undress or get under the cover.

She stretched her stiff body, desperately trying to recollect what had happened the night before. The headache was intensifying, but the memory seemed to have gone.

"Check what you're missing!" Irina stormed in, looking delirious, wrapped in a hotel bathrobe. Her make-up was badly smudged over her face, and she was sporting a large lilac bump on her forehead. "What did that bastard take?" she shouted.

For a second, Tatiana thought that Irina was losing her mind, but then the image of bright purple socks and a tanned hand up her thigh made her shudder. Automatically she touched her earlobe. "My earrings," she mumbled. "And my watch, and the bracelet," she said, looking at her wrist.

"Anything else? Check again!" Irina was frantically pacing the room. "My jewellery is gone and the cash from my purse. Not much, two grand or so. But," she said while posing, holding her finger up, "he didn't open the safe—and that's where I put the rest of the money, our passports, and the new necklaces we bought."

When Tatiana got up, she felt the room spin. Catching her balance, she reached for the water bottle. After a few gulps, she regained her focus. She came closer to study Irina's bump.

"Are you hurt?"

"Ah, it's nothing. I wasn't favoured enough to be put on the bed. Woke up on the floor this morning. Must have hit the side table on my way down. What a bastard! He must be a pro! He must have put something into that bourbon. That's why he insisted on us drinking it!"

Tatiana walked into the bathroom. She found her old sun-and-moon necklace and her simple gold wedding band on top of the vanity unit. Luc clearly hadn't deemed them valuable enough.

How nice of him—he left me my memories.

Returning to the bedroom, she asked, "What do we do now? Shall we call the police?"

"Are you crazy?! You want to tell the cops what happened last night? Maybe you should call your husband too? Tell him that you were robbed by the guy you'd taken to your room to have sex with. And did you, by the way?" Irina crossed her arms.

"Did I what, sleep with him?" Tatiana quipped with irritation. "Well, I can't remember. I was drugged like you. But I'm fully dressed and wearing tights, so I'd say no, I don't think so."

How dare she talk to me like that, like it wasn't her suggestion to bring him up to the room in the first place!

"Oh, Kitty, let's try to calm down." Irina put her hands up as a sign of peace. "Crap happens. No police. We have to get it together and check out now—we can't miss our flight. We'll figure out what to tell the boys on the way. I'm thinking Maks won't even notice I'm missing a few things. And if he does, I'll just tell him that they were stolen from my handbag at the airport."

Downstairs at the reception desk, a smiling Rob was preparing their bill.

"Ah, thank you, Rob." Irina kept adjusting her fringe to make sure it covered her bruise. "We met a gentleman last night who said he was staying on the tenth floor," she continued casually. "Is it possible to leave him a message?"

"Certainly. What is the gentleman's name?"

"Luc, with a *c*."

"And his surname?" Rob smiled politely.

"I can't remember," Irina stated. "He is tall, tanned, with dark hair and a ponytail."

"I can't recall any guest matching the description," Rob replied. "I am not supposed to, but I can check the guest list." He began scrolling down his monitor. "There is no one with first name Luc, I'm afraid. Is there anything else I can help you with?"

"No, that's OK. Just give us the bill, please. We're in a hurry." Irina nodded to Tatiana as if to say, "I knew it."

"Hey, look at our bar tab from last night," she said in Russian. "The bastard didn't even pay for our drinks—he put them on our room. Ooh, he was slick." She presented her credit card with a folded hundred-dollar bill tucked underneath it to the grinning Rob.

By the time the women boarded their plane, Irina was acting as if the Luc episode had never happened. Tatiana had mixed feelings about it. She didn't appreciate looking like an idiot who had been taken advantage of.

Not so much of a princess, after all. He fancied my diamonds more than he fancied me!

But on the other hand she was relieved. She didn't fancy

the sensation of being used for sex. *I guess one-night stands are not for me.*

Tatiana flicked through the options on the small screen in front of her and chose a pre-recorded news channel. Sinking deeper into the wide seat in first class, she put on the headphones. "Former casino maintenance engineer Mr Cong-Rodriguez in connection with complaints from a number of Las Vegas casinos ..."

The impeccably dressed American newsreader had a face like a mature Barbie doll. Tatiana was studying her far too perfect features, only half listening.

"...wish to question Mr Cong-Rodriguez after a number of slot machines were found to be landing on an unusually high proportion of winning combinations, resulting in a loss for several Nevada State establishments ..."

The man in the blurred black-and-white photograph had a small goatee and dreadlocks. Tatiana looked closer at the screen and laughed.

I would recognise you anywhere, "Mr Cong-Rodriguez"! What a name you've chosen! Looks like you've managed to break that system after all, to crack their winning combinations! I guess you're living your dream.

She felt a tiny stab of jealousy.

Good luck to them in finding you, Mr Zero! Number Twenty-Three won't tell a soul.

Chapter 30

"Honey, I'm home!" Oleg shouted in English, imitating a catchphrase from the movies. His enthusiasm bounced off the empty walls of their new house.

"I'll be down in a minute," Tatiana called back, trying to match his excitement. Over the past few weeks, Oleg had been returning early from work.

Ever since their house had been finished, he had thrown himself into organising his private sanctuary—the study and music studio.

Oleg spent countless hours arranging and rearranging his books, records, and posters. A beautiful white grand piano took prime position in the centre of the music room. Often at night, when Tatiana was struggling to fall asleep, she would hear the distant tinkle of keys.

Oleg was in his element, playing his favourite songs and finding time to compose new ones. He seemed so content and happy that Tatiana envied him. Her husband's life seemed to be a graph, with "Time" and "Achievement" steadily rising across it in a diagonal line.

The only time in the past month when Tatiana herself had felt great without the use of her usual stimulants was the day of her thesis presentation. The hard work had paid off. After overcoming her nerves, she'd delivered a confident speech outlining the main points of her subject.

When Tatiana was finished speaking, she looked at the three professors at the long, red-velvet-covered table and an almost forgotten feeling came over her. She was finally proud of herself.

When her university mentor began to talk, she understood by his warm, welcoming tone that she had managed to pull it off. The committee was impressed with Tatiana's thesis on Tolstoy's linguistic style. She passed with excellence.

But that feeling of triumph had faded soon after, and her burning question of what to do next still remained. She tried to push it away.

Tatiana boycotted the graduation ceremony to avoid bumping into Lena. She told the university she wasn't well.

After Tatiana's deliberate escape to New York, it looked like her friend had gotten the message. A few weeks after returning from the trip, Tatiana had plucked up the courage to tell her husband Irina's version of the story about the airport robbery.

"Why didn't you tell me before?" Oleg raised an eyebrow.

"I was embarrassed. And I wasn't sure how you'd take it, Oleg," Tatiana replied insecurely.

"My reaction. Hmm." Oleg looked cross. "How about," he said in a threatening voice before pausing, "we go shopping this weekend and replace all that was stolen?" He roared with laughter, looking at Tatiana's mortified expression.

"Ha! Got you! You should see your face, Sunny!"

Tatiana stood in silence, not knowing how to react.

"I couldn't care less about those little things! You'll get bigger and better diamonds. We just had a fantastic week, and I want to treat my wife."

"Really, Oleg? Congratulations! But you don't have to buy me more things." Tatiana lowered her eyes, overcome by guilt.

He was in such an upbeat mood, she didn't want to shake it. The business was moving forwards, and the house—his pride and joy—had been completed on schedule. Tatiana would never dare tell him she didn't like it. For her, it was too big, too bare.

The rooms with high palatial ceilings were so vast that the regular-size furniture inside them looked small and lost. It felt as if the house had been designed for a fairy-tale giant.

Tatiana's things were still piled in numerous suitcases inside her personal dressing room. She had yet to unpack, politely refusing Natasha's offer of help.

"I'm still deciding where everything will go," she'd explained.

Natasha had responded with an agitated whirr of the vacuum cleaner. She was obviously keen on putting the house in order.

Where does she find dust three times a day? Tatiana wondered, aimlessly roaming through the empty rooms and corridors. She could hear the hollow sounds of her own footsteps resounding off the polished marble floors.

The phone rang on Saturday morning, when she and Oleg were getting dressed to hit the city for the promised shopping spree.

"Stripey, it's your grandmother—she's in hospital." Tatiana could detect concern in her father's voice. "She had an accident—fell down the stairs to the cellar."

"Is she OK, Dad? When did this happen?"

"Yesterday. She's broken her hip, but she's in high spirits, according to her doctor. I've just spoken to the hospital. She's a fighter, your grandma!" Nikolai Ivanovich said with conviction.

"Which hospital is she in? I'll be there as soon as I can." Tatiana was overcome with worry.

"That could be problematic, Stripey. She was in her country house, so they took her to the Central Hospital in Tula."

"It's OK, Dad. I'll come today." Tatiana was adamant. "Are you and Mum going?"

"We're leaving to catch the train now."

"Wait. Let's go together. I have a car. I can pass by and pick you up. See you in a hour!" Tatiana put the phone down and turned to Oleg. "It's my grandmother. She's in hospital. Sorry, I need to go. Can I take Vasily?"

"Of course, no problem." Oleg agreed immediately. "If there's anything that Maria Petrovna needs, just let me know. Make sure she gets the best care. I can make some calls. We can transfer her to Moscow." Oleg glanced at his pager. "I'll be in a meeting with Maks if you need me. Page me."

"OK, thank you. I will. See you tonight." Tatiana shook her head.

His plans have changed instantly! We were to spend the day together ...

After a quick search through her boxes, she changed into comfortable jeans and trainers and then raced down the polished stairs in search of Vasily.

Chapter 31

Tatiana's grandmother's ward was light-filled and spacious. It occupied the top floor of the modern inpatients' building. Tula's Central Hospital was built on a prime spot near the train station. Behind the original white mansion with neoclassical columns lay a mature, leafy park. The hospital had been built in the nineteenth century, thanks to generous donations from the public. The elegant building belonged to a time when Tula was still a flourishing industrial town, world-renowned for its gunsmiths and ironmongers.

Over the years, unassuming and functional buildings had been added on to the hospital, but the extensive park remained its most prominent feature. On that warm summer day it was basking in sunshine. The place looked tranquil and comforting.

"What a beautiful park you have here, Grandma! I'll take you down when you feel better!" Sitting by the bedside, Tatiana reached for her grandmother's hand. It felt small, dry, and frail. She found it strange to see the tireless Maria Petrovna in this still environment—motionless and covered up to her chin with a washed-out duvet that had a hospital ink stamp on it.

Grandma's skin looked almost yellow against the white of the pillow, and her lovely round face seemed to have shrunk, making her once stub nose stick out from hollow cheeks.

Fighting the lump in her throat, Tatiana continued cheerfully. “Mum and Dad are downstairs talking to your doctor. They’ll be up soon. I’ve brought you some fruit yogurt. Shall I feed you?”

“Tanyusha, I’m so happy to see you. You didn’t have to come all this way for me.” Maria Petrovna smiled kindly. Her warm voice was unchanged. “I’ll get better soon, you’ll see. They’ve promised us a hot summer. There will be plenty of cherries in the garden, so I’ll make you your favourite cherry dumplings and jam.”

“Maybe you want a drink, Grandma? I’ve got a juice carton with a straw.” Tatiana reached for the shopping bag.

“Thank you, my darling. I don’t want anything.” Grandma shook her head.

“But you should eat—to get your strength back,” Tatiana insisted.

“Don’t worry. I’ll be back on my feet in no time, you’ll see.” Maria Petrovna gently clasped Tatiana’s hand. “Take all this fancy food back with you, Tanyusha. I’m not used to it, and there’s no fridge here anyway—it will get spoiled. Tell me, how’s Oleg doing these days?” She looked searchingly into Tatiana’s face.

“Oh, he’s fine. Busy as usual. We’ve moved to the new house now. You’ll come and visit us, won’t you?” Tatiana smiled.

“Of course I will.” Maria Petrovna nodded faintly.

“Oh, actually, Oleg’s offered to transfer you to hospital in Moscow if you’d like—the very best. We can arrange an ambulance to take you,” Tatiana said, remembering her earlier conversation with her husband.

Maria Petrovna shook her head. “Say thank you from me, but I’m not going anywhere. The doctors here are just as good. Did you know that I met your grandfather at this hospital, right after the war? I was a nurse. I worked in the old building back then.”

Maria Petrovna closed her eyes and swallowed. She slowly

raised a hand and wiped a single tear from the corner of her eye. Tatiana noticed that even that small move took a lot of effort.

"It's OK. I understand, Grandma. The journey to Moscow might be hard on you anyway. We'll come and visit here. I've graduated, so I'm officially on holiday now!" Tatiana said.

"I heard you did very well. Congratulations, Tanyusha. We're all so proud of you." Maria Petrovna smiled. "So what's next for my clever granddaughter? Maybe you'll study some more. You're too young to have a baby. There's no rush."

If only she knew, she would be so ashamed of me. Tatiana lowered her eyes. In her head she could hear the awful clank of the metal instruments.

"I don't know yet, Grandma. I haven't decided," she muttered.

"Tanechka, listen to what I have to say." Suddenly Maria Petrovna's voice grew stronger. "You're not yourself lately. I have noticed it. You look so sad. And because you're putting on a brave face, I can guess it has something to do with your husband. Am I right?"

Hesitantly, Tatiana nodded.

"Is he not treating you well? Has he done something to you?"

"Oh, no. It's not like that," Tatiana protested. "He's just too busy. Always. He doesn't have much time for me. I don't even know why he needs a wife," Tatiana added meekly, nervously twisting the corner of the duvet between her fingers.

"I'm not worried about him," said Maria Petrovna. "He's a very strong-willed young man. A man like Oleg will never be lost—with a wife or without. My heart aches for you, darling girl. You should be happy. And if he doesn't make you happy, then he doesn't deserve you."

"Maybe I don't deserve to be happy, Grandma. I've done a lot of wrong things. I am probably being punished for them!" Tatiana sighed.

"Nonsense, Tanechka! Don't even talk about yourself like that. It upsets me. You are a very good, sweet girl. You've always been! And everyone deserves to be happy!" Maria Petrovna paused, gathering her strength. "Do you remember who said, 'Man is created for happiness like a bird for flight'?"

"It was Korolenko, Grandma. Please take it easy. This excitement is a bit too much for you." Tatiana straightened her grandmother's bedcovers. They kept silence for a few moments, and then Tatiana changed the subject. "Tell me about yourself, Grandma. You got married to Grandpa when you were young, and then you had your children. You stayed faithful to him even after he died."

"Those were different times, Tanechka, hard times. We didn't have much of anything, especially through the war. You are a new generation. Your life is supposed to be better than ours. Marriage is not everything. You have choices, opportunities. That's what we've fought and worked for." Maria Petrovna paused.

"Your granddad would want you to have fun, too. He was such a merrymaker! Nikolai is a bit too serious, if you ask me. He doesn't take after his father." Both women gave a giggle.

"Yup. He takes the world very literally. He's a true scientist," Tatiana agreed.

"I don't understand the times we're living in," her grandmother said. "I can't watch TV anymore. What's going on? People getting shot on the streets. Bombs going off in the cars. What are they killing each other for? Who is the enemy? What do they want—more money? Power?" Maria Petrovna stopped, finding it difficult to speak.

"I'm worried about you, Tanechka. Oleg is a rich man. The new rich—isn't that what they call them? Are you safe?"

"I am, Grandma. You don't need to worry. Oleg takes security very seriously," Tatiana answered reassuringly.

Does she know about Vlad?

Her fingers began fiddling with the bedcovers again.

"OK, my darling. Sorry if I've said something silly." Maria Petrovna rested her head back on the pillow. "I'm old. I'm allowed to speak my mind. I just want you to be happy, my sunny girl. And you need to figure out how to achieve this. Go and do what you have to do." Maria Petrovna closed her eyes. "I'm a bit tired now. I'm going to rest for a bit."

"Ok, Gran. I'll go and find Mum and Dad. I will come again soon." Tatiana stood up and planted a gentle kiss on her grandmother's dry, shrivelled cheek. She couldn't help thinking that Grandma was giving her a blessing.

Chapter 32

Maria Petrovna died the following week. The sharp whirring ring of the telephone woke Tatiana on that Friday morning. Once she glanced at the clock, her heart throbbed in a grim premonition. Six thirty was never a time for a casual phone call. She rushed to the landing to pick up the receiver.

"Stripey, I'm sorry. Your grandmother passed away a few hours ago." Her father's voice was flat and strained.

"But how, Dad? I thought she was getting better! You told me not to come this week, saying that she seemed to be on the mend. You said they might even discharge her!" Tatiana cried out in anguish.

"I know. I'm so sorry, Stripey. She developed acute pneumonia three days ago. She probably didn't want to alarm us. She always underplayed things. You know your grandmother." Nikolay Ivanovich chuckled and then paused.

"I just wanted to say goodbye," Tatiana said quietly.

"I know, kid. I did too. But we got here too late. They called us last night when she was already unconscious. Your mum and I came over as soon as we could, but it happened too quick."

Tatiana could hear her father struggling to speak. She was overwhelmed with pity for him. "I can be with you in three hours, Dad. I just need to find Vasily—and Oleg as well." Only now, Tatiana remembered noticing that Oleg's half of the bed was untouched.

"Oh, Stripey, no need. Stay put. We're going to make all the arrangements. Sergey is here too. I'll call you later." Nikolay Ivanovich hung up.

Tatiana dialled a number. After a few rings, Vasily picked up. "Hello," he croaked and cleared his throat. Her call had obviously wakened him.

"Vasily, where are you? And where's Oleg?"

"Good morning, Tatiana Nikolaevna," Vasily said, making an effort to sound alert. "Oleg Borisovich is at the meeting. He diverted his calls to the car phone."

"What meeting, Vasily? It's half past six in the morning. Give me a break!" Tatiana hissed with anger.

"He went in last night. It must have overrun," Vasily replied hesitantly.

"Where is this meeting? Where are you now? Don't lie to me."

"I'm parked outside some building on Tverskaya Street, Tatiana Nikolaevna. Oleg Borisovich often has meetings here. That's all I know." Vasily breathed out anxiously.

"OK, thank you for telling me. I will need you today. But I guess that's out of the question now since you haven't slept," Tatiana said calmly. "Tell Oleg when you see him that my grandmother has died."

"I'm so sorry, Tatiana Nikoloevna. My deepest condolences." Vasily sounded genuinely moved.

"Thank you." Tatiana put the receiver down.

Of course, those apartments that he's renting on Tverskaya! He doesn't sleep in the office as he tells me. I wonder who I would find there if I rushed over this minute?

She savoured the possibility of catching Oleg red-handed. She even imagined the look on his face. *Who will be there with him? What if it's someone I know?*

Remembering Ksenia's lush smile and perfect legs, Tatiana winced.

But she has a famous boyfriend! It must be one of those novelty accessories that Irina warned me about.

Irina had recently caught Maks with a skinny and glamorous clothes horse. *That's whom I might find there, a stunning young model so impossibly tall that she would tower over Oleg in those ridiculous heels they wear. Ha! He would barely reach her shoulder!*

The whole image made Tatiana snigger. But she knew she would never go over. Confronting someone so superior to her in the physical beauty department would be a hurtful and humiliating experience.

What am I even thinking about? My poor grandma is lying there dead, under those horrible covers with the hospital stamps, and all I'm concerned about is my husband's whereabouts?

She remembered her grandmother's gaunt yellow face and their final conversation.

She was trying to tell me something about my life. She wanted me to take charge of it. She probably knew she was saying goodbye.

Sitting on the floor of the empty hall, Tatiana hugged her knees and wept.

Chapter 33

"I'm sorry, Sun, but I won't be able to come to the funeral. Something very important has come up. There's a problem with our account in Geneva. Maks and I have to go personally. We have to be there first thing tomorrow morning. I'll get the evening flight back, I promise." Oleg had called her on the phone. He hadn't even come home for three days, blaming his absence on a work overload.

"It's OK, Oleg. I understand. Banking problems are more important than my grandma's funeral. To you, anyway," she replied calmly and hung up. She wasn't even trying to be sarcastic; she'd meant what she's said. She simply didn't care anymore about what Oleg was doing or where he was going. It was as if the quota of her anguish and frustration was full. And that feeling was liberating somehow.

On her way to the funeral, Tatiana watched the changing sunlit landscape along the Varshavskoe Highway that linked Moscow with Tula.

Despite the car's air conditioning blasting at full power, her body felt uncomfortably warm under the tight black dress. The mercilessly blazing rays of the July sun seemed to be magnified by the glass of the windscreen, penetrating right through her clothes and even the dark lenses of her oversized shades.

Vasily was unusually quiet, tactfully giving her the space

to grieve. But somehow in his silence Tatiana could sense his disapproval of his boss's absence. She knew that Vasily came from a close-knit family. He always mentioned his parents and wife with respect. Missing a close relative's funeral was completely unimaginable for him.

From a distance, Tatiana watched the long colourful rows of flowers, garlands, and wreaths spreading over the stalls. The impromptu market covered both sides of the lengthy drive leading to the gates of Tula's largest cemetery.

She climbed out of the car outside the small yellow church, silently cursing the heat and the blinding sunlight.

Everything inside felt unreal. She couldn't shake off the sensation that she was watching a hazy slow-paced movie with a barely audible soundtrack. She saw a small funeral procession, her mum in a black shawl, her dad and Uncle Sergey looking alike and very pale, the priest with a curly ginger beard—a tall figure in an ornate cassock with an enormous gold cross on his chest. They all seemed to be acting their parts in the low-budget art-house drama.

Her grandma's open coffin, upholstered in pink, stood facing the elaborate iconostasis, and the barricade of thick candles was burning on the stand behind her head.

Grandma, covered to the chin with a silky white shroud, with a small icon of Mary and Jesus under her folded hands, looked unrecognisable. She was yellow, tiny, and stiff. Like a poor wax copy of herself, she looked strange and disturbing, resembling the worst wax sculptures Tatiana had seen at Madame Tussauds.

Tatiana didn't really register what the priest was saying. At the end of the ceremony, she, following the others, stepped forwards to kiss Maria Petrovna's stone-cold forehead. Then the coffin was carried outside towards the freshly dug grave.

Walking at the end of the procession, Tatiana was relieved to put her large shades back on. She watched the two sweaty gravediggers swinging their shovels, dispatching big heaps of soil back into the hole, covering Grandma in her pretty pink box.

Viktoria Andreevna was sobbing quietly on her husband's shoulder, her eyes swollen and her face wet.

Tatiana excused herself early from the wake party at Maria Petrovna's house. It felt very strange being there in her grandmother's absence, especially with all those people around. It seemed that the whole village had crammed in.

She sleepwalked to the car and nodded to Vasily. The return journey took them six hours. Tatiana didn't utter a word the whole time. Vasily played soft jazz on the radio and kept his silence in return.

The traffic around Moscow was almost stationary. When they finally reached the dacha in the late evening, Tatiana was surprised to discover a long line of cars parked in their driveway. The windows of the house were brightly lit, and she could hear excited voices from the back patio.

A jittery and overjoyed Irina greeted her. "Oh, Kitty! You're back! So sorry to hear about your poor grandma. Come here." She swung her arms open for a hug.

"I hope you don't mind. We organised a small gathering to cheer you up. There are only close friends here, I promise." Irina pulled Tatiana by the hand, leading her towards the kitchen.

"Nice dress, Kitty. Classy. Who's it by?" she said, continuing to chat. Tatiana was silent. Irina dragged her to the counter. There, on top of the shiny black granite, were two neat lines of white powder arranged carefully. "Ta-da!" Irina held out a cut cocktail straw. "Surprise! It's the right time for you try this kind of medicine." She winked at Tatiana." We don't need to tell your husband, it will be our next little secret! " Irina nudged her with her shoulder playfully."I don't like to use it often," she continued as if making an excuse." But you need a pick-me-up, Kitty. You've had a shitty day."

"Thank you for the thought, Irina, but I want to take a shower first. I'll be down soon. Enjoy yourself." Tatiana squeezed out a smile and walked out of the kitchen. Passing by the library, she glanced through the door to see Oleg and Maks bent over

Oleg's new pool table, their cues in their hands. Half-full whisky glasses and lit-up cigars in the crystal ashtray were on the cabinet nearby. She could swear she saw a thin white line next to it as well.

That's a nice little secret we all seem to share here. Oh well, who am I to judge? She thought bitterly.

The two men were talking animatedly and loudly, slapping each other on the shoulder. Music was blaring from the speakers. Oleg didn't notice his wife standing by the door.

Tatiana retreated upstairs. After a short while, she, dressed in jeans and a T-shirt, came down, pulling one of her large suitcases. She closed the front door tightly behind her. No one saw her leave.

Tatiana walked towards the security lodge to find Vasily.

"Please take me to Kropotkinskaya," she said.

Once inside Grandpa Ilya's apartment, Tatiana felt her legs give way, unable to support her body any longer. She slid down to the floor in the corridor, her back against the wall.

Burying her face in her hands, she began to sob. She wailed uncontrollably, her shoulders shaking violently. These were the tears of loss, despair, and profound self-pity.

When she finally managed to stop weeping, Tatiana stood up and walked to the kitchen. She poured herself a glass of water and emptied it in a few thirsty gulps. In the living room, she picked up the old telephone's receiver and dialled a long-distance number.

"Lena," she said, clearing her throat. "It's me. Can we talk?"

"Oh, sorry, do I know you? I think you may have me confused with a long-lost friend!" Lena was definitely upset with her.

"I know, I've been a shitty friend lately. You're absolutely right to hate me. But, please, can you hear me out?" Tatiana pleaded.

"What's happened? Isaeva! Something bad? How bad?" Lena shouted into her ear as Tatiana broke down again. "You're freaking me out!"

“We buried Grandma today,” Tatiana managed, sniffling.

“Oh, I’m so sorry! I had no idea that Maria Petrovna—” Lena’s voice softened.

“But that’s not why I’m calling you,” Tatiana cut in, composing herself. “It’s Isaev. I think I’m done.” Her voice began to tremble again.

“Oh my God! What did he do to you? What happened? Talk to me!” Lena yelled. “Stop crying into the phone for a second and talk to me!”

After a few moments Tatiana regained control over her speech. “It’s not about what he did to me, Lena. It’s ... not that simple. It’s more like what I did to myself. I’ve done some horrible things in this marriage,” Tatiana said with remorse. “Do you have time now? Do you want to hear?”

“Fire away. It’s been a long time coming,” Lena replied. “You owe me your honesty. And remember, I’m practically a journalist, so you can’t shock me!”

“I know. You’ve researched public toilets, so you must be brave!” Tatiana smiled for the first time in days. “OK, listen, it’s like this ...”

The two young women talked and cried and laughed for hours that night. At the end of their conversation, Lena drew a conclusion: “I will help you, Dobrova.” Tatiana jolted at the sound of her maiden name. “Let’s try to do this ...”

Chapter 34

The summer weather was short-lived. The sticky heat of early July ceased all too soon, giving way to cold winds and grey rain clouds. It had been raining for the past three days. Wrapping herself in a raincoat, Tatiana struggled to believe that on the calendar the summer was still in its zenith.

The chilly humid air made her feel cold all the time. Even inside, warming her hands over a cup of tea, she didn't unbutton her mac. The expansive VIP lounge of Sheremetyevo International Airport was almost empty that afternoon. There were just a few businessmen propped up in the leather chairs, rustling pages of their newspapers and sipping the complimentary alcohol.

There was a slight commotion at the reception desk. Tatiana turned her head. Oleg breezed in, the loyal Chip and Dale two steps behind him with walkie-talkies in hand. In the usual scanning manner, they inspected the hall.

Tatiana hadn't bothered to learn the names of the other two bodyguards, who were both new and huge. They stood still by the entrance, keeping their gazes fixed on the three receptionists in airport uniforms behind the desk. These women seemed to have seen it all before and carried on with their work impassively.

Tatiana knew that outside the building two black cars with

blue sirens on top were waiting for Oleg and his entourage. He had beefed up his security recently, Tatiana guessed, all due to the increasing number of shoot-outs and contract killings. "Crazy times we're living in!" Oleg had commented once after watching a news clip full of bloody corpses. "Crazy but exciting, Sunny!"

Today, he looked trim and smaller than usual, all dressed in black—a thin cashmere jumper, shiny formal trousers, and trendy, thick-soled boots. In contrast, his clean-shaven face looked pale and his tensely pressed lips betrayed a life of excitement that was gradually turning to fear.

Watching Oleg take his seat across from her, Tatiana felt a tiny stab of empathy. For a second, her husband seemed vulnerable and defenceless. But then, of course, he spoke.

"Terrible weather out there, Sunny. You couldn't have chosen a worse day to travel."

"You're not going to blame the traffic, are you, Oleg? With those sirens of yours, you don't do traffic jams, surely?"

"Of course not, but it's pouring with rain, so we couldn't drive very fast, not even in the emergency lane."

"It's no matter. My flight is delayed by an hour anyway. Thanks for coming. You want some tea or maybe a bite to eat?" Tatiana crumpled a starched napkin in her hand.

"Yeah, I'll have a soup or something." Oleg looked around for a waitress. He located her at the bar and made a gesture.

"We have an excellent fish soup today," reported the girl with the deep red lips, seemingly ignoring the presence of the security personnel and smiling at her two customers broadly. "And for madam, I can recommend our special crab salad."

"OK. Salad and soup then." Oleg nodded before asking Tatiana what she wanted.

It would have been strange if he had.

"So, what was so important about seeing me now?" asked Oleg. "I thought we'd said our goodbyes over the phone. You'll be back in ten days, right? And as I told you, I might come and visit you in London this weekend, if you're not too busy catching up with Lena." Oleg took a large sip of water from the glass bottle next to him.

"About that," she said, holding her breath.

Be brave. Just a few tiled steps down. Close your eyes and dive under that damn wall.

"Oleg, I don't think I'm coming back in ten days." Tatiana lifted her head and looked straight at him.

"You want to stay longer? No problem. It's a full business-class ticket. You can change the date easily." Oleg shrugged his shoulders, completely unaware of his wife's inner struggle. "You need more money then? Send me Lena's account details and I will make a transfer."

"No, Oleg. I don't need more money. What I'm trying to say is that maybe I won't be back."

I'm swimming in the open now. There is no way back.

"What do you mean? You're going there forever?" Oleg sneered.

"It's more like I'm leaving you," Tatiana pronounced clearly.

"I see." He gave her a long testing look, and then his expression changed. "I guess this is something you've been planning for a while. I know you, Sunny. You're not a spur-of-the-moment kind of person. May I ask why? What is wrong with your lavish existence? What's missing from your life? Not enough designer gowns?" As she'd expected, his voice was heating up. "Or perhaps I've made you work too hard? Building the house, cleaning, washing, and cooking for me? Digging up the garden?"

"None of that, Oleg," Tatiana said. "I—" She tried to continue.

"What is it then?" Again, he didn't let her finish. "I know what your problem is. Shall I spell it out for you?" He was almost shouting now. "You're bored and probably feel useless. You're jealous of me because I have a purpose, a passion, in my life. That's why you constantly imagine things that aren't even there."

"Oleg, raising your voice at me won't change anything. You can't just shout over me any longer. You're right, I do feel worthless sometimes, but *you* are the reason. You try to dominate me in everything, as if feeling superior is your prime goal." Tatiana felt heat pounding in her cheeks.

"Nonsense. I give you all the freedom in the world. You can do whatever you please. I don't even check on you. But instead of doing something constructive, you choose to get high with your 'friend' Mikko. I've never even asked you what kind of relationship you have with him."

"Me and Mikko? Ha!" Tatiana chuckled. "You're so ignorant, it's not even funny. The guy's totally in love with you. He's gay, Oleg!"

"Oh. I didn't know that." Oleg shrugged it off. "That's beside the point. It could be him, or it could be someone else. I've given you my trust."

"No. You just don't give a shit. There's a difference," Tatiana said, cutting in.

"Sir, madam, would you like your food now?" The waitress stood over them with a tray in her hands, her teeth shinning under scarlet lips. Oleg and Tatiana both paused to give a small polite smile.

"Yes, please." Tatiana welcomed a much-needed break from the storm. The conversation wasn't going as she wanted. But then again, it was her husband she was fighting with, the man who didn't lose.

They sat in silence for a while, pretending to enjoy the meal. Tatiana's taste buds seemed to be in shock. She couldn't even smell the crab and mango pieces on her plate.

"OK, Sunny." Oleg was first to speak. "What if I told you that I don't want you to leave, that I'm prepared to work on whatever it is that upsets you in our relationship? Surely we can talk it over. What is it that you want? To see more of me? I can come home every night, no matter how late my day finishes. Is that it?"

"Oleg, I don't want you to make me promises you can't keep. I wouldn't ask you to change for me. It would be too much. It won't work. And it will only make you unhappy." Tatiana shook her head.

"OK. What do you want? Tell me now, and I'll try to make it happen."

"I knew you'd ask me that. And I'm sorry I don't have the answer anymore. A while ago, I thought it was important for me to uncover the truth, to know whom you're meeting and what it is exactly that you're doing with Maks and all those shady guys I see at the office. I even thought it was important for me to know what really happened to Vlad."

Tatiana paused and looked searchingly at him. Oleg held her gaze. He didn't blink. "And most of all," she went on, "to know who else you spend your nights with." Her words began to trail off.

"But now? What's changed?" He urged her to continue.

"Now? I've come to realise that ... it's more important not to live a lie in the first place." Tatiana sighed. "I'm not so ... curious anymore. ... I just don't want ... this." Her bottom lip began to tremble. She bit on it and fell silent.

"Why, Sunny? It's never too late. Ask me now. Try it. I dare you," he pleaded. "And before you start, I had nothing to do with Vlad's death. Nothing. You understand? He was my friend. My mentor. And I'm sick of the whispering behind my back. It was an accident, but people don't like to see it that way. They like sensation, conspiracy, and all that crap. Am I making myself clear?"

Tatiana nodded. She resigned herself to the fact that she would never know for sure how and why Vlad died.

"Now then. Fire away. Ask me." Oleg seemed like he wanted to confess.

"OK." She took a deep breath. "On the morning when my grandmother died and I called Vasily in the car, who was with you in that apartment? And why are you renting it in the first place?"

"First, renting a place was Maks's idea. I don't know what's going on in his marriage, but I think that both him and Irina have plenty to hide from each other." Oleg paused. "As for your other question, it's going to hurt. Rocket. I was with the Rocket."

"What?" Tatiana convulsed in astonishment.

"Yup. I was seeing her for a short time before I met you. We sort of kept in touch. She's a funny girl. She doesn't mince her words, that one," Oleg said.

"That she doesn't," Tatiana agreed, remembering the detailed tales of her friend's sexual exploits. But Tatiana knew for sure—she felt it with all of her being—that Oleg was still lying. He intended to hurt her by saying it was someone that she knew. She believed that Irina's version of events was more likely, that men like Oleg and Maks had the need to accessorise themselves with glamorous women who would normally never even look in their direction were those men not so powerful and wealthy. It was a question of prestige more than anything else.

"OK, let's say it was the Rocket. What about Mila and Ksenia? Have they been in those apartments, too?" she asked.

"Mila? Who's that?" Oleg struggled to remember. "Oh, that needy one from our honeymoon. And Ksenia? Oh, no, Sunny. You should know me better. I'm not the admirer of silly women. I chose you, remember." Oleg's attempted playfulness fell short.

Tatiana regarded him carefully. He'd always been a master of conviction.

Don't try to flatter me now. You simply don't care about all these women. They are just passing episodes, stepping stones for your ego. They aren't beautiful enough or desirable enough in the eyes of others to be anything more.

That's it. I get it. It's all about your image. Your supremacy. Your power.

Tatiana shook her head and then asked her husband, "Why do you need me, Oleg? What is it you see in me?"

"Come on, Sunny. You're my wife. You're smart! You're pretty! You've been with me through thick and thin. You married me when I had nothing!" He shrugged as if he was stating the obvious.

"So, you value my loyalty then?"

"Well, of course I do!"

"Like a dog," Tatiana muttered and looked away for a brief distraction. She spotted Chip and Dale sitting a few tables away with a large plate of sandwiches between them, looking less tense than usual. Oleg's two new bodyguards were still standing by the door, clearly not yet having earned the privilege to snack on the job.

"OK, my turn." Oleg took another gulp of water. "Let me ask you something. It's been playing on my mind lately. Why didn't you keep the baby? I think I regret it—"

Tatiana's heart sank. That was the question she had been hoping to avoid.

"You didn't try to stop me!" she exclaimed. "I'm not blaming you," she added more softly. "The truth is, I didn't want ... to have a baby with you. ... I couldn't see you ... as a father—" The uneasy silence hung between them.

"Wow. Wow, Sunny." When Oleg finally spoke, his voice came out strained. Tatiana could swear that his face looked a little paler. "I didn't know you hated me that much."

"I don't hate you," she whispered. "Not ... anymore." She shook her head. "Not now, I mean."

"So, you must have decided back then?" Oleg cleared his throat. "I mean, you've been thinking about leaving for a while, but you kept me completely in the dark. It's a bit unfair, don't you think?" His voice rose to a high pitch. She noticed that his eyes had begun to tear.

"I'm sorry, Oleg. You're right. I should have ... talked to you sooner," she began, pressing her fingers against her eyelids. For some reason she didn't want Chip and Dale to see her crying. Sniffling and busying herself with going through her handbag, she fished out a handkerchief and a folded piece of paper. She blew her nose and then put the paper in front of Oleg.

"What's this?" His voice was still trembling.

"It's our divorce certificate, Oleg." Tatiana tried her hardest to stay calm.

"How did you get it? It must be fake."

Barely registering his arrogance, she said, "No. It's absolutely legitimate. Look. There is a registration number and the judge's stamp. As of yesterday, we are no longer husband and wife. We are officially divorced."

"I can just tear it up and that will be it." Oleg held the document with the watermarks closer to his face, studying it.

"Of course you can," Tatiana agreed. "This is your copy. You can do what you like with it. I have mine, and there is the official record at the registry office.

"But I didn't sign anything."

"You didn't have to. I did it all for you."

"How much did you pay?" Oleg hissed. "Who did you bribe with my money? I didn't know you had it in you."

"I'm flattered that I could surprise you with anything." Tatiana smiled bitterly. "It didn't cost much. I just called on a favour from an old friend. We were at school together."

"So, you thought it through then?" Oleg seemed to regain his composure. Now she could detect a quiet menace in his voice. "How are you planning to survive in London? Surely you still need my money? Or maybe you already have an English millionaire waiting for you, courtesy of your slut friend?"

"Lena is not a slut, as you well know. She's a woman who can take care of herself. Not your type at all," Tatiana protested. "That's why you never liked her. She doesn't need a man to provide for her.

"There is nobody waiting for me there. Only Lena," Tatiana continued. "OK. I confess, I've sold my jewellery, everything except for this." She opened the top button of her mac and pointed at the small sun-and-moon necklace.

"That cheap thing?" Oleg seemed surprised.

"It's always about money with you. This was always your best gift; it reminds me of when things were good. But technically, yes, I've used your money. I've used it to pay for a year of school over there. I'll be studying English and marketing. I transferred the balance ... to Lena's account. I'll live with her at the start, and after that, we'll see. ... I'll get a job. Lena says there are vacancies for Russian teachers. Apparently some British businessmen are keen to learn the language."

"And what if it doesn't work out for you?" Oleg gave her an intense look.

"Then I'll come back, Oleg. But not to you." Tatiana poured water in her glass.

"So that's it then." He exhaled. "How could you? How could you throw away all these years? Everything we've shared. Everything that's happened to us?" There was so much raw pain and honesty in his voice then that Tatiana couldn't hold back any longer. Tears began flowing freely from her eyes. She reached out her hand and placed it on his.

"I'm very grateful for all we had, Oleg. I know you tried; so have I. But it just didn't work. For me, Oleg. I'm talking about me." She nodded her head, feeling the tears trickling down her nose. She no longer cared what Chip and Dale might think.

She looked into Oleg's eyes, desperately wanting to be heard—not understood, just heard.

"I'm so sorry ... for everything I've done wrong. I've reached the point ... I'm in a bad place. ... I hate myself. ... I hate the person that I've become ... I can't go on feeling like this. ... I need to change." She sobbed. "I have one last favour to ask from you. I'm begging you ... from all my heart." She gulped for air. "Let me go ... please."

Oleg took his hand away and looked down. He let out a big sigh and raised his head. "I'm working on my new album. I kept it as a surprise for you. I was going to dedicate it to you. What a fool!" He chuckled bitterly.

Tatiana buried her face in her hands.

"OK, stop crying, Sunny. Enough of that, don't you

think?" Oleg tapped the table. He seemed to have regained his composure. "To sum up our meeting," he went on, "you're not leaving me as far as I'm concerned. You're going to study in England, for a year at least, or maybe longer. I want you to keep me posted. And if you need anything at all, if you're ever in trouble and short of money, I want to be the first one you'll call, day or night. Understood?"

Tatiana nodded. She was sniffling.

"What about your parents? What did you tell them?" Oleg seemed to remember.

"I told them the truth. They were shocked at first, but I think they understood. Can my dad call you ... to pick up my things?" Tatiana reached again for some water.

"Of course. Anytime. That goes for your parents as well. They can rely on me for anything." Oleg paused. "I guess I'll have to break the news to mine at some point. They will be devastated. They like you very much. You know it."

"I know. Say goodbye from me." Tatiana fought back the tears, but she began to cry again. "And Oleg, it's important to me that you know. ... I stayed faithful to you ... through all our time together. Except once ... well, almost once. I tried ... to cheat on you in New York. ... I wanted to get back at you, but I really sucked at it. I was drunk and got robbed. And not at the airport. Sorry. And thank you."

"Stop thanking me, silly." It was his turn to grab her hand. "I hope you come back to me." His tone changed to sensual and demanding.

Stay strong, Tatiana commanded herself in her head. She looked down at his fingers holding her wrist, examined the touch of his skin against hers, and was relieved to feel nothing.

She let out a sigh. "Oleg, think positive. You'll be better off without me and my whiney questions. You'll be free to roam around as you please, and you won't have to use those apartments for late-night meetings. You can have them at that huge house you've built." Tatiana tried to sound chirpy.

“Let me decide what’s best for me.” He released her hand hesitantly.

“Mrs Isaeva, your plane is boarding. Please let us escort you to the gate,” said one of the receptionists, who had appeared to the table.

Tatiana and Oleg both rose from their seats. Tatiana put her bag over her shoulder.

“Well, goodbye, Oleg.” She leaned forward to give him a kiss. He stood still, as if unable to move.

“Bye, Sunny. I’ll call you?” he muttered under his breath.

Tatiana took a small step back, as if wanting to see him better. For a second, she studied his familiar face, his furrowed brow, the faint scar on his forehead, his pursed lips. She looked at him, smiled, and slowly shook her head. Noticing a glint of panic in his eyes, she softened the blow. “Maybe. Or perhaps I will call you ... sometime.” She turned away from him and walked towards the door. She knew she was lying.

Finished with their sandwiches and now working on a huge bottle of Coke, Chip and Dale looked up as she passed and gave her a respectful nod.

The two new guys by the door didn’t even acknowledge Tatiana. They were staring intensely over her head, waiting for their boss’s signal.

The receptionist held the door open from the other side. Tatiana increased her pace. Looking straight ahead, she stepped over the threshold.

Epilogue

2005

"Good evening, ladies and gentlemen. Welcome aboard this British Airways flight from Moscow Domodedovo to London Heathrow. Our flying time this evening is estimated to be three hours and fifty minutes."

She closes her eyes and sinks deeper into the seat. *Nice to be going home. Four days in Moscow in the middle of winter is more than enough. I am not accustomed to freezing temperatures anymore. How did I once survive here? I remember wrapping up in endless layers.*

The captain's voice is still murmuring in the background. "We'll be undergoing a quick de-icing procedure ..."

The mild British accent, she can't place. The smooth hypnotic tone washes over her as if saying, "Hey, just sit back and relax. You are in my capable hands."

And I'll be doing just that, in the comfort of business class. Thank you, James.

"I've used our air miles to upgrade you," he'd told her when booking the flight. "Besides, it's only you going, not all of us. Hope it's nothing serious with your mum."

His hopes had been realised: all of the tests, including a biopsy, had come back negative. Mum was fine.

Dad had panicked prematurely, but she was still glad she'd

gone. In the mornings she'd accompanied Mum to her hospital appointments, and in the evenings the three of them ate supper in the kitchen, just like in the old days.

I can't wait to get home.

She misses them, her lot—James and especially the kids, Maria and Alex.

I can't wait to kiss your little heads, breathing in your innocent smell of No More Tears shampoo.

How to pass the time? There is always a choice between reading something glossy and mindless or watching a romantic movie—a love story, something sad and compelling, the kind of film that James finds terribly boring but which I can have a good cry to, especially since no one around would notice.

She looks around. The cabin is practically empty. There are just a handful of passengers, most of them male. *Must be businessmen.*

"Paper, madam?"

A very tanned and well-groomed flight attendant smiles down at her, his impossibly white teeth shining brightly.

"Yes, please," she replies, embarrassed to ask for a gossip magazine straightaway. She grabs a newspaper instead. She picks the one with the biggest picture on the front, hoping it will have fewer words. Under the title she reads the date. "January 25".

Oh yes, how could I forget? It was a very special day for me once. We used to celebrate it when we were students.

"Would you like a glass of champagne with your meal, madam?"

His smile beaming, the flight attendant leans over to place a napkin-covered tray in front of her, his well-toned muscles bulging under the uniform shirt.

"Oh yes, please. I would."

Did he read my mind? I just thought of celebrating.

The cold bubbles tickle her tongue.

I can't believe I didn't like champagne when I was younger. Obviously, tastes change for the better.

She picks up the newspaper and begins turning the pages. A small article in the business section catches her eye. "Prominent oligarch in bid for UK's top advertising firm ... oldest British institution ... offices in London, Manchester, and New York ... new Russian head ..."

She takes in the facts quickly and stumbles over the surname, the name that used to be her own.

Of course it's him. What a coincidence! I was just remembering our special day. We were so young—just a pair of kids.

Evidently he's doing fine. I never doubted that he would be.

"Duty-free goods, madam?" The buff flight attendant is back.

"No, thank you." She shakes her head politely.

He gives a nod and strides down the aisle, pushing the trolley in front of him. The boring arrangement of liquor bottles and cigarette boxes is decorated with an elegant vase holding a small bunch of red carnations.

"Cabin crew, thirty minutes to landing," the captain's voice says over the sad song and the credits. She sniffles, tracing a finger under her eyes in case her mascara has run.

That was just the kind of movie I needed, gentle and sorrowful. James wouldn't have approved. Far too sentimental for him. I can't wait to see him.

She checks her watch and sets it three hours back.

The captain has said thirty minutes. Good time to go to the bathroom.

She stands up and stretches discreetly, looking around the whole cabin. There is a couple at the back that she hasn't noticed before. They must have boarded after her.

She glances at the youthful pretty woman with impeccable make-up and imposing diamond studs in her ears. She is unmistakeably Russian.

Then she briefly gazes at the man next to her. He holds a newspaper close to his face, a platinum wedding band visible on his right hand. So he is Russian too.

The man puts his paper down and says something to his wife.

Can it be? It is the same tense stare, the same lips pursed into a thin line. She can even see a small scar beneath the man's receding hairline. Only the lines on his forehead have gotten deeper.

She turns her back to the couple and darts to the front of the cabin. Once behind the locked cubicle door, she tries to catch her breath.

She can feel her pulse pounding in her temples. She looks in the mirror.

Yup, my face is all red! Damn!

She gives her face a splash of cold water and then dabs it with a tissue.

What are the odds of that? I've just read about him in that newspaper. I don't think I'm ready to see him. Will I ever be ready? Too late for that now. There is nowhere to hide in this place. I will have to come out. And he will see me.

She sways her arms a few times and walks in place, trying to get rid of some nervous energy. Then she stops and keeps still, attempting to control her breath. She closes her eyes.

That's it. Concentrate on the breathing. Inhale deeply, pause, and exhale. Take yourself to your happy place, just like in yoga class.

She pictures her own front door, black and glossy, with an antique brass knocker and a matching squeaky letter drop with empty milk bottles in the rusty holder in front of it. Her front door opens slowly to reveal two happy little faces in the dark hallway. And then the light goes up and there is James. He smiles as his strong arms reach out to embrace her.

That's my happy place.

She opens her eyes and checks her reflection.

My cheeks are still flushed, but never mind, I look younger like that. I'm ready now.

She walks out and takes a few measured steps towards her seat. She looks ahead to meet his stare. He is gaping at her, his expression frozen in disbelief.

She gives him a half nod and sits down.

Now it's his turn to be in shock. I've dealt with mine.

"Please, madam, fasten your seat belt. We'll be landing shortly."

The tanned steward is getting bossy, but it's a relief. No one can leave their seat now.

What can I possibly say to him anyway, "Sorry that I didn't call you for eleven years"?

The plane has landed, but she doesn't rush to get up.

Let them all go.

The usual commotion sweeps through the cabin, the overhead lockers click open, and the hand luggage is pulled down. Coats are reunited with their owners.

On top of that noise, she hears a loud remark in Russian. "Just give me the bag, Sunny!"

Some things never change. She giggles to herself and coughs into her fist. *Well, good luck to you ... Sunny.*

After a few minutes, everything goes quiet. The cabin is empty. She can picture the passengers racing one another up the connecting arm to the terminal building as if there is a prize for the first one to cross the border.

She picks up her bag and leaves the plane among the steady stream of economy-class travellers. She walks along the endless glass passage towards the arrivals hall.

She passes through the channel "UK/EU Nationals only", avoiding a look at the long zigzagging queue under the sign "All Other Passports".

She is thankful that the terminal is so busy.

He can't possibly see me.

And then she hears it, over the heads of the crowd, a familiar voice calling out, "Happy Tatiana's Day!"

Acknowledgements

My deepest gratitude goes to Jill Dawson, the most elegant writer, a real lady, and the best mentor any newcomer can wish for. Thank you for giving me confidence and courage to write in my second language.

A special thank you to Lucy Boon, my first editor, critic, and collaborator. Thank you for making sure that *Tatiana's Day* reads well.

To my first readers, my sister Natasha and my dear friend Irina M. Thank you for your honest responses, kind remarks, and enthusiasm.

To Alexandra Sokolova, a very young and promising graphic designer, thank you for making my dreams about having the original book cover come true.

Thank you to the highly professional and dedicated team at iUniverse for making the publishing experience both smooth and enjoyable, especially Sarah Disbrow for being a wise and friendly voice at the other end of the phone.

To my parents, thank you for being there for me my whole life. I know that I can always rely on you. Thanks to you, I am a better mum.

And thanks to my wonderful family: my husband, George, and my charismatic, maddening kids, Sasha, Misha, and Nikita. I love you guys. Always.

Katia Perova grew up in Moscow. She studied Russian literature and English translation at the university. England has been her home for the past twenty years. She currently lives in Buckinghamshire with her husband and three children. This is her debut novel.